THE
BROI

ALSO BY CASEY KELLEHER

THE
BROKEN

CASEY KELLEHER

Bookouture

Published by Bookouture in 2018

An imprint of StoryFire Ltd.
Carmelite House
50 Victoria Embankment
London EC4Y 0DZ

www.bookouture.com

ISBN: 978-1-78681-379-4
eBook ISBN: 978-1-78681-378-7

For Tara & Seán

CHAPTER ONE
2003

A noise close behind her, startles her.

Glancing back, Nancy Byrne strains to see through the darkness. Staring down the long, narrow alleyway that she'd just hurried down, there's nothing there. It was just her mind playing tricks on her. The eerie silence all around her magnifying every creak and rustle.

There's no one there! she tells herself firmly. *You're being paranoid, Nancy. You're a Byrne. Man the fuck up and start acting like one.* She berates herself, purposely ignoring the shiver of trepidation that trickles through her as she eyes the flickering street lamp much further back. The eerie strobe effect only highlighting the dark shadows that dance beneath the thick mist of rain that pelts down.

Cursing herself. *What was she doing out here on her own in the middle of the night, walking the towpath of Brentwood lock at this ungodly hour of the morning?*

Of course there is no one else out here.

All the sane, normal people of London are tucked up safely in their beds, asleep, it seems. Just where she should be. She is soaked through too, she suddenly realises, as she sweeps her hair out of her eyes. Strands of it sticking to her forehead, wet and limp against her clammy skin.

When had it started to rain?

She hadn't even noticed until now, so consumed by her heartache and grief that she was oblivious to anything going on around her. The black tailored suit that she wore to her father's funeral today – yesterday now – wet through, clinging to her tiny frame. She is just exhausted. She hasn't slept for days. She needs to get home, to crawl safely into her bed.

That thought almost makes her smile at the irony at her sudden need to get back there when, just a few hours ago, it had been the one place that she hadn't been able to escape from quickly enough.

Home.

With its swarms of well-wishers and so-called friends of her father's that had all out-stayed their welcome back at the house for his wake.

Her father's murder had sent shock waves across their entire community. His sudden demise changed everything, and Nancy had seen it in all of their faces. How the looks of sympathy passed between them as they repeated the same old clichéd words of condolence. As if saying how sorry they all were for her father's sudden death, how shocked at the brutality of it all, would somehow make Nancy and the rest of the family feel less burdened by their loss.

Then there were all the stories she'd been forced to sit through. Anecdotes of the Infamous Jimmy Byrne. Tales that even Nancy had never heard before. Each one more elaborate and embellished than the last, as if everyone was trying to one-up each other on who knew him better, who was closer to him. Every unknown tale only expanding the ever-growing gap between her and her father; so much so, that Nancy had begun to feel as if she'd never really known her father at all. She wasn't alone.

No one had really known her father, and that was the sad truth of it.

All the lies he told, the secrets he kept.

Her whole world had exploded. In just a few short weeks, everything that she thought she knew had crumpled around her to nothing.

That's when Nancy had escaped. That's when she'd left them all to it. Just as the walls had begun closing in on her.

Though out here, away from them all as she walked in the cold night air, she was feeling just as claustrophobic.

The blackness and silence closing in on her too.

She needs to get herself straight, she thinks. She has to, for the sake of her family and for the sake of her father's businesses. It was all going to be down to her now and walking around London under darkness would be the least of her worries. Her father had lived his life on a knife edge. Enthralled in the danger and violence of London's criminal underworld, he'd become the notorious Jimmy Byrne. A kingpin of a world built on crime and violence. He'd built himself an empire, together with his business partner, Alex Costa, buying out numerous properties and businesses across London.

Nancy knew where most of her father's vast wealth came from. She wasn't stupid. He liked to call it his import and export business, though really they were shipping drugs. Large quantities of cocaine which were being distributed all over London. That's what had placed her father firmly on the map as one of London's most legendary, feared faces. He'd had an army of men working for him and he'd made sure that his family had all reaped the rewards of his success over the years.

Nancy had been blessed.

Living a lavish lifestyle in a big mansion over in Richmond. Herself and her brother's education had been paramount to her father. Insisting on enrolling both his children in one of the best private schools that money could buy. Her grandparents and mother had all wanted for nothing either. Her father had set a precedent. Only the best cars, the best food, the best life for his family. Nothing was ever too much for any of them.

That all fell on Nancy's shoulders now, as she had known it would eventually.

That's why her father had involved her in his business dealings from such a young age. Letting her run his books for him, and balance up his accounts. Showing her the ins and outs of some of the deals he made. He was getting her prepared for her inevitable future of taking over the family businesses. The infamous Byrne Legacy. Though neither of them had ever imagined that any of this would have happened so soon.

Hearing a bird flying above her, Nancy looks up. It will be morning soon. She must have been out here for hours, she thinks. So lost in her thoughts, in her grief, that she'd completely lost track of all time. Though, she takes comfort from the fact that the night's sky will be replaced with dawn shortly.

The darkness is starting to freak her out. Playing tricks with her mind. Making her think that she can see and hear things that are only illusions. She's just being silly, she knows that. Though no amount of scolding herself can stop her heart from beating so wildly inside her chest. No matter how hard she tries to convince herself otherwise, she is unable to shake the feeling that someone is following her.

Of course no one is following her. She's just being stupid, paranoid. She's walked the length of Brentwood's canal towpath and hasn't seen a single soul for miles, as if she was the only person out here tonight.

Which she might be, she thinks warily.

Up until now there'd been nothing but an eerie silence. Unworldly in London, she thinks, to not even hear the noise of traffic whizzing by somewhere off in the distance. Still this had been exactly what she wanted earlier: to be alone with her thoughts so that she could try and get her head straight. Only it has backfired, it seems. It is too quiet now. Walking around in the pitch-black dark is starting to make her feel anxious.

At least earlier, when she'd strolled through Richmond High Street and up past Kew Gardens, past the pubs and late night wine bars that had long ago shut up, after turfing out the last of their intoxicated customers, there had been people around. In their droves. The noise and joviality of the people she passed had only irritated her further. Reminding her that life goes on.

Nancy had only wanted to disappear then. To hide away somewhere on her own, to silence their loud chants and laughter. How dare everyone around her be so happy when her world had ended?

Strolling along the canal, consumed with her thoughts and memories of her father, as she'd eyed the reflection of the moon shining down onto the water's surface, as if following her, for a short while, she'd felt as if she had company. Being alone had helped. Only, her mind had started running away with itself. Her grief had started to eat away at her.

She just couldn't get her head around the fact that her father was really dead. That he'd never be coming back. This was real. He was gone forever. That image that she had of him splayed out on the cold ground of Tilbury dockyard ingrained in her mind. Murdered in cold blood.

Death would always be tragic when a loved one was concerned, she imagined, but murder was simply soul-destroying. So unjust, so cruel. Her father's life snatched away in a heartbeat. Her dad, just taken from her.

There would be no grief, no mourning for her now, Nancy knew that. There couldn't be, not until the murderer was punished for ripping her father away from her life so viciously.

How could one action, one gunshot, rip someone's life clean away and in turn, destroy hers too?

Leaving her completely broken.

Shivering, Nancy blinked back her tears. She'd vowed not to cry. Not yet. Not until her father's death had been avenged. And it would be avenged, there was to be no doubt about that. She would see to that personally. Reminding herself of all of this, Nancy fought to regain her composure once more.

Breathing more freely again now. Furiously, in fact, as she gulped down huge lungfuls of air, continuing her way towards the end of the alleyway, her grief quickly replaced with anger.

More than that. A hot, burning rage inside of her. That was the most fucked-up part of all of this. Nancy knew who pulled the trigger.

She knew who killed her father.

Which was all the more reason why she'd needed to be alone tonight, to clear her head. To gain some clarity on all the thoughts that consumed her as she walked for what felt like miles. Alone in the dark, passing canal boats and bridges, then further along, the old abandoned warehouses. The huge piles of litter and junk that had been dumped there. Shopping trolleys, old bikes. Rubbish everywhere. It had felt a bit like a ghost town.

She hadn't realised how far down she'd ventured until she stood alone outside one of the abandoned depots. She remembered how her father had brought her here once as a child. How he'd told her that the Grand Union Canal went all the way from Brentford to Birmingham. Nancy hadn't known how far that was back then, but her father had made it sound impressive.

Unlike the reality of the canal path today.

The run-down buildings, dark and desolate. Her eyes drawn to the broken windows. Boarded up, mostly, though some windows were smashed and exposed. Who knew what or who was lurking about in the squalor around her? Using the old buildings as crack dens or squats. Peering out at her through the pitch-black gaps that used to be glass. Who was she kidding, pretending to be all big and brave?

She'd felt foolish then and scared suddenly, walking around out here all alone in the dead of night. The place seemed so sinister. Unsafe. If anything happened to her, she'd thought, no one would hear her screams. No one would even know she was here. So she'd turned off the towpath; she'd taken a short cut through the long, narrow passageway that led back out onto the main London streets.

Only now she is here, she can't shake the feeling that she isn't alone at all.

She is being followed.

Picking up her pace as she continues, Nancy wills the daylight to come. Walking so fast that she feels out of breath, her lungs tightening inside her chest.

Looking up, even the moon has abandoned her now. Nowhere to be seen. She hopes that it is still up there somewhere, hiding in the night sky behind the tall wraiths of the trees that thickly line two towering walls either side of her. Still floating along beside her.

That was a joke. As if the moon was going to bring her any real comfort.

It is just her now.

Or is it? she thinks as the noise comes again.

Louder this time. Nearer.

A creaking behind her.

She moves quicker, not bothering to turn and look behind her. She doesn't need to: what she needs to do is get the hell out of here and fast.

She is almost running. Out of breath, her chest burns but it isn't her pace making her lungs constrict inside her ribcage. Concentrating on her heels clicking loudly against the cold concrete beneath her, she homes in on another noise behind her then. There is no mistaking it this time.

Footsteps.

Recognising the crunch of a stone underneath a heavy footfall. This time the sound directly behind her, she is certain of it.

She turns, half hoping that she can berate herself once more for being so weak and pathetic. Only, shaking her head, as if doing a double take she homes in on the large dark silhouette of a man just a few yards behind her, and she realises she isn't being paranoid at all. His huge frame is lit up by the flickering street lamp further back. Dressed in black, a hood pulled up around his face.

He was so close now that he could almost touch her. Hurt her?

Catching a flash of his steely glare as he lurches towards her, she recognises the malice there.

Nancy runs.

Her heart thuds so loudly inside her ribcage that it feels like it will explode out of her chest. Stumbling unsteadily in her heels, she silently curses herself for not changing into something more comfortable before she left the house tonight, as she fights to stay upright on the uneven pavement beneath her. Her feet are swollen and sore from walking for so long. Though, in hindsight, she hadn't foreseen being chased down a dark alley by some scary-looking madman.

Ahead of her, she can see the break in the wall of overgrown bushes and trees that line the alleyway. She is almost there. Almost back out on the main road. Back out in civilisation, and the well-lit Brentford High Street. Only another thirty yards or so to go. She'll be safer out there, she can call for help. Only, she is out of breath and her assailant is gaining on her. The pounding rhythm of her heart thuds inside her ears, matching the footsteps that pummel the concrete behind her.

SLAP SLAP SLAP.

Whoever it is, they are so close now that she can almost feel them. She can hear them breathing. Panting.

When the blow that she has been dreading finally comes, it floors her, slamming her body down onto the cold, wet pavement. Nancy lets out an almighty scream as the air explodes from her lungs with the force of the impact. Her face is smashed against the uneven ground, a hefty thud as her head makes contact with the pavement, the pain making her cry out once more.

Desperate to get up, to get her attacker off her, she realises that she can't move, weighed down by the enormous, heavy bulk of the man on top of her, pinning her down to the ground as she struggles for breath. She turns her head to the side, fighting for air. She licks her lips, feeling the warm liquid streaming down into her mouth from her nose, recognising the metallic tang of blood.

Another pain then, searingly sharp as her head is yanked back. Screaming once more, as her attacker wrenches her up by a large clump of her hair that feels as if it will rip from her scalp.

'Get off me.' The words leave her mouth as a threat, an order, but spoken out loud, they sound more like a desperate plea. A whimper. Before a large hand clamps firmly over her mouth, silencing her.

'Shut the fuck up and listen, you stupid little bitch.'

Bristling at the venom in her attacker's words, the real threat that lingers there, Nancy does as she is told, shunning the instincts telling her to fight back, the feeling of wanting to claw at this fucker's face, and scratch his beady evil-looking eyes from their sockets.

But there is no point in even trying. She is no match for this man, overpowered, crumpled beneath him, bleeding and hurt. She can barely move, barely breathe. He is four times her size and, by the sounds of it, he knows exactly what he is doing.

Instead, she realises, she'll have to play along. Try and be smart about her next move. The last thing she wants to do is antagonise her attacker any further.

She feels him lean in closer. His hot breath on her face. His skin almost touching hers.

Her body prickles with fear as she wonders what he is going to do to her.

'This is your only warning. Stop looking for information. Your father is dead, it won't bring him back.'

Nancy was physically winded at his words, the little breath she had inside seeping out of her. This was about her trying to find out information about her father's killer?

This was a premeditated attack?

Now she is petrified.

She wrinkles her nose in disgust at the strong whiff of rancid breath as the man continued speaking, his spittle landing on her cheek with every forceful word.

Helpless, all she can do is try and take in every detail: the size of his frame, the sound of his voice. Anything that will help her figure out who the fuck this man is.

'We won't tell you again. Stop digging, or we'll bury you too!'

Feeling her hair pulled back for a final time, Nancy winces as her attacker grips the back of her head before slamming her down with great force so that her face whacks against the pavement once more.

The sound of her skull cracking against the rickety walkway floor is the last thing Nancy Byrne hears before she blacks out.

CHAPTER TWO

'That was the thing about my Jimmy. The stubborn fucker only did things his way. Even when he was a boy, he wouldn't listen to anyone. Even told the headmistress of his primary school to fuck off once after she scolded him for not sitting quietly while she was reading the class a story, so he did. Only five years old he was. The mouth on him even back then.' Shaking his head, Michael Byrne laughed to himself, before downing the last of his pint of ale. Blissfully unaware that he wasn't fooling anyone, Michael was thoroughly enjoying himself now.

In his element at being centre of attention as he stood surrounded by a group of Jimmy's friends and business associates that had come back to the house for Jimmy's wake, he was getting a bit carried away with himself and the fabricated stories and memories of his one and only child, that probably hadn't even happened. Who the fuck knew? Michael certainly didn't. He'd left Joanie to do all the child-rearing bollocks.

The truth was that he and Jimmy had hated each other's guts.

As far as Michael was concerned Jimmy had always been a horrible, obnoxious bastard especially when it came to their relationship. Jimmy had treated his own father worse than scum. Publicly too. He'd done nothing but belittle and berate Michael at every opportunity and the older and more powerful he had become, the worse Michael had come off.

Jimmy had hated Michael with a vengeance, and made no disguise of the fact. In return, the feeling was most definitely mutual. Michael had hated Jimmy too.

Only it didn't bode well to talk ill of the dead, did it, and in his intoxicated state even Michael Byrne knew that. Especially seeing as most of Jimmy's nearest and dearest were some of London's most notorious faces.

Not only would it look bad on the family if Michael told everyone what he really thought of his spiteful narcissistic son, but his Joanie would have no qualms in stringing him up by his balls from the lounge's light fittings if she heard him speak out of turn about her precious Saint fucking Jimmy. Especially on the night of the man's funeral.

Only, that was the best thing about tonight.

There was no one around to keep tabs on him anymore, was there?

He was a free man again.

His Jimmy was dead, and lately Joanie wasn't in any fit state to distinguish her arse from her elbow. The woman had turned into a mute since she'd heard the news of their son's death. Barely holding it together. Which had turned out to be a right result for Michael as it happens. All week, she'd hardly muttered a single word to him. To anyone, in fact. It was pure bliss. Michael Byrne could do and say as he pleased, and no fucker would stop him.

He grinned.

Draining his glass triumphantly, he stared around the room. Aware that he was surrounded by some of the hardest, most ruthless bastards in London. All of them paying their respects to his Jimmy, and in turn giving Michael the time of day because of his apparent loss.

'That was his biggest downfall 'en all. He always wanted to be centre of attention did my Jimmy. He wanted all eyes on him at all times... The only person that one ever listened to was his mother. Making out to you lot that he was a proper hard bastard, but the truth was he was a right old mummy's boy. Old Joanie loved that.' Oblivious to the looks that were being shared around the group, he continued. 'It was almost incestuous at times, those two. They were thick as bleeding thieves. You try living here with them two like that. From the day that boy was born I became the black sheep in my own family. Couldn't do right for fucking wrong around the bleeding pair of them. It was always Jimmy and Joanie – those two should have fucking married each other. That would have been a match made in fucking Heaven.'

Unaware that he was showing himself up, that there was now an undercurrent in the room, Michael grinned jovially as he saw Jack Taylor walking towards him, but the expression on the man's face told him everything he needed to know.

He'd crossed the line.

'I think you've had enough, don't you?' Jack Taylor said, as he swiped the pint glass out from his hand. Aware of who was watching how this was going to play out, Jack kept his cool, his tone neutral as he spoke though the anger in his words was clear enough even for Michael Byrne to take the hint. 'You better rein it in. This is a wake, not a fucking party. It would serve you well to remember that.'

'Like I need reminding,' Michael said, spittle around the corner of his lips as he spoke. He wiped it away with the back of his hand. 'Remember?' he blurted out, shaking his head sadly. 'I buried my only son today. That isn't something that I'd forget in a hurry.'

'All I'm saying is if your Joanie sees you like this, you know she'll lose her head.'

'Oh behave, Jack. That woman's already lost the bleeding plot, hasn't she? Her precious son's dead. That's enough to tip the woman over the edge, trust me. She lived for him and only him. She never gave a fuck about me.'

Jack looked thoroughly pissed off, and in the two decades the man had been a friend and business associate of Jimmy's, Michael had never seen him look so angry.

Michael actually liked the man. They all did. As a well-respected detective inspector now for the Metropolitan police, he had helped the Byrne family out of a tight spot or two, many times over the years. The last thing he wanted to do was upset Jack Taylor.

'I'm sorry, son!' Michael said, doing his best to try and act sober as he played his trump card as the poor, grieving father. Making out that his behaviour was down to being riddled with grief. That he wasn't in his right mind. 'I'm not thinking straight, you know. I still can't really believe that he's really gone. That he's never coming back.'

Jack nodded, though he felt anything but sympathy for the man before him. Michael was clearly too stupid or too drunk to realise that he wasn't fooling anyone.

'I'm hurting…' Michael continued to sob, though as Jack searched his face, he could see there were no real tears there.

'I know you are, mate,' he said playing along, hoping to appeal to Michael's softer side. 'But you've already pissed off your Nancy. She stormed out about an hour ago, and if Daniel or Joanie hear you talking like this, there will be hell to pay…'

To his surprise, Michael nodded.

'You're right, Jack. You won't hear another peep out of me,' he said as he looked around the room at the group of men that had only minutes ago been huddled around him, hanging on his every word.

The group were dwindling off now. Glad of an excuse to get away from the man. Bored with his conversations and the fake niceties they had to bestow upon him.

People were beginning to leave.

He was glad.

From here on in, everything about their lives was going to change, for better or worse. Though Michael couldn't see how things could get worse, if he was honest. Certainly not for him anyway.

Watching as Jack Taylor made his way back in to the kitchen, he tried to hide the happiness that bubbled away inside him.

Life goes on as they say, and life for Michael Byrne was going to be a hell of a lot better now that his Jimmy was dead and buried.

CHAPTER THREE

Chad Evans had been a nervous wreck when he'd first got in his punter's car tonight, but he needn't have been so worried.

His tip-off had been spot on.

If he wanted to get work here in London, then the derelict industrial badlands of King's Cross was the place to find it. Or, as it turned out, the work would find him.

He'd only been walking York Way for a little over fifteen minutes when he'd been picked up by some guy in a swanky-looking motor. The bloke hadn't said much, but then they'd both known that neither of them were there to do any talking. His first punter had only requested a blowie. Which was a right result and, even more so, when he hadn't even argued when Chad had slid a condom on the guy. Another right old touch, especially after some of the stories he'd heard from his new boyfriend Joey.

In fact, thinking back to some of the horror stories that Joey had told him about his chosen vocation, it wasn't any wonder that Chad had been crapping himself tonight.

His first night on the job, and all he could think about were the sick and twisted punters that got their kicks from hurting prostitutes. Joey had said how one poor sod had been kidnapped right here. A few weeks back now. How he'd been bundled into the boot of a car, before being badly beaten up. He might have been killed too, if he hadn't managed to get away.

Still, Joey reckoned that was just a one-off.

He'd told Chad to trust no one. Not even the cops. They were the worst apparently. Picking prostitutes up for streetwalking, only to get girls and guys in the back of their motors and insist on some form of payment in kind to help them turn a blind eye to the offences they'd been pulled for. The officers knew that they could take whatever they wanted and there would never be any reprisals.

Chad was doing his very best to keep his wits about him. Though, so far, his job seemed pretty easy.

This punter had hardly spoken a single word in fact, clearly not interested in the conversation, which was fine with Chad as it meant he could get on with the job in hand, or in mouth as it were.

The easiest fifteen pounds he'd ever made. Then he'd be off to find his next punter, he thought as he bobbed his head up and down on his customer's lap.

Giving a complete stranger oral sex for money wasn't quite as awkward as he'd first imagined it would be, as long as he didn't think about what he was doing too much. Instead, he tried to think of nice things, like his Joey.

It had been pure fate meeting him.

Chad had been in London just a few weeks, after running away from his home in Manchester, when they'd finally met each other. Though, London hadn't turned out to be the magical place that Chad had expected. He'd been hoping to find himself a nice little job and a small flat somewhere and to make a fresh start for himself.

Only starting out again in London had been much harder than he'd anticipated. With no job and no money behind him, the small amount of cash he did have had gone in just a few days and he'd been forced to sleep rough on the city's streets.

It was only by a chance encounter that he'd got talking to a man at a bus stop one evening. His Joey. The fact that he earned his money as a male prostitute didn't bother Chad one bit, in fact, it only spurred him on to give it a go too. There was good money to be made after all.

Though, so far, it had been a lot easier than he'd imagined it would be. Chad had just blagged it up until now. Fake it until you make it, he lived by that. Pretending that he'd done this a thousand times before. He'd even managed to direct this punter down this quiet little lane which led to the disused railway arch they'd parked up underneath.

The place was perfect. With not a single soul for miles, there was no chance of getting caught by an unsuspecting passer-by, or worse still, Old Bill.

Maybe Chad had found his calling after all, he thought, suppressing his smile, his mouth still full.

He could feel the man beneath him building his rhythm up now. Thrusting inside his mouth, he was almost there, at the point of no return. Chad braced himself seconds later as the man shuddered. The thrusting stopping abruptly.

Chad sat up and wiped his lips, watching as the punter did his flies back up, and adjusting his hair in the rear-view mirror. Another perk of his first job was that the punter was actually quite a looker. Tall, dark and handsome. If he had met him in normal circumstances, the only reason Chad would have kicked this one out of bed, would have been to fuck him on the floor.

He was a bit quiet now though. Moody almost. Cool and composed, though the intense look on his face as he stared at his own reflection in the small mirror showed that he was really concentrating on something. As if he was thinking something through.

Chad wondered if he should ask him, just to make polite conversation, but then he remembered Joey's advice and thought better of it. *Always listen, but never, ever start asking the punters questions. They don't take to that very well. It makes them suspicious. Makes them feel as if you are digging for information on them.*

Speak only if you're spoken to.

Well that was all well and good, only, so far, this punter hadn't said fuck all to him. To the point that it was starting to feel awkward. Deciding not to break any of Joey's 'golden rules', Chad stared out the window instead. Taking in the view of London under the hue of orange street lamps spilling out way off in the distance.

It was strange how suddenly London could appear so still. How he could feel so estranged from the city from here. As if they were a million miles from everyone and everywhere. Only they weren't. They were parked up in the middle of the badlands. London's largest building site.

Right in the heart of it all, amongst the old railway lines and disused warehouses.

Joey had told him that this was where the new Euro tunnel terminal was being built. Right here at King's Cross. That big changes were coming. That people were flocking here in their droves. Yet the building work had only just started, and everywhere Chad looked were rows and rows of steely, half-finished buildings, all adorned with an armour of scaffolding poles around them. Accessorised with cranes and bulldozers, all left abandoned, motionless, under London's darkened night skies.

The roads around here were completely deserted. There was no one around for miles, which felt strangely beautiful and eerie at the same time.

Creepier if Chad had been all alone, he guessed.

The driver of the car had gone completely silent now. Sitting and staring straight ahead out of the windscreen, not moving, and Chad wasn't sure what to say or do.

He guessed the bloke was probably suffering from a bout of regret at what they'd just done. A closet gay who'd just lived out his fantasy with some strange rent boy he'd picked up while driving home late at night. Or perhaps he's married? Or he's got a boyfriend, and now he's feeling full of guilt. Whatever it was, he was acting weird, and Chad just wanted to get back to the main road so he could scout out his next punter.

Proud of himself for going through with this, he was pumped. He'd done his first job and made his first bit of money. Though technically he hadn't been paid yet.

'You okay to drop me back?' Chad asked. Then on getting no reply he quickly added. 'I can walk. You can just pay me. It's not far, I'll make my own way back.'

Again only silence ensued.

The man didn't move, didn't so much as flinch. He gave no indication that he'd even heard Chad speak. His eyes remaining focused, his gaze fixed straight-ahead.

That steely silence in the car now filled Chad full of anxiety. Not sure how to play this out. The man was starting to freak him out. His gut twisted at the sudden thought that something wasn't quite right here. They were out in the middle of nowhere, surrounded only by darkness.

No one knew that Chad was even here. In this car. With this man.

Thinking back to the story he'd been told about the man that had been attacked just weeks prior, Chad started to feel scared. Convinced that he was just overreacting, being paranoid even, he decided that he was just going to cut his losses and get the fuck out of here anyway.

Looping his fingers around the door handle, he was going to put this job down to experience and not worry about the measly fifteen quid that he would have earned from it.

The man was still staring ahead. Not moving. Not speaking.

Chad eyed the door handle once more. *Yeah, fuck it. It wasn't worth the aggro.* This bloke was starting to creep him out.

He pulled at the handle, getting ready to leg it as soon as the door pinged open. The door didn't move. There was a loud click, telling him that the central locking was on.

A loud click that alerted the punter next to him that he'd tried to escape.

The man turned his head then. As if he'd just snapped out of his trance. His steely eyes boring into Chad's. Full of loathing.

That's when Chad felt the first real wave of fear sweep over him. The feeling replaced very suddenly with an almighty thud, as the punter smashed into the side of his face with his fist.

The punch caught Chad off guard, snapping his neck backwards, and slamming the side of his head into the glass of the passenger door.

His ears were ringing now. The blow knocked him senseless. He was still conscious, though he knew that he wouldn't be able to fight back. Chad wasn't cut out to fight. With few options, the only thing he could think to do was to just lie against the door where he'd landed and play dead. Hope that the punter would think that he'd knocked him out. Praying that it would be enough to deter this fucking psychopath from dishing out any more blows.

So that's where Chad stayed. Slumped against the door, his eyes closed.

Waiting.

A few seconds later he heard the sound of the engine starting up, and that was when the real fear crept in. They were moving again, travelling further out across the badlands. Not back the way that they had come, like Chad had hoped. He'd been praying silently to himself that the man had got his kicks and would drop him back where he found him. Even if he didn't pay him. Chad no longer cared about the money.

Only, Chad knew deep down that the punter wasn't dropping him back. He felt sick then, tasting the burning bile at the back of his throat. The deep pit of dread that had replaced his stomach.

He was trapped inside this car with no idea where he was being taken.

He was at this mad fucker's mercy now.

He wondered at the irony that on his first night at working the job, he had fallen prey to exactly the type of nutcase that Joey had warned him about.

The car sped up.

Forty. Fifty. Sixty miles an hour. Chad wasn't sure but, opening one eye, he peered out of the window and eyed the rickety dirt track that ran adjacent with one of the old railway tracks.

He was going to have to fight back, he realised with dread. He had to. What other choice did he have?

He could do it. If he just leaned over now and caught the driver by surprise. He wasn't much of a fighter, he didn't have it in him, but he could claw at the man's face, maybe grab the man by the throat. Pull his hair even, whatever it took. They'd probably crash, and the chances were he wasn't going to leave this car unscathed. But at least he'd have some chance of getting away. He wouldn't be at such a disadvantage.

All he had to do was be brave and do it. Lean over, and strike out. For once in his life, be courageous.

Only Chad didn't get the opportunity.

The driver struck first.

He heard the click of the central locking being released and then in one quick sudden moment, the man leant over and opened the door. Grabbing hold of Chad, before launching him out.

The heat of the car replaced by the cold, rushing wind as suddenly Chad's body flew through the air.

Screaming with fear and panic, Chad reached back to grab onto something, anything. The door, the chair, anything that would save him.

Nothing could.

A twisted look of horror in his eyes, as he realised too late what was happening. That he was flying through the air at speed. Plummeting towards the steel railway beams.

The last thing Chad felt was his body slamming into the thick metal tracks. An explosion of pain as his body flipped over, smacking against every bit of steel and concrete with force.

Mangling his body beyond recognition.

Chad Evans never felt anything again.

CHAPTER FOUR

Pounding her fists against Alex Costa's front door, Nancy knew he was home, she could hear the loud thud of music radiating out through his fancy apartment's walls. His stereo blaring, even at this ridiculous hour of the morning.

His neighbours must love him, she thought as she scanned the corridor. Her eyes flashing wildly with fear and panic towards the elevator and stairwell, secretly terrified that someone might have followed her back to Alex's apartment.

Nancy tried again.

This time, banging her fists even harder against the panelled door, not caring that her hands were red and swollen.

'Alex! It's me, Nancy. Open the door.'

She had no memory of how she got here. No recollection at all. Alex Costa's apartment had been the closest place she could think of to go to. Only a few miles from Brentford Canal, though in the dead of the night and the state that she was in, she wasn't sure how she'd even made it here.

She must still be in shock. Both adrenaline and fear pumping around her body. The last thing she could remember was dragging herself up off the cold, wet pavement. Her attacker had been nowhere in sight. Long gone, he'd left Nancy out cold on the ground.

She'd felt disorientated, at first, when she'd realised that her clothes were all wet and torn. Her knees bleeding through the jagged rips in the material of her trousers after they'd taken the impact of her fall. Knowing that she couldn't go home, that her family would only make a big drama over tonight's ordeal – the last thing Nancy had wanted was her nan Joanie and her sanctimonious mother Colleen making a fuss over her – she'd had nowhere else to go but here.

'Alex, I know you're in there,' Nancy shouted once more, half tempted to kick the door to get his attention. Only thankfully she didn't have to resort to such measures. Seconds later the front door opened, and Nancy recoiled at the state of the man before her.

'Jesus, Alex,' she exclaimed catching sight of him standing in the doorway.

Alex Costa was a mess. Dishevelled, still wearing the clothes he'd worn to her father's funeral yesterday, only now he had the remnants of what looked like splashes of alcohol and tomato sauce all down the front of him. His skin looked sullen and grey. His eyes puffy and swollen. His pupils dilated to the size of saucers. His forehead dripping with sweat.

'You look worse than me!' Nancy added, watching as Alex tried to hold himself up against the doorframe, his body still unwittingly swaying as he stood there frowning at Nancy. He was drunk, she realised. Paralytic and, judging by the look of confusion on his face, he was wondering why she was here at his apartment at this time of morning.

Nancy was beginning to wonder that now herself.

Though still wary that her attacker might be lurking nearby, Nancy didn't wait for an invite inside; instead, she pushed her way in.

'Oh, please. Do come in,' Alex slurred, his voice heavily loaded with sarcasm as he closed the door behind her and followed Nancy through to the lounge. Staggering as he went.

'If I'd known I was going to have guests I would have tidied up a bit,' he said as he saw Nancy wrinkle her nose up at the chaos and disarray of his apartment. The music was still blaring loudly. The floor strewn with empty bottles of Scotch that had been carelessly tossed on the floor now that they were empty. The place stunk too. A stale stench lingered in the air around them. Body odour? Food? There was a strong bitter aroma of alcohol in the air too.

'Housework hasn't exactly been high on my list of priorities lately!' Alex said, without apology, as he bent down and dragged the half-eaten pizza that was hanging out of its box off the sofa and onto the floor. Kicking it underneath with his foot. 'Here, take a seat. I must have dozed off…' he said, suddenly realising that he was currently wearing half of the pizza's toppings. His shirt covered in tomato paste and stringy bits of mozzarella cheese. He'd spilt his drink down himself too. He must have passed out. That's why he hadn't heard Nancy banging at the front door.

'Typical, the first time in over a week that I've managed to fall asleep and you wake me up.' Alex slurred, his voice making light of the fact that he was annoyed that Nancy had turned up unannounced.

Only, suddenly he realised that Nancy looked a state too. Her clothes were ripped, and a stream of blood trickled down her face.

'Fuck! What happened to you? Did you have a fall or something?' he said, noting that the girl had clearly been crying, which was to be expected after burying her father he guessed.

'I went for a walk, down along Brentwood Canal,' Nancy said. 'I was attacked.'

Every part of her was hurting from where she'd been flung down so roughly. Her cheek was grazed and her lip was swollen and she could feel the trickle of blood dripping down her forehead from the cut above her right eye.

'Attacked? By who? Did you get a good look at them?'

Nancy shook her head.

It was dark, and he had his hood up. I couldn't see his face…'

'Fuck!' Alex said, shaking his head. His expression of concern then, as he walked over towards his stereo system, unsteadily on his feet, and turned down the pounding music, before walking from the room and returning with a wet flannel.

'Here, stick that on your face,' he said, almost sympathetically, until he added: 'You're dripping claret all over my carpet. Jesus, you look a state, Nancy.'

'Likewise,' Nancy muttered under her breath, the smell of whiskey fumes coming from the man making her recoil. 'You smell like a brewery.'

'Yeah, well. It's been a fucking tough week, what with your dad…' Alex left the rest of the sentence hanging between them. As if he could barely bring himself to say it out loud.

Your dad's death.

Jimmy Byrne's dead.

'I fucking miss him, Nancy,' Alex said, crumbling before her onto the floor, as he began crying hysterically, the alcohol and the intensity of his grief seemingly colliding the moment he'd set eyes on Nancy.

Shit! She shouldn't have come here. This was the very last thing Nancy needed to hear right now. She was doing her damnedest to try and stay strong. Her father and Alex had been close. She got that. Best friends, working together for over two decades, the two men had been inseparable. There wasn't a birthday party or Christmas that Nancy could remember without Alex Costa being there.

Uncle Alex, that's what she and her brother Daniel used to call him when they were small.

The rumours she'd heard about him and her father recently couldn't be true. They were more like brothers and, judging by the state of him now, Alex Costa was clearly taking her father's death just as badly as she was.

'We all do,' she said, her words sounding colder than she really felt them; Nancy couldn't console this man in front of her. She couldn't even console herself.

She was too numb. Too cut off from her own emotions.

'I'm sorry. I shouldn't have come here,' she said getting up.

Debating on making her way home, she thought about the attacker again. He might still be out there. Waiting for her, and this time she might not be lucky enough to get away.

Jack Taylor.

Why hadn't she thought of him earlier? She should have gone straight to Jack. He'd know what to do. Jack always knew what to do.

'Do you think you could call Jack for me, Alex? Maybe he could drop me home?' Then on second thoughts, realising that the man probably wasn't even capable of making a phone call, Nancy added: 'Or I can call him. If you let me use your phone?'

Alex waved his hand in the air, making out as if he was more than capable, even though he could barely see straight now. His vision blurred, the room was spinning.

Somehow though he made the call.

More than happy to oblige. Of course he'd call Jack Taylor. Hopefully the bloke would hurry the fuck up and get his arse around here, and he would take Nancy with him when he left. The sooner Nancy fucked off the better. He didn't want to be around anyone right now. Least of all one of Jimmy Byrne's children. Nancy being here, in his apartment, was only making him feel worse.

'He's on his way.'

Nancy nodded. Grateful then, though she realised that Alex had called Jack for as much his own benefit as he did hers. He didn't want her here, as much as she didn't want to be here either. She was clearly disturbing him from festering all alone with his thoughts in this shithole of an apartment no doubt.

'You want a drink?'

Nancy shook her head; only, Alex didn't notice, or at least, if he did, he decided that she needed one. Making his way over to the side unit, he poured out two glasses of Scotch. Slopping his drink all over the floor as he turned and walked uneasy on his feet towards her.

'Drink it,' he said, indicating the glass in his other hand. 'It will help with the shock.'

Nancy grimaced, but did as she was told. Instead of refusing it, she held out her hand and accepted the glass gratefully, seeing as a drink and a flannel were clearly the only means of sympathy Alex had to offer.

Bringing the glass to her lips with a shaking hand, Nancy swallowed the drink down in one, savouring the immediate burn. Relishing the heat in the back of her throat. Her father drank this shit all the time, and normally Nancy couldn't stand the stuff, the acrid smell of Scotch made her want to be sick, but tonight the alcohol was the only thing that seemed to get anywhere near the deep chill that cut right through her.

The cold, shock. A mixture of the two no doubt. She needed something, anything to take the edge off her nerves.

She'd been terrified tonight.

All alone out there with some madman. She was lucky to still be alive, she thought, remembering how he'd slammed her head down onto the cold hard ground. The malice in her attacker's voice as he had threatened her.

'What were you doing out wandering the canal by yourself in the middle of the night? Don't you think that's a bit stupid?' Slurring, Alex's words were almost inaudible.

'I'm sorry?' Nancy said, bristling at his condescending tone. Alex was twisting this around onto her? Making out that her being attacked was her fault. That she'd somehow brought it upon herself. 'This wasn't just a random attack, Alex. Someone followed me. They knew who I was. It was deliberate.'

'What did they want then?' Alex said, half listening now as he spread a line of cocaine out on the table.

Nancy shook her head, disgusted. Alex was off his face on coke too, she realised, and yet he still had the cheek to call her out on *her* behaviour.

She didn't answer. Watching as Alex bent down and hoovered up a line of coke that he'd prepared for himself, Nancy didn't want to have this conversation with someone who was clearly preoccupied with getting higher than a proverbial kite tonight.

Feeling Nancy's eyes burning in to him, the disapproval coming off the girl in waves, Alex smirked. 'Do you want some?'

She shook her head.

'How long did Jack say he would be?' she said, hoping that he would hurry up. She'd just been attacked. Just had her life threatened, and Alex Costa couldn't give a shit about her. He was too far gone. Too busy shoving shit up his nose and drinking himself into a stupor.

'Not long,' Alex said. *Not quick enough.* Glancing at the clock on the wall before pacing the room, visibly agitated that Nancy was here. Alex didn't know what to do with himself.

The knock on the front door couldn't have come quickly enough for either of them. Relieved that Jack had arrived in record time, Alex went to let him in.

'Where is she?' Jack's voice travelled through the apartment.

Staying seated on the settee, Nancy could hear the genuine concern in Jack Taylor's voice. His sympathy making her want to cry.

Holding herself together as Jack strolled into the room seconds later, Nancy could see the shock and panic in his eyes as he looked at her.

'Shit, Nancy! What the fuck happened to you? You're bleeding? Do you need me to take you to the hospital? Are you okay?'

Nancy lost it. Unable to pretend that she was okay any longer, she burst into tears. Her body shaking with each wracking sob.

Jack was there then. Beside her on the sofa, wrapping his arms around her as she cried. He could have kicked himself for not playing it cooler, but seeing the state of the girl, her face all cut and swollen, the blood, he hadn't been able to disguise his concern for her. She was clearly visibly shaken up, her face streaked with jagged trails of black mascara that ran down both her cheeks.

'Alex said that you were attacked?' Jack said, a few minutes later when Nancy's tears had finally subsided.

'I'm fine. Really.' Placing a trembling hand up to the cut to apply more pressure on her face to stem the blood flow that Nancy thought had stopped, she knew that the fear in her voice betrayed her. Who was she kidding? She wasn't fine at all. She was scared. Genuinely.

'It was probably just some drunk hanging out by the canal and trying his luck. Walking down there on her own, Nancy was an easy target for some fucking scumbag druggie to try his luck. Whoever it was probably thought that they could rob her so he could pay for his next fix,' Alex spat, still annoyed that Nancy had brought her dramas to his door, tonight of all nights.

Not only did he have her sitting here, but Jack Taylor too. Alex just wanted them both to hurry up and leave. So he could be alone with his grief. The Scotch and cocaine were surging through his bloodstream now. Psyching himself up again, making him feel on edge.

Pouring himself another drink, he offered one to Jack, but Jack shook his head.

Which suited Alex just fine. More for him. 'Suit yourself,' he said before going to open another bottle.

Nancy raised her eyes now that Alex was out of sight. Nodding down to the table, to the remnants of cocaine and the empty bottle of Scotch from earlier, she didn't need to say anymore than that. Jack got the message loud and clear.

'He's a fucking mess, Jack. I've never seen him like this before.'

Jack nodded, knowing more about Alex Costa than he was prepared to let on to Nancy. The man wasn't his priority right now, she was.

'Are you okay? Did you get a good look at whoever it was?'

Nancy shook her head.

'It was too dark, but it wasn't a random attack, Jack,' she said. 'Someone followed me. They knew who I was, and they were trying to scare me off. Trying to shut me up…' she paused, knowing that she'd said too much.

Jack could see it too. That Nancy was holding something back.

'Is there something you're not telling me? What do you mean they were trying to shut you up?' he said, his eyes furrowed with confusion.

'I don't know.' Nancy closed her eyes, trying desperately to remember the exact words her attacker had said to her. Everything had happened so quickly tonight. It all seemed like a blur now.

'He pinned me down to the floor. He was on top of me. I couldn't breathe. I felt like he was suffocating me…'

'Shit, Nancy. He didn't *do* anything to you, did he?'

She knew what he was implying. Rape.

'No, thank God.' Nancy opened her eyes, mortified that she was even having this conversation but also relieved that she could shake her head in answer. She had been scared for her life tonight. Remembering the pain as her assailant ripped her hair from her head, before slamming her head down against the cold hard concrete. She must have been knocked out then, because when she'd come back around her attacker had been nowhere to be seen.

Nancy knew that she had to give Jack Taylor more. The man wasn't stupid, and he would find out eventually.

'He told me to leave things alone. That I needed to stop digging for information on my father…' she said, remembering the assailant's last words before she'd blacked out. *Stop digging. Or we'll bury you too.* The threat in his words clear. Nancy knew that it was to be her only warning.

The next time she might not be so lucky.

'"Digging"? I don't understand. Why would someone threaten you? We made enquiries, but we didn't find anything. I told you that.' Jack stared at Nancy, his eyes questioning her, as he wondered what it was he was missing.

Nancy pursed her lips, feeling guilty now.

'Look, Jack, don't take this personally. I know you did your best, but I had a couple of my father's other contacts look into some information for me…' she said, knowing full well that Jack would be offended that she'd gone behind his back. 'I just wanted to be thorough. I wanted to make sure that I'd checked out every eventuality. That there wasn't something we'd missed. Something that could lead us to my father's murderer.'

As the Met's lead detective inspector in Jimmy Byrne's murder investigation, Jack hadn't been able to find anything. Not a shred of evidence, not a single clue as to who could have been behind her dad's killing, and Nancy knew how it angered him just as much as her.

'But I looked into it,' Jack said, clearly annoyed that Nancy hadn't thought him competent enough to look into Jimmy Byrne's death himself. 'I already checked out every lead we had, Nancy. I had my men search every fucking square inch of that dockyard. Ten times over. The tech guys ripped that laptop apart, yet they still came back with fuck all. The only glimmer of hope that we had in finding out any information was from Marlon Jackson, but your brother, unfortunately, put paid to that.'

Nancy closed her eyes again. Remembering how just a few days earlier her brother had fired a bullet through Marlon Jackson's brain in revenge for her father's murder. Marlon had been about to talk, Nancy was sure of it. Only her brother had prematurely silenced him in his eagerness to get his revenge.

Only, now Nancy wasn't so sure that's what that was at all.

'If anyone can find out who the fucker was who killed your father, it's me. You know that. Why did you feel the need to double check? Don't you trust me?'

Seeing the insult and disappointment on Jack's face, Nancy knew that she'd hurt his feelings – that was the last thing she had wanted to do. That was partly why she hadn't told him that she had other contacts looking into it all in the first place.

'I didn't want to offend you, Jack, but can't you see? I had to at least try and find out who killed him… I guess I just wanted to make sure that we had covered everything. That there wasn't some piece of evidence that we missed. I called in a few favours from a couple of my dad's other contacts. I didn't think it would cause any harm,' she said, searching Jack's face for some understanding.

He was quiet for a moment. Then he nodded as he let what Nancy was telling him sink in. Ever the reasonable one. 'And did these other contacts of yours find anything?'

Nancy shook her head. She'd been waiting for this question. Debating whether she should just come clean and tell Jack and

Alex everything that she knew. That her hunch had paid off and her other informant had uncovered information that even Jack hadn't been able to find out.

Only, she couldn't bring herself to do it. Something was stopping her. Her intuition? A gut feeling? Her contact had found out who her father's killer was, and now that Nancy knew, she wasn't sure what to do with the information. She felt awful for lying, especially when she knew that Jack would only want to help her if he found out the truth.

But she was still having trouble processing it all. She was still trying to make sense of all this madness that had gone on around her.

'No. They couldn't find anything either. It's just like you said, whoever it was that killed my dad, they were smart. They didn't leave anything for us to go on. There's no leads, no clues, nothing. They covered their tracks well.'

Jack nodded in agreement.

'Well who the fuck knows what Jimmy got himself involved with? Or who he got involved with. That man had that many skeletons, his closet could have rivalled a fucking graveyard,' Alex spat, interrupting Nancy and Jack's conversation. He'd had enough of the bullshit tonight.

'Fucking hell, I don't know why you care so much,' he slurred, ignoring the shocked look on Nancy's face at the venomous words he spat. 'Come on, it could be fucking anyone that killed him. Who fucking really knows anything about Jimmy Byrne anyway? Not you!' Alex pointed at Nancy. 'His own daughter.' Then turning his attention to Jack Taylor he added: 'Or you! His confidant. The man that dug him out of the shit more times than I can care to remember. And what about me, huh? His best fucking mate?' Alex laughed at this. The irony of the words Jimmy had always used to describe him. 'That's what he called me. The man that he was secretly sleeping with for the past twenty years. A friend. What a fucking joke. That man has no idea of the destruction and heartbreak he's left behind him.'

He knocked back his drink, enjoying the anticipation of the numbness that he knew would instantly come. He left his statement lingering in the air. The tension in the room palpable.

'That's all I was in the end, another of your father's guilty secrets. He loved me though, did you know that?'

'Twenty years? Is this true? Did you know about this?' Nancy said, looking at Jack nervously as Alex's words rang in her ears as she realised that the rumours that had been doing the rounds were clearly true.

Jack shook his head, but his movement held no reassurance to her. Then glaring at Alex, he gritted his teeth. 'That's e-fucking-nough, Alex. Now's not the time—'

'That's just it though, Jack. There never was a good time, was there? Jimmy Byrne and his fucking sordid secrets. The man ruined everything and, in typical Jimmy fucking style, he's not even here to pick up the pieces,' Alex spat, before staggering over to sit down on the opposite side of the room.

'You knew didn't you?' Nancy searched Jack's eyes for an honest answer.

'Ignore him, Nancy. He doesn't know what he's talking about. He's drunk and talking shit.'

But Nancy wasn't buying it. Something had gone on between Alex and her father, her contacts had already informed her as much, and judging by Jack's reaction, he knew about them both too.

Her contacts had already informed her that her father had been having an affair with Alex, but twenty years? Her entire life? Nancy couldn't even process that.

'I wasted twenty fucking years of my life, and for what? It was all just lies. Jimmy only ever cared about himself. How many other men was he fucking, huh?'

'That's it, we're leaving,' Jack said, standing up and wrapping the blanket that was on the chair behind them around Nancy's shoulders.

Nancy felt as if the room was spinning. She felt physically sick. The hot acidic bile that had lingered in the pit of her stomach was now in the back of her throat. Threatening to pour out of her.

It was one thing hearing the rumours, or facts as they were, but another to hear it straight from Alex Costa's mouth.

Her father and Alex? *Uncle Alex?*

The ugly truth.

She could see the raw pain in Alex Costa's eyes. The same pain that flashed before her. The genuine grief that tormented him so. He was heartbroken, bereft and that's why he'd got himself into such a state tonight, on the night of her father's funeral.

'Come on, Nancy,' Jack said, placing an arm around her and leading her out of the room.

Nancy didn't argue.

In fact, she couldn't get out of Alex Costa's apartment quickly enough.

CHAPTER FIVE

Pulling the blanket tightly around her shoulders, Nancy Byrne allowed Jack Taylor to lead her through her quiet darkened house.

'It's colder in here than it is outside,' Jack quipped, shivering as they both made their way through to the kitchen.

He was right, the house, now empty of people, was freezing cold. The icy chill that lingered in the air made Nancy's skin prickle and her teeth chatter. At this early hour of the morning the house felt so empty, as if it had been abandoned. But she knew that her grandparents and her mother were all asleep upstairs in their beds. Daniel too.

'Well at least they've all buggered off to bed. I was half expecting to walk in here and catch your grandad still on a bender. Pissed as a fart he was earlier.'

Nancy rolled her eyes at that. He'd been bad enough when she'd stormed out of here earlier; no doubt he'd drunk himself into a coma by now and, judging by the state of the place, it had been some send-off.

The place looked like a bomb had hit it.

Staring around the kitchen, Nancy couldn't help but think that the place didn't look much better than Alex's apartment. With the huge pile of dirty cups and plates that were stacked high in the sink, overflowing it onto the countertops. Dumped there, to be cleaned up tomorrow, Nancy assumed, her eyes scanning the kitchen sides, cluttered with half-eaten platters of food. The few remaining sandwiches on each tray were crispy and congealed-looking. Dumped down between the mass of empty wine bottles that adorned the rest of the free space. Bottles of her father's favourite Merlot and Dom Perignon.

Champagne at a funeral? Nancy squeezed her eyes shut tightly, guessing, rightly, that only her grandfather would have been so crass and thoughtless to crack open bottles of bubbly the night of his own son's funeral. Celebrating her father's death under the guise of grieving. The man hadn't fooled anyone, especially not her.

'I've never seen this place look such a mess,' Nancy said, contemplating tidying some of it up, and then deciding against it. She didn't have the energy. Not tonight. She'd deal with it all tomorrow.

'Do you want me to clean the place up a bit?' Jack asked following the younger woman's gaze around the bomb site of a kitchen.

'No, it's fine.' Nancy shook her head. Not wanting Jack to go to anymore trouble than she'd already put him to tonight. Nor did she want him to make any sort of noise that might wake her family up. The last thing she needed was any of them seeing the state of her, and making a fuss about her being attacked – and they would make a fuss. Especially her nan Joanie. She'd be mortified if she saw the state of Nancy's battered-looking face. 'I'll call the housekeeper tomorrow and ask her to come back. Nan told her not to come in this week. She said that she wanted to do it all herself, you know, to keep herself busy. Only she's not able for it.' Nancy shrugged, recalling how determined her nan Joanie had been. That was the hardest part about all of this: Nancy had never seen her nan so broken. The woman had completely fallen apart, right before her very eyes.

It was heartbreaking to see. Her nan had always been so strong, so feisty. They'd always joked that that's where Nancy had got those traits.

Nancy was the only one trying to keep it together right now, it seemed.

'Okay, well if you won't let me help clear up a bit, at least let me make you a nice hot cup of tea before I go. Sit down,' Jack Taylor insisted, not giving Nancy any time to refuse, before strolling over to where the kettle was.

Nancy did as she was told.

Thank God for Jack, she thought. Sitting down at the kitchen table, she pulled the blanket up around her as she watched Jack busy himself pouring her a drink. It was a nice feeling, she decided. Letting someone look after her. Especially after the night she'd just endured.

Jack Taylor was a good man. His presence in the house reminded her of her father. How he always looked out for her and her family, and even now that her dad was gone, Jack was still here, still doing his bit. It was admirable really. Nancy knew that he must be hurting too. Of course he was. Watching as he stirred the tea and popped some biscuits on a plate, Nancy couldn't help but smile then.

Catching her eye as he put Nancy's cup and plate down on the table next to her, he looked perplexed.

'What?' he asked.

'Biscuits too. A proper little housewife. You're good at this, you know, looking after people.' Nancy pointed to the neatly arranged selection of biscuits. None of which she'd eat. She didn't have the appetite for them. Then realising that she probably sounded condescending, as Jack blushed and looked awkward, she added: 'I'm only playing. Thank you. Seriously, Jack, I'm glad I called you tonight. I don't know who else I could have called. Alex was nigh on useless…'

Jack couldn't argue with that.

Taking a seat next to Nancy, they both sipped their scalding hot tea in silence, the events of the night playing out separately in each of their minds.

Nancy spoke again first.

'Did you know about my father and Alex all along?'

Jack stalled on answering, thinking about lying to the girl, not wanting to add any more angst to how she must already be feeling. Only, he knew that he had to tell her the truth. He owed her that much. Besides, he figured out, rightly, that not a lot got past the likes of Nancy. The girl was too shrewd. She'd know straight away that he was lying; in fact, the way her eyes were burning into him, the way she was reading every part of him, Jack knew this was a test.

Nancy was willing him to be straight with her. What else could he do? Alex Costa had put the truth out there, there was no more denying it now. Cautiously, he nodded.

'The thing is with your father, he was a very private man,' he said honestly. 'But, yes, he and Alex had been close for a very long time.'

'Since before my mother?' Nancy asked, thinking back to when she'd been a small child. All those times that Alex had been there, lurking around in the background. An honorary Byrne family member.

Jack nodded again.

'Shit,' Nancy said simply. She wondered if Colleen knew the truth about her father. That would make sense. Why her mother had been so difficult and detached from them for all those years; why she'd spent the past two decades drinking herself in and out of oblivion.

What else didn't she know?

'If it's any consolation, I think your father always felt ashamed of who he really was. That's why he hid it from everyone. From the world. But he did love Alex, and Alex loved him too. Very much. That's why the man has gone to shit since your dad's death. Fuck, we all have in one way or another. Each of us hanging on as best we can. But Alex has taken it really hard. I think he's having some kind of breakdown.'

Nancy nodded sadly.

'I had no idea.' Her voice small. Hurt that her father hadn't trusted her enough to confide in her.

'Only, Alex is letting his personal feelings affect the business now too. If we're not careful, the whole lot could go down the pan. Trust me, people will be watching us closely from here on in. There'll be a lot of big faces around London just biding their time until they swoop in and take what your father and Alex worked so hard to build up. Especially if they see how weak Alex is right now.'

Nancy sighed. She'd been thinking the very same thing earlier tonight when she'd been down at the canal. About how many of her dad's contacts could be trusted. That's how this game worked. Her father had always said as much. *It's dog eat dog, and the devil takes the hindmost.* People would be trying to worm their way in on the Byrne territory now that her father was dead, and Alex was clearly incapable of running a bath, let alone a business. Only, Nancy wasn't going to just lie down and let people take what was hers.

'That's why I've decided that, for now, I'm going to take over,' she said, the force of her words shocking even her. 'That's what my dad would have wanted. That's why he took me on board in the first place. So that I could be part of all of this. So that one day I could run things,' Nancy reasoned. Though in fairness no one thought that day would come as soon as this. 'I worked alongside my father for long enough to know what was going on. I know exactly what he was involved in, and if Alex Costa can't step up to the plate, then I'm going to have to.' She was determined now. Watching for Jack's reaction. For that look of doubt to flash in his eyes. But Jack didn't flinch. He didn't even register a second of doubt. Instead, he nodded.

'Well, no offence, but a fucking amoeba would do a better job of it than Alex Costa is capable of right now!' Jack said with a grin, trying to lighten the mood. Though he'd made a mental note tonight to keep an eye on Alex Costa from here on in. Everything about the man's demeanour worried Jack.

The man wasn't stable. Far from it. He was unhinged and, judging by the state of him tonight, he was out of control too. That didn't bode well in this game. It gave people the illusion that they were weak, that they weren't coping. The empire that Alex and Jimmy had worked all those years to build together would all turn to shit. Then Jack would lose out on his cut too.

'I'll help you in any way I can,' he said. He meant it, too. He'd had a nice set up with Jimmy and Alex; just because Nancy was going to be running things from here on out, didn't mean that needed to change anything. Jack would still do his bit, and still get his cut of the profits. Nancy would need him now.

'Are you really okay?' he asked, wondering if Nancy's sudden bravado was all part of an act. 'I mean, *really* okay? You know you don't have to put on a brave face around me, don't you? I don't want to scare you, Nancy, but there's some pretty nasty things going on around London at the moment,' he said cautiously.

They'd had several murders in the area that Jack had been made aware of and, so far, no leads as to who was behind the killings. All they knew so far was that the targets were young gay men. Most of them working in the sex trade; though that didn't mean that Nancy was completely unassailable. It wasn't safe to be walking around that canal for anyone, especially in the middle of the night on their own.

'Yeah, of course,' Nancy said with a nod, appreciating Jack's concern. She genuinely didn't feel the need to pretend around Jack. Clasping her hands tightly around her mug of tea, she savoured the warmth that spread up through her fingers into her hands. She felt colder than ice tonight. Unsure whether the chill that cut her right down to her bones was from the frosty night air, or the shock of her attack. Alex Costa's revelation thrown in for good measure too. 'I'm fine. Really.'

Jack didn't look convinced, recognising Nancy's cold hard stare, the way her jaw locked between her words as she spoke; she had the same hardened look of her father, that same steely glare. Just like Jimmy had looked when he was riled about something.

'Honestly, Jack.' Nancy sighed, sensing his disbelief. Jack's silence spoke volumes. 'I'm a big girl. I can look after myself. Whoever it was tried to scare me but, unfortunately for them, I don't scare easily.'

Jack smiled then. Never a truer word had been spoken. He'd seen it for himself, first-hand. How Nancy would waltz through her father's offices and warehouses, ignoring the admiring glances she received from some of the younger men that worked there. Not showing a fraction of intimidation at being a young woman in such a male-dominated world. She always acted as if nothing intimidated her. As if no one would get the better of her.

But then, she'd always had her father's protection. She didn't have that now.

'Whoever it was caught me off guard. Maybe Alex was right, after all. Maybe it was foolish of me to walk around the canal on my own, in the middle of the night. I won't put myself in that position again, and next time, if there even is a next time, I'll be ready.'

Jack nodded, not wanting to tell Nancy what he was really thinking. That there would *always* be a next time. Especially in their world. People would be on the take now, ready and waiting to move in on what Jimmy and Alex had spent years building up. Snatching whatever minuscule offerings were there for the taking. Unless Nancy really stepped up, the business would be fair game.

'I can do this,' Nancy said with certainty then, and Jack couldn't help but grin, shaking his head at the determination in her voice. It was the same tone he'd heard a thousand times before from Jimmy – the same tenacity and determination.

She was a Byrne through and through.

Even still, the attack tonight must have shaken her.

'Are you sure you didn't recognise whoever it was that attacked you? His voice, his mannerisms? Is there anything you can think of? Anything at all?' Jack said once more, the detective inspector in him unable to let Nancy's assault tonight go.

Nancy shook her head.

'I've been wracking my mind ever since it happened. Trying to analyse the sound of the man's voice, the menace in his tone. He was so close to me, I don't think I'll ever forget the smell of his rancid breath, or his cheap aftershave. But I didn't recognise him,' she said, starting to feel more angry than scared about her earlier encounter. It had been too dark for her to see anything, and she'd been too petrified to think straight.

The attacker had been counting on that. Whoever it was tonight had made their point. Though if they thought that Nancy was just going to let it all lie, they clearly didn't know her at all.

'Well, whoever it was, I'm sure that's the last you'll see of them now. Especially as, like you say, you didn't find out anything about your dad's killer. They can't threaten you if you don't know anything,' Jack said again, drinking back his tea, his eyes not leaving Nancy's as she simply nodded back at him.

The sound of Joanie Byrne's voice suddenly filled the kitchen as the woman entered the room.

'Well this looks very cosy!' she said, as she padded across the cold marble kitchen floor, her dressing gown pulled tightly around her slim frame, her obligatory curlers rolled neatly on the top of her head. A creature of habit, even when her head was all over the place.

'Sorry, Nan, we didn't mean to wake you…'

'Ahh, you didn't, child. It's almost half past four and I haven't slept a wink all night myself. Been lying there staring at the ceiling listening to your grandad snoring for England in the next bloody bedroom. How I didn't go in there and smother him I really don't know. Not that I would have slept much tonight anyway, I guess… Jesus, Nancy! What happened to your face?' Stepping closer to where Nancy was sitting, Joanie suddenly caught a glimpse of her granddaughter's face. The dimly lit table lamp had masked it from a few feet away, but now up close there was no mistaking the cut on the girl's face. The swell of her right eye. Her voice fraught with panic then, she'd always been so protective of her Nancy. She loved the girl as if Nancy was her own daughter. 'What in God's name has happened, Nancy?'

'She fell,' Jack said, quickly. Hoping to save Nancy from a tirade of questions and sympathy. Only Nancy spoke at the same time. In unison.

'I was attacked, Nan.'

The room fell silent as Joanie looked questioningly from Jack to Nancy. The pair of them looking sombre now as the older woman tried to process what she'd just heard.

'Attacked? By who? Are you okay?' Joanie's voice shook. Stepping forward to hug Nancy tightly to her, the woman wrapped her arms so firmly around her granddaughter it was as if her life depended on it. 'Who would do such a dreadful thing? On the night of your father's funeral too?'

'Who indeed?' Nancy said sadly. 'I'm okay though, Nan, really. It looks worse than it is. Just a few scrapes and bumps. It was my own fault for walking down Brentford Canal on my own in the first place.' Insisting that she was okay, breaking away from the woman's hold. Playing down the attack as much as she could. The last thing she wanted was her nan fussing over her.

The woman had enough to deal with right now without Nancy adding to her worry.

'We should call the police,' Joanie said, for the first time in her life not sure what else she should do. 'Report it,' she said now, horrified. Just the idea of someone hurting her one and only granddaughter making her blood run cold.

'Jack *is* the police.' Nancy laughed then. Trying to ease her nan's hysterics. 'Honestly, Nan, it's nothing. Probably just some silly drunk trying his luck to mug me; only, he soon scarpered when he realised I didn't have my handbag with me.'

Unconvinced, Joanie narrowed her eyes, scrutinising Nancy. The girl was lying to her. She had always been able to tell when Nancy tried to palm her off with a fib. The girl had the same mannerisms as her father, and Joanie had always known when Jimmy was lying too.

'Is that so?' Joanie cast her stare to Jack then, instead. Her eyes boring into his, as if challenging him to lie to her once more tonight.

But Jack knew better than to deceive the woman. So, instead, he just shrugged his shoulders, not wanting to get involved in a spat between the two women.

Nancy could be a stubborn cow when she wanted to be, but she wasn't fooling anyone, certainly not Joanie. The old woman didn't miss a trick.

'Will I wake your brother? Or your grandad? Not that your granddad will be much use to you. He's not much use to any of us really.'

'No, Nan! I'm fine, honestly. There's no point waking everyone up and making it into a big drama. It's my own fault. I should never have gone off on my own tonight. Really, I'm fine. I just need to get my head down and get some sleep.'

'If your father was here, he'd know what to do.' Joanie started crying then. 'My Jimmy would take control of things like this. He always knew what to do. How to keep us all safe.' That's who they'd always depended on when the shit had hit the fan in this household. Her Jimmy. Only, he was gone. The realisation hitting Joanie once more like a physical blow to her stomach. She slumped down onto the seat next to Nancy, unable to hold back her tears.

'Nan. Please don't cry,' Nancy said as she reached for her nan's hand, placing her palm over the top of it. 'We'll all be okay, Nan. In time, you'll see.'

Joanie nodded. More than anything else in the world, she really wanted to believe that, too, but how could she? Her son hadn't even been in the ground for twenty-four hours and already his daughter had been attacked.

There would be worse to come. Joanie was certain of it. She'd been unwittingly part of this lifestyle for long enough to know that there was no honour amongst thieves when it came to making money. It was every man for himself.

Still, the last thing she wanted to do was scare Nancy any further than she already had been tonight.

'I don't know what I'm going to do without him here,' she wailed.

Nancy felt her own tears then. Spilling out, down her cheeks. Her own loss magnified by the grief and pain that she could see so clearly in her nan. How, overnight, her nan looked as if she'd aged a decade. Her eyes sunken, their sparkle gone. The lines on the woman's face etched deeper into her skin than Nancy ever remembered. As painful as her father's death had been to Nancy, Joanie's pain ran far deeper. No mother should ever have to witness her own child's body being placed into the ground.

'I've only just put the kettle on, Joanie. Let me make you a nice cup of tea,' Jack said then, sensing the moment between the two women, and wanting to make himself useful.

'Tea? What was it with everyone these days that, no matter what happens, they think a cup of poxy tea is some kind of solution? All the tea in China isn't going to make me feel better. What I want you to do, Jack, is get your arse down to Brentford Canal and look for the bastard that did this to Nancy.' Joanie looked at Jack expectantly, the disappointment on her face blatantly obvious.

'The fucker's probably long gone now, Joanie...' Jack said, and then, on seeing the stern look on Joanie's face, the fury in her eyes, he took the hint. 'Of course I'll go.'

Pulling his leather jacket around his broad shoulders, he nodded, as Joanie knew he would. 'Are you all right now, Nancy, if I get off?'

'Thanks for bringing me home,' Nancy said, making eyes at Jack as if to apologise to him for the fact that her nan wouldn't just let this go.

'Try and get some sleep. I'll pop back tomorrow and see how you're doing, okay?'

The two women sat in silence as Jack left.

'If anyone can find the bastard, Jack will,' Joanie said, her voice full of certainty. Satisfied now that someone was at least doing something to try and find out who attacked Nancy. 'Now come on, drink up and let's get you off to bed, my love,' she said, pressing her hand against Nancy's arm, breaking the younger girl's thoughts. The poor girl looked exhausted. They all were. The events of the past couple of weeks had been too much for any one family to have to go through.

Nancy nodded. Even though she knew that, as tired as she was, there would be no sleep for her tonight. How could she when they were all lying in their beds, blissfully unaware that her father's killer was known to them all.

A murderer amongst them.

That was why she'd been attacked tonight. That's why she was being warned off. She'd lied to Jack and Alex when she'd said her contacts hadn't found anything. They had. Nancy knew who her father's killer was, and she wasn't going to sleep again, nor grieve properly for her father, until he'd been dealt with once and for all.

She promised herself that.

CHAPTER SIX

Ignoring his children's continual cries as they echoed around the tiny bedsit, filling both the tiny space and his head, Gem Kemal slumped down onto the chair at his kitchen table. A defeated man, he stared around the grotty, cramped bedsit that he and his family had been forced to call home for the past three years. This was it. He worked himself into the ground, day in day out, and this was all they had to show for themselves.

Miyra and the children were the only things that kept him going. The only reason that he managed to drag himself out of his bed each day and face his two jobs. All so he could keep this roof over their heads, and a roof was pretty much all his money stretched to. The rent here was extortionate. The landlord, yet another opportunist cashing in on Gem and Miyra's desperation to live in England, charged them a small fortune for the privilege. The place was not much more than a slum. The walls of the bedsit were thick with black mould. The carpets threadbare. There were two single beds that the four of them were forced to share; Gem and Miyra each sleeping with one of the children. Gem could barely remember what it felt like to share a bed with his wife alone anymore.

Exhausted from working the night shift at the club, he forced himself to summon up some energy for the busy morning that he knew he had ahead of him. His boss had called him in again, for a so-called meeting, which only meant a day of running errands, Gem expected.

'You look tired, Gem!' Miyra Kemal said, rubbing her husband affectionately on the shoulder before busying herself making him a warm drink, just as she always did when he came home between shifts. The fact that she'd been up all night with their two sick children not even factoring in her head. Gem still had work to do, she was tired, yes. But she could try and sleep this morning.

Gem loved that about Miyra. How his wife always put everyone else ahead of herself. So selfless, and giving. He loved this time of the morning, too: 6 a.m., just before the sun was up, when they both stole a rare few moments together before Gem ventured back out to work.

'How did last night go?' Miyra asked, heating up some water in a saucepan on the camping stove that Gem had bought for them after the electricity board had disconnected them for not keeping up with their payments.

'Same as every other night,' he said, not wanting to burden Miyra with the minor details of his workload. Miyra didn't need to hear any of that.

Pushing the pile of unopened and unpaid bills to the edge of the table, away from him so he didn't have to stare at them any longer, Gem rubbed his throbbing head. Out of sight, out of mind. Wasn't that what the English liked to say? Though with the threat of the landlord kicking them out, and the amount of debt they had hanging over their heads, their money troubles were never out of mind.

'You wouldn't believe the amount of money that the club's bringing in, Miyra. Alfie Harris must be making a fortune.' Gem shook his head in wonderment. 'And look at us. Living here like this.'

Miyra knew not to comment. Her husband did this some-times. Vented about their misfortunes. Ranted for a while. Of course Miyra could believe it. That's the way it had always been.

They were immigrants, and immigrants in London were treated like shit. Like nothing. But it was starting to really bring Gem down.

That's why people employed illegal immigrants in the first place. They didn't need to concern themselves with health and safety, or human rights, they could treat their workers how they wished. Make them work every hour of the day for a pittance and no one would dare to complain about the conditions in which they were forced to work. Not if they wanted to stay living in this country undetected.

'It's soul-destroying how hard I work, and how little appreciation I get for my efforts. I'm one of the most hard-working men at that club. Alfie Harris knows my worth; he knows that when I work the door he barely gets any trouble. Who wants to mess with a six foot two, crazy-looking Turk?' Gem spat, trying to make a joke of it all, as he let his words trail off, catching the flash of concern sweeping across his wife's face.

He could feel the anger building inside of him. So unjust, so unfair was his treatment, it was taking all he had to try and contain it. The last thing Miyra needed was more to worry about.

'I'm sorry!' he said. 'Ignore me. I'm in a bad mood.'

His wife had enough to contend with stuck inside these four walls, day in and day out. The children constantly squealing and crying. Hungry and bored, and even worse now they were both sick with the flu.

She had a lot on her plate, too.

'I shouldn't complain. At least I have a job, huh!' Though even Gem didn't believe the fake optimism in his words. Without a work permit, he had to take whatever he could get.

London was so corrupt. Since he'd arrived here just a few years ago, Gem had seen and heard things that had shocked him to his core. The place was overrun with criminals and there was deception and deceit going on at every darkened corner. Everyone seemed to be on the earn. He'd seen it himself first-hand at the clubs he'd been working at. The drugs, the girls, all sorts of deceit and villainy going on.

Though the only people making any real money from it all were the main players. This latest club he'd been working at the past three months was making an absolute fortune. Well, Alfie Harris, the owner was, and a few of the main dealers there too.

Gem was lucky to make minimum wage, and it galled him because he was the one working on the front line, working as part of the club's security team. He dealt with both the punters and the dealers first-hand, yet got little for his efforts. Alfie Harris was a shrewd man, Gem knew that. Which is probably why the bloke was so rich.

Changing the subject now, annoyed that he seemed to be working every hour, yet getting nowhere, Gem looked at his wife. 'How have the children been?' Staring over at his children that Miyra had placed inside the playpen in a bid to try and contain them from climbing all around the room. The sound of them both snivelling and crying tearing through his brain.

'They had a bad night. Emin's got a temperature. He kept us both up all night. Hopefully he'll be better today; though I think Azra might have caught it now. She hasn't stopped crying all morning.'

Gem nodded. He'd promised his wife that he wouldn't get involved in anything illegal, but maybe that had been a mistake. What sort of life was this for his family? Trying to earn an honest wage wasn't getting them anywhere. It was as if they were on a hamster wheel, going round and round in circles and getting nowhere fast. Miyra and the children were stuck inside this bedsit day in, day out. All of them miserable and hungry. Exhausted from the mundanity of their lives.

He felt it too. He was exhausted. Drained. All he wanted to do right now was crawl into his bed and fall into a deep, unrelenting sleep.

'You should try and get some rest today too,' Gem said, hoping that when he went to work Miyra would do just that.

His wife seemed tired. Quieter than usual, as she fussed around the kitchen, her back to him. Making him his morning cup of tea. He watched as she held onto the worktop as if to keep herself upright as the pot on the camping stove bubbled away. Her tiny figure like that of a child. Miyra had always been slim. Only, now he could see the outline of her bones underneath the thin fabric of her clothes. Jutting out, making her look malnourished and frail.

Watching as Miyra poured the boiled water into the cup and stirred the tea, before turning and carrying it over to where he was sitting, Gem's gaze moved to his wife's stomach. Her belly was nothing more than a small, bloated swell. As if she'd eaten too much food. It was hard to believe that a small baby resided in there.

Miyra barely looked pregnant, let alone almost eight months gone.

Taking the cup from her gratefully he smiled at her. His eyes lingering on her small, deflated breasts then. They should be full by now, but still her milk hadn't come in, and Gem knew that caused Miyra a head full of worry.

'I've had to reuse the last tea bag. There's no sugar either.' Her words sounded like an apology as she turned to take a seat herself. She suddenly felt heady, her vision blurred, and she stumbled as her legs suddenly went from beneath her.

Gem was up on his feet then.

As Miyra hit the table, sending the tea flying, the tepid liquid pouring out across the tabletop and dripping into a pool on the floor, Gem hooked his hands under his wife's arms, struggling to hold her upright.

'I'm okay,' Miyra insisted, though her disorientation was clear in her eyes as Gem guided her to the chair next to her.

'Sit, Miyra. Please.'

'I'm fine…' Registering that she had just fainted Miyra did as she was told, suddenly grateful of the seat beneath her bottom, steadying herself by placing her hands on the kitchen table in a bid to regain her balance. 'I'm just dizzy. I'm okay. It's normal in pregnancy…'

Gem shook his head, disbelievingly. Angry at himself for putting Miyra in this situation. What sort of husband was he? Unable to care and provide for his wife and children.

'Normal? How would we know what was normal? How do we know that you and the baby are really okay?'

All of this was Gem's doing. He knew that. He was the one that had forbidden Miyra to attend any hospital appointments. They were immigrants. No one could be trusted. Doctors, midwives, nurses. None of them. They'd all talk. Poking their noses into matters that didn't concern them. Prying about their other children, and their financial situation. About whether or not Gem and Miyra should even be here in England.

It was too risky.

They'd get sent back to Turkey. They'd be made an example of. Gem couldn't allow that to happen. So somehow Gem had convinced Miyra to just trust that all was well.

And so far it had been. Miyra had what the textbooks referred to as an easy pregnancy. But things hadn't been so easy for her lately. She was struggling now and with such a small bump he couldn't help but think that maybe the baby was struggling too. Gem felt guilty for that. He'd married Miyra and vowed to love her and protect and provide for her for all of their days; only, so far, he'd broken those promises.

He loved her, of course, fiercely. But he'd neither provided for her nor protected her.

That saddened him greatly.

England, the place where dreams came true? That was all lies. This country was a place of nightmares, and he'd fallen for it. He'd dragged Miyra over here from Turkey so that they could have a better life. Only, the painful truth was, now they had no life at all. Here in England they were treated like rubbish. Disrespected. Talked down to.

'You need to rest, Miyra. You're doing too much.'

Miyra nodded obediently, even though, they both knew that rest for her would be impossible. How could she rest while Gem was out working every hour? She had no choice but to look after the children. When this baby came along, it would be even harder. Though, of course, his wife didn't voice those thoughts. She never did. Miyra never allowed a single complaint to leave her lips.

'You're hungry, Miyra,' Gem said, acknowledging what they both knew was true. The reason why Miyra was feeling weak and faint. 'The babies are hungry too. I will sort something out today.'

He sank back down opposite his wife. The defeat in his voice that of a broken man, but he had to keep fighting. His wife and children were depending on him. He'd have to take some money from the club's tills.

It shamed him to even think about stealing from his workplace, to think how low he had sunk but the truth was that was just how desperate he had become now. He'd done it before and he would do it again.

What other choice did he have?

When he'd first started doing it, Gem had always intended to put back the money he stole, once he'd been paid, but his wages just never seemed to stretch that far to allow him the opportunity. It had become a habit. Topping up his wages every now and then. Hoping and praying that no one noticed the money had been taken.

And so far they hadn't.

'I'll bring something back for you all. I promise.'

Miyra simply nodded, but he could see the look in her eyes.

Gem wasn't due his money yet; they still had another five days to go until he was paid, and he couldn't call in any favours. He already owed money to Alfie Harris that he had subbed him.

That was the hardest thing for Gem to bear, the look of disbelief in his wife's eyes. She may not voice her complaints but they were there. Lingering under the surface, unspoken. Her silence speaking volumes. That Miyra had already resigned herself to the fact that they would all be going hungry today was clear on her face, and it pained Gem to see that his wife had no faith in him.

Sometimes he wondered if it would be easier if Miyra was angry at him. If she blamed him, as he blamed himself for the shitty existence he had bestowed on his family. She could have chosen anyone but, for some reason, she'd chosen him, and Gem still had days now when he couldn't believe his luck. He had nothing much to offer her, only love, and boy did he love her. More than anything, with every part of his being.

That's why he was working so hard. This was all for his family.

'I've got to go,' he said, eyeing the clock on the wall above them. He couldn't afford to be late again. When Alfie Harris summoned a meeting, you got there on the dot or else.

Picking up the cup that had fallen, Gem mopped up the spilt tea. Wiping the table dry, he made his way over to where the children were both playing loudly in their playpen now. He held his arms out to them, picking them both up, glad that their crying had stopped.

'Come,' he said to his wife, as he led her into the bedroom and placed the children both down on one of the beds, kissing them both on their foreheads gently before he tucked them in and then turned his attention back to Miyra. 'Lie down. The children are tired. Get some sleep while you can. I'll be back soon.'

Miyra nodded gratefully. Hoping that Gem was right and that the children would settle. At least if she slept for a little while she wouldn't feel so hungry and dizzy.

'I'll figure something out for us,' Gem promised, as he watched his wife lie back on the bed, closing her eyes gratefully before placing her hand protectively on the small round of her stomach.

And he would.

No matter what, Gem was going to have to find some way of trying to fix this for them all.

They couldn't go on as they were.

Things were going to have to change and soon.

Gem was determined.

CHAPTER SEVEN

'What the fuck do you mean the shipment's not come through? It was due this morning!'

'No, it was cancelled…' Scott James said, stepping forward. The only man in the warehouse brave enough, or maybe stupid enough, to answer back to Alex Costa. Especially when the man was in this ferocious mood.

Alex had only been here twenty minutes and already he'd managed to tear the office apart. Ranting and raving, as he dragged out all of the files from the cabinets, clearly not happy until he'd completely ransacked the place. *Christ knows what he's looking for*, Scott thought, but he was the mug that needed to try and rein the bloke in before he really did some damage to the place.

'Boss, you're going to do yourself an injury in a minute. You need to calm down. We can sort this…' Scott said trying to reason with him as Alex almost pulled the huge metal cabinet down on top of him. Pushing it back upright, Scott could see that all eyes were on them now. The other workers had downed tools and were having a good old gawp as Alex Costa lost his shit in front of them all for the second time this week.

Sensing the other workers' apprehension of getting involved in their boss's outburst, Scott knew that they were all doing the sensible thing of keeping the fuck out of it. Which is what Scott should have done, really; only, it was Scott's job to oversee things in the warehouse. Deal with any problems and, unfortunately for him, Alex Costa had become a huge fucking problem.

'Calm down? Calm fucking down? Someone's royally fucked up and I won't calm down until I find out who it was that took it upon themselves to go ahead and cancel the shipment?' Alex Costa was raging. 'I can't get hold of any of the fucking couriers and I've got every bastard in London ringing me, hassling me for their gear. What have you all been doing down here, huh? I'm not paying you to sit around and scratch your arses. What? Do you need a fucking babysitter? Someone to give you step-by-step instructions. Fuck me, monkeys take better direction than you lot.'

Alex Costa was rambling now. His slurred speech and blood-shot eyes told Scott all he needed to know. That and the stench of alcohol that came off the man in waves. Their boss was drunk, and knowing Alex Costa, as they all did, probably off his face on cocaine too. He was acting deranged. Unhinged. This was the second time this week he'd turned up here in this state, but this time Scott knew that he had to put an end to Alex Costa's erratic behaviour. It wasn't good for business.

Watching now as Alex slumped down into the office chair, exhausted from the chaos he'd created, opening the top drawer of the desk and reached for the bottle of Scotch that he kept there. Not bothering to get himself a glass, he undid the cap and glugged it back. Then he glared back at Scott, as if challenging him.

'What the fuck are you lot looking at, eh?' He caught the condescending looks he was being thrown from his own workforce, all standing around outside the office, peering in through the large glass front. 'You all having a good fucking look, are you? Go on, someone be brave and say what you're really thinking. I know you all would have heard the rumours by now. About me and Jimmy. Only, they're not rumours, and I don't give a fuck what any of you think,' Alex spat, glaring at the men each in turn. 'Looking down your noses at me. You don't know shit.'

'No one's thinking anything, Alex, we're just concerned about you, that's all.'

Alex was off his seat then. His face puce as he shouted. 'Bullshit! You think I don't know what you've all been saying about me. The comments and jokes. Nothing goes on in this place without you lot ripping the shit out of everyone. You're all two-faced cunts the lot of ya! You're all happy to have your pockets lined with my fucking money at the end of the month though, ain't ya! Well how about you all go and fuck yourself. I ain't paying none of you until I find out who went behind my back and cancelled today's shipment. One of you imbeciles has cost me a shit load of cash.'

Throwing the bottle of Scotch against the wall with all his strength, the glass and liquid exploded against it, which was the moment that Scott made a leap for Alex Costa, throwing the man down onto the desk, just as chaos amongst the workers erupted then too. The rest of the workers were enraged by Alex's threat; Scott was going to have a riot on his hands if he didn't put this to bed and quickly.

The men were no longer willing to be spoken to in such a way by their boss. They'd given Alex Costa a free pass the first time he'd come in here drunk and shouting abuse at them all, because of Jimmy. They all knew he was hurting and, to be fair, most of them were too. But patience was starting to wear thin now. Alex Costa wasn't the only one to be affected by Jimmy Byrne's death.

'Alex you're a fucking mess, mate. Go home and sort your head out,' one of the men called out, trying to appeal to Alex's more diplomatic side. Going on his actions tonight, though, he was beyond being understanding.

'I want my fucking money. We've been manning this place all week, and following orders as always,' another bloke shouted.

Trying his hardest to hold Alex Costa down, as the man hit and kicked out beneath him, he could see the other workers losing their shit now too. Disgruntled about not getting paid what they were owed, Scott knew they all had good reason to be angry.

'Alex can't take over from Jimmy. He hasn't got it in him,' another worker said, as the men around him all jeered in agreement. 'He's only going to run this business into the ground. Look at the fucking state of him; the bloke couldn't run a fucking egg and spoon race let alone an operation like this one.'

'Look, all of you, just back off. Let me sort this out, yeah!' Scott shouted, doing his best to restrain Alex, though the man was giving as good as he got. Hitting out. Kicking his legs up. As pissed as he was, he was still as strong as a bloody ox.

Nancy Byrne couldn't have timed her arrival any better.

'Well this is a lovely welcoming reception. Ooh, I see you laid on drinks too. You really shouldn't have!' Nancy said, stepping into the office and eyeing the state of the place. Scotch dripping from the walls, shards of glass all over the floor, and paperwork everywhere. It looked as if they'd been burgled.

The entire warehouse fell suddenly silent then.

Nancy Byrne was the image of her father. The same pale skin and steely eyes. She had the same commanding presence that Jimmy had too. Teamed together with her flaming red hair and her indisputable beauty, she held every man's attention in the room; they gave their boss's daughter the respect she was due. The respect that they knew she demanded.

Even Alex Costa had stopped his tirade.

Straightening himself up, as Scott James released his hold on him, he sat against the edge of the desk, as if having to support himself.

'I'm sorry to call you out here, Nancy. I didn't know what else to do,' Scott said, apologetically, hoping that he'd done the right thing. Normally he would have sorted out any kind of situation without involving anyone else. He was more than capable. Only, he'd never had to sort out his own boss before, and he figured Nancy would want to know what was going on here tonight.

He had no one else to call.

Nancy nodded understandingly. Though her eyes didn't waver from Alex's. The man looked even worse than the last time she'd seen him. Unwashed and unkempt, a shadow of his former self, the man looked like a tramp.

'You did the right thing, Scott,' Nancy said simply, reassuring the man as she sensed the ever-growing tension in the warehouse around her. It was no wonder that all the men here were disgruntled. Nancy had caught the tail end of the abuse that he was dishing out and to say that she was less than pleased about it would have been the understatement of the century. She was fuming.

'Now, do you want to tell me what the fuck is going on in here?' she said, directing her question at Alex this time.

'Some fucking prick has cancelled the shipment. I was just telling all these fuckers that they wouldn't be getting jack shit from me until I found out who it was.' Straightening up his shirt, suddenly self-conscious, Alex wasn't prepared to back down. Not when he knew that everyone's eyes were on him, that they were all lapping up the way that Nancy was talking down to him.

'Is that so?' Nancy said, nodding as if she understood. She stepped forward to pick up the phone. Dialling a number, she spoke briefly to someone at the other end, before hanging up just a few moments later.

'Well that's good news for everyone here then. The mystery's been solved. Apparently, Alex, it was you who cancelled it. I just spoke to the courier directly. He said you called him a couple of days ago and told him that you didn't need anymore gear from him. He said you were rude as fuck to him, too. That we're lucky he'd even consider doing business with us again.' Keeping her voice controlled as she waited for the penny to drop. For Alex to realise that some time this week in his paralytic state he'd taken it upon himself to make some very foolish decision that had ended up affecting them all.

'No fucking way…' Alex started, but his voice didn't sound certain. There was a tremor of doubt there; Nancy could hear it too.

Nancy stared at Alex, her eyes shrewd. Burning with fury, only somehow she managed to keep her cool. 'Right, lads. I'm sorry about the mix-up here today. The shipment is coming in tomorrow now. So it will be business as usual. I really appreciate you all keeping the place going the past few weeks, especially with everything that's gone on. Your efforts haven't gone unnoticed by me, and I'll be seeing to it that you all get a little extra in your wages this month.'

'Thank you, Nancy, we really appreciate that,' Scott James said, feeling sorry that the girl had to contend with all this drama when she clearly had more important things to deal with right now. 'Only, it's not business as usual when Alex keeps getting himself in this state. We can't work like this. It's not fair on us all having to tiptoe around him…' Scott intervened, feeling brave now, hoping that Nancy was in the same mind as they all were.

Nancy nodded.

'Scott, do me a favour and drop Alex off home, will you,' she said, before addressing Alex directly. 'I can't have you here in this state. Go home and sort yourself out. Take some time off,' she said, dismissively. Her mind made up of what had to be done here.

Alex didn't bother to argue. He knew that he'd gone too far this time.

Sensing the looks of pity that were being thrown her way from the workforce, that Nancy was here contending with this bullshit when she clearly had more important matters to deal with right now, Nancy made a point of standing taller. Her head up, her voice loud and assured as she addressed the room. She hadn't come here for sympathy. She'd come here to get this place sorted out once and for all, and Alex Costa had just made things ten times easier for her.

'From now on you all answer to me. Nothing and no one comes in or out of this place without you running it past me first, do you understand? I'm running things around here from here on out.'

Seeing the sea of faces around her nod in agreement, she finally relaxed. 'Good! Now someone do me a favour and get this shithole cleaned up!'

CHAPTER EIGHT

'Joanie, you're staring at a blank screen, you silly old fool.' Coming through from the kitchen, clutching his pint of ale in his hand, Michael Byrne was happy from his fill of the lovely dinner that Colleen had made for them all. He'd been looking forward to retiring to the lounge for the evening and watching the footie in peace, only, Joanie had beat him to the television set it seemed.

Sitting on the settee, her eyes fixed on the blank screen that she hadn't even bothered to turn on, a minor detail that Michael doubted Joanie had even noticed. The woman wasn't with it at all and her behaviour of late was really starting to unnerve Michael.

At first he'd made the most of his wife's sudden melt down. Embracing the fact that Joanie was preoccupied, so entangled in her grief to pay him the slightest bit of attention. It felt so liberating suddenly that Michael could do and say as he pleased without Joanie breathing down his neck every five minutes, scolding him, and trying to control his every action. It had been almost amusing watching this strong, fiery, woman reduced to nothing. Meeker than a little mouse. No longer shoving her opinions down all of their throats. No longer henpecking him into doing a million little jobs around the house each day, just to keep him busy and make herself feel as if she was the one in control.

Joanie had always been the one in control, but not any more as it would seem.

Jimmy had been their only son. They'd tried for more children after him, but they'd never succeeded in producing one. Michael had always thought that it was a blessing, to be honest. He never really took to parenthood. As a baby, Jimmy only ever wanted his mother's affection; he had no interest in Michael. So Michael had left Joanie to get on with it. Spoiling their one and only child. Plying him with every toy, the latest fashion. Showering him with love and attention.

Whatever Jimmy wanted, little Jimmy got and, as the years had gone on, the worse it had become.

His Joanie had created a monster.

Saint fucking Jimmy.

A spoilt little shit, that had grown up to be a bully and an intimidator. Even as a grown man, Jimmy had never found out what it was like to want something. To *really* want something. Not like Michael had spent his life doing. His Jimmy had everything handed to him all his life on a silver platter by Joanie.

The woman had lived solely for him. Him and their two grandchildren, of course. Nancy and Daniel. But even the grandkids weren't able to soften the blow of Joanie's grief.

The woman had become nothing more than an empty shell.

Not eating, not sleeping. She barely even bothered to speak.

Oh, and how Michael was enjoying every second of her beautiful silence so far. Only, the woman's moping and self-pity was starting to become tiresome. Joanie was practically rendered useless. No longer house-proud, the woman didn't bother to clean and tidy their home anymore, nor did she prepare and cook any of their meals.

Though all wasn't lost. Colleen had taken over where Joanie had left off, and Michael had to say that, so far, he was impressed. After all the years that Joanie and Jimmy had spent treating his daughter-in-law as if she was worthless – nothing. The pair of them had taken great delight in berating and taunting the woman for the entire time she'd been part of this godforsaken family. Joanie especially. Yet, Colleen must be a better woman than his wife could ever be.

Not only had she stepped up to the plate now that Joanie needed help, the woman had done it so graciously. She hadn't held a grudge, or taken her opportunity to throw everything back in Joanie's face, which, by all rights, she could have done. No one would have blamed her, not after everything she'd endured and suffered at the woman's hands.

Michael had seen the extent of the poor girl's bullying and mistreatment with his very own eyes. For years she'd suffered the brunt of Joanie's sharp tongue and cruel ways.

It took a strong woman to let that go.

Which was exactly what Colleen had turned out to be. Colleen Byrne had shown her true colours and Michael, for one, was pleased. Not only did it show her strength of character but it also saved him from the effort of having to do everything for himself. Colleen had stepped up and was doing a great job of holding things together, and for that alone he felt eternally grateful to the girl.

Colleen had changed beyond recognition these days. No longer drinking or taking any medication, she was totally clean. The tension between the two women had completely disappeared in an instant too. Colleen hadn't even thought twice about looking out for Joanie, especially after she'd seen the state the woman was in. Joanie was barely able to look after herself, let alone any of them.

That's when Colleen had really come into her own.

Taking over where Joanie had left off, the woman was a natural. Not a bad little cook either, Michael had thought. He'd spent the week feasting on dishes like pie and mash and shepherd's pie, just simple meals, mind, but Michael Byrne was a simple man and that suited him just fine.

But Colleen was out in the kitchen now, clearing up after dinner so that meant Michael was going to have to deal with Joanie himself.

'Come on, Joanie, love, why don't I run you a nice hot bath, eh? You can go and have a soak and then fix yourself up a bit,' Michael said softly, trying his best to snap his wife out of her permanent sombre mood.

He stared at the woman that he'd been bound to for all these years. Till death us do part. The words more like a threat than a promise, permanently hanging over him. Joanie looked so small and vulnerable sitting there, her tiny frame swamped in her huge dressing gown. A trail of gravy all down her front. Her hair matted, flat, to her head. Her skin lined and grey looking. It was as if Michael was only seeing her for the very first time. She looked old without her usual face full of make-up and her hair styled to perfection. It was as if Jimmy's death had aged her. Gone was the glamorous old Joanie. In her place sat an old, haggard woman.

Only a week since Saint Jimmy's burial, though to look at Joanie it could have easily been a decade.

Joanie looked broken beyond repair, and Michael almost felt sorry for her. As much as Joanie and Jimmy's relationship had riled him over the years, the woman was lost without him.

'Come on, love,' Michael said, hoisting Joanie up onto her feet, guiding her out of the room. 'You'll feel better if you make a bit of an effort. Sitting around all day in that filthy dressing gown is enough to give anyone depression. Me 'en all seeing as I'm the one that has to bleeding well look at you. Come on, let's get you up those stairs, huh?'

But Joanie didn't move. Instead she just stared at her husband as if the man had two heads growing from his shoulders. As if she'd just woken up from a sudden trance, her eyes boring into the man that she'd spent most of her life with. Reading him, just as she always had done, like an open book. The man was that transparent she could see the wall behind him.

'I'll feel better, will I?' she scoffed. 'Is that what you want, is it? Me to feel better. How selfless of you.'

Michael was quiet then. Unsure what his error was this time; he'd only been trying to help. He didn't know why Joanie was so suddenly angry with him.

'Come on, Joanie, I just thought it would do you good…'

Women. He'd never understand them.

'There's not another reason that you're trying to shoo me off upstairs, out of the way, is there?' Joanie said, raising her voice, before grabbing at the remote control on the table, and frantically pressing the buttons. Changing the channels until she found what she knew she would.

'Oh would you look at that, Michael. The football's just about to start. Fancy that,' Joanie spat. Staring at her husband in disgust. She knew exactly what Michael Byrne was all about. Making out as if he gave two shits about her when the only person Michael ever cared about was himself.

'Oh come on, Joanie. So what if my match is on? You know I've never missed a game,' he said, caught out. Though he had no idea why he had to apologise for simply living his life.

'Yes, Jimmy's dead. By Christ don't I know it. He was my son too, Joanie. But we can't all just fall apart over it, life goes on…' As soon as the words left his mouth, Michael knew he'd made a grave mistake as his wife locked eyes with him, the disgust and anger etched on her face.

'The gall of you! Standing there with a pint of ale on the table next to you, and that jovial look on your face as you eagerly await your next football fix. You don't give two fucks that our only child has been murdered, do you?' Joanie spat, doing all that she could to stop herself from smacking the man's head clean off his shoulders. 'Why aren't you suffering, huh? Why aren't you a broken man now that our son is dead?' Joanie was screeching now. Her face turning a deep puce; her eyes flashing with the anger and torment that had consumed her since she'd watched her one and only child placed down in the ground. 'Dressing your so-called concern up like sympathy, Michael, making out that you're doing your best by me, when you and me both know that the only reason you want to pack me off upstairs to the bathroom is so you can watch your stupid bloody football match. Nothing has changed for you, has it? Life just goes on the same as always. You're one selfish bastard, do you know that? You never gave a shit about my Jimmy.'

Unable to control the rage that surged through her then, Joanie launched herself at her husband. No longer in control of her actions or emotions, as every morbid, desperate feeling poured out from inside of her. Her anger exploding with every slap and punch that she administered to the back of her husband's head, as he fell to the floor under the force of the attack.

'I wish it was you that was dead. Not my Jimmy. Not my boy.' Sobbing now, a trail of snot hanging out of her nose. Her eyes flashing with pure hate. Her fists locked as she continued to lash out. 'I wish it was you that died instead of him. I wish you'd been bastard murdered!'

'Get off me, you mad fucking bitch,' Michael squawked, trying to cover his head with his arms to protect himself from the torrent of blows that the woman was raining down on him. Shocked at the force of strength behind them.

'Jesus! What's going on?'

Colleen was in the room then, too, unable to believe what she was witnessing, the sudden commotion as her two in-laws physically fought in the middle of the lounge. Michael was trying desperately, without success, to restrain his wife, which only made Joanie screech and hit out more. Wild like a banshee, as if she wasn't even aware of what she was doing.

Colleen pushed her way in-between the couple. Using her body to try and shield Michael as she grabbed hold of Joanie's shoulders.

'Joanie, darling. It's okay. I'm here, Joanie. It's okay.' Staring at the older woman dead in the eye, Colleen kept her tone soothing and calm as she coaxed her back down from her rage.

It worked.

She could see it in Joanie's eyes immediately, how the woman's expression suddenly changed as she snapped out of her trance-like state. Staring down at Michael, she looked momentarily confused, as if wondering how he had got there. Why he was cowering on the floor. His hands still trying to shield his head, a trickle of blood dripping from his nose.

Then she started wailing loudly.

She'd done this?

What was happening to her?

Joanie shook her head, she felt dizzy. Light-headed. She had no recollection of attacking the man in front of her. None at all.

'I didn't mean to… I don't know what happened…' Her voice small and pathetic as she continued to sob. Her cries filling an otherwise silent room.

'We know you didn't, Joanie. You're not yourself at the moment, that's all. Come on, love, let's get you upstairs. I'll run you a nice hot bath and then you can have a little lie down.' Seeing the angst and the confusion on the older woman's face, Colleen offered her a small comforting smile.

Joanie didn't argue this time. Nodding her head obediently she allowed her daughter-in-law to lead her from the room.

Exchanged a look with Michael as she passed the man; Colleen's concern for the woman was clear in her eyes.

Joanie really wasn't right at all.

'I'll make sure she's okay,' she mouthed before closing the door behind them.

Alone now, Michael Byrne collapsed on the sofa. His head throbbing as he wiped the remnants of blood that had splashed down onto his top lip, away with the back of his hand.

The woman had fucking lost the plot.

If it wasn't for Colleen coming to his aid just then, she would have probably battered him senseless. Talk about irony: the only person that seemed to be capable of getting through to his wife had been the one woman that Joanie had spent a lifetime hating.

Michael just hoped that his daughter-in-law could talk some sense into his wife because one thing was for sure: he didn't know what the hell to do with her anymore. Joanie was getting worse and worse with each passing day.

Downing his much-needed pint in one, Michael Byrne shook his head in despair.

Joanie Byrne had been a mad bitch before their son's death, but now the woman was well and truly off her fucking head.

CHAPTER NINE

'Oi, I saw that!' Bridget Williams shouted as she clocked the new girl, Ruth Lewis, trying to pull a fast one.

Leaning over the front desk and dipping into the till, before shoving a twenty pound note down the front of her minuscule knickers. The thieving bitch clearly thought that no one was watching her, but Bridget Williams had been keeping a close eye on the girl and the silly little cow had lucked out today. Suspicious from the off, her instincts about the new girl had been spot on and now she'd caught her red-handed.

'You thieving little cow! I knew it, you're nicking money!' Storming down the hallway, Bridget was fit to kill. 'Put it back. NOW.' Grabbing the younger girl roughly by her wrist, Bridget swung Ruth around with the force of a woman twice her size.

'Ow, you're bloody hurting me!' Ruth whined, trying, but failing, to shrug the older girl off her. 'I ain't got nothing.'

'Ladies, calm down.' Lee Archer stood up from the desk then, trying to placate the two women as they fought; though he might as well be a mute for the amount of attention they paid him.

'I saw you with my own eyes.' Bridget shook her head, unable to believe the utter gall of the girl's barefaced lying.

Ruth smirked.

'Well, no offence, Bridget, but you are getting on a bit, maybe you need those eyes of yours testing,' she said with a smug grin, knowing that her comment would sting the older girl, just as she intended. 'The few regulars you have in certainly do!'

'Tell her, will you, Lee? I didn't take anything, did I? You've been sitting there the whole time, haven't you?' Turning to their minder, Ruth Lewis threw Lee Archer a pleading look, fluttering her heavily made-up lashes in his direction, hoping the man would use the only two brain cells that he'd been blessed with and help her out.

Lee nodded obligingly. Just as she knew he would, despite the fact that he'd been too busy staring at her arse to notice what her hands were doing inside the till. Men! They were so fucking simple that it was almost hysterical.

'She's telling the truth. I would have seen if she took anything.' Lee Archer shrugged. Hoping that he wasn't going to have a full scale fight on his hands. He'd only stood in here for the evening to help Daniel Byrne out. When the bloke had called him up and offered him a night's work here at the brothel on Bridge Street, Lee had almost bitten his hand off for the opportunity. Not only was he working for one of the Byrnes, which was the ultimate job as far as he was concerned, but he was earning a good bit of wedge for tonight too and, on top of that, being surrounded by a host of scantily clad beauties.

He'd even chanced himself at bagging a freebie or two if he played his cards right. But the job wasn't cracking up to be what he'd envisaged. Women and their fucking theatrics. Lee had never seen or heard anything like the arguing that went on here amongst the girls. This lot were off their fucking rockers. Give him a room full of warring men over bickering women any day. At least with men, they didn't hold grudges. They said their bit, and then they moved the fuck on.

Unlike these two, who seemed to be caught up in some kind of never-ending grudge.

'All this bickering ain't good for business,' Lee warned, nodding towards the closed doors that lined the hallway next to them. They had a full house tonight and the last thing he needed was two of the girls tearing each other's hair out while there were punters listening in. It would only take one of the old buggers to mention it to Daniel Byrne and Lee would be out of a job quicker than these girls could get their knickers off.

'Can't you just try and get along, ladies?'

'"Ladies"?' Bridget laughed. 'This scrawny mare wouldn't know a lady if one smacked her square in the face, which, if she carries on the way she's going, is exactly what's going to happen.'

Grabbing the girl's skin tighter she leant in, and sneered: 'Do me a favour, darling. Stop with all the doe-eyed, brainless bimbo bullshit. It might wash with people who think with their dicks instead of their brains,' Bridget shot a look to Lee Archer, leaving the man with no doubt to whom that little dig was intended for, 'but it won't work on me. I know you've been taking money, and I'm not having it. Put it back. That's your final warning.'

Some of the other girls had started coming out of their rooms, hearing the loud commotion, the raised voices of the two women arguing, all eager to find out what was going on.

'We don't need an audience, ladies.' Lee Archer rubbed his head, this was all he needed. A full scale bloody lynch mob as he tried to usher the girls back into their rooms without success. 'There's nothing to see; it's just another fucking drama.'

'Another *drama*? Is that what you call this little slapper stealing our hard-earned money?' Bridget spat, her eyes flashing with fury as she glared at Ruth. Aware that everyone behind her was listening, Bridget was going to make sure that everyone knew what this little bitch had been up to. 'You might have your eyes on this little tart, but your gaze is lingering in all the wrong places, mate.' Then turning to Ruth, Bridget eyed the girl with disdain.

'What are you doing huh? Taking clients into the back room and giving them the full service, but only declaring to us that all you've given them is a blowie or a hand job. Then pocketing the difference? That's the oldest trick in the book, darling, and it ain't how we do things around here.'

'Well, if it's the oldest trick in the book then I'll take your word for it, cos you would know. You washed-up old slapper,' Ruth said tartly, aware that all eyes were on her, determined to save face.

Bridget was on the girl then. Making a grab for the younger woman's knickers, determined to find the money that Ruth had stashed away so she could prove to everyone what a thieving little cow she was.

Only, Ruth had no intention of letting Bridget call her out in front of the entire house. If she wanted to keep her job, she was going to have to fight for the privilege. Literally.

Belting Bridget hard around the face, she smiled triumphantly. Until Bridget hit back with an almighty punch. Bridget was on top of her then. Raining furious blows down on any part of the girl's body that she could get to. Ruth's only way of defending herself was by clawing at the older girl's face. Which only made Bridget more angry. Wrapping her fist around a chunk of Ruth's hair, she dragged the girl awkwardly down onto the floor. Revelling as Ruth screamed out in pain as the huge clump of hair came away from her scalp.

Lee had no choice but to intervene then.

'For fuck's sake!' Out of his seat now. Trying to break up the two feuding women as they writhed around on the floor in front of him, punching and kicking each other as they both screamed obscenities at one another. He could hear all the other girls that worked here too, standing behind them, all chanting loudly and egging the two girls on. The place was in utter chaos. Even the punters had started coming out of the rooms to see what on earth was going on.

Finally, Lee Archer lost his shit.

'FOR FUCK'S SAKE!' he shouted as he manoeuvred his huge frame between the two women, trying to break up their fight. 'Can you all just calm the fuck down.'

His sentence was cut short, as one of the feuding women caught him right on the nose with a sharp jut of her elbow. Catching him unawares, his nose exploded with pain as the blow knocked him to the floor.

Landing with an almighty thud, the room was silenced.

For a second he thought that it had taken getting lamped by one of the girls to stop all the bullshit, and as much as it bloody hurt, it was worth it. But he quickly realised that the sudden hush in the room around him had nothing to do with him at all.

A voice boomed out: 'Does someone want to tell me what the fuck is going on here?'

A female's voice? Stern, cutting. Whoever it was had managed to stop Bridget and Ruth's ruck with just one sentence. The rest of the girls had fallen silent too.

Shit!

Still splayed out on the floor, Lee turned his head to the side to clarify that he'd already guessed exactly who it was. His suspicions confirmed as he clocked the sight of the black patent high heels. His gaze moving upwards, to the knee-length black dress peeping out from the long beige Mac. Wincing as his eyes finally rested on Nancy Byrne's face as she loomed over him. The scowl told him only one thing: she did not look one bit impressed.

'Nancy?' Lee said weakly, catching sight of Jack Taylor then too. The older man standing in the doorway behind Nancy, his eyes flashing with amusement as he stood back and let Nancy Byrne deal with the chaos that had erupted around her.

'Where's Daniel?' Nancy asked, her tone curt as she scanned the room for her brother. Daniel was supposed to be here tonight, keeping an eye on the place.

'I dunno. He said he had some business to deal with and asked me to step in,' Lee said, wiping the blood from his nose with his sleeve.

Nancy bristled. Typical Daniel. He'd said he wanted to help out with their father's business, but so far he'd done nothing but cause her more problems. He had one job to do tonight, and that was to look after this place, yet he couldn't even do that right.

Nancy was pissed off.

Between Alex Costa and the warehouse, and Daniel and this place, it was becoming very clear who was going to have to run everything.

Her.

'I've got it sorted, Nancy. You just walked in at a bad time…' Mortified that Nancy Byrne had turned up before he'd had a chance to calm the situation down, Lee was well aware that he looked like a prize moron right now; he was desperate to redeem himself. Daniel Byrne had offered him an in, and if Nancy got rid of him now, he'd never live it down. Being lamped one by a girl and donning a broken nose was bad enough. 'There was a bit of an issue, but I'm sorting it.'

'You are, are you?' Raising her eyes in disbelief, Nancy shook her head. 'Only, if this is your idea of sorted, Lee, then me and you have got a big problem.'

Staring at the two dishevelled women before her then. Their faces red and blotchy, covered in scratches where the women had torn strips from one another, gouging each other's flesh with their nails. The youngest girl looked as if she'd come off a lot worse.

'You gunna fill me in?' Nancy said eyeing Bridget, hoping that maybe the woman could shed some light on the situation. Bridget had worked for her father for years. A loud brash Irish girl with a heart of gold, her father had always said. Though looking at the state of her now, Nancy wasn't convinced.

'This little cow has been stealing from the till. I caught her red-handed, sticking cash down her drawers.'

'Is that so?' Nancy eyed Ruth, noting that the younger woman made no attempt to deny the allegations.

Guilty as charged.

This place had been one of her father's biggest earners for years, Nancy knew that because she was the one that did his books for him. Tallying up the fortunes that came through this front door, Nancy knew exactly what the place was worth. Though right now, looking at it, it wasn't worth shit to anyone.

Taking in the sight of the two women, Lee standing there looking gormless behind them, the rest of the girls all watching, Nancy knew that she had to sort this mess out once and for all. These girls would run rings around her if they thought for a second that she was soft, and they could do whatever the hell they wanted.

'So, you're new, are you?'

Ruth nodded. Mistaking Nancy looking her up and down as admiration, the girl smirked. 'That's right, and I'm one of the best earners in here. She's making it up. Chucking out stupid allegations because she's jealous of the fact that, since I started working here, all her punters prefer me,' Ruth said with confidence, unsure who this woman was, but willing to impress her all the same. Before glaring over at Bridget triumphantly. Believing that her place in the house was safe.

Only, unfortunately for Ruth, Nancy caught the girl's snide look, and wasn't one bit impressed. The girl was clearly on a fucking wind-up and, unlucky for her, Nancy wasn't in the mood for games tonight.

'Well, I tell you what, Ruth, I'm going to give you the benefit of the doubt.'

Ruth beamed at that. Staring at Bridget as if she'd just totally trumped the girl, her face soon fell at Nancy's next sentence. 'I'm going to let you keep that twenty quid so you can pay for your taxi home. You're sacked.' It was Nancy's turn to smirk now.

Not one to suffer fools gladly, Ruth Lewis had just blown any chance she had of continuing to work here. God knows what Alex Costa had been thinking employing a low-life like this girl. Nancy could see through her from a mile off.

'Sacked? Er, I don't bloody think so,' Ruth Lewis retorted, having no intention of letting some rich stuck-up girl tell her what to do. 'Alex Costa hired me. I only take my orders from him.' Standing firm, Ruth was certain that Alex Costa would put this stuck-up cow in her place once he heard what had gone on tonight.

'Well, that's hilarious, darling,' Nancy scoffed, her smile genuine now that Ruth Lewis was about to come unstuck. 'See, Alex isn't in charge around here anymore. I am. Nancy Byrne, babe. Pleased to meet you, or not. As the case may be,' Nancy said, thoroughly enjoying making her formal introduction. 'Now why don't you get your scrawny arse off my property before I have you forcefully removed?'

Ruth paled. Realising her error way too late. Nancy Byrne, the notorious Jimmy Byrne's daughter. Shit!

All eyes were on Ruth. Waiting to see how she handled herself. Well she'd show the lot of them, bunch of jealous, stuck-up bitches.

'Make me!' Ruth challenged the girl, knowing full well that Nancy wouldn't dare.

She was wrong on that account too.

'With pleasure, darling,' Nancy said, grabbing Ruth by a fistful of her hair, frogmarching the scantily dressed woman out into the hallway, before dragging her down the stairs. There was an alleyway that ran down the back of the flat where the rest of the residents around here stored their rubbish. It was the perfect exit for the girl, Nancy thought as she opened the back door and launched Ruth out of it.

'I never want to see your face around here again. Do you understand?'

Ruth stood on the pavement, unable to speak. Nancy Byrne was a ruthless bitch and as much as she wanted to try and save face, the woman had a hardness about her that Ruth found unnerving.

'Now sling your hook.'

Her point well and truly made Nancy went back upstairs to find all the girls still standing around.

'And what the fuck are you all doing standing around gawping. Haven't you all got work to do? Go on, move your arses. The show's over. Get back to work or you can all join your little mate out there. Sort your punters out, and then get this place cleaned up.'

Then she turned her attention to Lee Archer.

'I don't know what my brother was playing at leaving you in charge but you're out too.'

'Nancy, please. You've read this all wrong, sweetheart,' Lee piped up, desperate for one more chance to try and keep his new job.

'Don't fucking "sweetheart" me,' Nancy said, irritated by the man's patronising tone. Nancy nodded at Jack Taylor, who until now had been standing watching the wrath of Nancy Byrne with much amusement. The girl certainly didn't stand for any shit.

'Do me a favour will you, Jack, put the rubbish out for me, will you,' Nancy said giving Lee one last look of contempt. 'This place is starting to stink.'

Nancy Byrne had spoken and her word was final.

CHAPTER TEN

'You want me to come back, Mr Harris?' Walking into Alfie Harris's office, Haluk Demir hadn't been expecting to see the nightclub's boss sitting behind his desk. Not at this time of the morning. It was almost ten o'clock. Normally Alfie Harris was nowhere to be seen at this time of the day. Especially if he'd been working here the previous evening.

Haluk had been hoping to get in and get his work all done quickly so that he could get home. But having to work under his boss's watchful eye would mean that probably wouldn't happen now. Haluk would have to do his full shift.

Not that he should complain, really, that was what he was being paid to do and, to be fair, he actually enjoyed working in the club. Especially as his section was the main staff quarters downstairs. Away from the chaos of the main club where the other group of cleaners all had to work together, scrubbing the sticky dance floors that were coated with all kinds of spilt liquids. Mostly alcohol, though there had been plenty of times they'd had to clean up vomit. And never mind the spillages of God knows what, that they had to clean off the club's fancy velour VIP booths, or the state that the main customer toilets were left in.

'If you're busy, I can go and do something elsewhere?'

'No, come in. It's fine. I'm just sorting out a few bits of paperwork. I'm almost done. Don't mind me.' Alfie waved the man in. Distracted, still staring down at his computer screen, his eyes not even acknowledging Haluk's presence. His head down, as he continued to type into his computer.

The man looked stressed, Haluk decided. Seeing the expression on Mr Harris's face, etched with agitation, the deep furrow in the man's brow that his boss clearly didn't want to be disturbed.

Eyeing the piles of money stacked up on the desk that Alfie had been counting, he watched as the man picked one bundle up and re-counted it, before sighing, as if his sums weren't tallying up, before recounting it all over again.

Haluk knew not to pry. He was nothing more than a lowly cleaner. He was well aware of his place in the club's pecking order.

'I'll try not to disturb you too much!' he said dutifully.

Haluk had always prided himself on his work. Immersing himself in it, he always set about doing the best job that he could possibly do. Cleaning everything immaculately. Every speck of dirt and dust dealt with. He enjoyed it too. Just because he was 'just a cleaner' didn't mean that he couldn't take pride in all that he put his hands to. Even more so today, seeing as Mr Harris was present in the room. Haluk wanted the man to think good of him, to see that he was working hard.

Emptying the bins and the numerous ashtrays that were dotted around the room, he cleaned and polished the office until it shone.

'Is it okay if I plug the hoover in, Mr Harris, sorry, I don't want to disturb you…'

'Of course. I'm done here now anyway. I'll get out of your way.' Still seemingly distracted as he switched off his computer, Alfie Harris walked over to where his safe was on the back wall. Tapping in the numbers, with his back blocking Haluk's view, he put the money bags neatly inside, before closing the door behind him.

'Have a good night, Haluk,' the man said, shrugging on his jacket.

Watching as his boss left the office, and closed the door behind him. Haluk was glad of the solitude once more. He waited, listening to his boss's footsteps fading away in to the distance.

Then nothing, only silence.

Running his hand over the man's desk, pulling out the chair, Haluk sat down for a minute. Casting an eye around the room, for just a few seconds, pretending that all of this was his. The expensive computer in front of him. The fancy ornate sofas. The drinks cabinet full of bottles of liquor. The safe full of money.

His eye going to the gap in the safe's door then.

It wasn't shut properly.

Haluk eyed the office door. Firmly shut.

Getting up, curious to see what was inside Alfie Harris' safe, Haluk stepped closer. His heart beating rapidly with each step. Anticipation, excitement and fear all rolled into one as he reached out and opened the door. Peering inside.

Spotting the money bags that Alfie Harris had just placed inside, he roughly counted it up. There were thousands of pounds here. Just sitting here inside this little metal box. Inches away from his fingertips.

He should just close the door, he thought to himself rationally. He could leave a note for Mr Harris telling the man that he'd done so. Showing the man that his intentions were good. That he was ever the trustworthy, honest employee.

For what though?

Mr Harris didn't give a shit about a man like Haluk. A lowly cleaner, invisible to all. Three months Haluk had worked here, cleaning Mr Harris's office, and today had been the most conversation the two men had ever engaged in. Alfie Harris didn't even know his name. He only employed so many Turkish immigrants at the club because he knew he could get away with paying them all the bare minimum.

This money could change his whole life.

He should take it, he thought. Not all of it. Just one pile.

Mr Harris probably wouldn't even notice that the money was missing. To a man like Alfie Harris it was just pocket change; to Haluk, though, it would make him richer than his wildest dreams.

Unable to resist, Haluk peered inside the bag closest to him. Thumbing the money that sat on the top of the pile, he stared in awe at the fortunes inside. His heart was thudding loudly in his chest now. Unable to believe that he was even contemplating stealing this money. It was a crazy idea, he thought.

Do your day's work, Haluk, and go home. You're not a thief.

Then another part of him thought, *but what if he was?*

What if he was done with being a good, honest hard-working man that never saw any kind of payout for the hours that he so painfully put in. Cleaning this nightclub every morning, and then spending the rest of his days cleaning public toilets and office blocks.

He'd never make this much money in his lifetime.

This could change his life.

All he had to do was reach out and take it.

Listening carefully, he strained to hear if there was anyone outside in the corridor. Anyone around.

Nothing. Only silence.

The only noise came from above him. A faint thud of footsteps as the other cleaners swept and moped the dance floors upstairs. He could hear trays of glasses clanking together as they were pushed through the glass washer.

Nothing down here. Silence, interrupted only by his pounding heart inside his chest.

Allowing his fingers to curl around the bag, Haluk slipped the package inside his jacket pocket, before quickly shutting the safe behind him. Gathering up the hoover then and the rest of the cleaning products from where he'd dumped the cleaning caddy down on the floor, Haluk made his way out of the office.

Shoving everything inside the cleaning cupboard at the end of the hallway, he took a deep breath to gather himself.

Shit! What are you thinking, Haluk? You can't do this.

His conscience getting the better of him.

A thief, a liar. This wasn't him, he didn't steal.

He should put it back, he decided, wiping the sweat that was forming on his brow along with the sticky droplets of perspiration he could feel shimmering on his top lip. He cursed himself now.

Was this really how low he'd become?

Walking back to the office, Haluk took the money out of his pocket with every intention to put it back where he had taken it from.

Only he couldn't.

Shit!

He'd closed the safe behind him. He didn't know the code.

Staring at the desk, he wondered if he should just leave it there. But then what if Mr Harris grew suspicious of him? What if he worked out that Haluk had gone into his safe? Or worse than that, what if someone else came in here and took the money before Alfie found it tonight? Staff came and went in here all day long. Haluk would probably still get the blame. He was the last person in here; he'd be prime suspect.

Haluk would lose his job then anyway.

No, he'd done it now. There was no going back, so he shoved the money deep inside his pocket and prayed that Alfie Harris would never be any the wiser.

Taking the stairs two at a time. Hurrying now, it was stuffy in here. Loosening his collar as he reached the top of the stairs, he couldn't wait to get outside and breath in the cool morning air.

He was almost at the main door. Almost there, when he caught a movement in the corner of his eye.

Stepping out of the shadows was Gem Kemal. The club's head of security.

Why was he still here?

Haluk's heart was now pounding so hard, it felt fit to burst. Something about the look on Gem Kemal's face told him that he'd somehow been caught red-handed. But the man couldn't possibly know that Haluk had just stolen the money, could he?

'You in some kind of a hurry?' Gem Kemal said, stepping out. His huge frame blocking the doorway as he stood there with his arms folded tightly across his chest, the stern look on his face.

'I was just leaving. I'm all done,' Haluk said, his voice shaking with nerves as he stared around the club and realised the place was completely empty now. The trays of glasses abandoned on the bar tops. The mops and brushes discarded in the middle of the floor.

All the other cleaners had gone.

But no one had told Haluk to go too.

Then he saw Alfie Harris standing with his back against the bar. His face devoid of any kind of expression, but something in the man's demeanour told Haluk Demir that he was in a whole world of shit right now.

They knew. How? He didn't know, but without a doubt they knew.

Haluk felt suddenly sick. His stomach twisting inside him, a sinking feeling in the depths of his gut.

Alfie Harris finally spoke.

'You get everything you need, did you?'

'Er. I don't know what you mean… I've finished my shift…' Haluk froze. Pulling his jacket in around him tighter. The money bag digging sharply into his ribs.

'We think you might have something that doesn't belong to you,' Gem Kemal spoke now, stepping towards the man. Eyeing Haluk's jacket where the money was concealed.

They knew! Shit, they knew.

Haluk wanted to throw up. He should never have been so stupid to do what he did. Karma always got you in the end, and this was his. Caught red-handed, he'd lose everything because of this one costly mistake.

'Empty your pockets.'

Without so much as an argument, Haluk did as he was told. Taking out the bag of money from his inside pocket he passed it over to Gem. He turned to his boss.

'I'm so sorry, Mr Harris. As soon as I took it, I realised my mistake and I tried to put it back…' Haluk's voice was quivering in fear, trembling as the words tumbled from his mouth.

Only, Alfie Harris wasn't buying his excuses.

'Save it,' he ordered, not wanting to hear the lies and bullshit that he knew the man would try and shower him with. 'You know what, Haluk? I wanted to give you the benefit of the doubt, I really did.' Alfie Harris shrugged. 'But money has been taken out of my tills for weeks now, the books just aren't adding up and when I called Gem in and told him about this little problem here at the club, he suggested that it might be you. Said he'd had his suspicions about you for a while. Taking money from the club when no one was looking. Dipping into my tills. There was only one way to find out for sure, so I set you up, and you fucking took the bait.'

Haluk looked at Gem, puzzled at what he was hearing. Then back to Alfie Harris.

'But sir, I haven't taken any money from your tills. This is the first time I've ever stolen anything in my life. I'm so sorry for what I have done. Please believe me.'

Alfie Harris nodded. 'Oh, I bet you are sorry, but nowhere near half as sorry as you're going to be once I've finished with you.'

Alfie Harris was beyond annoyed and he didn't believe a word of Haluk's lies. This bloke had been fleecing him for months. Fucking people! You gave them so much as an inch, and the bastards would try and take a mile. Never satisfied with what they had, it galled Alfie that people actually believed they had a right to take what was his. He'd worked his bollocks off for this club. He'd put everything he had into it, and it was starting to pay off.

Only now he had his own fucking staff stealing from him.

Treating him as if he was some kind of cunt.

'See, I like to think I'm a very fair man, Haluk. Giving all you illegals a bit of cash in hand work. Cutting you a bit of slack when others wouldn't dream of it. Only, none of you can be trusted, can you?'

Mr Harris had indeed been generous. Haluk had fucked up massively. He was crying now. Tears of shame and fear pouring down his face at how low he had stooped today.

'Get him out of my sight,' Alfie said speaking directly to Gem, acting as if Haluk wasn't even standing there. As if he didn't matter. Invisible once more. 'I want him dealt with properly.'

Gem stepped forward, only too glad to oblige.

Grabbing the man tightly by his neck, he dragged Haluk out through the back doors of the club so that he could execute the man's reprisal without any form of interruption.

He felt a flicker of guilt then.

When Alfie Harris had called Gem in today and told him of the money that had been going missing, Gem had thought that his game was up. That his boss was onto him. Only he'd quickly passed the buck and set Haluk up, lucky for him, Haluk had taken the bait just as he'd hoped. Not many men would be able to resist the temptation of an open safe, full of money.

Alfie Harris was not a man to be fucked with, that had just been made plainly clear.

As Gem led Haluk out the back alleyway to give the man the biggest kicking of his life, he shrugged away the tiny flicker of remorse he felt.

Someone had to take the fall, though, and Gem was just glad that fucker wasn't going to be him.

CHAPTER ELEVEN

Sitting on the edge of her friend's bed, Amber Richards could tell by her miserable-looking reflection in the mirror that Megan Harris was in a foul mood this evening. That, and the fact that Amber had been here for almost fifteen minutes and the two girls had practically sat in complete silence. The only noise in the room was their favourite Sugababes album playing in the background on Megan's mini hi-fi system, and the fact that Megan wasn't even bothering to sing along spoke volumes in itself.

'You sure you're okay, Megs?' Amber said, knowing her friend well enough to know that she was anything but all right.

'Yeah, I'm fine,' Megan said bluntly, pretending that she was just concentrating on applying her make-up in the mirror. Too angry to talk.

Though Megan wasn't fooling anyone. Least of all Amber.

'It wouldn't have anything to do with that leggy blonde sitting in your kitchen, drinking wine with your dad, would it?' Amber said boldly. Knowing that's exactly what Megan's problem was. Though why her friend had got in such a mood about it, she couldn't seem to fathom.

'Did you see the state of her?' Megan turned and looked at Amber, raising her eyes at her friend's bluntness. Of course her bad mood had everything to do with her father's new girlfriend, Jennifer Dawson. 'She's only what, seven or eight years older than us, Max! She's too young for him!'

Megan was fighting back the tears that were threatening to fall now. Embarrassed that she felt so upset that her father had finally brought his girlfriend home to meet her. It wasn't just that he had a girlfriend. He'd had loads over the years, of course he had. But he'd never brought one home with him before. He'd never cared enough about any of them that he'd wanted to introduce them to her.

'She was practically draped over him when we walked in on them. Seriously. Who does that?!' Megan said wrinkling her nose at the memory of leading Amber into the kitchen to get a drink when she'd first arrived, only to find her father and his new bird locked in an embrace, up against the sink.

Megan had taken an immediate dislike to the older girl on sight. Despite the fact that her father had seemed so happy. So loved-up. He hadn't even noticed that Megan and Amber had come into the room at first. At least when he did, he'd had the good grace to look uncomfortable about his behaviour. Immediately stepping away from Jennifer so that he could make the necessary introductions.

Jennifer had been all smiles and compliments, but Megan didn't bother reciprocating. Instead she'd got her and Amber both a drink, before quickly making their excuses not to join them. They'd both been hiding away up here instead ever since.

'Well, it didn't look like there were any complaints coming from your dad, babe! In fact, he looked proper loved-up if you asked me! It's cute, in a way. Isn't it? Seeing him so happy?'

'I guess.' Megan shrugged.

Though the last thing Megan thought it was, was cute. Megan had never seen him like that before, and it stirred up something inside her that she hadn't even realised she'd feel until now.

Jealousy.

For sixteen years, she'd had her dad all to herself, ever since her mum had upped and left them both when Megan had been just a baby. Just the two of them, and now suddenly there was another woman in the house to contend with.

A woman who her dad seemed to be totally wrapped up in.

'I mean, come on, who wouldn't be loved-up though? She's bloody gorgeous,' Amber said honestly, not realising that it was the last thing Megan wanted to hear. 'Did you see what she was wearing? She looked a bit like that supermodel Gisele that's everywhere right now. Only even prettier, don't you think?'

Megan shrugged. Not wanting to agree with her friend, though there was no denying that Jennifer Dawson was indeed beautiful. Dressed to perfection. Her hair and make-up pristine. When they'd walked into the kitchen, the whole room had been filled with the woman's warm laugh and the sweet smell of perfume. It was as if she had cast some kind of spell on everyone in the house, her mate included.

'It did look serious, didn't it?' Megan said, knowing that Amber would tell her the truth. 'I mean, he's never brought a girlfriend home before and I know he's had girlfriends, it's just… they've never been serious enough that he's wanted to introduce me to anyone, and he said that he's taking the weekend off so they can spend some proper time together. He *never* takes time off work!'

It was more than just that though.

Her father had been acting different lately. Megan had been trying to convince herself that he was just busy with his new business venture, but she knew that it wasn't just that. Even at home, he seemed so preoccupied. Always on his phone, and when he wasn't on that, his head seemed to be elsewhere.

This girl had really got to him, and it made Megan feel suddenly insecure. As if she had another woman vying for her father's attention, and she was worried that she'd be somehow forgotten.

'Maybe it is serious then! Your dad did look pretty happy to be fair. Who knows, eh? Does it bother you if it is?'

'I guess not,' Megan lied, shrugging her shoulders as if to play down her fears, silently scolding herself. She was being pathetic. Her dad had every right to be happy. He'd spent his whole life devoted to her. He was a great dad. The best. Playing the role of both father and mother. Megan had never wanted for a thing in her life. He'd always been there for her when she needed him.

She knew he deserved to be happy.

'I just guess that I wasn't expecting her to be so young, that's all.'

'Well, I think she looked nice. It could be worse, Megs. He could have hooked up with some right old nag. Then you'd have something to really moan about. Besides, just think, if this does all work out that girl could end up as your stepmum. How cool would that be? You could borrow all her fancy clothes! Maybe you could try and bag me those Christian Louboutins that she was wearing. I'd simply die if I got to borrow them!'

Megan rolled her eyes at Amber's exaggerated plea, smiling at her friend's typical response of always managing to see something that she could get out of a situation.

Amber giggled too then, glad that she was finally cheering her friend up.

'You know, Megs, this could work in your favour in more ways that you think.' Amber was on a roll now. She'd come over tonight with a proposition for Megan, and now it seemed she'd made perfect timing. 'If your dad's all loved-up and wanting to spend time with his new girlfriend, he's not going to mind you staying over at mine for the weekend, is he?'

'He wouldn't mind me staying at yours anyway?' Megan said, narrowing her eyes. Wondering what Amber was getting at.

'Of course not. Only. We won't be staying at mine. We can go out! Properly out.' Amber was grinning, deliriously excited about her plans. All she had to do was get Megan to agree to them. 'You know that bloke I've been texting, Reece Bettle? Well he's only said he'll sort me out with some fake ID for us both so that we can get into a club tomorrow night.' Unable to keep the excitement from her voice, Amber hoped that her friend would be up for the idea. She'd promised Reece that she'd be there, no matter what, and she didn't fancy rocking up on her own as Billy-no-mates.

'He said he'd have a word with his friend on the door for us too. That we'll easily get in… What do you reckon? You up for it? Tomorrow we can spend the day getting all dolled up, giving each other makeovers? Then we can try our luck getting into a club. Go on, Megs, it will be a right laugh.'

Megan raised her eyes, unsure about Amber's plan.

'He might let me stay at yours for the weekend, but there's no way my dad will let me go to a nightclub,' she said, already defeated and thinking the negative about Amber's little plan.

'Of course he won't, you moron! You're only sixteen! That's why we're not going to tell him!' Amber laughed, rolling her eyes sarcastically. 'This is your dad that we're talking about. The man who doesn't let you go anywhere, jeez! I reckon we're the only two girls left in our year who haven't managed to blag our way into a nightclub yet.'

Alfie Harris was one of the most overprotective parents Amber had ever come across. The man didn't let Megan out of his sight without at least fifty questions. Amber had thought it was sweet, at first, especially as her parents couldn't give a shit about her or any of her siblings' whereabouts half the time. They were mostly just glad that their kids had buggered off out somewhere and left them both in peace.

There was a whole world out there, though, that Megan and Amber had yet to discover.

'Please, Megs. It will be amazing, I promise. You and me on the dance floor. Having a couple of cheeky vodkas. We'll have such a laugh.'

'I dunno, Amber. You know what my dad's like. What if he checks up on me?'

'What, with Jessica Rabbit down there keeping him busy? No offence, babe, but I doubt your dad will even notice you've gone this weekend.'

Megan nodded, Amber's words hitting a nerve, just as she knew they would.

She was right, of course. Her dad had been so preoccupied lately. Firstly with his new business venture, now with his new girlfriend. He probably wouldn't even give her a second thought. Maybe Amber was right. Maybe she should go out and have some fun for a change. She was bored of always staying in and being the 'good daughter', especially when her father clearly had double standards, picking up women that were less than half his age. Pissed off at her dad and not wanting to stay in and watch as he made out with some slapper, Megan nodded in agreement.

'Okay! I'll come,' she said. 'But you can come downstairs and back me up when I tell my dad that we're going to be at your house all weekend. You know what he's like. The last thing I need is him driving around there and catching us out.'

Amber grinned then. Gripping her mate's hands, she squealed with excitement.

'You are on, Megs! Oh my God, we are going to have so much fun!'

*

'We'll walk, Dad, it's only fifteen minutes away,' Megan Harris said, pleading with her dad not to embarrass her any further by constantly insisting on driving her around as if she was ten years old again.

'It's dark outside. It will take me five minutes,' Alfie Harris reasoned. Having given in to Megan's request to let his daughter stay at her friend Amber's house for the weekend, he was having a lot less luck persuading the girl to let him at least drive her there so that he knew she got there safely.

'Honestly, Mr Harris, it's really kind of you to offer, but it doesn't take long to walk, and we'll both be together. It's not like she's walking on her own,' Amber said, playing along as the sensible friend.

'Yeah, come on, Dad!' Megan pleaded, willing him to stop being so overprotective. He was showing her up. Amber would take the right piss out of her once they finally got out of here this evening.

'But I took the weekend off. I was hoping we could spend some quality time together. The three of us?'

'Oh come on, Alfie, she's sixteen. She doesn't want to be hanging out with us oldies. Let her go out with her friend,' Jennifer Dawson said then, winking at the two girls, letting them know she was on their side. 'They're both smart girls. Like they say, it's not far and they'll stick together!'

It was an olive branch. They all knew that. This was Jennifer's way of showing Megan that she was giving the girl some moral support.

Megan smiled back at Jennifer but her grin didn't reach her eyes. She wasn't born yesterday. The girl was just involving herself in the conversation for pure effect. Playing the good cop, bad cop routine in a desperate bid to win her over.

Only, her dad was hanging off the girl's every word.

'Okay, okay!' Throwing his hands up in the air, laughing. Outnumbered. Faced with all three women staring at him now, insisting that he let Megan go.

'But the second you get to Amber's I want a phone call so that I know you got there safely, okay?'

'No worries, Mr Harris. We'll call you as soon as we get there,' Amber said quickly as Megan gave him a quick kiss on the cheek before he could change his mind, before throwing a curt goodbye to Jennifer.

The two girls quickly left the room.

'See, she's not that bad. She had your back in there.'

'Yeah, I bet she couldn't wait to get rid of me!' Megan said bitterly.

CHAPTER TWELVE

'Follow me, my friend,' Gem Kemal shouted over the loud thud of music that pounded out from the speakers behind them, as he guided Daniel Byrne through the throng of people that crowded the nightclub's main bar and dance floor.

Reaching the VIP booth that sat on the platform overlooking the entire ground floor, Gem offered Daniel Byrne a seat.

The man looked impressed.

'Fuck me. The doors only just opened, ain't they? This place is heaving,' Daniel shouted as he took in the spectacular sight of the club's clientele: the scantily clad hordes of girls dressed in a uniform of tight micro-mini skirts, cleavage-busting tops and stiletto heels, which might have been the height of fashion for the early 2000s, but personally, Daniel Byrne couldn't see the attraction of all the women wanting to be clones of each other. There was no individuality, he thought, eyeing a group of girls all standing in a cluster, with their chunky striped highlighted hair and their obscenely large hooped earrings. The men were not much better, with their designer clothes and their matching designer stubble. Sauntering around the place with their popped collared shirts.

The club's atmosphere, however, was electric. The music was pulsating its way throughout the building. The bass bouncing wildly off the walls and the floors, vibrating right through Daniel's body as he spoke. 'I heard this place was supposed to be the bollocks.' He raised his eyes in agreement now, seeing first-hand that the rumours were indeed true.

From outside, The Karma Club hadn't looked anything particularly special; the place was no more than a deserted Victorian warehouse, situated in the heart of North London's King's Cross badlands. The club was nestled between the old railway arches at the back of a darkened redundant workers' yard, tucked away out in the middle of fucking nowhere, but then Daniel guessed that was all part of its appeal. The main clientele seemed to be London's spoilt little rich kids. All that money, and yet they chose to get their rocks off in an old abandoned warehouse. Irony at its' very best.

'This is the place to be, Daniel,' Gem said proudly, pointing over to one of the girls that just walked in surrounded by a small entourage. 'See the girl in the tiny red dress? You must recognise her?'

Daniel shrugged. The girl looked vaguely familiar.

'It's Kate fucking Moss. You know, the supermodel. We've had all sorts in here. Leonardo DiCaprio, Jude Law. Most nights, we've got half the premier league's footballers in here too and they love to spend their cash, let me tell you. I'm surprised you haven't been here yet yourself, Daniel? This place has made Alfie Harris a very rich man.'

Daniel nodded in agreement at Gem's words. He'd heard that Alfie Harris was coining it in these days. The Karma Club was the talk of London right now, and considering that the place had only opened three months ago, it had already seemed to take on a life of its own.

His dad had cashed in early, making sure that his and Alex Costa's gear was sold on the premises. Daniel was well aware that his family had been making a tidy little sum out of the club's success and, by the looks of things, there was much more money still to come.

'All of London's beautiful people under one roof.' Gem grinned as he watched Daniel's reaction. The man was taking it all in. Then, nodding to the waitress to bring him over a drink, Gem ordered one for Daniel too.

'See the DJ over there?' Gem nodded towards the booth. 'Georgie Kissking, please tell me you've heard of him? 'Course you have. Everyone's fucking heard of him. He's one of the best DJs in the world. The fucking godfather of dance music. Alfie Harris flew him in from Ibiza and gave him exclusive residency. You know what that means, don't you? These kids are literally lining the pavement outside to get their arses in here, for him alone. Tickets to get through the doors are like fucking gold dust.' Gem shook his head in wonderment. 'Alfie Harris reckons he's going straight now he's got this place, and with the money he's making, he's got a good chance of staying clean.'

Daniel smirked then. 'Yeah, I saw him plastered all over the entertainment pages of the newspapers last week. Busy kissing some boy bands' arses outside the club. Proper fancies himself as some sort of local fucking celebrity, these days. But it's all good publicity, and I guess that's why this place has just taken off. Every fucker wants a piece of it.'

'Some men have all the luck, while others, like us, have to make our own,' Gem reasoned, but the bitterness in his voice was easy to spot.

Alfie Harris had well and truly landed on his feet, and it pained Gem to see someone making so much money with so little effort when he had to work his arse off as head of security, spending months overseeing Jimmy and Alex's interests, distributing their gear via a couple of the doormen that were set in place, and all Gem was bringing in was a meagre hourly wage.

Sinking back in his chair, he took a mouthful of the Jack and Coke that the waitress had just brought over for them both. All the while keeping an eye on the main door, making sure that Alfie Harris didn't come swanning in and catch him sitting on his arse talking to Daniel when he should be working.

He still couldn't believe that the man had actually taken the weekend off work, and left him in charge of the place. Gem had clearly proved himself trustworthy when he'd helped him deal with the cleaner who had been supposedly stealing off the man.

Gem had deliberately set this meeting up right under Alfie Harris's nose. *Hiding in plain sight*, wasn't that the term people used? As far as anyone was concerned, Gem Kemal was paying his condolences to Daniel Byrne. No one need be any the wiser what they were really talking about.

Eyeing Daniel with a vague curiosity, Gem lit up a cigarette before holding out the packet towards his companion, who shook his head.

'So, why did you ask me here tonight? I take it you didn't call to give me a show-and-tell of the fucking club, Gem?' Daniel said, wondering what this sudden little meet up was all about.

'You know what, that's what I like about you. You're just like your father. You don't take any bullshit. You're straight down the line.' Remembering the other rumours that he'd heard about Jimmy and Alex, Gem winced, realising his ill choice of words as soon as they had left his mouth.

Only, Daniel didn't seemed one bit fazed.

'"Straight down the line"? Come on, Gem, I'm sure you've heard all the rumours that are flying about. My old man was more bent than a bleeding butcher's hook.'

Gem laughed, relieved. A loud cackle escaping his mouth despite himself. Glad that Daniel had taken his turn of phrase in good humour, and that he wasn't easily offended. The last thing Gem wanted to do was wrong-foot the man. He also wasn't going to insult him by lying to him.

'Of course I've heard the rumours, Daniel. It was all anyone spoke about for days. I'd have had to have been living in a bubble to not have heard them. Only, I don't care what your father got up to in his personal life. It's none of mine or anyone else's business.' There wasn't much going on around here Gem didn't know. He had eyes and ears all over London. Knowledge was power – and Gem made it his business to know everything.

'I had a lot of respect for your father, you know. He came across as if he was indestructible, but I guess death comes to us all in the end,' Gem said, shaking his head as if he was still trying to let Jimmy Byrne's demise sink in, before laughing to lighten the mood. 'Your father was ruthless though. And smart too. Which is why I asked you here tonight. I figured that maybe you'd be interested in a little proposition I've got for you.'

Daniel laughed again. 'Well I hate to disappoint you, mate, but me and my father were worlds apart.'

Gem shook his head.

'You're a Byrne, Daniel. And I see him in you. There's more to you than meets the eye.'

'Go on, then.' It was Daniel's turn to sit back now as he read Gem with intrigue. Knowing full well that Gem Kemal only called him here tonight because he was his father's son. The man clearly had no idea that Daniel had fuck all input in the family business. Not yet anyway.

It was his sister Nancy who was running everything now, though perhaps Gem wasn't aware of that little fact. Though, that Gem was assuming that Daniel, being the only son, would be the one to rightfully take over his father's business did resonate with Daniel too. That was exactly how it should have been. So maybe he and Gem were on the same page after all.

'I want to change things up here at the club, and start making some real money,' Gem said simply, finally laying his cards out on the table. 'As head of security it means I have access to the entire club. I already have my men in place on the team. Why should men like Alfie Harris be the ones making a fortune when I'm the one doing most of the groundwork? That's why I want to start bringing in my own gear.'

'Why? We're already shifting gear at the club, using the supplier that my father and Alex put in place. Has there been a complaint about the product?'

'There haven't been any complaints as such, no,' Gem said holding his hands out honestly.

'Then why try and fix something that isn't broken?' Daniel said, wondering what Gem would stand to gain by changing an operation that was already in play.

'Because the figures speak for themselves. Your father had us selling cocaine. He refused to allow any other substances into the club.' Gem shrugged. 'These kids are bored with cocaine. They want something more than that. I have it on good authority by one of my top dealers that these kids want a different kind of buzz than what a gram or two of coke can give them. I'm talking MDMAs. GBH. Special K,' Gem said, speaking with enthusiasm. 'Pills, Daniel. That's the way we stand to make some real money.' He sat forward in his chair, eager to convince Daniel of his business idea. 'Your father always said that he didn't want to be held responsible for fucking up any kids with that shit.' Gem shook his head in wonderment. 'The irony being that that shit is exactly what the kids of today all *want* to get fucked up on. This is our opportunity to branch out.'

He had him now, he was sure of it. Sensing Daniel's intrigue, Gem grinned.

'I have some contacts in North London. Some Turkish friends of mine that I know will be happy to supply me with enough pills for us to trial them here at the club,' Gem said then, finally getting to why he'd called the meeting this evening. 'But I can't do it on my own. I need your backing. A Byrne. With your name behind me, we won't have other dealers coming in here trying their luck.'

'What about Alfie Harris? It's his club. Does he even know about any of this?'

Gem shook his head. 'Look, Harris ain't interested in the drugs side of the business. He never has been. He's strictly all about the club.' He shrugged. 'Your father and Alex put the pressure on him when the place first opened, and Alfie was made to go along with it all. The man made a fortune from the proceeds, though. It wasn't as if he wasn't reaping the benefits. We don't need to tell him shit.'

Daniel nodded, knowing better than anyone how shrewd and persuasive his father could be when he had wanted. If he had wanted in on the club, no one would have stopped him. Not even the nightclub owner.

'I'm serious, Daniel. Come in on this with me. If you don't, someone else will and that's a big risk for me. There are too many snakes out there. Who do you trust, eh?' Gem said, shaking his head, before toking on his cigarette once more and then slowly exhaling a white plume of smoke.

Daniel remained silent. *Who do you trust indeed?* he thought. His father had always been reluctant to get involved with the Turks. He used to say that they were too reckless. The influx of Turkish gangs in to London were renowned for their vicious temperaments. Though Gem Kemal didn't seem that type.

The man seemed legit.

And Daniel knew that Gem was bang on the money, too, when it came to what this club should be selling. He only had to look around the place to see that. This was the noughties, after all. His father had always been stuck in some kind of time warp of the 80s and 90s. Times had changed now, and the clubbing scene had without a doubt moved on. His father would never touch Ecstasy or heroin, but Gem was right. There was clearly a massive market for the stuff.

Seeing Daniel quiet now, deep in thought, Gem continued talking. He almost had Daniel convinced, he was sure of it.

'I want us to work together, Daniel, because, together, you and I will be a force to be reckoned with. We can test the product out the first time round using my suppliers and, if you're happy with the turnover, we can think about importing our own supplies together. I already have my men here in position at the club to sell it all for us.'

'So, where do I come in then?'

'If this is a success, we use the couriers that your father and Alex have in place to bring us our new products. We use their warehouses and the dockyard.' Gem corrected himself. '*Your* warehouses and dockyard. We can keep the same drop-off points too. Nothing will change, but we'll be supplying a much better product. My only stipulation is that we keep this between only you and me. We need to be discreet. We can't let any of this get back to Alfie Harris.'

Daniel nodded, able to see the logic in Gem's proposal. His father's sudden demise had shaken up the underworld, that was for sure. The reality was, a lot of people in London right now, Gem included, saw his father's death as some kind of golden opportunity. The tide had turned and every one of his father's contacts were suddenly seeing the market as a free-for-all. Of course, it was only going to be a matter of time before someone else tried to elbow their way in. That was the way things worked around here. With the rumours rife about Alex Costa losing his head, and the fact that he and Nancy were both so young, the Byrne empire was an easy target now.

Maybe Gem was right. If they joined forces with him, Daniel could start building his own workforce. He'd have backup then, and judging by the success of this place, Gem clearly knew how to control the masses. Glancing around The Karma Club once more, drinking in the electric atmosphere, he could see the positives in Gem's plan for them both.

Though there was one thing standing in their way.

'What about my sister, Nancy?' Daniel said, as he tried to work out the logistics of how they could run the operation together when Nancy had a habit of sticking her oar in and trying to take over every situation. 'She won't go for any of this. She hates the drug side of the businesses. In fact, I think she's thinking about stepping away from this side of the business altogether.'

Nancy had already made her intentions more than clear. She wanted to concentrate on several brothels that their father had set up, those, and the numerous properties that their father had invested in over the years: the swanky apartment blocks and lucrative office spaces dotted all over London.

'I didn't realise that you had to answer to your own sister?' Gem said with a wry grin to show Daniel that his comment was said purely to wind him up. Then, seeing that Daniel was being serious, he added: 'This arrangement doesn't include your sister, Daniel. Let's get that straight from the off. If we are to go forward with this, you and me, then that's one of my conditions. I won't work with a woman. Let her step away. That's even better for us.'

Daniel grinned then. Liking Gem Kemal's logic even more.

Women could be a royal pain in the arse, but his sister Nancy was the ultimate. Gem was right; if Nancy was thinking about stepping back from the club and the drug scene, there would be no harm in Daniel pursuing it, would there?

This could be the chance he'd been looking for to finally strike out on his own. To step out of his sister's shadow and get the recognition that Daniel knew he deserved. His sister may have always been the golden child in their father's eyes, the one that could do no wrong and would succeed no matter what, but their father wasn't here anymore.

Daniel Byrne was more than capable of running his own empire, and one day he would.

Fuck his father's wishes. He'd cut Nancy out.

That would be payback then, for all the times that his father had put him down, and belittled him.

Everyone had underestimated Daniel, but not anymore.

'So what do you say, Daniel, do we have a deal?' Gem said, smiling expectantly as he waited for Daniel to come around to his way of thinking.

'Okay, I'm in.' Daniel nodded. Picking up his glass and holding it out to Gem's so that they could seal their deal with a toast. He quite fancied working alongside the Turks, those fuckers were just as fucking mental as he was. They would make the perfect team.

Daniel Byrne was a force to be reckoned with and it was high time that his sister Nancy – and the rest of London for that matter – started to take note of that fact.

'To us, my friend! New business partners.'

CHAPTER THIRTEEN

Sitting on the bed, looking down at her hands, Joanie Byrne stared intently at the sore red welts that had formed from where she'd just pounded them against her husband's skull.

She couldn't remember any of the attack she'd inflicted on him. Not a thing. Though the shocked looks on Colleen and Michael's faces when she'd come round from her little episode had told her all she'd needed to know. The scariest part of all was that it wasn't until Joanie had heard Colleen's voice that she'd even realised she was lashing out at Michael. It was as if she had slipped out of her body into another realm.

As if she'd been in some kind of trance.

Knowing her useless excuse of a husband, Michael probably deserved a smack or two, of course. The way he'd been parading around the place, acting as if he didn't give two shits about their son's death, Joanie felt no remorse for giving him a good old clout around the head. Her husband was the epitome of everything she despised in a man. A self-centred coward. That's all he was. But what could she do about it? She was married to the man. Tied to him for all of her days.

And now, when she needed him the most, he was doing what he always did so well: taking advantage of the fact she was suffering. Well, she may not be able to cope with the bastard right now, but she would remember all of this. His constant drinking, all those snide little digs that he made. When she was feeling more herself again, Joanie would make that bastard pay for his insincerity.

But now she needed to concentrate on herself. On the pain inside her, which crippled her every minute of her waking hour. *What was happening to her?*

She felt as if she was slowly losing her mind with grief. Trying her hardest not to cry then, as she listened to her daughter-in-law busying herself in her en suite, running her a bath, Joanie sighed to herself. Who'd have thought it? The only person that she could depend on these days was the one woman that Joanie had spent the last twenty years despising.

She felt truly awful, especially now that Colleen was doing nothing but run around after her, and staying at her side constantly, making sure she was okay. Joanie could barely think about all the spiteful, nasty things she'd said and done to the woman over the years.

Fighting and scoring points against each other.

It all seemed so pathetic now. How Joanie had somehow convinced herself that Colleen was some kind of threat to her and Jimmy's relationship. That the girl had come along and tried to snatch her son away from her.

Now they'd both found out the truth about her Jimmy, about his hidden sexuality, the irony was that Colleen could never have done such a thing, even if she'd wanted to. It felt like such a waste. All those years that Joanie had spent bullying and manipulating the woman, she felt wrecked with guilt about it now.

'Okay, Joanie, I've ran you a nice bath, and I've put some fresh towels on the radiator for you to keep them warm. Do you want me to give you a hand getting in?' Colleen asked politely, hoping to God that Joanie would say no and spare her the sight of seeing the mother-in-law naked.

'I'm sure that I'll be fine. Thank you,' Joanie said, her words clipped, embarrassed to be such a burden on the woman.

Colleen nodded.

'Well I'll leave you to it then. Tell you what, I'll go and fix you some tea. I'll have it ready for when you get out.'

Colleen's kindness was too much for her. Joanie started sobbing.

'Joanie?'

'Why are you being nice to me?' she said through her tears, unable to catch her breath as she tried to talk. 'I treated you appallingly. All these years. All the things I've said to you.' Joanie meant every word of it too. She might not be in the best state of mind at the moment, but she could clearly see what was going on all around her. The grandkids were preoccupied trying to help out with all of Jimmy's business dealings, Michael had been his usual typical unhelpful self, which only left Colleen.

By rights, Colleen should have left Joanie alone to suffer. She should be the one revelling in Joanie's misery and heartbreak. Just like her own husband bloody was. Instead, Colleen had become her rock.

Who else would Joanie have if it wasn't for her?

'The past is the past, Joanie. Let's just leave it there, yeah?' Colleen said then, not wanting to distress the woman any further than she already was. 'We can't change what happened now; we just have to move on.'

Joanie nodded. Though a small part of her wondered how Colleen could so easily just forgive and forget. The woman's life had been made a living hell. Joanie had done that. She owed the woman so much, at least some sort of an explanation. But the words sounded pathetic even to her own ears.

'I used to think you were a threat, Colleen. That was my problem. I was so scared of Jimmy finding a happiness with you that I could never give him, of him needing you more than he needed me.' Joanie had the good grace to look ashamed of herself, remembering the depths she'd gone to drive a wedge between

Jimmy and his new wife all those years ago. 'I'm sorry for the way I treated you. Really I am.'

Colleen sat down on the bed then, too, beside Joanie, genuinely taken aback by the woman's admission. Joanie had never once in twenty years shown her an ounce of remorse for the way she'd treated her, and never in her wildest dreams did she ever imagine she would get an apology from Joanie.

Jimmy's death had changed Joanie into someone that Colleen didn't recognise anymore.

'Look, Joanie, none of us are perfect. I know I haven't been the best mother in the world to Nancy and Daniel. I spent most of their lives walking around this house in a drunken haze. In fact, if it wasn't for you stepping in and doing such a great job bringing those kids up, God knows what state they'd both be in now. I have my own guilt to deal with. None of us are perfect. I was an awful mother, but a mother all the same, and I can only imagine the pain that you're in right now, losing your one and only child.' She placed her hand on Joanie's. A small gesture that let Joanie know that the dynamics between them had changed.

They were calling it a truce. Both of them. Starting again.

And Joanie was glad about that. Seeing the genuine tears that glistened in Colleen's eyes, she knew that Colleen meant every word that she said. Though Colleen's pain cut Joanie deeply. The reason she'd never been a mother to those two children of hers was because of Joanie. She'd made sure of that, sabotaging Colleen's every chance at her relationship with Nancy and Daniel. Placing a wedge firmly between them.

She'd wanted Nancy and Daniel to only ever need her. Jimmy, too. That was how spiteful and vindictive she could be.

What sort of a woman did that? Denied a mother her own children?

'Will you ever forgive me? Or at least forget?'

Colleen patted Joanie's hand, unable to find her voice, and Joanie couldn't blame her. Not normally good with her emotions, she felt awkward now, her apology leaving her feeling somewhat vulnerable.

'I'll go and get that bath,' she said then, leaving Colleen alone with her thoughts.

She owed Colleen so much now, she realised that.

Joanie just hoped that one day her daughter-in-law would forgive her.

CHAPTER FOURTEEN

Standing next to her brother's bed, the narrow stream of light beamed in from the hallway, illuminating Daniel's face just enough so that Nancy could see him breathing. Enough so she could see his chest rise and fall as he slept so soundly. So deeply.

How could he sleep so soundly after what he'd done? she thought, as she wrapped her finger tightly around the trigger of her father's Smith and Wesson that she'd taken from his safe. Aiming it at Daniel's head.

The house was completely silent now.

Everyone fast asleep in their beds.

Nancy was enjoying the stillness. She'd needed some time on her own to think things over tonight, to try to work out what she was going to do, especially after the day she'd had. Finding herself in her father's office at the front of the house, she'd sat in his chair for what had felt like hours. Just staring at his photographs on the wall.

The Byrne family.

Her mother, her grandparents, Daniel. Even Alex.

All of them staring back at the camera happily, smiling. Blissfully unaware that the Byrne family was nothing more than a rickety house of cards, a sham, ready to topple at any given moment.

Jimmy's facade.

She wondered how much of their lives had been real.

Her father had loved her, she was certain of that. Despite all the lies and deceit, she knew that deep down in her soul. Though about the other things – about him and Alex, about the other men – for years she had no idea at all. Her father had hidden his secrets well. Buried them, in fact, so deeply that no one would ever find out the truth.

But the truth always came out in the end, one way or another. As it would with the other secrets that now tainted this house.

Steadying her arm, she pointed the gun at Daniel's head. Right in the middle, between his eyes. Her brother had been behind her attack the other night too, Nancy was certain of it. One of his vain attempts at trying to warn her off from finding out too much. In typical Daniel style, he'd sent someone else to do his dirty work for him.

But Nancy knew everything. She'd had it all confirmed by her father's reliable sources at the Cyber Crime Unit that Daniel was involved.

Her brother, the blackmailer and murderer.

She'd found out more than even Jack Taylor had been capable of. She was the only one who knew. The only one really aware of how low her brother Daniel was prepared to stoop to get what he wanted. The extremes he would go to protect himself. The man had since shown no sorrow or remorse for what he had done. No regret for ripping their family apart. For murdering, in cold blood, the only man that Nancy Byrne had ever loved.

Now he was going to die.

Trying to control the shake of her hand, she willed herself to do it. To fire her father's 'old faithful', as he used to call it. The gun that he kept in the house for their own protection.

The irony, Nancy thought as she aimed it at Daniel's head. The very person he'd needed protection from had been sleeping under their roof all along.

Her finger twitched.

One squeeze of the trigger was all it would take, and his brains would explode all over the pillow and headboard behind him. Or slam a bullet into his chest, just as he had done to their father.

One press and it would all be over.

It felt surreal to watch his face, so relaxed. The complete oblivion that his own sister was about to kill him, that she was standing over him with the power to rip his life away from him while he was lost in his dreams.

She could do it.

She had to do it.

Pull the trigger! she instructed herself.

Wincing as she recalled the past couple of weeks since her father had been murdered. How Daniel had made them all believe that Marlon Jackson had been involved. How they'd held the man in one of her father's warehouses and how she'd watched as Daniel had executed him too.

She felt sick to her stomach at that. Knowing now that Daniel had played them all. He'd killed Marlon to silence the man. Afraid that Marlon would give his game up.

Oh, Daniel was good. She'd give him that.

He played them all.

Their father had massively underestimated Daniel, it seemed. Her brother was smarter and far more devious than any of them had given him credit for.

Nancy felt her tears, unable to hold them back as they spilled out involuntarily. Pouring down her cheeks against her wishes. Brushing them away with the back of her hand, her other hand still holding the gun.

There would be time to weep once this was over and, when she finally did allow herself to properly cry, she was saving her tears for her father. Not for her brother.

She should wake him, she thought. Let him really suffer. Make him feel the pain and torment that he had inflicted upon her, upon them all.

Pull the fucking trigger!

Only, she couldn't do it.

Instead she stood there, frozen to the spot, her arm stretched out in front of her. Shaking violently as she realised that she couldn't go through with his murder.

She was too weak, too pathetic to go through with it. Her conscience eating away inside of her, telling her that if she did this, if she went through with it, then she'd be sinking just as low as her brother.

She'd be a cold, callous murderer too.

Her nan Joanie would never cope with another death in the family, the woman was barely coping now, and what would happen to Nancy? With Daniel dead, she'd end up in prison. Who would look after her father's businesses then? Who would make sure that everything was run just as her dad would have wanted?

She couldn't go through with this.

Angry at herself for not having the guts to just shoot the fucker in the head, and wipe him off the face of the planet, she hurried from the room, feeling the bile rising up in her throat again. The red hot rage that pulsated through her veins at the injustice of it all.

That Daniel had somehow got away with everything.

CHAPTER FIFTEEN

'Where the hell were you last night? You were supposed to be over at the flat on Bridge Street,' Nancy asked, annoyed to find her brother sitting at the kitchen table, calmly eating his breakfast, completely oblivious to the amount of aggro he'd caused her by disappearing the night before, and how he'd driven her to the edge.

The fact that she'd almost killed him.

'I've been busy!' Daniel said, not bothering to look up from texting on his phone.

Nancy eyed the glass of Scotch next to him. Disgusted that Daniel was drinking already, so early in the day. Not that it perturbed her. It didn't matter how lairy and volatile Daniel could be, especially when he had a drink inside him – he didn't intimidate her in the slightest. In fact, right now, the only thing she felt towards her brother was severely pissed off.

'Well you left that prat Lee Archer in charge and by the time me and Jack got there, the girls were tearing each other's hair out. Literally! What the fuck are you playing at, Daniel? The one thing I asked you to do, and you couldn't even do that right.'

Daniel had asked to be included in the businesses, and Nancy had included him, only he'd thrown it back in her face. She geared herself up for one of Daniel's excuses, for her brother to try and dig himself out of it with some pathetic reason why he hadn't kept an eye on the place like she'd asked him to.

But Daniel wasn't in an apologetic mood, it seemed.

'Oh, give it a rest will you, Nancy. It's a poxy brothel. It's not exactly difficult to keep a few tarts in line, is it?! I'm sure that Lee had everything in hand.' Daniel rolled his eyes then. 'Besides, I ain't stupid! The only reason you asked me to keep an eye on the place is so that you could pack me off out of your way. Well I had other plans. Some business of my own that I needed to attend to. Not everything has to be run by you!'

'Is that so!' Nancy said, shoving her handbag on the kitchen side, before going to the fridge and pouring herself a glass of orange juice. She couldn't stomach any food, not with the mood she was in.

'Well, who does it have to be run by then, Daniel? Because this is a *family* business. We're carrying things on just as Dad would have. You don't get to just start throwing your weight around and making decisions behind my back. That's not how things work around here.'

Daniel shook his head, his mouth curled into a twisted smirk.

'And how *are* things run around here, Nancy? You tell every fucker to jump and we all ask how high? Is that how you want it? You shouting the orders and I just comply, like some personal fucking lackey? Only, that's bullshit too. This was our father's business, you're right. But no one's put you in charge. I have as much right to make decisions as you do.'

Nancy took a mouthful of her orange juice, allowing herself a few seconds to breathe before she launched her glass at her brother's head. He could be so pig-headed at times. Thinking that he had a right to do as he pleased. That he could worm his way in to a business that he knew nothing about.

'You don't know what you're doing, Daniel. That's the problem. You didn't help out with the business when Dad was alive, and you haven't got a clue what you're doing now that he's gone.' She stared at him, the hatred that she felt towards her brother all-consuming. They wouldn't even be here now, having this conversation, but for Daniel.

'You fuck things up, Daniel. You always did, that's why Dad never involved you in the first place.'

Nancy hit a nerve.

'The reason why I never got a look in, was because you always stole the limelight, Nancy. Little Miss fucking perfect. You're so stuck up your own arse it's a wonder you can see daylight. Dad didn't give me a chance because he was too blindsided by you. His precious little fucking Nancy!'

'Oh, shut up, Daniel. Dad didn't give you a chance because he knew you were a fucking liability,' Nancy shouted back, sick to death of her brother's 'poor-me' attitude. 'That's the real reason. Now he's dead and this business will only survive if I'm in charge. I know what I'm doing, Daniel. I've let you come on board, but if you keep insisting on fucking things up, and not doing as I ask, then you're going to be out.'

Daniel nodded, letting Nancy know that he heard her loud and clear. But the twisted smirk on his face seconds later told her that her threat had been in vain.

'See. There you go again. "You're in charge. If I don't do as *you* ask." When are you going to get it, Nancy? You don't tell me what to do. You don't tell me jack shit.'

Daniel sat back in his chair, full of confidence as he glared back at his sister. 'He fucking underestimated me, and so are you!'

Nancy had heard enough

'That's just it though, Daniel. I'm not underestimating you. I know *exactly* what you're capable of. Exactly the lengths you'd go to save your own arse.' Nancy's eyes flashed with fury as she finally laid her cards out on the table, hoping her brother would just put an end to all this lying and deceit and admit what he had done.

She'd had enough of all the pretence.

'I know all about you. All your filthy little secrets,' she spat. 'I know what you did!'

Their eyes locked then.

Nancy could feel her heart beating erratically in her chest, her ribcage tightening, waiting for her brother to put his hands up and admit it: that he had killed their father.

But Daniel was a coward until the end.

'That's why you had me followed, isn't it? So you could shut me up. The attack the other night. It was you, wasn't it? Go on, admit it! I fucking dare you!'

Daniel laughed then, his face crinkling in amusement.

'Fucking hell, Nancy. That must have really put the shits up you! You're fucking paranoid, love! Maybe you should go and see someone about that!'

He was mocking her now, and they both knew it. Skirting around the truth, just like he always did. Her brother was completely gutless.

That only made Nancy hate him even more.

'You are going to pay for what you've done, Daniel. I promise you that.'

'Is that so?' Daniel said, getting up off his chair, not intimidated by Nancy's threat in the least. If anything, he found her threat highly amusing. If his sister was so intent on making him pay, she would have done it by now.

'What are you going to do, Nancy? Kill me? We both know you haven't got the balls for that. So what then? The police. Only, there's no evidence. No witnesses, only your word.'

Daniel shook his head and made a sad face, pouting his lips. 'Oh Nancy! Please! You're not well, Nancy! Your head's all fucked up. The police will say that too. How the poor little rich girl isn't coping. You think they give two shits about a murdered gangster's daughter? You think they give two shits about him? Someone did them a favour.' He smirked once more.

'So, the way I see it, Nancy. We're in this together for the long haul. Only this isn't just your business to run and I won't be answerable to you. So stay off my fucking back. I mean it,' he said, before finally storming out of the kitchen.

Leaving Nancy Byrne standing there alone.

A lump in her throat.

Wishing to God that she'd shot her bastard of a brother when she'd had the chance.

CHAPTER SIXTEEN

'Well, this is just fucking handsome, Colleen. I tell you what, this girl can't half cook!' Michael Byrne piped up at the end of the dining table as he happily swigged his beer. 'As much as I love my Joanie's cooking, don't get me wrong, Colleen here isn't far off. She's a blinding cook.'

In his element, Michael sat at the table with a pint in his hand and a huge grin on his face. He was unaware that his granddaughter Nancy was glaring at him, trying her hardest to bite her tongue before she said something that she'd regret. She couldn't remember a time in her life when she'd seen the man happier.

Her grandad seemed to be permanently drinking and glued to the TV these days. It was like someone had finally let the man off his leash. It sickened her that he could be so insensitive to carry on, jovial and full of life, when everyone around him was clearly struggling. Though her grandad probably hadn't picked up on the tension around the table, especially between her and Daniel.

'Do you want some more potatoes, Sam?' Colleen said, as she passed the plate over to Sam Miles, pleased to get the chance to finally meet one of Daniel's friends. She couldn't recall her son ever bringing anyone home before now.

'Oh, no, I'm good, thank you, Mrs Byrne.' Sam grinned. 'There's enough food on my plate to keep me going for the rest of the week.'

Colleen smiled at the young man's politeness. He wasn't the type that Colleen would have seen as Daniel having much in common with. Sam was quiet and easy-going, the complete opposite of Daniel. In fact, her son's behaviour lately was starting to worry Colleen; in particular, his excessive drinking.

Watching him as he downed his third glass of wine, already half-cut, Colleen had a sneaky suspicion that he'd been drinking long before lunchtime too. He and Nancy hadn't spoken a single word to each other either, and Colleen knew there was an undercurrent of hostility between them. She just hoped that Daniel didn't take it upon himself to make matters worse today.

The whole point of cooking this meal for everyone had been to restore some normality within the family. Though Colleen knew that, with the Byrne family, there really was no such thing as normal.

'This is a lovely roast, Mum!' Daniel said in agreement with Sam, as he rudely shovelled a huge slice of roast beef in his mouth before pouring himself another glass of white wine. 'A bit fancy for a Saturday lunchtime though, isn't it? What's the occasion?'

'Thanks! No occasion. I just thought it would be nice for your nan to have us all together around the table. You know, after everything that's happened,' Colleen said modestly, glad that someone was enjoying her efforts. Unlike Nancy, who was sitting there pushing her food around the plate in silence. She hadn't eaten a single bite.

'You not hungry, Nancy?' Colleen asked, trying her hardest not to look offended that her daughter wasn't even going to attempt to eat the food that she'd spent the past two hours cooking.

She'd been so looking forward to today. In her head she'd envisaged how it should have been all those years ago; cooking a proper family meal, with her son and daughter sitting at either side of her. All talking and laughing and enjoying each other's company.

In reality, the tension in the room was palpable – everyone sitting at the table with their own personal crosses to bear.

Though if Colleen was being really honest with herself, she was simply glad that Nancy had even accepted her offer of dinner at all. Colleen knew why she'd agreed to it though. The same reason they all had. For Joanie's sake. The woman needed her family around her more than ever right now.

'No. I've not got much of an appetite. You know, after "everything that's happened".' Her tone full of sarcasm. Finding it hard to swallow even a mouthful of the food that Colleen had cooked, Nancy pushed her plate away.

Jack shot her a knowing look, warning the girl to go easy on her mother. Clearly Colleen had gone to a lot of effort today, he thought, looking at the beautifully set dining table. Joanie's best china plates and the freshly cut flowers everywhere. The food was delicious too. Roast beef with all the trimmings. He knew how hard it was for Nancy to be in her mother's company, but Nancy just didn't seem to want to give the woman a chance.

Nancy shrugged back at him, before taking a big swig of her wine.

Boy, she needed a drink. She was finding this all so much harder than she expected. Sitting here at the table with her family all around her. Trying to act normal, to pretend that everything was okay, when it was anything but.

Daniel. Her grandad, and now Colleen. All of them fake as fuck. Sitting around the table playing happy families.

Especially her mother. Who was the woman kidding? Colleen making out that it was all for her nan Joanie's benefit.

It was sickening to watch. Acting all holier than thou. Colleen making herself indispensable to them all, out of the sudden goodness of her heart. Well, Nancy could see straight through her.

'Well, if you're not eating it. I will. Waste not want not! Huh. That's what you always used to say, Nan, isn't it?' Daniel said, putting on a fake Irish accent to mimic his nan as he leaned over with his fork and grabbed a big slice of meat off his sister's plate, before shoving it into his mouth and continuing his sentence with his mouth full. 'This is well tasty, Mum! Almost as good as yours, Nan!' Daniel winked at his nan then, catching the small smile that he'd hoped she'd give him.

Nancy bristled.

Mum.

For the past twenty years, she and Daniel had never called Colleen 'mum'. No one else at the table seemed to notice the familiarity between Colleen and Daniel, or at least, if they did, no one reacted.

'Ah, you're a toerag, Daniel.' Joanie grinned, her grandson's humour breaking her trance. She'd been sitting at the table in silence up until then. Her head had been pounding for days. 'This is a really lovely dinner, Colleen. We don't get together as a family often enough,' she said, staring at the seat at the head of the table where Daniel sat. The place where her Jimmy used to sit.

'Are you sure you're all right, Nan?' Nancy said, sensing the tears that threatened once more. Joanie had barely spoken two words all afternoon. Nancy couldn't help but think that her nan was suddenly looking older and smaller than ever before. As if she'd disintegrated in every way possible these past few weeks.

'Oh, I'm fine,' Joanie lied. Not sure what was wrong with her. Grief? Or old age? Joanie was too proud to admit that she was struggling. Even now, she felt as if she was slowly losing her mind.

All she wanted to do was crawl underneath her bed covers and give in to sleep. Pray that she wouldn't wake up so that she could be with her Jimmy again. But she was here instead, pretending that everything was okay. What other choice did she have? Besides, her family still meant everything to her. She wanted so much to enjoy her dinner with them all, at least.

'I was just thinking how lovely it is to have you all here. That Jack is here, too. And Daniel's nice young friend, too.'

'He's my boyfriend, Nan,' Daniel said then without missing a beat, as he squeezed Sam's hand.

Sam bristled, moving his hand away as he sensed everyone's awkwardness and shock at Daniel's sudden announcement. Daniel hadn't even told him that he was going to tell his family about them both today.

'And a lovely friend he is too,' Joanie said, thinking that she had misheard Daniel. Though the silence around the table told her that she hadn't misheard him at all.

'No, Nan. I said he's my boyfriend. I'm fucking him.' *This was more like it*, Daniel thought, popping a whole roast potato in his mouth as he took in the look on everyone's face at the table. Thoroughly enjoying the collective awkward reaction.

Michael Byrne spoke first.

'Fucking hell, boy, you don't mince your words do you? Pardon the pun,' he said, choking on his food at his grandson's announcement. 'Though I guess it's in your genes, isn't it? Seeing as your father was partial to a bit of—' Seeing Joanie and Nancy glaring at him, Michael stopped himself before he said something crass. Before ending his sentence. 'To men. He liked men.'

'Jesus, Daniel, you could have warned me that you were going to tell everyone,' Sam whispered through gritted teeth, mortified that Daniel had just blurted out that they were in a relationship. His family were clearly shocked and, to be fair, Sam couldn't blame them. They'd only been seeing each other for a few months now; today was the first time that Daniel had invited him to meet all of his family properly. Talk about springing it on them.

'It isn't a big deal though, is it! No point fucking lying about it. I mean, you only have to look at my old man to see what a fuck up that all was,' Daniel said slurring his words as he picked his drink up; in his element at being centre of attention. 'Dad knew about me. I bet he didn't tell any of you though, did he?' Daniel continued, as he looked from his nan Joanie to Michael and then to Colleen. His hunch immediately proved right. None of his family had a clue.

Despite the fact that Sam was fidgeting awkwardly in the chair beside him, Daniel had no intention of shutting up now. He'd already done eighteen years of that.

'Surprise, surprise. Another one of dad's filthy little secrets, eh? I wonder how many more the old man had?'

'What are you talking about?' Joanie said, confused.

'Dad knew I was gay. I told him. But he was ashamed of me, you see.' Daniel laughed then. A twisted smirk that held no amusement. 'I was fourteen years old when I finally plucked up the courage to tell Dad. Do you know how much guts that took me? To admit my deepest, darkest secrets to the big fucking Jimmy Byrne. And do you know what he said to me? He said that I was an attention-seeker and that I was making it up. Then he actually laughed at me.'

Daniel's face was twisted with pure hate now at the memory.

The room had gone silent. No one at the table dared to speak, still shocked at Daniel's sudden outburst and the venom with which he'd spoken of his father.

'And do you know the most sickening part of all of this was that, all along, he knew that he was gay too. He made out he was ashamed of me, but all that time he was just ashamed of himself. Fucking hell. He made me feel as if I had something wrong with me. As if I was sick in the head for even thinking about boys.

Men. When he was a raving fucking poofter all along. What were the chances, huh!'

No one was eating now.

Seeing the distraught look on Joanie's face, and knowing full well that Nancy was already fit to blow at her brother, Jack spoke up.

'That's enough,' he said, not willing to sit there and listen to Daniel's rant any longer. As much as Daniel was clearly hurting, he was speaking with such venom and spite that this could only end badly. Joanie Byrne had gone so pale she almost looked transparent, and Colleen had tears streaming down her face at discovering her son's angst. Someone had to try and rein Daniel in, and it may as well be him.

At least Daniel might actually listen to him.

Only, he wasn't prepared to tonight. Not in the mood he was in.

'Oh, fuck you, Jack. That's what he did. Silenced me. He didn't want to hear it either. Well, you don't tell me when it's enough. You don't tell me shit. He spent his life living a fucking lie. I'm not doing that too.'

'Bullshit,' Nancy said, her voice firm, hissing through gritted teeth. Trying her hardest to contain her temper.

Daniel smirked, glad that he'd riled up his sister.

'That's the problem with this family, Nancy. No one wants to hear the truth. You all want to float around in this make-believe fucking bubble. Wasn't that Dad's philosophy? Pretend it ain't happening, then you don't have to deal with it. That's why he let mum walk around the house like a fucking zombie for all those years. Smacked off her head on pills and drink.'

'Oh please, don't blame Dad for *her* actions,' Nancy spat, her eyes blazing at Daniel and his audacity.

'Maybe Dad was right about some things. You are an attention-seeker, and you don't care who you hurt when you open that
mouth of yours.' Nancy was fighting with the demons inside of
her now, scared that if she stayed here for another second that she
would blurt out everything that she knew about her brother, and
that would only break her nan's heart beyond repair. The woman
was already struggling. Finding out that it was her grandson that
had murdered her son would probably tip Joanie over the edge.

Nancy couldn't do it.

'We don't give a shit if you're shagging the Pope, Daniel.' Then
picking up her full glass, Nancy held it up, making her point loud
and clear. 'Here you go. A toast, everyone. To Daniel and Sam.
Hope you're both deliriously happy together. There? You happy
now? Did you get the reaction you were after?'

Slamming her glass down on the table, she glared at Daniel
with such hate now. 'Don't you ever, EVER talk about my father
out of turn again. Or, I promise you, it will be the last thing you
ever do.'

With that, Nancy fled from the room.

Dinner was well and truly ruined.

*

'Fucking hell, Daniel. That was awkward,' Sam Miles said as he
shook his head in wonderment and followed Daniel out to his
car, almost running to keep up with him. Though to be fair, he
couldn't have got out of Daniel's family home quick enough.

Talk about intense.

Meeting the Byrne family had turned out to be one of the most
cringeworthy experiences of his life and a part of him couldn't
help but feel that he'd just been used somehow.

'You could have told me that you were going to be making
a fucking debut from your bloody closet today. At least I could

have prepared myself.' Though Sam highly doubted that anything could have prepared him for the way in which Daniel had announced their news. In fact, part of him thought that Daniel had probably planned this all along. Dragging Sam along with him today so that he could make his shocking announcement in style.

Nancy was right. It was as if Daniel revelled in everyone's shocked reactions. As if he'd purposely wanted to wind them all up.

Still it was done now, he guessed. Daniel had finally told his family about him. Which, in a way, could only be a good thing, Sam supposed. At least now he knew that Daniel must be a little bit serious about their relationship. He must care about Sam more than he let on if he'd just come out to his entire family.

'My sister's a cunt,' Daniel said, his words coming out in a slur. Glad that he'd put the stupid cow in her place. He was sick of Nancy always looking down her nose at him. Treating him like he was nothing. When the truth was Daniel was more like his old man than any of them.

Especially Nancy.

'That she may be,' Sam said, not entirely agreeing, but going along with Daniel so that he didn't cause yet another argument between them both. 'But your poor nan and your mum. They both looked so shocked. Could you not have broken it more gently to them?'

'They'll get over it.' Daniel shrugged, too drunk to care what his nan and his mother thought about him.

'Where are we going now? Back to mine?' Sam said hopefully.

He and Daniel had hardly spent any time together lately and he understood that Daniel needed his space, what with everything that had happened in recent weeks. Losing his father the way he did and now trying to help run all the businesses. A selfish part of Sam just wanted Daniel back the way he'd been when they'd first got together. Before Daniel had started drinking excessively and disappearing off out all the time without him.

'Nah, later maybe. I've got some business to sort out first. You coming? Or you want to go back inside with that lot of fucking loons?' Daniel asked raising his eyes back towards the house.

Sam laughed then, despite himself.

'Course I'm coming. Here, let me drive. You're off your bloody head,' he said, running around and getting into the driver's seat, taking Daniel up on his offer, before his boyfriend changed his mind.

Daniel Byrne had no idea that he was the biggest fucking loon of them all.

CHAPTER SEVENTEEN

Pulling up down one of the side roads just behind Drayton Gardens in Camden, Sam Miles turned off the ignition as the two men sat in silence. Staring up at the grey concrete-looking council estate, the place looked every bit as depressing as Sam imagined it would be to live there.

He watched as a group of young lads all poured out of the main front door of the building, not bothering to move out of the way so that an elderly lady was forced to press herself up against the wall to let the boys all pass her. They stood there, eyeing up Daniel's motor.

'Fucking hell. I'm glad we aren't getting out. We'd only come back to find those lot have pinched our car stereo!'

'The stereo would be the least of your worries around here, Sam,' Daniel said, reminding himself that Sam Miles had a lot to learn. Despite the fact that they'd both came from wealthy backgrounds, his boyfriend had lived a somewhat sheltered life. Living over in affluent Chelsea with his rich parents. He had no idea about the poverty and survival of living in a run-down council estate. How could he? He'd come from a stable, loving family. Unlike Daniel, who knew the score when it came to dealing with the more sordid parts of the city. His father was a gangster, it didn't get much darker and seedier than that. 'See those fuckers there, they'd take your motor for a joyride and then torch the thing just to fucking spite you,' Daniel said, eyeing the group so that they knew he wasn't intimidated by them.

If you didn't live in Drayton Gardens then you had no reason in being here, and the gangs that patrolled the communal grounds and gardens were all now standing around and taking a keen interest in the two men sitting in the fancy-looking Beamer.

Though Daniel Byrne wasn't just anyone.

These fuckers would learn that the hard way if they tried any funny business with him.

'Fucking scrotes the lot of them. Giving us the stares.'

Sam nodded in agreement, though Daniel's words were starting to unnerve him. This grimy estate was worlds apart from the London he was accustomed to. He looked up at the rows of washing streaming from the windows and balconies, the groups of youths that huddled in the doorway smoking gear and drinking out of cans, threatening and intimidating every person that passed them as if it was some kind of a game.

And the rubbish. There were bits of it strewn everywhere. Stinking nappies. Half-eaten kebabs.

Sam wrinkled his nose in distaste and was glad when the man that Daniel was waiting for finally came out through the main doors and approached the car.

Sam just wanted to get the fuck out of here.

'All right, lads,' Jenson Reed said before staring up and down the street, making sure that there were no Old Bill about. That lot were about as discreet as a poke in the eye with a sharp stick. Seeing the coast was clear he leant down on the open window of the driver's side and peered in at Daniel.

'Fancy fucking motor this, must have cost you a mint.'

'Yeah it did, so get your fucking grubby mitts off the fucking paintwork, yeah!' Daniel said, leaning over Sam and swatting Jenson's hand away from his pristine motor. This car was Daniel's pride and joy. The only reason Sam was driving it was because he was too drunk.

'All right, mate, keep your hair on.' Jenson grinned, throwing his hands up in one swift exaggerated movement.

Daniel smarted.

Jenson Reed.

So this was the main dealer that Gem was using at The Karma Club to dish out their shit. Jenson Reed must have been at least a decade older than Daniel, though you wouldn't have thought it the way the man was dressed. In his cheap Adidas tracksuit, and bright white high top trainers, baseball cap tilted on the side of his head, the man was a walking, talking cliché. He was putting on an accent, too. Trying to sound more street than he actually was. A proper wide boy.

He'd only set sights on him for a few minutes and already the man was instantly rubbing Daniel up the wrong way. Acting far too familiar and far too cocky for his liking.

According to Gem, though, Jenson had worked on the doors of London's biggest nightclubs and the man had a list of loyal punters the length of the dingy fucking tower block behind him. The bloke shifted a shit tonne of gear, according to Gem, so for now Daniel would go along with the plan.

For now anyway.

Eventually, Daniel would be running the show himself. He'd find a way to cut Gem Kemal out, too.

'So you've got some gear for me, have you?' Jenson said, glancing at his watch as if he had better places to be.

'Oh, sorry. Are we inconveniencing you? You got somewhere more important you need to be, do you?' Daniel said, raising his eyes. Indignant at the disrespect this fucker was showing him.

'I have as it happens. I've got a right tasty little bird waiting for me. You know the score…' Jenson winked at Daniel, and something in the bloke's demeanour told Daniel that Jenson was actually making a dig at him. As if he'd heard the rumours about his father being gay, and he was being sarcastic.

The little prick wouldn't be brave enough or stupid enough to pull a stunt like that though, surely?

'Here.' Daniel leant over and passed Jenson the bag of gear that he'd just picked up from Gem's contacts over in Islington, a shady-looking Turkish gang, dealing all sorts out the back of one of the kebab shops on Islington High Street.

'Fuck me, Daniel. You're taking a risk, ain't you? Picking this lot up and delivering it to me personally? Your old man used his lackeys for all that.'

'That's all well and good, Jenson. But you see, unlike my old man, I like to make sure everything's done to exact precision. There's no room for fuck-ups. This way, there's fewer of us involved,' Daniel explained, realising that Jenson wasn't much better than the scummy Turks he'd just dealt with. He'd gone from one bunch of fucking dregs to another, he thought, eyeing the state of Jenson Reed.

Jenson didn't appear to notice. He was too interested in the bag of pills that Daniel Byrne had just handed him. Nodding approvingly at the contents, he smirked.

'About fucking time too. I'm always getting asked for Special K and Es. I got a lot of people interested in this lot. We'll make an absolute killing.'

Daniel nodded. The bloke was a prize prick, but that was just what he wanted to hear.

'I get a little taster out of this lot, don't I? Gotta do a bit of quality control before I start dishing the shit out.'

Daniel pursed his mouth, taking in the way that Jenson was grinding his teeth, his pupils huge. The bloke looked as if he was already off his face.

'Aint you had enough? Fucking hell, are you some kind of cunt or what? Talk about fucking unprofessional. This is a fucking massive deal we have going down. One on which you stand to make a good amount of profit. I don't want you off your fucking tits tonight. Do you understand? Sort yourself out!'

Jenson grinned. 'Oh, you don't need to worry about me, mate. This stuff don't even touch me these days. I've become immune to it all,' he said unconvincingly.

'Yeah, well you won't be used to this shit. It's supposed to be the best out there. Potent shit, but worth every penny. Don't fuck this up.' Dealers were the lowest of the low as far as Daniel was concerned. Just as bad as the druggies and addicts. All of them slaves of their poison.

'Touchy!' Jenson sneered, not showing Daniel Byrne that he was one bit bothered by the man. He knew who he was, of course he did. Jimmy Byrne's son.

But who the fuck was Daniel, eh?

Jenson had never even heard the bloke's name until recently. Yet here he was, acting the big bollocks because of who his father had been, only, Daniel didn't scare him. Not one bit. Jenson was the real soldier here. Working out on the front line, dealing directly with the punters that came into the club.

'You know what, Daniel, you should try a couple of these too, you know. They might help you lighten the fuck up. You on the rag or something?'

'Fuck off, Jenson, you prick,' Daniel said, refusing to bite. Right now he could happily get out of the car and lamp the guy one.

'Right, we done here, Daniel?' Sensing the row that was brewing, Sam started the engine. Daniel had been so volatile lately, who knew what the man was capable of if someone tipped him over the edge – which, right now, was exactly the way that Jenson was heading.

'Yeah, we're done,' Daniel sneered. 'Just do your fucking job, Jenson. Sell the gear, and don't be fucking obvious about it when Alfie Harris is around, do you get me?'

Jenson nodded. He wasn't going to say jack shit to anyone. Not with the money that he stood to make from this little lot.

'Whatever you say, "boss?"' Jenson grinned now. 'Though I wouldn't want to be in your shoes when Alfie Harris finds out that you are dishing out pills in his club. He'll go mental.'

'I ain't distributing pills. *You* are. So let's hope he don't get to fucking hear about it. Now fuck off, away from the motor,' Daniel said finally, nodding to Sam that they were done here.

*

Placing the package in the inside pocket of his jacket, Jenson stuck his fingers up at the car as it sped off into the distance. Instantly taking a dislike to that stuck-up prat, Daniel Byrne, he half hoped that the man would catch sight of him in his rear-view mirror.

That would be funny; Daniel and his sidekick trying to chase him all around the estate. He'd have to catch him first. Jenson couldn't help but smile to himself as he made his way to his bird's house so that they could both test out some of his new merchandise.

Despite his prick of a boss to contend with, today was turning out to be a good day indeed.

CHAPTER EIGHTEEN

'Good evening, young ladies!' Standing at the main doors of The Karma Club, Jenson Reed grinned at his choice of words. *Young* being the operative, he thought to himself as he eyed the two girls in front of him, tottering up the steps in ridiculously high heels that they could barely walk in. These two wouldn't look amiss wearing school uniforms, he thought with a wicked smirk.

Still that didn't stop these girls trying their luck to get in by dressing older than they actually were. And boy had they both made an effort. All dolled up, in revealing clothes and faces full of badly applied make-up. It was almost comical how girls still didn't seem to cotton on to the fact that the harder they tried the more obvious they looked.

'Embryos in Wonderbras.' That's what Jenson and the other doormen at the club referred to girls like these two. In fact they probably didn't have much they could offer to even a Wonderbra. They were probably still padding their tops out with tissue paper.

Bless 'em! Still, he had to give it to them for at least having the nerve to try and get past the doormen. His boss had had a strict photo ID-only policy on the door but, in all fairness, as long as they passed his inspection Jenson wasn't that fussed if a few younger girls tried their luck getting in. In fact, if his new potential customers just happened to be pretty, young girls, he certainly wasn't going to be turning them away. For him it was yet another perk of the job.

Give him a young dumb girl any day of the week, unlike older birds that were a bit more clued up, and didn't stand for any bullshit from blokes like Jenson. The younger girls were naive as shit.

'I take it you both have some form of photo ID on you?' Jenson smirked, wondering how far he could go with this.

'We're both eighteen. I've got ID. I can prove it.' The taller of the two girls, Amber Richards, stepped forward confidently, putting on her most convincing display of being pissed off at having to prove her age. As she reached into her clutch bag for the ID card that she'd been hoping not to have to use, she pouted stroppily as she placed it in the doorman's hand. 'Happy now?'

Wrinkling his nose as he examined the photo card, Jenson was trying his hardest not to laugh. He prided himself on being able to spot a good fake from a mile off and this one was so bad that he doubted it would even fool a fucking blind person. Staring down at the photo, Jenson guessed that the girl was about fifteen. Sixteen, tops. Though the date of birth said different.

He looked back at them both.

Pretty girls. Really pretty. Even with their faces caked in dodgy make-up.

Jenson shook his head in wonderment. Christ! It was no wonder some men were so easily duped these days. These young girls all passing themselves off as over eighteen. Swanning about the clubs half dressed, letting men old enough to be their fathers buy them drinks and God knows what else – but the moment they had sex with someone, everyone made a big deal about the men being out of order. If anyone was getting played, it was the fellas.

These girls knew exactly what they were doing. Conniving as fuck.

That's why Jenson didn't feel bad about the way he treated half of them. Why should he? The girls were going to go after some poor unsuspecting fucker, it may as well be him. At least he'd make sure he got something out of it in return.

Handing Amber's ID back to her, Jenson eyed the other girl. She looked younger, and not nearly as confident as the first girl.

'And what about you?' he asked, raising his brow questioningly. 'You got some ID, too, have you?'

Megan Harris nodded. Unable to find any words, she was shitting herself now. Praying that none of the doormen would recognise her face. Trust Amber not to mention the fact that it would be The Karma Club where they were meeting up with her new boyfriend tonight. She'd waited until the taxi had dropped them off down the road to break that bit of news to Megan. When it was too bloody late for Megan to protest about it, unless she fancied traipsing halfway across London on her own.

Praying no one on the door recognised her, she diverted her gaze and looked at Amber instead, but she guessed rightly that it only made her appear even more nervous.

She could have killed her friend now.

Amber said they'd have no problem getting in here tonight. That they'd both just slip past the doormen unnoticed. That Reece Bettle had squared it with his mate, but Megan wasn't so sure now. Amber had spun her a right line, convincing her that, after sorting out their fake IDs for them both and plastering her in so much make-up she felt as if she was wearing a mask, they would get past the bouncers without any trouble. Her hair felt tight and awkward on top of her head, twisted up into a tight bun. Amber had told her that she looked more sophisticated now, only Megan wasn't convinced.

'Go, on, Olivia,' Amber said, nudging her friend's arm as she used the fake name that was written on the ID card. 'Show him your ID.'

Rummaging around for it in her bag, Megan realised that her hands were shaking. Part of her wanted to say that she'd lost it, or left it at home. Any excuse to save them both from the humiliation of this bouncer sending them both away while an entire queue of people stood behind them watching.

Megan knew that she couldn't do that though. Amber was counting on her to get in tonight. She'd had her boyfriend, Reece Bettle, make the ID cards up for them especially. He'd promised her that they were good copies, too. That they'd have no problems getting in; though, watching the way that the doorman's eyes had scanned Amber's card, his gaze lingering on the small print as he tried to work out her age, Megan wondered whether Amber's new boyfriend had stitched them both up.

If the doorman wasn't convinced by Amber's fake ID, he'd be even less convinced by Megan's. Hers had a fake name on it, too, and she had forgotten what her surname was supposed to be. Olivia something. Western or was it Westport? Shit! She couldn't remember.

How she had let Amber talk her into this, she'd never know.

'Here.' Handing it over, Megan made a conscious effort to steady her hand as she shot a worried look at her friend.

The two girls waited then, as the bouncer's gaze flickered to and from the ID cards and then back to both the girls, eyeing them both with scrutiny.

He was on a power trip. He had to be, Amber thought, as she watched the man enjoying the authority that he had over them. Purposely taking his time in deciding whether or not to let them in. Well, she'd had enough of the man's petty games.

'Are you done or what, cos I'm freezing my tits off out here,' she said, tapping her foot in agitation as she tried to call the bouncer's bluff by making out that she was not impressed with him holding them up from going inside. 'You asked for ID and you got it. What's your problem?'

'All right, gobby!' the doorman said with a smirk.

Then looking back at Megan, or Olivia, as he believed she was called, Jenson Reed softened. The youngest of the two girls was much nicer than her older, trappy mate. She was the prettier too, he thought as he allowed his gaze to linger on the girl's toned figure. Wearing a tiny denim miniskirt and crop top, finished off by some ridiculously high heels that the girls were all wearing these days, she looked that tall, she was swaying.

He shook his head playfully, before offering the girls a nugget of his wisdom for future reference.

'You know, you really need to work on your confidence,' Jenson said. 'Firstly, your nerves totally gave you away.' He grinned at Megan, shaking his head in dismay, though he couldn't help but laugh at the girls' abysmal attempt at trying to pull the wool over his eyes. 'And secondly, I've seen some dodgy fucking fakes in my time, but these are probably the worst I've come across. You girls been doing arts and crafts at school have ya? Trying to earn yourselves one of those *Blue Peter* badges off the telly? Jesus! I've seen it all now.' Jenson tapped at Megan's ID. 'It says you were born in 1971. Now my maths is pretty fucking shocking, ladies, but that makes you thirty-two, and there's no way that both of you combined are as old as me.' Handing the ID back to the girls with a grin he added: 'ten out of ten for having the bollocks to try and pull it off.' He winked now. Enjoying the disappointed looks on the girls' faces as he handed back their IDs, letting them know that they'd been well and truly caught out.

Megan Harris was relieved. The longer she'd stood here at the doors of the club, the more she'd decided that this was in fact the worse idea that Amber had ever had. She was glad that they weren't going in now. She'd been petrified that she'd be caught out. 'Come on, Amber, let's go.' Grabbing her friend's arm in a bid to drag her away.

But Amber wasn't as easily dismissed as Megan.

'Hang on,' she said, shrugging Megan's hand from her arm. The Karma Club was one of the best clubs in London, and tonight she was supposed to be proving to Reece that she was more mature than he gave her credit for. Not getting in to this club tonight wasn't an option. If she didn't get in, Reece would dump her. He'd practically said as much. Complaining that she was too young to go anywhere with him, or get in anywhere. That she was always at school. He was getting bored, Amber could sense it and it wouldn't be long until he started looking at his other options elsewhere. And judging by the state of some of the other nigh on naked girls that Amber had seen going into the club tonight, he was bound to find someone to take her place. She had to get in tonight. There was no way that she was going to let some other little slapper make a play for her man.

'Oh come on, man, give us a break, mate. We're supposed to be meeting up with some mates. They're already inside.'

Jenson shrugged as if the decision was out of his hands – which they all knew it wasn't.

'Come on, Amber, leave it yeah?' Megan pleaded. Hoping that Amber wouldn't cause any more of a scene than she already had. 'Let's just go back to yours, yeah? My dad gave me enough cash for a takeaway. We can try and get some drink from the offie on the way home.'

Jenson laughed then. 'God, you two are a bit gullible, ain't ya?! Cor, Reece said you were a bit easy to wind up!' He winked, finally giving in and letting the girls know that he'd been having them on all along.

This was the friend on the door that Reece had told her about.

'Very funny!' Amber said with a smile, trying to hide the fact that she'd been seconds away from losing her shit with the man. Glad now that she'd somehow kept a lid on her temper, she knew every word of tonight was going to get back to her boyfriend. Well, at least she'd shown that she could hold her own.

'Good one. I knew you were only joking all along. I was just going along with it all,' she said now, smiling her most charming smile at the man. If this was one of Reece's mates, then Amber was determined to leave a good impression. She knew what lads could be like, influencing each other with just a few words. The last thing she needed was someone in his ear telling him to ditch her.

''Course you did,' Jenson said with a knowing look, before lifting the red twisted rope and allowing the two girls into the club.

'I'll be seeing you later, ladies!' he said then. 'I'll come and have a drink with you when we quieten down a bit later on.'

Jenson shot a smile at Megan, pleased to see her blushing at his obvious advances towards her.

He smirked, staring at the girls' arses as they sauntered into the club.

He'd done these two girls a good turn letting them both in here tonight, and it was only fair that at least one of them returned the favour.

And Jenson Reed would make sure that they did.

CHAPTER NINETEEN

'You do know that you haven't stopped looking at that clock tonight; you got somewhere else you'd rather be?' Jennifer Dawson scolded Alfie Harris playfully, shaking her head at the man.

'Don't be silly!' Alfie smiled, sitting back in his chair, full after the delicious meal that Jennifer had just cooked for them both.

'Oh, come on, Alfie. I know you, darling. What's on your mind? Is it Megan or the club that you're worrying about tonight?'

Getting up to clear the plates away, Alfie shrugged, knowing there was no point in lying to Jennifer. His head had been elsewhere all evening, if he was honest.

'It's not Megan, she's an angel. She's probably the one thing I've never had to worry about really. Even though, naturally I still do.'

''Course you do! You're her dad. It's only natural you're going to worry about her. But she's sixteen, and by the looks of it, you've done a great job in raising her,' Jennifer said, knowing that Alfie Harris had brought his daughter up single-handedly. He'd told her about his wife running off with another man shortly after Megan was born. That she was unable to cope with the responsibility of motherhood, so she'd upped and legged it, leaving Alfie holding the baby, literally.

Jennifer could only imagine the amount of women the man had dated since then. Though he'd insisted that he'd never once introduced any of them to his daughter, so she figured she must mean more to him than she'd first hoped.

'She's sixteen, though, babe. You got to let her have a bit of freedom. Girls need that,' Jennifer said, trying to offer Alfie some womanly advice. 'You remember what it was like to be sixteen, don't you?' She teased again, watching as Alfie smiled.

''Course I do! That's what bloody worries me so much!' he grinned, amused by Jennifer's banter.

'Look, I know yesterday wasn't easy for you, Jen. Megan isn't normally so off-hand with people. It's going to take her a while to adjust,' he said, trying to reassure the girl. 'I think you'll both hit it off like a house on fire in time.'

'I reckon we will too,' Jennifer agreed. 'She seems like a lovely girl, Alfie. Let's just give it time and not put too much pressure on her.'

Alfie relaxed then.

Jennifer was the salt of the earth. She really was.

And Megan would see that in time too.

'To be honest, I'm more worried about the poxy club. This is the first Saturday night I've not gone in since the place opened,' Alfie said, being truthful with Jennifer now. Wishing that he wasn't such a control freak and that, for one night, he could just take the evening off and enjoy it.

Especially given the company he was keeping. It didn't get much better than this; only, he'd already had one phone call from Gem this evening, asking a stupid question about the alarm system and it had set him on edge. It didn't feel right staying here at home, not when Saturdays were the highest profile night of the week at the club. But then, at the same time, he and Jennifer never got the house to themselves. This was a rare opportunity for Jennifer to spend some proper time with him. Away from the fancy restaurants, and the expensive hotel rooms they'd spent the past two months having to settle for.

With Megan staying over at Amber's this weekend, tonight they could just be themselves. Just the two of them.

There was no way that Alfie could run out on her now, to go down and keep an eye on the place. No matter how much he'd secretly thought about it. He'd done that to her last night. Popped in to the club, to check on the place, but in the end he'd stayed there for hours. The girl would do her nut if after all the effort she'd gone to, he upped and left her again. Alfie wouldn't blame her.

'Look, you said yourself. You trust Gem. He's the head of your security, isn't he? If there's an emergency, he can get you on the phone, can't he? It's all in hand.'

She stood up. 'And speaking of everything being "all in hand"…' she grinned then, before wrapping her arms around Alfie, and guiding him back to his chair. Leaning across the table, Jennifer poured him another glass of wine and handed it to him. Sipping hers then too, she smiled.

'You're a good man, you know that, Alfie. I wasn't sure at first. You know, after hearing some of the rumours I have about you, but you're nothing like what they say.'

Alfie couldn't help but laugh then. 'And what is it that they say?'

'That you were a very bad man back in your day.'

'Oi!' Alfie laughed again, aware of the twenty-year age gap between them both. 'You make me sound bloody ancient.'

Jennifer giggled at that; in her element winding Alfie up.

'You're a real softy, really. The way you are with your daughter. The way you are with me.' She put her glass down. Moving over to where Alfie was sitting, she straddled him, relishing the fact that they had this big old house to themselves. That they could do whatever they pleased without interruptions.

'I love that about you. How protective you can be, how caring you really are. I bet not many people get to see that side of you?'

'Yeah, maybe,' Alfie said, knowing full well that up until now the only person who had seen this side to him had been Megan.

Alfie Harris had been a notorious face in his time. But when it came to his daughter, he'd been the perfect gentleman and the best father he could be. He was like that with Jennifer, too. The girl was different to other girls he'd dated. This actually meant something to him. Fuck, it must have, to stop him from going into the club on the busiest night of the bloody week.

'I like it. In fact, I really like you.' Jennifer smiled down at Alfie, before leaning down and gently kissing him.

Which Alfie immediately responded to.

He loved the way that Jennifer only seemed to see the good in him. It made him want to keep it up, this new persona of his. Finally out of the game, the gangster way of life. He was happy going straight these days. Trading in a lifetime of crime and dodgy dealings to become a legitimate businessman and, what's more, his club had turned out to be a roaring success. He was a natural.

Like many other big faces in London over the last decade, Alfie Harris had invested wisely into the clubbing scene. He'd recognised a perfect business opportunity to pass some cash through. Only, what he hadn't anticipated was the club taking off overnight as such a success.

Things were on the up, in all aspects of his life, he thought, taking in the beautiful sight of his girlfriend, as Jennifer Dawson started to slowly undress.

Straddling him, she lifted herself backwards so that she was lying across the dinner table, almost naked.

'Well, babe. There's something that you should know about me,' Alfie said, taking off his shirt now, as he stared down at her.

She was sprawled out on his kitchen table, in only her black lace lingerie, looking sexy as hell.

'I'm still a very bad man sometimes, you know!'

'Oh, don't you worry, Alfie. I'm counting on that!'

Jennifer laughed, before pulling Alfie Harris down on top of her.

Determined to get all thoughts of her boyfriend's business out of his mind.

CHAPTER TWENTY

Staring over to where Amber and her new boyfriend Reece Bettle were now practically dry humping each other on the seat beside her, Megan Harris – or Olivia as she was having to answer to all evening, tugged down the material of the minuscule skirt that Amber had insisted she wore tonight. *Chic and sophisticated* Amber had said, only Megan felt anything but.

Megan had heard so much about her father's nightclub, and it was safe to say that she would have been more than impressed if she had seen the place under different circumstances. Though experiencing it first-hand, sneaking in her with fake ID and worried sick that her father might somehow just show up here and catch her out, Megan felt completely out of her depth.

She wasn't enjoying herself one bit.

It didn't help that she'd spent the entire evening being hit on by pervy old men that were old enough to be her dad. Even Reece's dodgy mates were at it. All of them trying their luck with her, figuring that if Reece was on some kind of a promise with Amber, then one of them clearly stood a chance with Megan.

Though they were all well and truly out of luck, as Megan didn't like any of them, Reece included. And she doubted any of them even liked her, seeing as not one of them had bothered to try and strike up any real form of conversation with her. They just sat there leering at her, making little comments between themselves while giving her the eye.

Reece Bettle was the worst one of them all. Letching at any girl that passed them. Megan didn't know what Amber saw in the bloke. Him and his group of little clones. All loud and gobby, and under the illusion that they were God's gift to women. They were the type of men that Megan's father had spent his whole life warning her away from and Megan was doing her best to ignore the lot of them, but sitting here on her tod all evening was becoming boring.

'Amber?' Megan interrupted, taking her chance as she saw her friend's head pop up for air between snogging the face off her new fella, before Reece-the-creep could pull her back down into another passionate embrace. 'I think I'm going to get off. This is boring. Are you coming?'

Megan squirmed as she watched Reece continue to paw over her mate, his hands sweeping greedily over her body as he copped a cheeky feel. Cupping Amber's boobs, all the while purposely keeping eye contact with Megan.

The bloke made her feel physically sick.

'Can't you just stay a bit longer, Olivia?' Amber said, throwing a pleading look to her mate, letting her know that she wasn't quite ready to leave as she gestured to Reece who was still feeling up her padded bra; though judging by the way he was panting, the wad of tissues she'd stuffed down there earlier this evening wasn't putting him off. 'Fifteen more minutes, yeah?' Amber said, shooting her mate another pleading look. Then making a point she added. 'I dunno why you're worrying, babe. We told your dad that you're staying at my house, and my mum and dad think we're at yours. We don't have to go anywhere—'

'What? You're free all night?' Reece said with a sly grin, before lunging at Amber playfully and ramming his tongue down her throat again.

Pulling herself out of the embrace, Amber laughed.

'Steady on, Romeo. I didn't say I was free *all night*. I said we weren't in a hurry,' she said, her tone pleading as she looked back at her friend. 'Come on, Olivia, just stay a little bit longer, yeah?'

Desperately trying to keep her cool and act mature, Amber was trying not to lose her temper with her friend, but Megan was really testing her patience. Amber had gone out of her way to try and prove to Reece that she was more grown up than he gave her credit for. Getting let into the club, drinking whatever drinks he bought for her, even though most of them tasted disgusting. She'd even let him stick his hands inside her knickers just now while they were kissing, and all Megan was doing was acting like a spoilt brat and sabotaging all her attempts at trying to act older.

Amber was beginning to wish she'd never brought Megan with her tonight.

'But you said we were going to have a girls' night?'

Amber rolled her eyes at Reece playfully then, trying to make a joke out of Megan's whining. 'I only said that for your dad's benefit.' Then turning to Reece. 'Her dad's a nightmare. Talk about overprotective. We only came here tonight because—'

'Amber!' Megan warned. Not wanting her friend to tell Reece anything else about her father. The last thing she needed was anymore unwanted attention from Reece and his cronies. 'My dad's not that bad. He just worries about me, that's all,' Megan lied, knowing full well that if her father found out about her being here in the club tonight, he'd have a full on fit. Beyond overprotective, Megan wasn't even allowed to go to her friend's house without him constantly checking on her, and he insisted on driving her everywhere. He'd only let her out this weekend without making too much of a fuss because he actually liked Amber. He thought the girl was an angel. A good influence on his daughter.

The irony.

If only he could see the girl now. Drunk in a club, and draped across a scumbag like Reece.

Though clearly Reece was the sole purpose of Amber insisting on coming here tonight.

'Oh come on, Olivia. Lighten up, girl. Maybe you should have a drink. Enjoy yourself a bit.' This coming from Reece, who, going by the state of him, and the slur to his voice, had clearly had enough for them both.

He was on something too. Megan had no idea what he'd taken but she'd seen him and his mates passing around a couple of pills. He'd been hyper ever since and she could see how dilated his pupils were now, how he ground his teeth between speaking.

'I'm good, thank you!' she said curtly, but Reece wasn't willing to take no for an answer. Picking up his drink, he thrust it at her. 'Go on. It won't kill you.'

Megan wrinkled up her nose at the smell.

'Don't smell it, drink it!' he said, feeling irritated. Olivia was behaving like a right stuck-up little cow tonight, putting a right damper on the evening. Amber had already hinted that she was able to stay out tonight, and Reece knew if he played his cards right he could easily persuade her to come back to his. But this whiny little cow was trying to get Amber to go home. The only way that he was going to persuade Olivia to stay out longer was to get her shit-faced. Only, typically the spoilt little cow wasn't going to comply. So he was going to have to try a different tack. Exchanging a look to one of his mates, Reece knew exactly what would loosen this girl up.

'Ain't you got any other mates that you could have brought out with you, Amber? Ones that haven't got poles stuck up their arses? This one's as boring as fuck…' He'd seen her type before. The girl wasn't just playing hard to get with them all. She *was* hard to get. Frigid as fuck no doubt, and acting her age. Most of the lads had lost interest in her. Now she was just someone for them to take the piss out of, and Reece was intending on having some fun with this one.

'Oi! She ain't boring.' Trying to keep the peace, Amber could feel the tension building between her best friend and her new potential boyfriend. If they pissed Megan off now, the girl would walk out, and Amber didn't fancy staying here all on her own with Reece and his rowdy mates. She needed her wingman, so, for now, she was going to have to try and keep Megan sweet.

'Go on, Olivia, try it. It tastes better than it smells. In fact, you can hardly taste the whiskey, the Coke masks it,' Amber lied.

Aware that everyone was staring at her now, Megan took the glass once more and put it to her lips, the vile smell wafting up her nose, making her want to gag. She wanted to say that she didn't want it, but the stern look on Amber's face told her that she didn't have a choice. She knew that her friend was losing her patience with her now too.

Taking a sip, she almost choked as Reece tipped the glass up so that the liquid suddenly poured faster into her mouth, making her gulp down more than she'd anticipated. Coughing and spluttering, she could feel the burning liquid as it hit the back of her throat. Then shooting up her nose, she felt her eyes water too.

'Don't tell me you ain't ever had a drink before?' Reece said disbelievingly as Megan continued to cough loudly as he and his group of mates watched on, laughing at her. 'Jesus fucking Christ, you two really are just kids!'

'Oi, leave it out. 'Course she drinks,' Amber said defensively. 'We only drink vodka, though, that way our parents can't smell it on us. To be fair to Olivia she has got a point. Whiskey is rank.' Catching Megan's eye, Amber offered her friend a small smile then, hoping that sticking up for her would win her friend back over.

'Voddies, eh? Why didn't you say?!' Reece grinned, smiling once more now he knew the girl's preference. 'I'm going to go and get you both a double. That all right for you?' Reece said to Olivia. His tone almost challenging.

'A couple of drinks, Livs, then we'll go, okay?' Amber said now, hoping that Megan would accept Reece's offer.

'Yeah. That's fine with me.' Megan shrugged. She didn't want a vodka. She didn't even want to be here, but she was just going to have to suck it up for now, especially if she was going to have to sit in Reece and his little idiot mates' company for another twenty minutes. A strong drink was the only way she'd get through it.

Watching as Reece gave Amber another one of his sickening sloppy kisses before he whispered something in her friend's ear and they both started laughing, Megan was glad when Reece and his mates headed off over to the bar. His public displays of affection were starting to make her feel nauseous. Shuffling up as Amber came over and joined her on the seat, Megan saw the smug look plastered to her friend's face.

'Well, what do you think?' Amber slurred, oblivious to Megan's dislike of her new fella, as she stared after him, her eyes not leaving Reece for a second.

'What do I think?' Megan said now, shaking her head, annoyed. For a smart girl, Amber really could be dumb sometimes. 'I think that Reece loves himself. I think his friends are all losers, and I'm bored out of my mind. Seriously. I thought we were supposed to be having a night out together, just you and me. I know you said you were meeting Reece, but you've been doing nothing but snog each other's faces off all night long, while I'm sat here like a spare part.'

'Oh come on, Megs. I thought you'd be happy for me,' Amber said, distracted then as she clocked Reece talking to the attractive barmaid behind the bar, convinced that Reece was eyeing up the pretty blonde.

Then she clocked a better look at the girl.

'Oh shit, Megs. That girl behind the bar. That's Sherrie Murphy, isn't it? From round my way,' she said, trying to peer across the crowded bar to get a better look at the girl. Certain that it was one of the girls from her estate: a couple of years older than Megan and Amber, though the girl knew who they both were.

'Yeah, that is her,' Megan confirmed. Both girls watched as Reece leant over the bar and said something to the girl, and the girl nodded, before staring over towards them both. She didn't look too happy.

'Shit, she's seen us. Do you reckon she's recognised us? Do you reckon she'll get us kicked out for being underage?'

'You don't think she'll tell my dad that I was in here, do you?' Megan said now, suddenly worried.

Amber watched as the girl continued to serve drinks, wondering if Reece had smoothed things over for them. He must have done, because the girl didn't bother to look their way again.

'Nah, she won't say anything,' Amber said, glaring back as she caught Reece's hand lingering a moment or two longer than it should have as he placed his money in Sherrie Murphy's hand and paid for their drinks.

'Cheeky bugger. Do you reckon he fancies her?' she said, suddenly seeing red at her new boyfriend having the cheek to flirt with another girl right in front of her face.

'Don't be silly, Amber. He's well into you. You both haven't left each other alone since we got in here. He's been too busy trying to suck the face off you to be interested in any other girl.'

Amber pursed her lips, not so convinced. She decided there and then that no matter what happened tonight, there was no way that she was leaving Reece here alone so that he could end up shagging that barmaid.

'Seriously, Megs, we're supposed to be having fun tonight. We got in. No one has recognised you, and your dad has no idea that we're here. You need to loosen up a bit, babe.'

'And I've already said that I'll stay for a few drinks, haven't I? I mean it, though, Amber. A couple more drinks and then we're out of here.'

'Okay!' Amber promised. Pleased that she'd managed to persuade Megan to loosen up a bit, she smiled as she spotted Reece walking back towards her, a tray of drinks in his hands. 'A few more drinks and then we'll go back to mine and chill out, just you and me. Cross my heart.' Mimicking drawing a cross over the centre of her chest with her forefinger, Amber shot Megan her sweetest, most convincing smile just as Reece got back and handed the two girls their drinks.

She looked at Reece then, and he winked at her. Letting her know that he'd executed his little plan.

Clinking glasses together, and downing their drinks in one, Amber smiled at her friend as she waited for the little happy pill that Reece slipped into her friend's drink to work its magic, ignoring the tinge of guilt that she felt at tricking Megan like this. It was for her own good really.

Reece was right. The girl needed to live a little.

The problem was that Megan's old man was so overprotective and cautious with his only precious child that he didn't let Megan have any fun. It was almost as if her friend had been conditioned to be sensible and boring all the time.

If anything, they were doing her a favour.

'How's that?' Reece said with a smirk as Megan put her empty glass down on the table. 'Feeling better?'

Megan shrugged, the drink instantly going to her head, though she wasn't going to admit it.

'Better than the whiskey, thanks!'

'Good. Maybe you'll start having some fun now, eh?' Reece said, throwing a knowing look to Amber, glad that the girl had gone along with his little plan of slipping an E into her mardy cow of a mate's drink. That would teach the miserable bitch to lighten the fuck up.

Only, he didn't bother telling Amber that he'd slipped half of one in her drink too.

Not that Amber needed to loosen up tonight, she was already a sure thing. Reece Bettle was certain of that.

'My mate from the door, Jenson, he said he might join us in a bit. I think he's got a bit of a thing for your mate here.' Reece grinned at Amber, then looked Megan up and down. 'Guess he likes the miserable, boring sorts?' He teased as he sat down in the booth.

'Who? The doorman that let us in here earlier? The one that was on a wind up, making out like he wasn't going to let us in?'

Reece nodded.

'Yeah, he's my flatmate. Sound as a pound, he is.'

Amber grinned at Megan then, mouthing the words *lucky cow*. Secretly hoping that this Jenson might be the one to put Megan in a better mood tonight.

'I dunno, he seemed a bit too old for me…' Megan said, being negative once more, which only made Amber roll her eyes in despair.

The bloke had been a right sort. A complete wind-up merchant, but good-looking all the same. Megan should be thanking her lucky stars that he had even looked at her twice. But of course she wasn't. As always, Megan was putting a negative spin on everything.

'Oh, she'll soon change her mind about that after a few more drinks.' Reece winked, making Megan think he was talking about the alcohol loosening her up. The girl had no idea her drink had been spiked.

Holding her drink up to her friend, before downing the rest of hers in a bid to keep up, Amber smiled over at Reece.

'Come on then get some more voddies in, Reece. Me and Olivia are going to show you boys what we're made of.'

CHAPTER TWENTY-ONE

Megan Harris was wasted.

It turned out that after a few double vodka and Cokes the club wasn't too bad after all and, in actual fact, as the night had gone on, neither were Reece and his cronies. Amber had been right, now that she'd relaxed a little, she was actually enjoying herself for once. Especially as Amber had made more of an effort to include her. The two of them had spent the past hour together on the dance floor, dancing to all the latest tunes together like a pair of maniacs. Megan couldn't remember a time when she'd felt so happy, so free, twirling around and around as the loud thudding base pulsed right through her.

She felt incredible, invincible, and she could tell that Amber felt it too.

They both laughed then. Catching each other's eyes, having the best night of their lives.

'Fuck, I need a drink,' Amber said, grabbing her friend by the arm, trying to coax Megan from the dance floor, though Megan didn't want to leave.

'Ahh, babe. Just one more song. Come on.'

'I can't, Megs. I need a drink. Come on, we've been dancing for ages.'

'Okay, let's get a drink, then we're getting back on it! These tunes are wicked.'

Following Amber as she led them both to the bar, Megan stood waiting patiently as her friend ordered them both two pints of water, relieved that Amber wasn't making her drink anymore vodka. Part of her was starting to feel woozy; she must have made herself dizzy from dancing. The room felt as if it was balancing just off its axle. The floor slanted and warped.

'Earth to Megan!' Amber said as she waved the girl's pint of water in front of her. 'Here, get this down you. God, it's so hot in here. I'm sweating.'

Megan realised she was too. She was barely wearing anything, yet she felt as if she wanted to strip off her clothes which were sticking to her as the tiny droplets of perspiration trickled down her back. Her face was glistening with a film of sweat. Wiping the hair that was stuck to her face out of her eyes, she took the drink and knocked it back in one, her eyes scanning the club as she did, looking at all the dancers around her.

The atmosphere in the club was electric.

And she was part of it.

Part of something amazing. That felt good. It felt more than good. For the first time in her life Megan felt as if she properly belonged somewhere. With all these happy, crazy people, dancing and laughing together as if they'd all known each other all their lives.

'I'm going to go and find Reece. You coming?' Amber shouted above the loud thud of music.

'I'm going to get another drink. I'll come and find you all,' Megan said, before turning back to the bar and asking for another glass of water. Suddenly she felt completely dehydrated. The heat of the club from all the bodies and bright lights were all making her feel a bit light-headed.

Fuck, she was so thirsty.

Packed tightly up against the crowded bar, the throng of people all squashed up against her was starting to make her feel claustrophobic. Especially the person right behind her, who was pressing into her so hard that Megan was about to turn around and tell whoever it was to back off.

But something about the way the firm hand pressed into the small of her back made her grin. Without bothering to turn around, Megan instantly knew who it was. Or at least who she hoped that it was.

'Here, let me.' Pushing his way forward, Megan grinned as she recognised the doorman from earlier.

Jenson Reed.

Reece had told her that he would be coming to look for her later, but part of Megan hadn't believed it, to be honest. The man was seriously good-looking, and the fact that he worked on the door meant that he could probably have his pick of girls in here tonight.

Why her?

Still, his hands didn't leave her body as he leant over the bar and whistled to get the attention of one of the bar staff; so, for now, Megan certainly wasn't complaining.

If anything, she was basking in his attention. Aware that groups of girls around her were all looking her way now with envy, wondering how someone like Megan could snag themselves a man like Jenson.

'What's your poison, darling?'

'I'll just have a water, thanks,' Megan said; then seeing Jenson raise his eyes at her, worried that she'd somehow just proved a point and shown herself up to be a silly, little kid, she quickly changed her mind. 'Actually, I'll have a vodka and Coke. A double, please.'

'That's more like it.' Jenson laughed, holding up his fingers and ordering one for himself while he was at it. 'They were some serious moves that you and your mate were throwing out there,' he said, nodding over to where he'd been watching Megan and Amber gyrating about on the dance floor.

Megan felt her face flush. She hadn't realised that she was being watched by Jenson. If she had, there was no way that she would have gone along with Amber's idea of who could throw the craziest shapes on the dance floor, like a pair of lunatics. She half hoped that Jenson had at least missed the silly dance off they'd had with each other, but going by the twisted smirk on his face, Jenson Reed had seen it all.

Megan blushed.

'Hey, fuck it. Don't be embarrassed. You look like you're having a good time and that's all that matters, huh?' Jenson said, passing the young girl her vodka and Coke, before necking his own.

'Thirsty?' Megan smiled, raising her eyes.

'I'm just trying to catch up with you.' Jenson winked. 'I've got a half hour break. A lot can happen in half an hour.'

Again Megan blushed, but this time it wasn't a feeling of embarrassment that overcame her, but something else. Something strange that she hadn't felt before, like a fluttering feeling deep inside her stomach. Tinged with something else. Excitement. Anticipation. She wasn't sure.

Copying Jenson, Megan drank her drink back in one, but the alcohol was stronger than she'd anticipated, and the heat of the place was getting too much for her now. Grabbing hold of Jenson's hand to steady herself from stumbling over, she tried to make a joke of it.

'Wow, that's totally gone to my head. I think I need to sit down.'

Jenson laughed then in agreement, watching Megan sway from side to side on her feet. Quickly guiding her over to where Amber and Reece's friends all sat in a corner booth. Ordering Reece's mates to budge up when he got there, Jenson helped Megan to sit down on the chair.

'Wow, this place looks beautiful.'

Staring around the club, her gaze rested on the spectacular light show above them. The psychedelic beams of colours all pulsed in time with the music before twisting their way around the dark abyss that was the club's blacked-out ceiling. Then there was a spray of twinkling white stars, so bright and magnificent that she couldn't take her eyes off them.

'Fuck me, Jenson, these girls are off their fucking tits,' Reece piped up, peering over from where he was currently busy with Amber; the girl wedged beneath him, more than up for a bit of a fumble.

He was glad to see that Megan had lightened the fuck up, too, by the looks of things. Staring up at the ceiling like a space cadet, in her own fucked-up little world.

Jenson grinned.

These young girls made it far too easy for lads like him and Reece.

Megan stood up then, unsteady on her feet, stumbling towards the steps.

'Hey. Hey. Where are you off to?' Jenson said with a laugh.

'I'm too hot in here. I can't breathe. I need some air,' Megan said, feeling suddenly out of it. She was burning up. Her body felt as if it was on fire. She was dizzy too. The room spinning wildly around her, making her feel as if she was floating.

Jenson was at her side then, wrapping his arms around her, as he led the girl down the steps. Catching her as she slipped.

'Whoa! Slow down, you'll end up doing yourself an injury,' Jenson said, hooking his arm around the girl to hold her upright as he carried on guiding her through the throngs of people standing around in the corridor down below them.

Seeing the long queue of girls standing outside the main toilet doors, Jenson led Megan down towards the staff ones instead. Behind him, Reece and Amber were following.

Reece mirrored Jenson's body language, his arms wrapped around Amber as they both laughed and joked together. Reece's girl looked a damn sight better than Jenson's bird did though.

Opening the door, Jenson walked in first. Letting Megan go into a cubicle on her own so she could take a few moments to sort herself out, he splashed some water on his face as he watched Reece and Amber making out in the other cubicle next door. The girl was too out of it to realise that Jenson was watching. Though Reece was doing it on purpose, winking at his mate as he lifted Amber's top over her head. Jenson started to feel turned on.

'You all right in there, Olivia?'

No answer.

Jenson knocked on the door.

'Olivia? Are you okay in there?'

Shit! Her fake name? Megan had forgotten about that. 'Yeah, I'm fine. Hang on.' Taking a deep breath, Megan was starting to feel queasy now. Her heart hammering inside her chest. Her skin was burning hot; the kind of heat you felt just before you threw up. Only she wasn't going to be sick, she told herself firmly. Not now.

Unlocking the door to let Jenson in, Megan Harris was anything but okay, only, she wasn't about to admit that to Jenson Reed any time soon.

CHAPTER TWENTY-TWO

Pouring the tea into the china teapot, Colleen Byrne placed the cup and saucer neatly on the tray.

Just so.

Nothing too much trouble for her dear old mother-in-law Joanie, she thought with a smile, glad to have finally found her purpose in this household. She hummed to herself as she looked for a pretty little teaspoon to complement the bone china. She could hear the television set blaring in the lounge, and she'd seen from the fridge that Michael was already on at least his fourth beer of the evening. Half-cut, Colleen supposed. He hadn't even bothered to check on how his wife was doing. Probably because he knew he didn't have to. Colleen would take care of it, just as she had been doing for the past week now. Cooking and cleaning, looking after Joanie; nothing was too much for her.

And to be fair it wasn't. Colleen was glad that she could be of service to her in-laws. In fact, it was an actual pleasure. She was still saddened by Joanie's admission of regret yesterday at how she'd treated her daughter-in-law for all those years. The raw emotion in her voice had caught her off guard. Like a punch to her stomach. Colleen had never expected to hear Joanie confess to her bullying ways. For all the times that her mother-in-law had meddled in her and Jimmy's marriage. For the way she'd treated her for the past twenty years.

It was abuse. Mental abuse. Manipulating, belittling. Bullying. Turning her own children against her.

Joanie apologising for her behaviour had been an admission that she'd been aware all along of what she'd been doing.

If Colleen was honest, it was something she never would have expected in her wildest dreams. She'd chosen to let it go. She wasn't about grudges, she decided. Forgive and forget, that's what Joanie had asked of her, but Colleen wouldn't even know where to start.

The damage had already been done.

Two decades Colleen had spent on the receiving end of her oppressive mother-in-law's torrent of abuse and torment, to the point where she had even started questioning her own sanity.

Until Colleen had been brought down so low that she'd even contemplated taking her own life.

That's how far Joanie Byrne had pushed her. Oh, Joanie had been smart about it. There was no denying that. Smart, just like Jimmy had been. Discreet in her ways, her abuse had been carried out under the surface, so subtle that there had been days when even Colleen had trouble distinguishing between what had been real and what hadn't. All those mind games that Joanie had played with her. All those lies the woman had told.

When Joanie had first started her hate campaign towards her, in the early stages of Colleen and Jimmy's relationship, Colleen had thought that she was just being paranoid, over-sensitive even, but she'd soon learned that Joanie had a game plan all along and the woman had executed her strategy well.

Succeeding in making Colleen's life a living hell.

The worst thing of all for Colleen was how Joanie had managed to turn Nancy and Daniel against her. Her own two children. That's how good the woman was!

Oh, yes. Joanie had pulled out all the stops, hiding bottles of vodka around the house. Concealing them in places that she knew

Colleen would find them so that when Colleen had come back from yet another of her numerous stints in whichever nuthouse or rehab clinic Jimmy had shipped her off to, she'd quickly fall off the wagon and fuck up once again.

Joanie Byrne had wrapped up Colleen's poison with a bow and served it to her with pleasure, and Colleen, too weak and desperate to know any better, had played right into the woman's hands.

Then there had been the pills.

The doctor had prescribed them, at first, to help with her panic attacks and night terrors, to ease the dark cloud of depression that loomed so constantly above her. Antidepressants. Sleeping tablets, painkillers. A real pick'n'mix for a pillhead. Just like the assorted biscuits that Colleen was piling onto the small china plate now. All different shapes and colours, all neatly displayed. The dainty little jug of milk and a sugar bowl nestled in beside it. Just the way that Joanie had become accustomed to for her nightly pot of tea that Colleen insisted she drank before she went to bed.

Looking after Joanie, just as she had once looked after her.

Content with the tea and biscuits all laid out so perfectly, Colleen pulled out the small plastic container of pills from her pocket.

Joanie always loved her evening pot of tea. She said that Colleen made it for her, 'just so.' That always made Colleen smile. Glad that her talents weren't wasted. That dear old Joanie appreciated the extra efforts Colleen had gone to especially for her.

Picking up the tray, Colleen smiled to herself as she made her way back upstairs.

No, she wasn't one to hold grudges.

Colleen was better than that.

How did the saying go? *Don't get mad, get even!* Well that's exactly what Colleen intended to do. The cheek of that woman, asking her to forgive and forget.

Forgive and forget?

Colleen was neither Jesus, nor did she have Alzheimer's. There would be no forgiveness for Joanie, and Colleen would never, ever forget.

There had been a time when Colleen had been weak and vulnerable, and Joanie had looked after her. Now the tables were turned and it was Colleen's turn to repay the favour.

Plastering the biggest smile on her face, she walked into the room and spotted Joanie lying in her bed, her old-fashioned pyjamas buttoned up around her neck, her cheeks flushed from the heat of the bath she'd just soaked in. Colleen placed the tray down beside her.

'Well don't you look a lot better this evening!' She beamed, poured the woman a large cup of tea. Extra milk, too, so that the woman could drink it down quickly.

'I feel a bit better, too,' Joanie said then, still coy from being so open with her daughter-in-law.

'Well, this will soon sort you out. A nice pot of tea, just the way you like it and some of those posh biccys. You'll feel right as rain again in no time. It's been a tough few weeks, Joanie, darling,' Colleen said sweetly as she passed the woman the china cup and watched as Joanie drank it back in one. Just as she always did, before holding the cup out for Colleen to pour her another.

Which Colleen was only too happy to oblige.

Strong, tough old Joanie Byrne.

Only, soon she'd be drugged out of her mind and acting every bit as crazy as she had accused Colleen of acting for all these years.

Passing Joanie her second mug of tea, Colleen smiled.

CHAPTER TWENTY-THREE

'Shit, man, are you okay?' Jenson asked stepping into the cubicle, eyeing Megan as she pressed herself up against the toilet wall.

The girl looked awful. Her hair was dripping with sweat, stuck to her forehead. Her cheeks were flushed bright red. Her pupils were dilated to the size of saucers. She looked as if she was buzzing off her tits, but she was doing her utmost to try and hide it.

'I'm fine,' Megan lied. Not realising that Jenson could see she was anything but. She felt like death warmed up. Her head was pounding and her skin was on fire. She could feel the sweat pouring off her now, trickling down her back. The crop top she'd borrowed earlier that evening from Amber was now stuck to her body, soaked through. A part of her just wanted to go home so she could crawl into her bed and sleep off all the vodka that she'd stupidly drunk.

In fact, she decided, after tonight she was never drinking again.

She must have poisoned herself?

She was burning up. A fever? She felt so sick now that she'd even considered asking Jenson to call her dad. Though she'd quickly come to her senses on ruling out that option. Her dad would murder her if he found out that she was here at the club. Drunk, and making out in the toilets with one of the club's doormen. He'd never let her out of his sight again, let alone out of the house, and she could kiss goodbye to her friendship with Amber.

'Do you need to sit down?' Jenson asked, watching as Megan swayed from side to side.

'No, really, I'm fine.' She felt embarrassed at the state she'd got herself in. She wished that she hadn't been so keen to make such a point now, downing all those vodkas just to impress Reece and his knobhead mates. So that they'd think that she wasn't such a bore.

'Honest, I'm fine,' she said, giving Jenson a small smile as she saw the concern on his face. She should be grateful that Jenson was even bothering to take the time to check on her. That he cared enough to ask her if she was okay. The last thing she wanted to do right now was put him off. Not when he was clearly making a real effort for her, when even Amber couldn't be arsed to check and see if she was okay, too wrapped up with lover-boy.

'I'm just hot. That's all…' she said, as she saw Jenson looking her up and down.

'That you are!' Jenson said with a laugh, as he leaned in for a kiss, his mouth covering hers, his body pressed up against her.

Though instead of the feeling of heady excitement at her first kiss, Megan felt as if she might throw up, her skin prickling from the heat that burned right though her. Trying to keep her mind off the thought of the bile that threatened to rise at the back of her throat, she was suddenly distracted, as the thin cubical wall started moving behind her.

Slow thuds, at first, turning quickly into rapid, rhythmical pounding.

'What the fuck is that?' Megan said as she heard the loud moans and groans coming from the cubicle next door. The words were out of her mouth before she stupidly realised someone was having sex!

Great! Now she really did sound like a little kid. As if she didn't know what sex sounded like.

Which of course she didn't, not first-hand anyway.

Though Jenson didn't seem to hold that against her.

'It's just Reece and your mate,' he said, waving it off as nothing. 'Having some fun, babe, like we should be doing.' Running his fingers across Olivia's forehead, down her nose. Resting on the tip of her thin, delicate-looking lips. Feeling a stir within him, as the young girl gazed back up at him, all wide-eyed and innocent looking.

Young girls like Olivia always did it for him, especially when they were off their tits like this. That was the funniest part of all of this. The fact that they rarely had any clue that they'd had their drinks spiked. It was a good little system that he and Reece had in place.

Reece rented out his room in his flat to Jenson, and in return Jenson gave Reece a steady supply of gear for his troubles. A touch, because whenever Reece then used his gear to snare a few birds, he always gave Jenson the heads-up on them.

Like these two girls tonight.

So young and naive, they had no idea that from the minute they walked in here they were being royally played. They'd feel stupid tomorrow, stupid and cheap, when they realised they gave it up to two lads that they hardly even knew in some scummy toilet cubicle, but Jenson and Reece would be long gone by then. The girls would be too mortified to show their faces around here again, and Reece and Jenson would do what they did best, and move the fuck on to their next conquests.

Talk about easy pickings.

'You sure you're okay?' Jenson said then, as he looked at this girl and wondered if perhaps Reece had slipped her more than just the half tab of Ecstasy that he'd said he was going to give her. The bloke had other shit on him too. Special K, GBH, and Ecstasy. Though looking at how off her face this girl was, Jenson wouldn't put it past Reece to have given this girl one of his special concoctions. He did that, sometimes, if a girl wasn't playing ball. Mixed gear up with shit his mates had got hold of.

He might come across as a charmer, but Reece was as sly as they fucking came.

'I'm fine… really,' Megan said, suddenly panicking that if she told Jenson that she was feeling ill then he might lose interest in her. Or leave her here alone, and Megan didn't want to be on her own. She was starting to feel scared.

Watching the girl's panicked expression, and the way her eyes darted around the cubicle at every noise, Jenson wasn't convinced. Though, she was adamant that she was okay. She wouldn't keep saying it if she wasn't, and Jenson still had twenty minutes to kill. They were both alone in the booth, so he might as well make the most out of it while he still could.

'You're so pretty, Olivia,' he said, sliding his hand up the girl's top, smiling to himself when the girl didn't stop him. That's how easy these girls were. Tell them what they want to hear and most of them were up for anything, he thought as he ran his hands over her small, barely there breasts.

'It's Megan,' Megan said, her voice small as she squirmed her way from where she was pinned between him and the wall. Trying to get some air. To breathe. To get Jenson discreetly off her. 'My ID. We changed my name so that my dad wouldn't find out… He'd go mad…'

Jenson shrugged, no longer listening. Olivia, Megan. Whatever. It was all the same to him. His hands were roaming her body now. All over her. Touching and grabbing.

And Megan wanted to tell him to stop, only she didn't know how to say it. She'd thought that she wanted this, but now that it was happening, or going to happen, Megan wasn't so sure. As nice as Jenson seemed and as much as she fancied him, she wasn't ready.

She could hear Amber and Reece laughing in the cubicle next door, the wall still moving in jolts as her friend and her boyfriend continued to have sex up against it.

This was her all over, wasn't it?

Typical, boring Megan.

Always so sensible, always so scared of everything.

The rate she was going, she'd probably never lose her virginity. Closing her eyes, she forced herself to allow Jenson to touch her, to let his hands roam across her body.

His hands slid down her thigh, his fingers gently tracing their way back up inside her skirt.

'You want this, don't you?' He smiled now, before kissing Megan's neck.

She made a noise.

A grunt.

A 'yes', he figured, as he felt her give in to him. Weakening in his arms. No longer resisting his advances.

He was pressing against her now with all of his weight, keeping her upright against the wall as he unbuttoned his jeans.

If Reece was right about this girl being prissy and uptight tonight, then he reckoned that he was right about the fact that she was probably a virgin too.

Talk about a right touch.

But she certainly seemed to have come around to the idea of having a bit of fun now, holding onto him, gripping the back of his neck tightly.

'I don't feel so well,' Megan whispered, as she buried her head in Jenson's neck, the overpowering scent of his musky aftershave almost choking her. She felt suddenly strange now. As if she was losing control. She could barely stand. Her legs had gone to jelly. Her body tingling everywhere.

Something was wrong. Really wrong.

Only, now she couldn't find her voice to say it, and Jenson was lifting her skirt up. There was a sharp searing pain as he pushed himself inside of her. One that should probably make her scream with agony. At least tell him to stop.

But she couldn't tell him. She couldn't do anything.

Convulsing wildly, Megan spasmed out of control as her body tried to reject the drugs that were inside her.

CHAPTER TWENTY-FOUR

Jenson felt Megan getting into it now, pushing herself against him, but her body was jerking all over the place as if she had never had sex before and didn't know what the hell she was doing. Jenson was losing his stride.

'Hey, slow the fuck down, babe,' he said, trying to steady the girl against the wall so that he could get his rhythm back. He could hear Reece pounding away in the next cubicle again too. That gobby girl, Amber, was clearly a goer. Re-enacting some kind of porno commentary with all her exaggerated moans and groans. Totally fake, just like she was. There was no way that Reece was giving the girl that much pleasure.

Still, it didn't stop Jenson getting off on the sound of it though.

As he built up his momentum, he knew it wasn't going to take him long to get there either. About to explode inside of the girl, he leant down, his tongue searching for hers. Just the way that he liked to come.

Only, Megan wasn't reciprocating the gesture, and looking down at the girl's face, Jenson suddenly could see why. Her eyes were bloodshot whites, pupils rolling to the back of her head.

Her expression vacant. As if she wasn't there.

Jenson pulled himself backwards, away from the girl, still gripping her arms with his hands, trying to work out what was wrong with her.

Megan began to slouch, her body slipping down the wall, jerking around like crazy.

'What the fuck?' Jenson shouted, panicking.

He'd just been inside of her, mistaking her enthusiastic thrusting for enjoyments, and all the time she was fitting. He felt physically sick. Releasing his hold on the girl, he watched as Megan sank down onto the floor, head jutting loudly against the wall, then banging against it over and over again.

'Fucking hell, mate, we having some sort of competition?' Reece shouted to his friend, jovially, 'cause if we are, your bird's fucking winning. What are you doing in there? Murdering her?'

'Holy fuck, man! Reece! REECE! You need to get your arse in here now.'

Hearing the panic and distress in Jenson's voice, Reece hoped this wasn't a wind up, he and Amber had been in full swing just then. He was almost at the point of no return.

'You better not be shitting me up, Jenson,' he said, reluctantly stopping what he was doing, and fastening up his flies.

'Hurry the fuck up. The girl's gone schizo on me. I think she's having some kind of fucking epileptic fit.' Jenson was frantically pulling at the door now, stepping over Megan to get the fuck out of there.

Reece and Amber were both there then. Standing dishevelled in the cubical doorway, Amber looking instantly sober, sensing that something really wrong was up.

'But she can't be. She's not epileptic?' Peering in through the gap to see what Jenson was talking about. 'Fuck. What's happening to her?' Amber screeched, catching sight of her friend writhing around on the toilet floor, her body jerking and twisting about, her skirt all pulled up around her waist, exposing herself as her body jolted repeatedly. A frothy liquid was seeping from her mouth. 'What did you do to her?'

'I didn't do anything!' Jenson said, shouting now, the panic evident in his voice. He should have known that the blame would come back down on him. 'She just started fucking freaking out. You want to ask your fucking boyfriend what he did to her, more to the point!'

'We need to help her,' Amber said, ignoring Jenson's comment and squeezing in through the gap of the door and pushing it wide open. 'Help me get her out there onto the floor. She needs more room.'

Seeing her friend in such a state, Amber was beside herself, while Reece and Jenson were just standing there, both of them staring at her without so much as moving an inch. Rendered useless, the pair of them stood there like spare parts.

Amber dragged Megan out of the cubicle.

'What the fuck are you trying to do to her?' Reece asked as he watched Amber struggle to pull Megan's body over.

'I'm putting her in the recovery position, like they showed us at school. In case she's sick. She'll choke to death.' Amber was crying then. Helpless, as the seriousness of the situation suddenly hit her. 'Megan? Can you hear me?' Tapping the side of Megan's face, Amber tried to stop her friend's head from jerking back. But there was no response.

'Why the fuck are you calling her Megan? I thought her name was Olivia?' Reece said then, clocking the change of name.

'Yeah, well. We lied. She didn't want anyone to find out who she really was. Her dad owns the nightclub. Alfie Harris. Fucking hell, Reece, stop standing there looking at her and help me. Please? What's the matter with her? What's happening?'

Staring into Megan's vacant-looking eyes, it was as if Megan wasn't even there. Just her body, still convulsing violently. A trail of sick streamed down from her friend's mouth.

Holding Megan down onto her side, so that she didn't choke, Amber started to cry. 'We need to call an ambulance. We need to do something.'

Reece was pacing the bathroom now. Marching up and down erratically, the palm of his hand on his forehead, the realisation hitting him – that he'd drugged Alfie Harris's daughter.

'Fuck that, man! They'll inform the Old Bill. Or worse, her old man. They'll find out it was us that gave her the gear. I'm not getting stitched up for dishing out Es,' Reece said, debating his options.

'Es? What do you mean? As in Ecstasy?' Amber said then, staring at Reece with a look of disgust. 'You never said anything about Ecstasy. You said you were just going to give her something to make her relaxed: happy pills you said.'

'What do you think Ecstasy is, Amber? You don't get a pill much happier than that! We've all had them tonight and none of us are freaking the fuck out!' Reece said.

'I haven't had one,' Amber screeched, as the realisation suddenly hit her then that she'd been feeling more than drunk tonight. Only, she had never suspected for a second that Reece would do that to her too. 'You gave me one too? You arsehole!'

'Oh, chill out, Amber, seriously you're overreacting. I only slipped half a pill in yours. Just a little something to get you in the mood.'

'Oh I'm in a fucking mood all right,' Amber said, shaking her head, suddenly terrified that she might have a reaction like Megan was having. 'What if this happens to me?' she said, her voice high-pitched with panic.

'Nah, you only ingested a quarter of the strength of the pills that Megan had. Fuck. I didn't know she was going to react like this, did I? I just thought I'd teach her a lesson, you know. Stop her from being so stuck-up and self-righteous. Looking down her nose at us all, as if she was better than everyone. I thought it would bring her back down to reality. So I slipped her a couple.'

Only, Reece hadn't factored on the silly cow OD'ing on the shit. She looked a right mess too. This wasn't going to fare well for him if he got caught supplying. What if she died? He'd get done for murder then, too.

'What the fuck was that shit, man?' Reece shouted at Jenson now, figuring if he was going to get in the shit for something, then he'd be taking this fucker down with him.

'It ain't the gear. It's quality shit. Trust me, I got it from a decent source,' Jenson said adamant. 'She's just having a bad reaction. Fuck knows, with all the vodka she's been knocking back. Maybe she's had some sort of chemical reaction?'

Reece was pacing the bathroom then. Unsure of what the fuck to do, there was no way he could take the rap for this.

'We all need to get the fuck out of here,' Reece said, grabbing at Amber's arm and trying to pull the girl away. 'Seriously, just fucking leave her there, Amber. Let someone else call a fucking ambulance; someone will come in here in a minute and then they'll stitch us up for this. We ain't got time to hang about.'

'Are you having a fucking laugh?' Amber said, tears streaming down her face as she realised how severe the situation really was. Megan was in trouble. Big trouble, and Reece was just going to ditch her. Leave her here writhing around on the cold, filthy toilet floor. Lying in a puddle of her own vomit.

What sort of a man did that?

'We can't just leave her. She's having some sort of a fit. What if she dies?' Amber was hysterically crying now sinking to her knees on the floor alongside her friend.

'Reece's right. You knew that he was going to spike her drink, Amber, that means that you are responsible for this too. The police will lock you both up for this.' Seeing Reece and Amber both in a state of pure panic now, Jenson realised he was the only one trying to remain calm. This was bad, really bad and this would all come back onto them.

'What about you? You fucking sold me the gear in the first place,' Reece said, not willing to be the one to take the rap for this. There was no way that he was going to let Jenson set him up to take the fall alone. 'What the fuck did we give her? You must have had some sort of a dodgy batch? You're to blame, too, you know.'

'Fuck this,' Jenson said, deciding that he didn't trust Reece not to fucking grass on him. He'd deal with that two-faced prick later. Grabbing at Amber, he pulled her roughly up onto her feet. 'Come on, Reece's right. Someone will walk in any second. These toilets are always busy. She'll be found in a few minutes and taken to the hospital before you know it.'

Amber stared at Reece. Her so-called boyfriend had already left her, currently heading out of the bathroom door to save his own arse.

'Come on, we've got to go. Trust me, the last thing you need is to get in trouble too. It's better this way. Olivia or Megan, whatever her name is, will be fine.'

Amber shook her head, unable to comprehend Jenson's words. What had she done? Why had she ever listened to Reece? He'd told her that spiking Megan's drink would just be a bit of fun, that there would be no harm in it. Reece had said that it would be a laugh, and Amber had only gone along with his idea because she wanted Megan to lighten up a little and have some fun. She'd never in a million years meant to hurt the girl. They were best mates.

'No, you go. I'll stay with her? To make sure she's okay.'

Jenson shook his head. Not a chance. Amber would sing like a fucking canary once the plod started asking her questions. All they'd have to do is lay on a little bit of pressure and they'd all be in the deepest of shit.

'If you stay, you're going to make the situation a million times worse. Stop being fucking stupid, and move, Amber. NOW. Do you not understand the fucking trouble we'll all be in, Amber? We'll do time for this. All of us.'

Amber was torn. She looked back down at her friend, her skin tinged blue now, her body still jerking on the floor. Amber knew in her gut that she should stay. Her friend needed her, and if that meant facing the consequences of her actions tonight, then so be it. But she knew what Reece and Jenson were saying was also true. They'd all get done for this. They'd go to prison. Amber would be sent to one of those young offenders institutes. Megan would be just fine when the ambulance crew arrived. The paramedics would make sure of it. Maybe Jenson and Reece were right: what was the point of making the situation even worse?

'Amber!' Jenson said, his tone commanding. If the girl didn't leave with them now, they were going without her. 'Come on.'

'I'm sorry, Megs. Please forgive me.' Amber mouthed through her sobbing tears, before turning on her heels and running as fast as she could.

CHAPTER TWENTY-FIVE

The loud shrill of the telephone ringing on the nightstand dragged Alfie Harris from his deep sleep. Leaning over to answer it before it woke up Jennifer, who was lying fast asleep in the bed beside him, he eyed the clock on the bedside cabinet, surprised to see that it was only just gone one a.m. He must have nodded off after Jennifer had persuaded him to have his wicked way with her for a second time that evening.

To be fair, he'd been exhausted even before they had finished dinner. Working at the club was starting to take its toll. Which is why he'd agreed to take the weekend off in the first place.

He was glad that he had now.

Tonight, with Megan staying over at her mate's house, Alfie and Jennifer had had the rare opportunity to actually spend some quality time together. At home. Not out at some fancy, stuffy restaurant, or in a wine bar surrounded by loud pretentious hangers-on. It had been just the two of them, a bottle of wine and a home-cooked meal, and boy, could Jennifer cook.

And for the first time in a very long time, Alfie had actually thoroughly enjoyed himself. Jennifer Dawson was a stunner in every way. Extremely witty and smart too. Alfie really liked her. It was funny because he hadn't been looking for anything serious, initially, but they'd been seeing each other for a few months now, and their relationship had become exactly that.

Alfie picked up the receiver. Annoyed that he couldn't seem to have just one night off without interruption.

'This better be good!' Snarling into the receiver at whoever the unlucky caller was, he made no disguise of the fact that he was in no mood for pleasantries.

'Boss, it's me.'

Alfie rolled his eyes on hearing Gem Kemal's familiar voice. He should have guessed. Gem Kemal had insisted that he had everything in hand down at the club tonight, only that was a fucking joke considering that this was the third phone call Alfie had received from the bloke in as many hours.

'You do know that I took the weekend off, don't you, Gem?' Alfie spat, well and truly irritated. He was in half a mind to shove his suit on and storm down to the club anyway. He was wide awake now.

'Seriously, Gem, this is the third fucking time you've called me? First the security system's code, and then wanting to know where the keys to the safe are. You're head of fucking security, Gem. You should fucking well know these things. What is it now, huh? Do you need instructions on how to wipe your fucking arse properly?' He'd left Gem in charge of the place because the man had assured him he could handle looking after the club for one night. Only, it had become apparent that the bloke clearly didn't have a clue what he was doing at all.

Watching Jennifer stir now, Alfie slung his dressing gown around him and quickly left the room so that he wouldn't disturb the girl's sleep. Closing the door quietly behind him, he was well and truly pissed off. He should have known Gem wouldn't be able to cope with running the place. Saturday night was the highest profile night of the week at the club. The place would be packed to its capacity.

He should be there.

'Seriously, Gem, right now I'd have difficulty believing that you could run a fucking bath, let alone my fucking club.'

'I'm sorry, boss, really I am, but we've got a huge problem down here, and I knew you'd wanna know about it ASAP.'

Alfie raised his eyes, the irony of Gem's words totally going over the other man's head. Talk about state the fucking obvious.

Alfie did have a huge problem. With Gem.

This had better be important.

'Go on…'

'We've had an OD, boss, in the toilets. They think it's Ecstasy,' Gem said, the panic suddenly evident in his voice as he relayed the dramatic events of the night that had just played out. 'Someone called an ambulance, and the Old Bill have just turned up too. They're crawling all over the place.'

'Fuck's sake!' Alfie interrupted, running his hand over the top of his head, as if trying to contain his frustration. 'Oh, that's just typical, isn't it? The one night I stay at home and pande-fucking-monium has bloody broken out!'

The Old Bill would be loving every minute of this. Snooping around his club while he wasn't anywhere near it. What a night to leave Gem Kemal in charge. Alfie should have known that something like this would happen in his absence. It was always the way. As much as he'd loved spending time with Jennifer this evening, he should have been at the club tonight. Keeping an eye on the place. This probably would never have happened if he'd been there. It didn't matter that he had the best team of security on the door and the top bar staff running the place, The Karma Club was his baby and he should be the one there overseeing that everything ran smoothly.

'There's more, Alfie. They've ID'd the girl but they reckon she's underage. Sixteen, at the most. Just a kid,' Gem continued, knowing full well that his boss would be fuming when he heard the rest of the details that he was about to divulge. Knowing how hot-headed his boss could be, Gem had been dreading making this phone call.

'Well what the fuck are you lot doing letting fucking kids in the club? I thought your doormen knew better than that. Everyone's ID'd on the door. That's fucking paramount, you all know that; so unless one of you lot has a death wish the Old Bill must be mistaken? Maybe she just looks younger than she actually is?' Alfie hoped that was true.

The last thing he needed was to have his license revoked for allowing underaged kids to somehow blag their way in to his club. Alfie had always made sure that his doormen were extra vigilant for that very reason. His staff knew how meticulous he was at making sure entrance was only permitted to over 18s. There was no way that any of his men would be dumb enough to let a kid in. It was more than their jobs were worth.

'That's just it though, boss, she did have ID on her. But the police reckon it's a fake…'

Alfie bit his lip. He just wanted Gem to shut the fuck up now. The more the bloke spoke the worse the situation was becoming. One thing Alfie did know was that someone hadn't done their fucking job properly tonight, that was for certain. Heads were going to roll for this, Alfie Harris would see to that personally.

'Well, at least we know that this girl didn't get Ecstasy from any of our men. She must have brought it in with her, or got it from some other fucker that somehow managed to get it past the doormen.' Personally, Alfie didn't have time for drugs at his club; they were nothing but a mug's game but they came part and parcel with the territory, he knew that.

The music and gear went hand in hand. That's what the club scene was all about.

Though Alfie Harris had never been keen on that side of the business, he'd allowed Jimmy Byrne and Alex Costa to run that side of things and, up until now, they'd never once had a problem. But then, they only sold the best quality cocaine that money could buy.

'Make sure the club's clean. The last thing we need is the plod tracing this shit back to our doormen or, even fucking worse, to me. If they find out who's dealing, we'll all be royally fucked. Get Jenson and Danno out of there,' Alfie said, deciding to get the two dealers that Jimmy and Alex had put in place as doormen as far away from the club as possible. So at least that way, there was no chance of this OD coming back in any way at his club. 'Tell them to knock off early. The last thing I need is the plod catching the doormen dealing shit.'

'Well, that's another thing, Alfie. I can't locate Jenson,' Gem said, the shake in his voice betraying him. 'I think he's already done a runner.'

Alfie Harris shut his eyes. Well and truly pissed now, guessing rightly that Jenson Reed had probably fucked off tonight to try and save his own arse, not because the stupid fucker thought that he'd be better off lying low. This whole situation was a fucking nightmare. The police crawling everywhere like cockroaches, one of his main dealers going AWOL and some kid ODing in the toilets.

It wasn't going to take Einstein to do the fucking maths here.

As of tomorrow, Alfie would be having words with Alex Costa and putting an end to the drug distribution in his club. He never wanted this sort of shit going on in his club in the first place, the only reason he'd ever gone along with the deal was because Jimmy Byrne and Alex Costa had made Alfie Harris an offer that he couldn't refuse. Literally.

He knew that you didn't say no to men like those two.

Jimmy and Alex ruled the fucking streets. If they told you to jump, you fucking jumped. Through hoops of fire if you had to.

Besides, in some ways, letting Jimmy and Alex take over that side of the club had actually done Alfie a favour. The deal he'd made with them meant that he didn't have to get involved in the drugs side of things, he could just concentrate on running his club.

That side of things were completely out of his hands. All Alfie had to do was turn a blind eye. Everything had been set up by Jimmy and Alex. They'd been the ones to arrange for two dealers to work in the club under the pretence of security: doormen, in actual fact. Hiding in plain sight, they had direct contact with all the customers on the way into the club.

Alfie had been promised that only the best grade of cocaine would be served up on his premises. That way, they knew that the clientele were kept happy and that there would be no problems, or comebacks. No turf wars with any other dealers. And they all stood to make a shitload of money. All Alfie was required to do was turn a blind eye and hold his hand out at the end of the month for a nice big wad of cash for his troubles.

Though the irony now was that Alfie didn't fucking need the extra money anymore. He had money coming out of his ears. In just a few short months, The Karma Club had become legendary in the clubbing world. Alfie Harris was pulling in more money than he knew what to do with. He was already in talks about opening up a second venue somewhere a bit more upmarket, like Mayfair.

With Jimmy dead, and Alex temporarily off the scene, now was the perfect opportunity to do so. But neither of the men were around to clear up any of the shit that had been left in their wake. Which meant that Alfie was going to have to take the brunt of the fallout from tonight. A position that he'd been promised he'd never be put in.

He'd made up his mind firmly. He was done with it all.

He didn't need this kind of aggro. He'd ask Alex to pull his men out. He'd get his own doormen in to run the place. Legit doormen who knew how to stop underage kids from worming their way in.

'You tell all your men that they are on my payroll and that when this is all over, I'm having one of their jobs for this fuck up tonight, because, trust me, if one of them have let some kid in and has given her some gear, there will be hell to pay. Do you understand?'

Walking back into the bedroom and turning on the light, Alfie ignored Jennifer's whining at being woken up so abruptly and how bright the bedroom light was.

'Get your clothes on, Jen. I'll drop you home. I'm going to the club. We've got trouble.' Chucking Jennifer her dress that she'd left in a heap at the foot of the bed, Alfie wasn't in the mood for an argument, and the expression on his face said as much. This was another reminder of why he hadn't been looking for anything serious when it came to women. His business always came first and tonight he was in the middle of dealing with a fucking nightmare.

Though give the girl her dues, Jennifer didn't argue with him. Alfie felt a tinge of guilt. Jennifer was a diamond. Any other bird would have lost their shit at this treatment.

Turning his attention back to the phone, making sure that Gem heard him clearly, he repeated himself. 'I'm on my way over. Don't let the plod anywhere near my office, or anywhere else for that matter. They haven't got a warrant, so they can't start snooping around the place. Can you at least get that right?'

'Yes, Alfie. Sure thing. Boss, there's something else. It's probably nothing… but I think I should run it past you anyway.'

'What is it?' He was sitting down on the edge of the bed as he pulled on his trousers, convinced that nothing Gem Kemal could say would make things any fucking worse.

'The girl. The one that's OD'd…' Gem said, his voice sounding suddenly cautious. 'Well, one of the barmaids, Sherrie Murphy, she thinks that she recognises the girl. Only, it's a bit of a weird one—'

'For fuck's sake, Gem, spit it out. Get to the fucking point, I haven't got all night,' Alfie shouted, about to lose his shit.

'Sherrie thinks that the girl might be your daughter, boss. She reckons it's your Megan. I mean, the girl's ID says her name's Olivia, so Sherrie might be talking shit. And I'm guessing your daughter is at home with you… I know it sounds stupid.' Gem winced, wishing he'd never said anything at all. Sherrie Murphy had been the one to find the girl in the toilets and had stayed with her until the paramedics had taken her out to the ambulance on a stretcher.

'She might have been a bit confused though, boss, she was in shock. She said something about another girl that had been with her. Amber or something—'

The phone went silent then.

'I knew that it was probably nothing,' Gem said, checking his phone was still working, and hadn't somehow lost connection.

'Boss? Are you still there?'

'Is Sherrie still there with you?' Alfie said, a real urgency to his voice.

'Yeah, she is. One of the other bar staff has just made her a hot drink.'

'Good. Don't let her out of your sight. Tell her not to say jack shit to the Old Bill either. Not a fucking word. And keep her there until I get there, okay?'

'Yeah, of course. No worries, boss,' Gem said catching the panic in his boss's voice.

'The hospital that the paramedics took the girl to, which one was it?'

'Erm, I think the paramedic told one of the coppers that they were taking her to St George's. Shit. Sherrie isn't right, is she? It's not your Megan that OD'd, is it?' Gem said now, finally piecing things together.

Only he was talking to a dead phone.

His boss had already gone.

CHAPTER TWENTY-SIX

Standing in the doorway of the kitchen, Jack Taylor had had a sneaky suspicion that Nancy would be working here at the brothel at Bridge Street. She'd said that she was going to sort this place out, and Jack knew that Nancy was a woman of her word. Sitting at the kitchen table, with the mountain of folders stacked up beside her, it seemed that she wasn't wasting any time in doing so.

Jack had been watching her for a few minutes now. So engrossed in the figures in front of her that she hadn't even noticed her glasses slipping all the way down her nose. Like a librarian, or a sultry-looking secretary.

'It suits you!' he said, with a smile.

'Shit!' Nancy jumped. Startled for a few seconds, though she quickly regained her composure. 'I didn't hear you come in. Fuck, Jack! You scared the life out of me.'

'Sorry. I didn't mean to scare you,' he said, feeling bad now for sneaking up on the girl. The attack that Nancy had endured a few nights ago had clearly left its mark, no matter how much she had insisted otherwise.

'It's a bit late, isn't it? Even for you?' he said, nodding over to the piles of paperwork that Nancy had been working her way through, before looking up at the clock. 'It's gone 2 a.m., Nancy. Don't you ever sleep?' Then he noted the bottle of Scotch. Jimmy kept it in the cupboard for when he was here sorting out business.

Nancy's eyes went to it, too. Holding it up as if to do a toast she shrugged.

'Sleep? Not lately.' She smiled, trying to make light of her admission, but Jack could sense the raw honesty behind her answer. 'I thought a few of these might help, but I don't think they are helping me at all. I can't bloody see straight let alone think straight,' she said with a small laugh, realising that she'd had way more to drink than she'd intended.

Jack looked concerned then.

As beautiful as Nancy was, there was no mistaking the dark bags under her eyes, nor how frail and thin-looking she was becoming. The problem was, Nancy was her father's daughter. Too proud to admit to anyone if she was struggling, and she was struggling. No matter how much of a brave face she put on for the rest of the world, Jack knew Nancy, and the girl was suffering greatly.

Her father's death had devastated her beyond repair.

Though Nancy, being a Byrne, was never going to admit that out loud.

'I thought that I could sort out some of the accounts. The incomings and the expenditures. The books are in chaos… I should have kept on top of it all, but my head's been all over the place since my dad…' Seeing the troubled look on Jack's face, Nancy stopped herself mid-sentence, not wanting to say out loud the words that, each time she spoke them, took her breath away.

Since my dad died.

Her stomach lurched at the words once more.

'There's just so much to do, so much to think about. The warehouse, this place, all my father's property investments and businesses.' She'd spent hours tonight going through the endless pile of files that were stacked up all around her. Tallying everything up as she double-checked everything. Running her finger down along the figures on the page, before jotting her own sums in the margin next to them. 'I thought I'd make a start with this place, though the books here just don't add up. This place is making a loss. A huge one, too, and it has only been a few weeks since my dad… If things keep going the way they are, we could end up having to shut it down.'

She was drunk, Jack realised as he heard the slur behind her words. The Scotch she'd knocked back tonight was only heightening her already fretting mind. Watching as she wrinkled her nose and looked back at the books again as if somehow the figures had changed since the last time she'd looked, he stepped into the room.

'It's just one great big headache,' Nancy said rubbing her hands across her face. 'I really don't know what I'm going to do here, Jack.'

'If anyone can do this, Nancy, it's you. Trust me.'

'Truthfully? You really believe that? Because from where I'm standing, it's not looking good at all. We've lost so much money. I'm not sure that I can do all of this on my own.'

'You're not on your own, Nancy!'

'Aren't I? I don't know when or even if Alex will be back running things here again, and I can't depend on Daniel to pull his weight, can I? So, this is all going to be left down to me now. I need to get it all sorted, otherwise we'll all be royally screwed.'

'Forget about Alex and Daniel, Nancy. You've got me. I'll help you in any way I can,' Jack said trying to reassure the girl. 'Alex just needs a bit of time out of it all. He'll be fine in a few weeks or so. And as for your brother, I genuinely think that he meant well leaving Lee Archer looking after this place. Maybe you should give him one more chance.'

'No way. You saw him earlier at dinner. He's a fucking mess. God knows where his head is at right now, but it's like he's on self-destruct mode.'

Nancy pursed her mouth. Still not able to bring herself to tell anyone what she knew her brother had done. That he was the one who murdered their father. Still annoyed at herself for not avenging her father's death when she'd had the opportunity. But Nancy knew it wasn't just that.

The second she opened her mouth and told everyone the truth – that Daniel had murdered their father, nothing would ever be the same again. She'd blow their entire world wide apart. Her nan's included, and Nancy really didn't think that the woman would ever come back from that revelation. Hence why Nancy was here in the middle of the night. Sat in Bridge Street brothel's kitchen on her tod, long after the last of the girls had gone home for the night. That's how desperate she was to try and keep her mind off her brother and keep busy instead.

'I've decided that I'm going to promote Bridget, and get her to run this place for me. She's been here long enough to know what she's doing; besides she was practically running the place single-handedly for my father and Alex Costa anyway. It's about time she got the recognition for it. I reckon if I offer her an attractive enough salary, she'll pull the place back around in no time. She's a good girl, and I trust her.'

'And you don't trust Daniel?' Jack said then, his question hanging in the air between them, knowing that her brother's behaviour at dinner today had riled up Nancy. Though so far, Nancy's silence on the matter was doing all the talking for her.

'Look, Nancy, I'm just going to play Devil's advocate here. But I think the reason that your brother has been acting the way he has lately, is because he's hurting. Just like you are. I know he's got a funny way of showing it, but we all grieve differently.'

Nancy shook her head. Not willing to listen to Jack making every excuse under the sun for her brother.

'That's crap, Jack, and you know it. Daniel's not grieving. Not like me and you are. Daniel doesn't give two shits about anyone except himself, that's the real truth right there,' she said then, her eyes blazing.

'Maybe you just need to cut him some slack.'

Nancy laughed, shaking her head.

'Cut him some slack? Please.' She raised her voice, the truth balancing on the edge of her tongue. 'You haven't got a clue what you're talking about, trust me.'

'Then tell me. If I haven't got a clue, tell me what I'm not seeing. Because I know there's something you are not telling me, Nancy. I can see it in your eyes. What is it? What's Daniel done that's so bad?' Jack pleaded with the girl, seeing how tormented she was about her brother. How angry she was with him.

'I just don't trust him,' she said simply. Wishing that it was so easy that she could tell Jack everything and unburden herself of being the only one who knew the truth about the evidence that her father's old contact had managed to find on him. How the computer that was used to blackmail her dad led back to the house.

The sordid video of her father having sex with a younger man before he was killed violently.

The trace had led right back to Daniel.

It could have only been Daniel.

But she couldn't find the right words to even start to explain, so instead, she lied.

'With the business. He'll fuck it up, like he does with everything. Ask yourself this, Jack, why the sudden interest in my dad's business's now anyway? Daniel was never interested in being a part of any of it when my dad was alive. And you know what else, my dad didn't want him to be a part of any of it either. He didn't trust him. That's the bottom line. His own father didn't trust him, and in the end he had good reason not to—'

'What do you mean?' Jack said then, perplexed, as Nancy realised that she'd been waffling.

The drink loosening her tongue. She quickly backtracked. 'What I mean is, I gave him a chance. I told him to look after this place and he couldn't even do that. He left someone else in charge of the place who had no clue what they were doing. He can't be trusted to do anything.'

Jack Taylor had no idea what her brother Daniel was really capable of.

No one did.

Only her, and it was taking every bit of willpower that Nancy had not to blurt out to the man in front of her everything she knew.

But she kept quiet about what she knew.

The sudden realisation dawning on her that she'd spent her entire life listening to her father say how Daniel wasn't smart enough, or shrewd enough, or determined enough, but actually her father had been wrong all along.

They all had.

Daniel had every one of them fooled.

He'd killed their father, and by doing so he'd ripped their entire family wide apart and the craziest thing about it all was that he'd got away with it.

He was still walking around, acting as if he was innocent, and what galled her even more was that she hadn't annihilated the bastard when she had the chance.

But that was the difference between her and Daniel. Nancy wasn't a cold-blooded killer. She wasn't a murderer, and she'd never stoop as low as her brother.

'This business really means a lot to you, doesn't it?' Jack said. Seeing the determination in Nancy's eyes, he could see that she was as passionate about the business as Jimmy had been. Nancy wasn't doing any of this purely for the money. There was more to it than that.

'I watched my dad work his fingers to the bone to build up what he had. He came from nothing, but he worked his arse off to make sure that we didn't. He made sure none of us wanted for anything. We had the best education, the best clothes, the best house…' She felt her tears then, though she blinked them away, refusing to get emotional again, not in front of Jack. 'This was important to him. This is what made him; it made me too. I need to keep everything going. My dad would have wanted that. And he would have wanted me to be the one to do it. That's why he involved me in the business in the first place. He always said that one day he'd leave all of this to me. The Byrne empire. Only, the day came sooner than any of us ever anticipated.'

Jack went to her then.

Wrapping his arms around her, he held her tightly.

Letting her cry in his arms.

The girl had been so strong for so long, he'd known it wouldn't be long until she broke. He was just glad that he was the one nearby when she finally did.

But the last thing he expected was for Nancy to reach up and kiss him. Softly, at first. Her lips warm, her breath hot on his skin. Jack pulled back, but Nancy kissed him harder. Her mouth searching hungrily for his.

As much as Jack knew that this was wrong, that Nancy was drunk, he couldn't resist her. Fuck, he didn't expect many men could. Nancy was beautiful. Way too young for him though, but she certainly knew what she was doing.

Unbuttoning his shirt, hers too. Jack felt himself getting swept away in the moment of it all. The excitement. He hadn't realised until now how much he wanted Nancy.

Kissing her back, he could smell the heady scent of her perfume mixed with the strong smell of Scotch on her breath. She was drunk, he reminded himself, doing the decent thing and breaking away from her.

But Nancy had other ideas.

Pulling him towards her, down on top of her on the kitchen table. Tugging at his unbuttoned shirt. Lifting her own top over her head.

It all happened so quickly, so passionately.

Seconds later, they were merely two bodies writhing as one. Entwined together.

Jack could feel Nancy's nails digging into his back, tearing down his skin as she moved beneath him.

An arch of her back, and then a long, trembling shudder.

Jack came then too, before collapsing on top of her.

The room silent now. Just the sound of their laboured breathing. The pounding of their hearts inside their chests.

'Shit. We shouldn't have done that,' Nancy said, getting up from where they'd lain, and getting dressed. Immediately regretting her actions. She felt embarrassed then. For initiating it all. For being so forceful, so self-gratifying.

'It was my fault. I should have stopped it.' Jack closed his eyes.

What had he been thinking?

Jack was almost forty. Nancy was twenty years younger than him.

She was drunk, too, and vulnerable. He should have known better. Only, his ego had taken over. Convinced not many men would have been able to resist Nancy Byrne, but he should have.

Nancy wouldn't hear of Jack apologising though. The man had done nothing but be nice to her, to look out for her. She'd done this, not him.

Though now she felt as if she should at least explain.

'I just wanted someone. For a few minutes. Someone of my own. To make me feel protected,' Nancy said then, before laughing. Scolding herself as she did so, for sounding so pitiful. Still shaken from the attack a few nights ago, she'd needed to feel safe. To feel a pair of warm, strong arms around her. To feel as if she really wasn't alone. 'God, how pathetic am I, huh? Sleeping with one of my dad's best friends. What a walking, talking cliché!'

Jack shook his head.

'It's not like that, Nancy. I care about you. You know that, and I'm here for you no matter what,' he said, hoping to reassure the girl. 'You're not on your own. You've got me. As friends, or whatever. I'm here for you. I just want to make sure that you're okay. That you're safe.'

It was Nancy's turn to close her eyes then, as the realisation suddenly hit her.

'That's why you came here tonight, isn't it? You're keeping tabs on me, aren't you?' Of course he was. Why else would he just show up here at stupid o'clock in the morning? 'Is that what you're doing? Checking up on me? Poor defenceless Nancy! Is that what you think?' Her voice cold once more, back on the defensive. 'You think I can't do this, don't you? That's why you're here. Why you're following me around and watching my every move.'

'It's not like that, Nancy! I just want you to be okay, to be careful.'

Nancy laughed then. Both amused and insulted at Jack's patronising comment.

'To be careful? Why? Because I'm a woman?' She smarted. 'Would you be skulking around the place if I was a man?' She guessed, rightly, that Jack doubted her capabilities to step into her father's shoes and take over from where the man had left off. 'Thanks for having faith in me. I can do this, Jack. I may be a woman, but that's not a handicap. I'm more than capable.

Though I guess if I was a man, you wouldn't have just had the added bonus of being able to fuck me!'

Even Nancy winced at that low blow.

'Shit. I'm sorry.'

Jack held his hands up then, calling a truce. He'd forgotten how fiery Nancy could be when pushed, but he also knew she didn't mean what she'd just said.

There was something between them. They both knew it deep down.

'Hey, I didn't say you weren't capable, okay. Shit, Nancy. If anyone can sort this mess out, it's you. I'm just saying be careful. Whoever it was that attacked you the other night might come back. That's all I'm saying… You need to keep your wits about you. There's been a lot of fucked-up things happening around here lately. People being attacked, or worse, murdered. People aren't always what they seem.'

Nancy couldn't argue with that. People really weren't what they seemed.

Wasn't that the truth?

'Look, I was vulnerable the other night and whoever it was that attacked me had known that. In fact, they'd depended on it.' Nancy shook her head, the disbelief of how easily she'd played into her attacker's hands. 'They caught me off guard, but let me tell you, Jack, they won't do it again. I'll be ready next time and if they think they can get the better of me, then they will have deeply underestimated me. No one's stepping in here and taking from me what my father has built. They'll have to kill me first.'

Jack winced, knowing without a doubt that Nancy meant every word she spoke.

'That's exactly what I've been worrying about.'

Nancy shook her head. Annoyed with herself for letting her guard down tonight too. With Jack.

'And tonight. Tonight was a mistake. We shouldn't have done that, but it was my fault. I was the one who initiated it. I wasn't thinking straight.'

Glad when the loud shrill of a mobile phone rang out in the room, interrupting them.

It was Jack's. Only he didn't move, didn't speak.

Instead Nancy nodded at him, as if to give him permission. 'You better get that, it might be important.' She half hoped that it was too. Some crisis at work that would mean Jack would be called away. She just wanted him to leave now. She wanted to be on her own. To drink herself into a complete stupor. To wallow in self-pity.

Nancy got dressed, listening in to Jack as he answered the phone, his tone short and curt.

Suddenly he was pacing the room. An urgency to his voice that Nancy recognised to mean that something was up.

'I'll be right there,' he said as he ended the call.

'Trouble?' she said, as he placed his phone back inside his pocket. Seemed her wish for him to leave had suddenly come true.

'You could say that.' Jack's expression now was deadly serious. 'That was Gem down at The Karma Club. Someone's taken an overdose. They're saying it's a young girl and that she's in a really bad way.'

'Shit,' Nancy said, praying to God that the drugs hadn't come through their suppliers. 'You don't think that this girl got her gear from one of our guys, do you?'

'I don't know…' Unsure of what the fuck was happening down at The Karma Club, the best thing for him to do now was get his arse down there, and find out for certain.

Nancy sensed his hesitation.

'What, Jack? Tell me?'

'Look, this is the last thing you're going to want to hear right now, but fuck it. You'll find out sooner or later anyway. Daniel.

He's changed the supplier at the club. He said that you didn't want any part in the club anyway. Not in the drug side of it all. So he's stepped it up.'

'What do you mean "he's stepped it up"?'

'I mean that he's distributing MDMA – Ecstasy. There's a massive demand for it in the clubs at the moment. If the girl did take something from one of ours then we've got ourselves a huge fucking problem—'

Nancy shook her head. Unable to fathom what she was hearing.

'What? You knew that Daniel had taken it upon himself to start making changes like that and you never thought to mention it to me?' Interrupting Jack, incensed that he'd kept this from her after all his spiel about being able to trust him. Clearly she couldn't if he wasn't telling her shit that he'd been hearing about her own business.

'Nancy. You've got enough on your bloody plate, and you're already gunning for him. I thought it was best to keep out of it. I was keeping an eye on him and when I got the opportunity I was going to try and talk him out of all this bullshit. I warned him to steer clear of all of this.' Jack sighed, annoyed that he hadn't done that in the first place. Fuck knows what Daniel had led them all into now. Maybe Nancy was right, after all. Daniel was a liability. He'd been intent on cutting Alex and Nancy out of that deal and taking this deal all for himself. Jack had warned him not to get involved in anything to do with drugs, but it seemed Daniel had gone and done the deal anyway.

The idiot.

All these months that Jimmy and Alex had been distributing their coke in the club, and they'd not had a single problem. Tonight was the first night that Daniel had executed his plan to start shifting pills and already the bloke was neck high in shit.

'Oh, you did, did you? Well, now look what's happened. Fat lot of good that did us all, eh?'

'They've just summoned Alfie Harris down there and from what I've just been told the man's like the fucking Antichrist.'

'Yeah, I bet.' Nancy nodded once more. 'He's never been keen on drugs being distributed in his venue. This will be the last thing he needs, all that negative press—'

'I think the last thing that Alfie Harris is worrying about right now is that poxy nightclub,' Jack said, his expression as deadly serious as his tone as he stared Nancy dead in the eye.

'Sorry, that was insensitive of me,' Nancy said, wondering herself when she had become so cold-hearted. 'The kid. Do you think she'll be okay?'

'I hope so, I really do,' Jack said. 'Fuck, Nancy. They think it's Megan. Megan Harris – Alfie Harris's daughter! She's only sixteen.'

'What?' Nancy said hoping to God that she'd misheard him.

But Jack didn't bother repeating himself. They both knew what he'd said.

'I'm going to go down there and see if there's anything I can do to keep the heat off. See what the rest of my lot have managed to dig up and have a word with the superintendent. See what they've found so far.'

Nancy nodded, unable to find any words now.

'This isn't good. If this comes back on Daniel, the Old Bill will throw the book at him.'

Again Nancy nodded. Watching as Jack Taylor stormed out of the office.

Then taking a seat in the chair behind her, she rested her head in her hands, the drama of the night too much for her to deal with.

Alfie Harris's daughter had been caught in the crossfire tonight. Some poor, defenceless sixteen-year-old kid.

Nancy felt sick then. The Scotch leaving a bad taste in her mouth as she leant over and threw up in to the wastepaper bin. Wiping her mouth with the back of her hand, she thought about Jack's last words.

How Jack had been concerned that the Old Bill would lock Daniel up for this. That was the least of Daniel's worries, Nancy thought. Alfie Harris adored his daughter. The girl had been the sole reason he had wanted out of the criminal way of life. It was one of the reasons why he despised the drugs side of the club. He'd always made no secret of any of that.

It would only be a matter of time now until Alfie Harris went on the warpath for this tonight. Daniel would be praying that he was locked up, as far away from Alfie Harris as possible.

They all would.

CHAPTER TWENTY-SEVEN

'Take as long as you need.' Guiding Alfie Harris into the private room on the Intensive Care ward, Critical Care Nurse Denton stood back and let the man have a few moments, allowing him to identify whether or not the girl in the hospital bed was his daughter.

So far, they had little information on who this patient actually was.

A young girl, aged fifteen to sixteen they'd guessed. The only ID she had in the bag that the paramedics brought in with them had turned out to be a fake. Fake name, fake date of birth. The police had been about to start making their time-consuming enquiries to try and find out the girl's real identity, but Mr Harris's arrival at St George's Hospital could provide the vital pieces of information on the patient that they so desperately needed.

'Megs?' Alfie Harris said then. His voice high-pitched, his throat constricting. Standing at the foot of the hospital bed, he felt his legs go from beneath him at the sight of his precious daughter, lying there so helpless looking. Stupidly believing that calling out to her would somehow allow her to miraculously answer him back. Gripping on to the metal bedpost to steady himself, he fought to gain his composure.

He felt Jennifer's hand on his shoulder then. For a second Alfie had forgotten she was even in the room with him. He hadn't been too sure about the idea of Jennifer rocking up at the hospital with him at first, but now, seeing his baby girl in the state that she was in, he was glad she had been so insistent on coming with him.

She was right in thinking that he'd need her support. He didn't think that he could do this without her.

'It's her. It's my daughter,' Alfie said then, his voice barely a whisper.

Consumed with shock and fear, Alfie had never felt so scared in his entire life. It was definitely Megan, one hundred per cent, though it had taken him a few moments to process the fact as he'd taken in the sight of her: skin, tinged with blue; the streaks of black make-up smudged all down her face; her lips, cracked and dried, parted by a large plastic tube that was hooked up to a large machine next to her; the IV drip that the nurse was placing in her arm; the loud chorus of beeping machinery echoing around the clinical room.

He barely recognised her, if the truth be told. In this state. But it was her all right. His little Megs. His beautiful princess.

'Can you confirm your daughter's full name, please?' Nurse Denton said, not wanting to bombard the man for information but she wanted to at least get the girl's name. Now they had her name they could obtain her full medical history.

Alfie nodded. His eyes not leaving his daughter.

'It's Megan Harris.'

He hadn't been prepared for this. After ringing Amber's home phone constantly, and getting no answer, he had raced to the hospital in record-breaking time, hoping to rule out what Sherrie had said. That it wasn't his Megan here.

But his worst nightmare had come true. It was Megan.

'What's happened to her? Is she going to be okay?' The tremor in his voice sounded almost alien. As if it belonged to someone else, far away. This couldn't really be happening. Not to him and certainly not to his beautiful Megan. His precious daughter, lying there helplessly, attached to a mass of tubes and wires.

'Has she taken any form of drugs before?'

'No. Never,' Alfie said with certainty. Though he could see from the nurse's neutral look that she was trained not to comment what she really thought: that a lot of parents didn't have a clue what their kids were really up to once they were left to their own devices. But this nurse didn't know his Megan.

She was a good kid.

She didn't do drugs.

'Is that what you think this is then? Drugs? Megan wouldn't touch anything like that.'

The nurse nodded. She'd heard that sentence too many times to even count.

'The paramedics that brought her in were told that she'd possibly taken MDMA – methylenedioxymethamphetamine – to give it its full chemical name. Or Ecstasy as it's more commonly known. Kids get up to all sorts these days, Mr Harris; even the most trustworthy ones are capable of making the odd bad decision.'

'Not my Megan. She's too smart for that. There must be some mistake.'

'Well, we'll know for certain when we get the toxicology report back. Until then we can't confirm exactly what she's taken nor can we verify how much of the drug she has in her system. But her body's showing all the symptoms of an MDMA overdose, so that's what we're treating her for.' Pausing, Nurse Denton let the patient's father have a few seconds to digest what he was being told. It was a lot to take in for anyone, especially someone who was so visibly upset.

'Your daughter has also consumed a large amount of alcohol, Mr Harris. She's suffered multiple seizures and the paramedics had to stop her from choking on her vomit on numerous occasions when they brought her in, so we decided to pump her stomach.' Nurse Denton moved around the bed, making sure that

Mr Harris was given all the information he needed, and that the man was taking in the severity of his daughter's situation. 'We've administered an activated charcoal directly into your daughter's stomach now through a nasogastric tube and while we wait for that to work in flushing out any further toxins, our priority is to reduce her temperature. It's been rising rapidly. Currently at 41.5.'

Alfie nodded, dumbly. Unable to take his eyes off his daughter lying there, looking so vulnerable in the hospital bed. Unable to focus, his brain was whirring as he tried to take in everything the nurse was telling him.

Nurse Denton could see that too. It was understandable. Seeing a child in this state was a shock to anyone's system, let alone a parent.

And Megan Harris really was in a bad way.

Though she was saddened at the realisation that she was starting to become immune to the sight now. As harrowing as a child in this state looked, Nurse Denton had seen so many patients in similar conditions a hundred times over. That was the grim reality of her job. She spent so much of her precious time dealing with youngsters that had selfishly dabbled with class A drugs, these days. The Critical Care Unit was inundated with overdoses and drug abuse patients. Completely overrun in fact. They had patients being brought in on a daily basis, in such increasing numbers that Nurse Denton was almost numb to it now. Almost.

Though her heart always went out to the unsuspecting, worried parents. All that stress and heartache that they were put through, all because of their child making an often stupid, thoughtless mistake. That's what galled Nurse Denton the most, that these patients' critical conditions were self-inflicted. That they were only here because they convinced themselves that nothing bad would ever happen to them. As if they were somehow invincible. How they didn't even consider the consequences or how much medical care and attention would be needed to nurse them well again. Round-the-clock care that could have been given to more worthy patients: patients that had ended up here through no fault of their own, with real life-threatening conditions. Still, Nurse Denton didn't voice this opinion, of course. Remaining ever the professional, her only duty now was to care for her patient.

'She's been sedated. We've intubated and mechanically ventilated her for now, until we can get her stats all back under control.'

'I don't know what any of that means? Is she going to be all right? She will be, won't she?' Alfie said then. He could feel Jennifer standing next to him, gripping his arm tightly as if to offer him some comfort. To remind him he wasn't on his own.

'Mr Harris, your daughter is extremely sick. She's currently in a coma and being kept alive with the help of a life support machine. We are doing all that we can. She's in the very best hands.'

'What about her mate, Amber? Was she brought in too?' Alfie asked, worried that Megan's friend would be in a similar state. He hadn't even thought about Megan's friend until that point. The two of them were inseparable. If Megan was in a bad way, then Amber might be in a similar state?

'Amber? I'm sorry, I don't know anyone of that name. Your daughter was brought in alone, Mr Harris. You're welcome to speak to the paramedics that were called to the scene but, as far as I'm aware, she was on her own when she was found. A barmaid found her and stayed with her until the paramedics arrived. Is that who you mean?'

Alfie Harris shook his head. Assuming that the nurse was talking about Sherrie Murphy. Fuck knows where Amber had got to then? He clenched his jaw. Why wasn't she with Megan? They should have been together. The pair of them. Fuck! None of this should even be happening.

'What the fuck's that?' he said then, as an alarm started beeping loudly, screaming out into the room, interrupting his thoughts.

'What's happening?' Alfie's voice rose in a panic as Nurse Denton hurried around the other side of the bed.

'It's okay. I just need to change the IV drip. The alarms are a good thing. They're letting us know exactly what's going on at all times.'

Alfie nodded once more. That seemed to be all he could do right now. Nod his head like a gormless idiot. Not knowing what else to do or say.

'Please tell me that she is going to be all right,' he repeated. This time his voice was barely a whisper, forcing himself to ask the one question that, now he knew all the details, he suddenly dreaded hearing the answer to. Never in all his days had he experienced such acute fear as he was right now. The thought of Megan slipping away from him. Losing her. He just couldn't even bear it.

Placing her hand on Mr Harris's arm, Nurse Denton wanted to offer this man words of reassurance, but she wasn't prepared to offer any false hope.

Megan Harris was in a very bad way.

There was a chance that she wouldn't be recovering from this.

'Mr Harris, your daughter is a very sick girl. The next twenty-four hours are critical. I wish there was something more I could tell you…' Then trying to help the man to feel at least useful so that he could focus on his daughter instead of his own fears, she nodded to the chair behind him. 'Take a seat. You can talk to her. She might hear you, you never know. There have been studies to show that sometimes they can… I bet she'd be glad to hear your voice.' Then looking at the woman who was with him, the nurse added. 'I'll get our porter to bring you one, too, if you'd like?'

Jennifer nodded gratefully. She'd barely spoken two words since she'd got here, but what could she say? There were no words. All she could do right now was be here for Alfie.

Watching as he sank down into the chair beside his daughter and gripped Megan's hand tightly in his own, Jennifer tried to hold back her tears as she heard him speaking so tenderly to his daughter.

'Megan, baby, it's your dad. I know you can hear me, darling. I love you, Megs. You're going to be just fine. You're going to fight this all the way, Megs, because you're strong, eh, just like your old man.'

He was crying now. Big fat tears, cascading down his cheeks, his shoulders shaking with each wracking sob as he spoke. As he said the words that even he was finding impossible to believe.

What if Megan doesn't make it? What if she dies? His daughter was all he had in this world. She was the only person that really meant anything to him.

He'd raised her single-handedly from a small baby, after he'd caught her skank of a mother cheating on him with one of his best mates. Alfie had thrown the woman out and dedicated his life to making sure that his daughter never went without anything again. It had been hard, at times, especially in Alfie's line of work. Wheeling and dealing in all sorts of dodgy business over the years. Associating with lots of unfavourable characters, and all the while trying to bring his daughter up in the best way possible.

To be kind and decent. To not have to struggle the way Alfie had at her age.

That's why he'd been so made up when The Karma Club had taken off just a few months ago. Finally, after all these years he could go legit. No more dodgy dealings and now he'd decided no more drugs either. Though it appeared he'd made that decision much too late.

His beautiful girl.

He was guilty of a lot of things. Being overbearing and strict as fuck with her, but he'd only ever been that way because he knew that the world was full of bad people. Evil fuckers that would hurt you in the blink of an eye if there was some kind of gain to be made for them. And now his deepest fears had finally been realised.

Megan had been hurt. Badly.

All those years of trying to protect his daughter and keep her away from people who might harm her, and the irony was that she'd found her way to trouble anyway. In his very own nightclub of all places. His daughter had taken drugs from people that Alfie Harris probably fucking knew. People that were probably on his fucking payroll. When he found out who, somebody was going to pay the highest price for their actions tonight.

Taking a deep breath then, Alfie wiped his tears away, and tried to pull himself together. If Megan could hear him then he needed to stay strong. To stay in control.

'Your dad's here, Megs. So when you're ready, you just open those pretty blue eyes of yours. I've got you, Megs. Do you hear me? I've got you.'

When this was all over, when his Megan was okay again, Alfie Harris was going to cause fucking murders over this.

CHAPTER TWENTY-EIGHT

Joop's Gentleman's Club in Soho was buzzing as per usual for the weekend. Full to capacity, packed with wall-to-wall buff males every direction he looked, Ross Nicolson was in his absolute element. This was what he deemed as a perfect Saturday night. It was all in an evening's work for him. Electric. Soaking up the atmosphere while he served all his fancy cocktails and flirted with all the punters.

The busier the bar was, the better. It meant more tips for him and, of course, it meant more options for him too. He could have his pick of the men in here, no doubt; his only dilemma was willing it down to just one contender. *Hmm, who was he going to let take him home and fuck him tonight*, he thought with a grin.

Eeny, meeny, miny mo.

Catching the eye of the tall dark stranger sitting in the corner of the room, alone in a booth, Ross had already found tonight's lucky partaker. This was the third Saturday in a row that the man had been in here. Choosing to sit on his own in the same spot, drinking the same drink too. *A Jack and Coke, man.* Simple, no fuss.

There was something about him that Ross just couldn't put his finger on.

Dark and mysterious-looking, a bit moody too.

The man had a real pull about him that Ross just couldn't resist. As if there was something intense about him, dangerous even. And judging by the many advances this man was receiving from all the other men around him, Ross wasn't the only one who felt the attraction.

Only, the man was acting as if he wasn't interested. Politely declining the many offers he received of people wanting to join him, making out that he preferred his own company. The entire time, seemingly unable to keep his eyes off Ross. Which, in turn, only stirred something deep within him.

Lust, desire, the need of a good hard fuck? Ross didn't know what it was, and he didn't care; all he did know for sure was that this bloke wanted him badly, he could tell.

'Course he did; how could he resist Ross's charms? Good-looking, fit and funny. He was vain as fuck too, but hey, who's perfect?

Grinning triumphantly to himself, Ross decided he was going to reel this bloke in. Playing hard to get probably drove his sort wild, seeing as men were literally throwing themselves at him, and there was nothing like a bit of healthy competition to spice things up a bit. Waiting for the perfect opportunity, for the man to look his way, Ross quickly turned his attention on the customer in front of him.

'You know what you need to try?' Ross said playfully. Leaning over the bar to the awaiting customer and rubbing the man's arm. 'Sex On The Bar. It's one of my specialties.'

'Is that so? Well, seeing as you insist.' The man laughed then, only too happy to allow the young, hot barman to make him one of his 'special' cocktails.

'Oh. I do insist indeed.'

Ross got to work then pouring several different shots of alcohol into the cocktail shaker, before adding some fruit juice and ice. The entire time he could feel the man at the back of the room. Watching him. And it was turning Ross on.

Sugaring the glass he poured the finished mixture in and slid it over the bar towards the man, along with a playful wink.

'You lick the rim first then you swallow it down whole,' he said brazenly, watching as the man eagerly did as he was told. Picking up the glass, he ran his tongue around the edge, his eyes on Ross the entire time before knocking it back in one.

'How was that?' Ross said, knowing full well that he could have served up this bloke a glass of cold piss and he'd still salivate over it. 'Orgasmic, huh?'

'That was something else,' the man said, handing over a twenty pound note and telling Ross to keep the change. His clammy hand lingering over Ross's. Letting Ross know in no uncertain terms that he was on to a sure thing.

Ross smiled.

Searching the back of the room again, hoping that the man was still watching him, Ross couldn't help but feel disappointed as he noticed the empty booth now.

His glass discarded on the table. Half empty.

The man had gone.

Shit!

Ross wondered if he'd played it all wrong. Maybe the guy was the jealous type.

Oh, well, fuck it. You win some you lose some, Ross thought, knowing the punter in front of him was a sure thing. He believed in having fun. Pure, unadulterated, kinky-as-fuck fun. And lucky for him there was no shortage of willing participants. He may have lost out on one main prize tonight, but there were plenty more where that one came from.

'Tell you what, Jerry. Why don't you get off? I can clean up here. Go on, it's been a long night mate,' Ross Nicolson said, hoping his boss would take him up on his offer so that he could stay back and have a couple of cheeky drinks on the house.

About to protest, to Ross's surprise, Jeremy Cooper nodded with gratitude. They had an event in here in the morning. A private function. Some fancy book launch that a local author was throwing. He could do with getting his head down, before he came back in tomorrow morning and started all of this over again.

'Okay. If you're sure?'

'I'm sure.' Ushering the man out of the bar before he could change his mind, Ross bid him good night before coming back into the bar and heading straight over to the optics.

Pouring himself a double vodka, neat with ice, he walked over to the booth and took a seat. Enjoying the silence as he drank his drink back in just a few mouthfuls. Glad of the peace and quiet as he sat there, looking about the place. The bar seemed so different at night, like this. When there was no one else around.

The rustic wooden floors, and leather studded booth seating. It had a library feel about it, he thought with a smirk. All they needed was some bookshelves. It was tired and dated-looking, but then it also felt homely and he guessed that's why the place had such appeal. The men that came felt comfortable here. A place where they could be exactly who they really were without having to pretend otherwise.

Ross knew all about that. He was a pro at hiding his sexuality from his family. Knowing only too well that none of them would accept it. Which is why he was so outrageously camp when he worked here. Flirting and showing an interest in any man with a pulse. It was all just a game to Ross. A way of getting out his truth that he'd been forced to compress inside him.

Fucking families.

His were the reason he'd moved here, to London, to get away from the lot of them.

Debating on having another drink, Ross decided he couldn't be arsed now. He'd put himself in a bad mood. He was just going to lock up and bugger off home.

Cleaning down the bar top, he remembered to check the toilets before he left and make sure that there were no unsuspecting buggers hiding out in there, getting their end away. Ross had well and truly learned his lesson last time when he'd inadvertently locked two fellas in the pub one night. Turning up in the morning to find two half-naked men curled up on the floor together. Both of them completely off their faces from drinking their way through his entire optics in his absence.

Tonight though, as he pushed back each of the cubicle doors, he was pleased to confirm that the toilets were indeed empty.

Grabbing his coat and the keys from the side as he made his way back through the bar, he heard the main door go.

'Jerry! For God's sake, I told you to go home. I'm capable of locking up, you know. You don't need to check up on me!'

Only, Ross stopped in his tracks then, as he reached the front of the bar and saw that it wasn't Jerry. It was the man from earlier.

The tall, dark, handsome stranger that Ross hadn't yet had the opportunity to properly talk to. Resigned to going home on his own and settling for a takeaway and quick wank, suddenly Ross's night was looking up.

'Fuck man! You scared the crap out of me.'

The man didn't speak. Instead he sat down in the booth, and slid back in the chair, making himself comfortable.

Ross grinned. This was good. The man had come back. *For him.*

'You want a drink? Jack and Coke, right?' Keen to impress the man, Ross poured out a double measure, and one for himself, too, before taking a seat opposite the guy.

Intrigued now.

'I saw you earlier,' Ross said, trying to engage the man in some kind of conversation, though he didn't seem very receptive.

Still not speaking, instead he gulped down his drink in one. His eyes not leaving Ross's.

Perhaps he was shy? Maybe he wanted Ross to take the lead. He'd clearly come back here for a reason, and Ross was going to make sure that he wasn't disappointed.

Walking over to the door, Ross locked it behind them. Then walking back over to the man, he stood in front of him. Over him. Taking the glass out of his hand.

The man didn't move. Didn't even flinch.

Taking that as some form of encouragement Ross dropped to his knees in front of him. Unbuttoning the man's trousers. His fingers fumbling clumsily over the button. Fuck! He hadn't felt this excited since he'd first lost his virginity.

Blokes normally made it too easy for him. Throwing themselves at him.

And normally Ross just went along with it. Fucking the men and pretending that they did it for him, when half the time they probably didn't even know how to do it for themselves.

But there was something about this bloke that was so different to all the others. He had an air of such mystery about him. As if there was so much more than met the eye. He looked a bit menacing too. Sat there, acting all cold and distant. Even now, as Ross took him in his mouth greedily, he wasn't giving anything away.

Though it wouldn't be long until Ross got some reaction out of him.

Shit. He didn't even ask the man's name, he thought then, feeling seriously turned on by the encounter.

This is what really did it for him.

No pretence. None of this getting to know each other bullshit.

Just hard, raw, passionate sex.

Ross could barely contain himself. Increasing the intensity of his mouth over the man's rock hard form, he could feel the man bucking beneath him. Enjoying Ross's well-honed skills, before a few seconds later he shuddered violently. Releasing himself.

Falling back on to the floor, Ross grinned triumphantly.

'Well, that didn't take long,' he quipped, though he recognised the want and urgency that had been between them both. That rare animal magnetism.

Ross undid his own trousers then, hoping that it was his turn next.

Only the man's mood had changed now, as he got to his feet. Still cold and detached, there was something else that flashed in his eyes.

Confusion? Disgust?

Staring down at Ross with a twisted look on his face.

'Hey, come on, man. I thought you wanted to have some fun?' Ross said, feeling used now. 'You not going to repay the favour?'

The last thing Ross had been expecting was a punch to the side of his head. The force of the blow knocking him to the floor. Dazed and confused. Wondering what the fuck he'd done to deserve that, Ross tried to get up but the man just kept coming at him. Kicking him and punching him.

His ribs cracking, his head feeling as if it was starting to cave in with each blow. He could taste blood in the back of his throat. Feel it trickling out of his nose. A hot mind-numbing pain all over his body as he burned from the stinging blows.

'Please?' he mumbled, not sure now if any sound was even leaving his mouth.

Trying to sit up, his hands cupped protectively over the top of his head.

Another punch came then, this time knocking his teeth out. Sending him flying back down on the floor.

Then a boot stamping down on his face.

Then darkness…

*

Walking down Dean Street, thoroughly annoyed with himself for leaving his phone behind at the bar, Jeremy Cooper couldn't wait to get home to bed.

A few hours' sleep and then he could head back down here early in the morning, armed with his usual bag full of croissants and a frothy cappuccino. After a busy week manning his bar, there was nothing else quite like a Sunday morning in Soho, just before the main hustle and bustle started again for the day. When half of London were still in bed. The Sunday shopping trade not due for another couple of hours.

He'd only left an hour ago and already Soho was quieter than earlier. There were still people around. Not as many. The main throngs of people all partying and cavorting, drinking and dancing, had made their way through the maze of bars and late-night shows scattered all around Soho. Filtering out now into just the odd small group of people making their way home for the night.

Just where Jeremy Cooper should be.

Instead he was making his way up the cobbled street towards his bar; irritated now he took in a deep breath of air. Though part of him couldn't help but think that maybe forgetting his phone was a blessing in disguise. As much as he appreciated Ross's rare offer of help last night with closing everything up, the chances were that he wouldn't have done everything properly. Not the way that Jeremy liked his bar clean.

Placing the key in the lock, he narrowed his eyes as the door instantly pushed open.

'For fuck's sake!' he said, annoyed that Ross Nicolson couldn't seem to do anything right as he mumbled away to himself. 'I should have known he couldn't be bloody trusted. Bloody man's an idiot. Who locks up for the night, and leaves the front door wide op?—'

The last word of his sentence didn't leave Jeremy's lips. Instead it was replaced with a stifled moan, as he stood frozen to the spot. His eyes fixed on the mangled body splayed out in the middle of the floor. The face unrecognisable now. The features replaced with a mushy red pulp of broken flesh and skin. A pool of deep red blood congealed around the man's head pouring out all across his beautiful restored oak floor.

Immobilised, his arms hanging from him limply as he went into shock, he let the keys that he was holding slip to the floor as he let out a loud, strangled scream.

Then Jeremy Cooper threw up the contents of his stomach.

Ross Nicolson was dead.

CHAPTER TWENTY-NINE

'Where the fuck are you?' Shouting down the phone, Jack Taylor was beyond pissed off. He'd been calling Daniel for the past ten minutes as he'd driven across London like a lunatic. Now, as he pulled up outside The Karma Club, spotting the police cars that were all lined up out the front, finally, Daniel Byrne had picked up the phone.

'Oh, that's fucking charming that is. Whatever happened to saying hello when you call someone, huh?' Daniel replied tartly. 'I mean it's only common courtesy, I guess, not the fucking law, but still—'

'Stop with the wisecracks, Daniel. We've got a fucking problem,' Jack said, deliberately stopping Daniel in his tracks with his smart-arse comments; he wasn't in the mood for it tonight. Especially not now that he had arrived at the club and was about to face his colleagues and probably have a world of mess that he needed to try and cover the fuck up on Daniel's behalf. 'Well, actually it's you who has the problem, Daniel! I take it you haven't heard yet?'

'Haven't heard what? Do you coppers only ever talk in fucking riddles? Cut to the chase, Jack…'

Jack closed his eyes in despair, recognising the slur in Daniel's words. The man was drunk. Again. Judging by the fact that there was no urgency in his tone to find out why Jack was ringing him in the middle of the night only confirmed that Daniel was indeed hammered.

Great! Just what Jack needed. To babysit that twat tonight.

Daniel being drunk was only going to antagonise the situation further if Alfie Harris went on the warpath. Which Jack Taylor knew would be a certainty. Time was literally of the essence right now, so he got straight to the point.

'That little plan you had about dishing out class As in The Karma Club. I warned you not to do it, didn't I? I told you not to get involved in shit you know nothing about. Well, you've really gone and fucked yourself, Daniel. Some kid's only gone and OD'd on fucking Ecstasy; only it turns out that this ain't just some kid. It's Alfie Harris's daughter. She's sixteen, Daniel. Do you know the shit you've just gone and fucking caused? The man is going to fucking annihilate you when he finds out that it was you that okayed the gear being sold in his club!'

The silence down the phone was deafening. The only sound, Daniel breathing.

Glad that Daniel had finally shut the fuck up talking and let the seriousness of the situation finally dawn on him, Jack knew he had the bloke's full attention, and about time too.

But Daniel just wasn't getting it.

'How the fuck am I to blame? How was I to know his fucking daughter was going to get hold of the shit?' Daniel said; as always, not willing to take the blame for his actions.

Jack pursed his mouth. *Typical Daniel.* The man's immediate response was always to find some other fucker to pass the buck to. 'If she's only sixteen then she shouldn't even have been in the club. Fuck knows which of the blokes served it up to her, but it has nothing to do with me.'

'Only, that's just it, Daniel. It has everything to do with you because you're the idiot who gave it the green fucking light to start flogging the shit in the club. You're the one who called off your father and Alex's supplier. You didn't even tell your sister. This is all going to fall back on you! Have you heard the stories about Alfie Harris when he was one of London's main players? The man might claim to be retired from all that shit these days, but fuck me, if anything happens to his daughter you can mark my words you'll be getting a visit from him sometime very soon, and you won't be walking away from it, Daniel. The man is a fucking lunatic.'

Jack waited for his warning to finally sink in to Daniel Byrne's thick skull. For Daniel to start begging for help, to sound contrite at least.

Only, Daniel wasn't going to do any of that. He was doing what he always did and throwing his toys out of the pram instead. Saving his own arse by threatening to take any other fucker around him down with him too.

'Well you better make this right then, Jack. Hadn't you?!'

'How the fuck can I make this right? It's already happened. This is going to come back on you, Daniel, there'll be fuck all I can do to save your arse now. You did this; you're going to have to deal with the consequences.'

'Is that so? Only, you've got some consequences of your own to sort out. Haven't you, Jack?' Daniel let his threat linger in the air between them both. The two men silent at either end of the phone. Knowing exactly what Daniel was referring to.

'Why don't we talk about where you were on the night my father got killed, Jack, eh?' Daniel said then, playing his ace card.

'You fucking piece of shit!' Jack snarled.

Daniel laughed.

'I bet your lot would love to hear all about that. Wouldn't they?' A bent copper hiding out in my dad's car. Watching as Jimmy Byrne got shot in the chest by his own son. And did you fucking help him? Did you fuck. You were too interested in the payout, weren't you? Taking half the money in return for your silence. Maybe I should just tell them all the truth, huh? Seeing as the shit's going to hit the fan anyway. Fuck it, I'll tell them everything. How you were in on my father's murder too. That you were an accessory. Fuck it, you were an accomplice.'

Slamming his fists on the steering wheel, Jack closed his eyes. Furious with himself forever thinking that Daniel would keep his mouth shut about what went on that night.

Of course he wouldn't.

Daniel only paid Jack Taylor half the money that he'd taken from his father that night, as a sweetener. It was insurance money to keep Jack from talking.

Jack had stupidly taken it, too.

Too much to refuse, two-hundred-and-fifty grand was; only, Daniel would use that against him forever now.

'You were never supposed to fucking shoot him, Daniel. You were supposed to take the money and fucking run. That was the deal. You said that you were just blackmailing him. You didn't say fuck all to me about murder. You did that. Alone.'

'But you were there, Jack. You saw it all. Yet you didn't fucking do anything about it, did you?'

Jack couldn't argue with that. It was true. He'd been so shocked at first. Watching as his friend had fallen to the ground. The blood pouring out of him, as he lay on the cold wet dockyard.

It all happened so quickly.

Daniel and Marlon racing out of there with the money. Leaving Jack crouching in the back of Jimmy's car. That had been the worst part about it all. How Jimmy had asked him to keep watch, as backup. But Jack had known the plan all along.

Daniel had told him it was foolproof. That it was only ever about the money. Jack never wanted his friend to get killed in the process. But once Jimmy had been announced dead, what else could he do? The damage had already been done.

They had the money.

Daniel's little plan to blackmail his old man had completely gone tits up, but no amount of regret or remorse would bring Jimmy back.

Jack only had two options after that.

Tell the truth about what happened and risk losing everything. His career as a DI. All those years of climbing the corporate ladder, for what? To lose it all now over Daniel Byrne's stupid bloody plan?

Or he could keep his mouth shut and say nothing.

Then, at least, in some ways, Jimmy's death wouldn't have been completely in vain.

Jack had walked away with quarter of a million.

Blood money.

He'd let his greed get the better of him, and he would now forever be at Daniel Byrne's mercy because of it.

'What about my sister, Jack? What do you reckon she will say when I tell her why you've really been following her about? That you got rid of any evidence that had been left at the dockyard that night. That you tried to get rid of the laptop, too, only you couldn't even do that, could you?' Daniel was in his element now. Putting Jack Taylor firmly in his place. The man was going to make tonight right no matter what. 'I wonder what Nancy will say when she finds out that you paid one of your dodgy fucking informants to follow her on the night of our father's funeral? That you arranged for her to be scared off. How did you word it again? Oh that's it, you were going to shake her up a bit. Threaten her to steer clear of making any more enquires. Only, you shit her right up, didn't you?' Daniel was really laughing now. This was the best bit of all. Jack Taylor had made a fucking holy show of his sister, yet Nancy had no fucking idea. Even now she was being played. Confiding in Jack, thinking that he was her confidant, when he was reporting back to Daniel all along.

For a girl who liked to think she was so smart, she really was completely clueless.

'Stupid cow thinks you're her knight in shining armour right about now, doesn't she? She's got no clue that the only reason you've been following her around like a bad fucking smell lately is because you've been making sure she isn't on to us. On to you!'

'You really are a piece of work,' Jack said through gritted teeth. Thinking of tonight with Nancy. How they'd made love. He knew she thought it was a mistake, and shit, perhaps it was, but something had changed tonight.

Jack had really felt something for Nancy, and he truly believed that she felt it too.

'You're in this with me, Jack, and don't you fucking forget it, mate.' Daniel grinned, knowing full well that no matter what happened with Alfie Harris tonight, Jack Taylor would have to make it right now. He had no choice. 'So you go in that club and you fucking sort this. You make sure that some other fucker gets landed with the blame for all this. I don't give a fuck who!' Daniel said now, his voice calm once more. 'In fact. Stick it on that twat Jenson Reed. The bloke's a fucking bellend anyway. It would have been him that gave the shit to the girl. Let him take the fucking fallout for it. Do whatever the fuck you have to, Jack, but do not let my name get dragged into this, because, if it does, I'm going to drag you down with me.' With that Daniel Byrne hung up the phone, his confidence that the situation was resolved to his satisfaction fully restored.

Jack Taylor would be a fool to go against him now.

CHAPTER THIRTY

'I didn't hear you come in!' Walking into his lounge, Sam Miles rubbed at his eyes and glanced over to the clock, pretending that he was still half asleep and that he hadn't been pacing the floor waiting up for Daniel to come home from another one of his drunken benders. Sam knew how much Daniel was getting pissed off with him constantly checking up on him, and asking questions, only he couldn't seem to help himself.

He'd never felt like this about anyone before.

They'd only been seeing each other for a few months. It had been casual, at first, but Daniel had quickly become intense. Wanting to be with Sam twenty-four-seven. Wanting to talk for hours, to go out and get pissed together. To fuck.

Sam had found it flattering, at first.

They'd both attended the same private school, and couldn't have been more opposite if they'd tried. Sam was the quiet one. The smart one. Top of the class with all his grades, he never imagined Daniel would even look twice at him, though somehow Daniel had.

Sam couldn't believe his luck.

A man like Daniel Byrne. So dark and mysterious, it set him on edge. Sam knew about the kind of family that Daniel came from. Everyone at the school had heard of the notorious Byrne family and, as much as his common sense had told him to steer clear, not to get involved, he'd quickly fallen hard for the man. Daniel had become like a drug to him.

But recently, their relationship had taken a rapid decline. Daniel had become really detached, not just from him, from everyone. Drinking all day long, suffering from acute bouts of anger and depression, the next minute full of excitement and wild ideas. They'd stopped spending any real time together, Daniel preferring to go out on his own, late at night. He no longer stayed over as often either, and when he did decide that he wanted to stay at Sam's flat, he didn't get here until the early hours of the morning. Even then he'd turn up half-cut and in a foul mood.

He never seemed to have any straight answers about his whereabouts either. If Sam asked him where he'd been or what he'd been up to, Daniel lost his shit, accusing Sam of trying to control him, of keeping tabs on him.

So instead, Sam just had to mind his own business, trying his absolute best to be patient with Daniel. Though no matter what he did it seemed he couldn't ever win, and it was getting harder and harder to try and ignore his boyfriend's erratic behaviour. The more Daniel acted as if he wasn't into him anymore, the more Sam Miles had started behaving like some paranoid bunny boiler of a boyfriend.

'Hey, are you all right, Daniel?' Sam said, seeing him sitting there in silence, staring at the floor as if he was in some sort of a trance.

Daniel's father's death had affected him much worse than he'd been letting on. To his family, to Sam. To himself even. The truth was, it was eating away at the man. Sam knew that Daniel didn't know how to deal with his emotions, not properly. So instead he'd started shutting himself off from people. Putting up a guard and not letting anyone in. Sam included.

Only, it was starting to drive a huge wedge between them both and Sam had had enough.

'Daniel, please. Talk to me?'

Looking at Daniel now, slumped on the sofa, the stench of drink that filled the room, knowing full well that even drunk as he was, Daniel wouldn't tell him shit about where he'd been tonight, Sam couldn't help himself. 'Who was that you were just talking to on the phone?' he said, his curiosity getting the better of him.

He'd been intending on playing it cool tonight. Not letting Daniel know that he'd had his ear pressed up against the bedroom door, as he tried his hardest to listen in to the heated conversation he'd been having. But Sam hadn't been able to catch much of the conversation. He'd only managed to hear a snippet here and there about Daniel's dad. Then Daniel had started raising his voice.

He was starting to wonder if Daniel was cheating on him. All these late nights out on his own. The whispered phone calls. Even now, overhearing Daniel on the phone, Sam had decided to go out and see if he was okay, but the conversation had quickly ended, and Daniel had flung the phone down on the chair beside him.

'It was no one. Mind your business,' he said then. Not bothering to look up. He wasn't in the mood for Sam and his constant fucking whining and insecurities tonight.

But Sam wasn't just going to let up.

'For fuck sake, Daniel, why can't you just tell me who it was?'

Walking towards him the first thing Sam clocked was the red stains on Daniel's knuckles. The spray of blood all up his clothes. That's when he realised things were far from okay.

'Fuck! What's happened to you? Are you okay?' he said as he neared, bending down and trying to take Daniel's hand; the panic evident in his voice now as he wondered what the fuck had happened. 'Shit. Have you been attacked? Shall I call the police?

Daniel waved him off. Up on his feet, not wanting any fuss, he shook his head, irritated. 'I'm fine. Stop with the fucking dramatics. What's with the twenty fucking questions, Sam? I don't need it right now. Do me a favour and shut the fuck up, will you!' Getting up from the chair. Away from Sam and his puppy-dog fucking eyes, Daniel paced the lounge, running his fingers through his hair. Clearly agitated.

Backing off, Sam nodded, sensing the volatile mood that Daniel was in, and knowing that he'd clearly had a skinful of drink too. He'd learned by now not to push the man. Something had happened tonight. Something bad and if he was going to find out what it was, then he was going to have to try a different tack.

'I'm just worried about you, Daniel. It's late. You've come home covered in fucking blood. Someone else's blood?' he realised then, noting that Daniel wasn't visibly cut. Confused, scared he added: 'Have you hurt someone?'

Daniel closed his eyes and took a slow deep breath. As much as Sam meant well, the bloke was starting to do his head in. He told Sam that he wanted to stay here tonight in order to get away from his overbearing family. From his stuck-up bitch of a sister. Only, now it seemed that Sam was on his case too. Probing him about every little thing he said and did. All Daniel wanted was a bit of fucking space. For Sam to shut the fuck up and leave him alone so he could sort his fucking head out. But Sam was like a dog with a bone when he had something on his mind, he just couldn't leave it be. Daniel knew he had to give him something. Anything.

So he lied.

'Look, I got mugged, okay. Some bloke jumped me on the way back from a bar, though he wasn't counting on me beating the crap out of him. I gave him a proper hiding, so calling the police wouldn't be the best move in the world. Just leave it, yeah?' Daniel said then, flashing a warning to Sam that told him the conversation was over. 'I'm going to go and get a shower and get

out of these things. Wash all the bloke's fucking claret off me. I'm
fine, okay. Stop worrying about me. Jesus. I'm a big boy, Sam. I
can look after myself, you know.'

Sam nodded, watching as Daniel chucked his jacket down on
the chair before staggering out of the room.

He waited…

For the sound of the running water as Daniel stepped into
the shower. Giving it a couple more minutes until he knew the
coast was clear, before he started riffling through Daniel's jacket
pockets. Unsure what he was looking for, but knowing that he
was looking for something. The only thing that he did know right
now was that he was starting not to trust Daniel. All these nights
of him going off out on his own. Late at night. Drunk. He must
have been going somewhere? With someone?

The question was, with who?

Pulling out a handful of receipts, he started scanning through
them, doing his best to piece together Daniel Byrne's night. Seeing
if his suspicions were founded. But he didn't find anything that
incriminated Daniel. A receipt from a place called Joop's earlier
this evening. Hours ago now, where he'd only bought one drink.

Out alone?

Sam wasn't convinced.

Still, he knew that he wasn't going to get any other information
from Daniel tonight. The man was like a closed book.

Shoving the papers back inside the jacket, he remembered a
little saying that his mother would often use when he'd had these
kinds of problems in his last relationship. When his boyfriends
had cheated on him in the past, and Sam had gone snooping down
their things looking for any incriminating evidence against them.

If you go looking for trouble, then you'll probably find it.

Only Sam Miles had no idea how much trouble he was about
to find himself in.

CHAPTER THIRTY-ONE

'It's all right, Sherrie, you're not in any trouble. I just want to know what happened, okay?' Alfie Harris said as he handed the young barmaid a tissue so that she could dry her puffy eyes, before eyeing the clock, and hoping that this wasn't going to take him too long. He didn't want to be away from the hospital any longer than he needed, but he knew that if he didn't deal with the situation immediately, he might not get the chance. He needed to find the culprit that dished out drugs to his daughter tonight, before they did something stupid, like fucking leg it.

He'd left Jennifer back at the hospital. She'd said she'd phone him if there was any change in Megan's condition, but the nurse had assured him that Megan would remain sedated for the rest of the night. He'd been going stir crazy just sitting at her bedside watching her.

Alfie Harris needed to get to the bottom of what the fuck had gone on. He couldn't just sit around, rendered useless. He needed to find the fucker that fed his daughter Ecstasy.

So far, though, Sherrie Murphy hadn't been much use. She was in a right old state. Sitting on the sofa in his office, bawling her eyes out.

Alfie knew he had to try a more gentle tack.

'You just tell me what you told Gem, okay darling…'

Sherrie glanced over at Gem, who nodded at her for encouragement as he sat perched on the edge of Alfie's desk. His arms folded across his chest.

It was almost 4 a.m. now, the Old Bill had cleared the club out early and Gem had been lumbered babysitting this blubbering wreck for the past two hours. He just wanted her to hurry the fuck up and tell Alfie what he wanted to hear so they could all go home, though he had an inkling that once Sherrie had told him everything she knew, home wouldn't be the place they'd be heading for.

'I wasn't sure it was them at first. Reece kept calling one of the girls Olivia. But I was sure that it was Amber and Megan he was with. But they were both really dressed up. Nice like. Though they both had way too much make-up on them. I could see Meg's blue eyeshadow from all the way over at the bar,' Sherrie said, trying to remember every last detail, just as Alfie Harris had told her. 'Reece and his mates were messing about, you know? Saying shit about the girls. I didn't hear it all, but I knew that they were taking the piss out of them. That they were planning on doing something—'

'Like what?' Alfie said, his jaw clenched, as he pursed his mouth. Trying to restrain himself from really losing his temper. 'What were they planning on doing, Sherrie?'

Sherrie looked embarrassed; looking to Gem again for some moral support, he nodded once more.

'I thought they were just joking around. You know how men can be when they're all together. They were saying that one of the girls – Olivia – was frigid. That she needed a bit of help loosening up. That he had just the thing to sort her out.' Sherrie started crying again then. Trying her hardest to explain, though even she knew how pathetic she sounded, wracked with guilt for not doing or saying anything earlier when she'd had the chance. 'Reece is forever chatting shit, and trying to make himself sound hard in front of his mates. He started talking about having loads of Es on him. Then they all started laughing. Is that what Reece spiked Megan's drink with, was it Ecstasy?' Sherrie said, staring up at her boss with wide eyes.

She could see by the look in his eyes that he wasn't best pleased with her, and after the state she'd just seen Megan in, Sherrie felt awful.

'He kept calling her Olivia, Mr Harris. That's why I didn't realise they were talking about Megan. If I had, I would have said something, I swear!'

'But you didn't.' Alfie was pacing the room. His stomach twisted in knots as he tried to contain the rage that was building up inside. He knew it. His Megan wouldn't have touched drugs. She wasn't that stupid. He'd been right all along.

Some little cunt had spiked his baby girl's drink.

Clenching his fists tightly, he wanted to smack Sherrie in the face for being so stupid not to speak up and tell someone what she'd heard. For letting whoever this fucking Reece was get away with this shit.

But Alfie had never hit a woman in his life, and he wasn't about to start now.

Deciding he'd take his anger out on this cunt Reece when he caught up with him instead, besides he needed to keep Sherrie sweet for now, and get every last bit of information he could from the girl.

'And it wasn't all talk, was it?' he spat.

Sherrie shook her head.

'I saw them all going to the staff toilets a little while later. I was busy serving drinks, but it must have been about fifteen minutes later when I saw the three of them coming out of there. They couldn't get out of here quickly enough—'

'The *three of them*?' Alfie said questioningly.

'Yeah, Amber, Reece and Jenson.'

'Jenson? The doorman? He was there too?'

The plot thickened.

What the fuck was Jenson Reed doing hanging out with Megan and Amber? The bloke was at least twice their fucking age. That must have been how the girls had got in to the club. If that prick on the door was involved in this as well, then Jenson Reed was in for a nasty shock too.

Sherrie nodded, knowing that Mr Harris wasn't going to appreciate the next snippet of information that she gave him.

'Jenson and Megan were all over each other. I think that's why they went down to the toilets together. Some of the staff do that, you see. They nip down to the loos to… be alone with each other or a punter that they've pulled.'

Sherrie let Mr Harris join up the dots. His staff toilets were used as a regular knocking shop.

Alfie bowed his head. Cradling it in his hands, feeling physically sick as he thought about his daughter being taken down there by one of his own doormen. One of the fuckers that Jimmy Byrne and Alex Costa had put here in place, as a fucking dealer.

On the one hand, he wanted Sherrie to keep talking, to tell him everything, on the other hand, he wasn't sure that he could stomach hearing the truth of tonight's events. His baby girl in some grotty toilet cubical with a man twice her age. Just the thought of it made his blood boil. He could feel the vein in the side of his temple pulsating. His jaw clenched shut.

Realising that Sherrie had stopped talking. That the girl felt just as uncomfortable as he was now, Alfie plastered on a fake smile, egging her to continue.

Sherrie took her cue.

'When Megan didn't come out, I thought I'd better check on her. You know, see if she was okay. But she wasn't okay. She was lying on the bathroom floor. She'd been sick everywhere and she was having some kind of a fit. So I called an ambulance and then I stayed with her until they came. I told them everything I knew.

They said that it would help if they knew what she had taken. I told them about the Es, but I wasn't really sure what she'd taken. I wish I could have been more helpful. I wish I could have stopped it.' Sobbing uncontrollably, Sherrie was clearly traumatised by the night's events. 'She looked so awful, Mr Harris. She will be all right, won't she?'

'Let's hope so,' Alfie said, his voice almost a whisper, fighting the rage that was building inside.

'I feel as if I'm partly responsible. That if I'd told someone what Reece had planned to do, I could have stopped it. Maybe Megan would have been okay?'

Only you fucking didn't, did you?! he thought angrily.

Though somehow he managed to contain his temper.

'You did good, Sherrie. Staying with her until the paramedics came. You looked after my girl.' The lie rolling so easily from his lips. As angry as he was with Sherrie right now, the girl's only real crime was that she was as naive as fuck. And Alfie needed her to keep talking. He needed to find out exactly where to find Reece and Jenson.

'What about Amber? How did she seem when you last saw her?' he asked, hoping that his daughter's friend hadn't just abandoned Megan when the girl had needed her most. Worrying that she might be in some form of trouble too.

Sherrie shrugged her shoulders. 'I didn't really get a good look, to be honest. They couldn't get out of the place quick enough. The three of them practically legged it.'

Alfie nodded once more. Disgusted with the realisation that Amber had purposely left Megan in that state, knowing how bad she was.

He took a deep breath.

'You want to go home?' he asked, his voice kind. Kinder than he actually felt.

Sherrie nodded.

She was exhausted. The drama of the night had caught up with her, and she'd cried enough tears for England. Home was exactly where she wanted to be right now. In her bed, away from all this.

'Then there's just one thing that I need from you, Sherrie, okay? One thing, then you can go, okay?' Alfie stared Sherrie dead in the eye. 'Do you know where I can find Reece and Jenson? Do you know where they might be?'

There were a few seconds' silence while Alfie prayed that the girl did know. He wanted to get this mess sorted out immediately, then he could get his arse back up the hospital and be with his Megs.

Wiping her snotty tears on the sleeve of her top, Sherrie nodded. 'Reece lives over in a flat in Drayton Gardens, just behind Camden Lock. Flat 15. Jenson rents a room off him.'

Alfie raised his eye, wondering how Sherrie would know the bloke's exact address.

She blushed. Looking embarrassed.

'I went back there a few times, a couple of weeks ago. Like I said before, Reece doesn't really take no for an answer.'

Alfie bit his lip. He hadn't even set eyes on this Reece before, and already he wanted to brain the cunt. Pressurising young girls. Spiking their drinks. Sherrie wasn't much older than Megan. Maybe a couple of years. Old enough to work the bar, but too young to be hanging around with the likes of Reece and Jenson by the sounds of it.

Still, he'd thought that about his Megan too.

How his little princess wouldn't be seen dead knocking about with no-marks like that, but he'd been wrong then too. All these years of keeping his Megan wrapped up in cotton wool, and it hadn't made one bit of difference. Trouble had still found her, and of the very worst kind. Maybe that was it? Maybe Alfie had been too overprotective. By constantly looming over his Megs like a shadow, he hadn't taught her how to stand on her own two feet. How to use her own judgement when it came to trusting people.

He'd worked so hard to stay straight these past few months, he'd even managed to surprise himself at how determined he was to change once he put his mind to it. He'd gone on the straight and narrow for his daughter's sake ultimately, not wanting to subject her to this lifestyle any longer than he already had.

It was ironic, then, that his daughter had just become the one reason that he was allowing himself to be pulled back into his former violent ways.

He was going to cause murders for this.

Alfie had heard enough. On his feet then. Desperate to get over to the flat before these fuckers Reece and Jenson did something stupid like a fucking runner and went AWOL, he nodded to the young girl.

'Get your coat and bag and we'll drop you home.'

Sherrie stood, feeling awkward, unsure whether or not to say anything. Her impulse got the better of her. 'I haven't been paid yet,' she said, her voice small. Knowing full well that she was pushing her luck. 'For tonight. I haven't been given my wages.'

Alfie shook his head at the girl's blatant audacity.

'Are you having a fucking bubble?' he said, looking at Gem for some clarity, disbelief written all over the man's face. 'You still think you're getting paid for tonight? Not a fucking chance. You're not working here anymore, Sherrie. You're done.'

'But I thought that if I answered all your questions… and I did help look after Megan. I called the ambulance. I stayed with her until the paramedics turned up. I thought you said that I'd done good?'

'You looked after her?' Alfie laughed then, though his humour didn't meet his eyes. 'Sherrie, you let some piece of shit slip something in my daughter's fucking drink. You knew what that scumbag was planning on doing. That makes you as bad as him in my book. But, lucky for you, that prick Reece will be taking the fallout for this. Him and Jenson and, trust me, they are going to fucking pay mercifully for what they have done to my daughter. Now, I won't ask you again. Get your coat and bag, like a good girl, and get the fuck out of here before I change my mind, and do something that I'll really regret.'

Hearing the threat in her boss's voice loud and clear, Sherrie nodded. She'd tried her hardest to put things right tonight, to look after Megan, and tell Mr Harris everything she knew. That's why she was walking away with minimal reprisals, she thought, she'd done as she was told.

She followed Gem Kemal and Alfie Harris out to the club's main doors. Though at least she was walking away unscathed, she thought, unlike Reece Bettle and Jenson Reed would be. Those two weren't going to be as lucky. By the look on Alfie Harris's face, the man was on the warpath, and Reece Bettle and Jenson Reed were two dead men walking.

CHAPTER THIRTY-TWO

Standing outside the dingy-looking flat in Camden, Alfie Harris stared up at the plaque on the wall.

DRAYTON GARDENS.

Nodding, he indicated to Gem that this was indeed the place that they were looking for. A shitty little council estate located just behind Camden Lock. This was the place that they were going to find the fucking scrotes that had put his Megan in hospital. That's if the two fuckers hadn't already upped and legged it.

He stepped back so that Gem could get to work at picking the locks of the main entrance door, but Gem turned and grinned at him.

'The lock's already been dismantled. Hacked at with a hammer or a crowbar most probably. Some little skank's gone and saved us a job!'

Gem pushed the door wide open with ease, before the two men slipped inside, making their way along the dark, pokey hallway and up a few flights of concrete steps. The dingy entrance was in keeping with the rest of this shithole. The place stunk too. Both Alfie and Gem making a point to hold their breaths as they climbed to the third floor, trying to minimalise the stench of rotten stinking nappies and piss at their feet. The place strewn with rubbish. Talk about a dump, the residents here clearly hadn't learned one of life's most fundamental rules: you never shit on your own doorstep.

Whatever happened to people treating their homes as their castle? Alfie thought with disgust, turning his nose up at the squalor that these people chose to live in. The fact that it was a poverty-stricken area, and these people clearly didn't have so much as two sticks to rub together didn't mean that they had to live like fucking animals surely? It didn't cost anything to have a bit of pride and stay clean!

Stepping over empty beer cans and discarded needles, he thought this place was the pits of the fucking earth, but it was nothing in comparison to the pure hell that he was going to send the two fuckers that they were paying a visit to.

Approaching the flat, Alfie pointed to the door up ahead. Flat 15, Sherrie had said. That was the one.

He put his finger to his lips, both of them listening to the thudding music that came from inside. The fuckers were home, and clearly still wide awake.

Though there was nothing like catching them with the element of surprise. By the time Alfie and Gem had smashed their way in, it would be too late for the scumbags inside to even think about tooling themselves up, or running away.

There would be nowhere for them to go.

Gem nodded down to the bottom panel of the front door that had been boarded up, as if someone had previously given it a kicking.

'Well, this makes it a bit easier, doesn't it? Fucking thing's probably hanging off its hinges already,' he said, keeping his voice low. Stepping back, he waited for Alfie's word so that he could put his foot through the thing.

Taking a second to prepare himself mentally for the onslaught that was about to follow, Alfie Harris knew that once they got inside, there would be no coming back from this.

Tonight, blood would be spilt.

Gripping the metal baseball bat tightly in his grasp, he thought about his poor Megs lying in that hospital bed. How the nurse had told him that even if she recovered now, which was looking highly unlikely, the chances were that she'd live out the rest of her days as a vegetable.

His little girl.

Not being able to feed herself, or wipe her own arse. Confined to a fucking wheelchair and needing around-the-clock care. All because some fucking scrote thought that it was okay to fucking mess with her.

Scrutinising the rest of the flats nearby, Alfie checked that there weren't any curtain twitchers doing their rounds. Though he seriously doubted that any fucker would be up at this time in the morning anyway.

It was almost 5 a.m. now.

Being Sunday morning, it was highly unlikely that any alarm clocks were about to go off and mark the start of an honest day's work. In fact, around here Alfie suspected that this was the case most days. None of the residents on this shitty council estate would know a thing about dragging their arses out of bed before midday around here, he guessed, no matter what day of the week it was. Personally he didn't give a shit about the neighbours seeing or hearing anything they shouldn't tonight. If the fuckers knew what was good for them, they'd turn a blind eye, or Alfie would pay them a visit too.

Still he glared at their windows all the same. Then, nodding at Gem, Alfie Harris gave the order.

Let the reprisals commence.

Booting the front door with his huge size 12 boots, Gem kicked the shit out of it. Sending long splintered spears of wood shooting across the hallway. The door smashed to pieces in just seconds. Just a slither of wood left, hanging limply off its rickety hinges.

They were in.

Storming into the first room ahead of them, straight into the lounge. Slamming that door off its hinges, too, as they burst into the room, screaming and bellowing loudly, holding the metal baseball bats over their heads. Catching a group of three lads off guard: the boys all sitting around the lounge smoking weed and playing on the Xbox. The room was dingy. The curtains drawn; the only light in the room was from the glare off the telly.

'Who the fuck are you?' one of them shouted with feigned bravado, as the group of lads all jumped to their feet. Shitting themselves, as the two madmen stood there holding the bats high above their heads, clearly not afraid to use them if they had to. Half wishing that it had been the Old Bill busting in here to raid the place now that they were faced with these two nutters.

'No, son, the question isn't who the fuck are we. It's who the fuck you are? Which one of you cunts is Reece?' Alfie bellowed, glaring through the smokey haze, seeking out the man. These lads were barely even adults. Seventeen, eighteen years old tops? Wrinkling his nose, the room stank of weed. These kids must be as high as fucking proverbial kites.

'Who's asking?' the boy said, shouting back. Clearly trying to buy his mate some more time. To warn him that there were people here looking for him.

'You stupid fuck!' Gem said, cracking the bat down over the kid's head, and knocking him out, sparko onto the lounge floor. The other two lads were rendered silent then.

In fear of their lives.

And so they should be, Alfie thought, with the mood he was in.

'Where is he?' he said, directing his question at the shortest lad in the room.

Taking one look at his mate sprawled out on the floor, passed out, a trickle of blood dripping down from his ear, he wasn't a grass, but he didn't fancy getting his head caved in either. He pointed.

'He's in the back bedroom. With his bird. They're in bed.'

'Right then, off you both fuck. Take fucking sleeping beauty here with you,' Alfie said, ordering the boys out of the flat, along with their now unconscious mate, before nodding at Gem to follow him through to the bedroom.

'You take that one. I'll do this one,' Alfie said as the two men simultaneously kicked in the two bedroom doors. Slamming them hard against the walls behind them.

A shrill scream filled the room then, which was when Alfie spotted Amber. Naked in the bed, with the duvet cover pulled up around her. Next to her, he assumed, was the infamous Reece.

The shock on his face clear to see.

Though, right now, just the sight of the pair of them made Alfie Harris's blood boil. In fucking bed with each other, while his girl was in a fucking coma in hospital.

This just got better and better.

'Get your clothes on. Now,' he bellowed. Pointing his finger, he could barely look at Amber. 'And you, you fucking piece of shit. Do you know who I fucking am?' he shouted, striding to the other side of the bed where Reece was and grabbing the fucker by his throat. Forcing him up against the headboard behind him.

It was all Alfie could do not to throttle the fucking life out of the filthy little scrote right there and then. But he didn't intend to make Reece Bettle's punishment quick, or painless.

'Is this what the two of you have been doing, is it? Shagging? While my Megan is fighting for her life in hospital, strapped up to a fucking life support machine?' Alfie shook his head now. 'You both fucking disgust me.'

Then turning back to Amber, as the girl quickly pulled some clothes on, Alfie spat: 'You haven't even asked me how she is, Amber. She could have fucking died. Fuck! She probably still will,' the emotion thick in Alfie's throat as he spoke the words aloud for the first time.

'But Reece said that she would be okay. That she just had a bad reaction. He said she'd probably be in overnight…'

Amber started crying again, realising that Reece had just told her what she'd wanted to hear. That he'd duped her into getting into bed with him, all the while her friend had been fighting for her life. 'I'm so sorry, Mr Harris, I didn't realise…' But deep down, Amber knew that Megan hadn't been all right. She'd just been kidding herself and now, faced with Alfie Harris at the foot of her bed, she looked riddled with guilt about everything.

So she fucking well should be, Alfie thought.

'A bad reaction? She's in a fucking coma. Who needs fucking enemies, eh? With mates like you. Leaving her on a fucking toilet floor. Go on, get your clothes and fuck off out of here. NOW!' he bellowed.

Hysterical then, knowing that she had severely fucked up, that she should never have listened to Reece in the first place, Amber did as she was told. Scrambling to her feet, trying to hide her modesty as she kept the duvet over her body and slipped her dress over her head, she picked up her shoes from the floor.

'And you, you piece of shit. I asked you a question. Do you know who I am?'

Reece nodded. Everyone knew who Alfie Harris was. He was one big, bad bastard. Or at least he had been back in his day. He watched Amber as she fled the room without even giving him so much as a second glance. Too busy saving her own arse now.

Selfish bitch!

This was all her fault.

It wasn't until it had been too late tonight, until Megan had already OD'd, that Amber had finally told him and Jenson the truth about who 'Olivia' really was: Megan Harris – the daughter of the notorious Alfie Harris. Reece couldn't fucking believe it. No wonder the girls had pulled a fast one and lied about Megan's name when they'd both tried to sneak into the club on

Alfie Harris's night off. The girl had seemed far too stuck-up and straight-laced to have a legend of a father like the owner of The Karma Club.

Everyone knew Alfie Harris. The man had been a bona fide nutter in his younger days. One of the hardest bastards in London. Rumour had it he'd worked for the Kray twins. Though Reece was never really sure, as most geezers over fifty claimed to have worked for the infamous brothers at one time or another.

Who the fuck knew?

All Reece did know was that he was the one that had spiked Alfie's daughter's drink and now the mad bastard was standing next to his bed with a nasty gleam in his eyes. One hand wrapped firmly around Reece's throat, the other wielding a metal baseball bat. Which meant he was well and truly up shit creek now, without a fucking paddle. He'd fucked the girl up, big time. Though he couldn't help but wonder how Alfie had found out so quickly that it had been him. Jenson had told him not to worry, that Alfie would never find out it was him who gave her the gear. But Jenson had been wrong about that.

Alfie Harris had found out, and only within a couple of hours of it happening too. The man must be as shrewd as fuck.

There was nothing Reece could do now other than beg for forgiveness. Though, to be fair, the pure hate and venom that radiated from the man in front of him didn't give him much hope that Alfie Harris was the forgiving type.

'I'm really sorry, mate. I had no idea that she was your daughter. Honest to God,' Reece said, sounding pathetic even to his own ears.

'Who gave you the gear?'

Reece shook his head. He'd always taken pride in not being a grass, but he also valued his life. Alfie Harris was after blood tonight, and he knew if he didn't come clean and tell him what he wanted to hear, it would his blood that got spilt over this.

'Did you smuggle the shit into my club, or were you sold it by someone? Fucking tell me now.'

The bat struck Reece's shin with an almighty blow. Cracking the bone on impact.

Reece screamed, praying that he hadn't just pissed himself; he'd never live it down if he had.

Alfie held the bat up above the man once more.

'Now you've got one more chance to tell it to me straight. Who sold you the gear?'

It was Jenson. Alfie was sure of it. But he wanted to hear it from this fucker's mouth directly. He wanted Reece to say the man's name.

And he did.

'Jenson gave it to me. He said that he had some new gear. That he was trialling it out. That it was good shit, the best. I didn't fucking know that this would happen. I swear to God, I would never have dished that shit out if I'd known your daughter was going to react that way.'

Gem was back in the room then too. Marching Jenson into the room with his hand on the back of his neck, his own baseball bat digging into the side of Jenson's head.

'Oh, perfect timing!' Alfie said, staring the man up and down as if he'd just wiped the fucker off the bottom of his boot. This was the man that had taken his daughter into his staff toilets.

His blood was boiling once more.

'We were just speaking about you, Jenson. Well, Reece was. I'll deal with you, you cunt, in a minute,' Alfie said before turning back to Reece and repeatedly bringing the bat down on his legs. 'You put that fucking poison in my daughter's drink. You fucking piece of scum.'

Ignoring Reece's pathetic screams for mercy, Alfie Harris took his time in shattering the man's kneecaps and legs until they were just two bloody limp pulps at the end of his body.

When Reece finally passed out from the pain, Alfie lowered his bat.

Then he looked at Jenson. This fucker was getting way worse than that.

Jenson knew it too.

Seeing his mate being beaten within an inch of his life, Jenson quickly weighed up his options. Which weren't fucking many. He could stay here and get the same treatment, only much fucking worse, he expected. Or, he could try and make a run for it. Only, with Gem standing so close behind him, the only way out of here was the bedroom's balcony.

Fuck it, Jenson thought, it had to be worth a shot.

Running to the glass doors and yanking them open – a cold rush of air hitting him as he managed to get his leg up on the concrete wall, ready to swing himself over. But his only hope of a getaway was quickly diminished as Alfie Harris leapt on him – was on him in seconds. Grabbing at Jenson swiftly by the fucker's throat, he yanked the man back down, holding him tightly before peering over the balcony himself.

'And where the fuck do you think you're going?' he snarled. 'We're three flights up and that's a long fucking way down.' Alfie whistled, guessing, rightly, Jenson's plan was to try and swing himself into the lower balcony beneath him.

That's how desperate he was to get away from him.

Glad that he was more than aware of the danger he now faced, Alfie grinned to himself. Hoisting Jenson backwards so the man's back was arched over the balcony wall, his feet both dangling off the ground.

'I want to know what the fuck you were doing selling Ecstasy in my club?' Alfie said, leaning in so close that his face was practically pressing against Jenson's now.

The man was forcing his head backwards, away from his attacker.

'I was told it was legit. That we were changing our suppliers,' he said. 'I just did what I was told. I was following orders.'

'Bullshit,' Alfie shouted. 'Did you know anything about this, Gem? Any rumours about cutting out our main suppliers?'

'First I've heard of it,' Gem said shaking his head. 'No one ran that past me.'

Alfie turned back to Jenson.

'Gem is the head of fucking security. Don't you think that if you were changing supplier, he'd know all about it? You better stop with the crap and start being straight with me, Jenson; otherwise, I'm going to help you make your way out via the balcony that you seem so keen to fucking escape down. Only, it might get a bit fucking messy. You know, when your head fucking explodes as you hit the concrete. Cracking your skull open like a fucking Kinder Egg. Brains and claret everywhere.'

Jenson shook his head. Left with no doubt in his mind that the man in front of him was perfectly capable of killing him tonight. Especially if what he said was true and Megan Harris really was on a life support machine. The man wouldn't have anything to lose.

Fuck risking his life to save some other man's back. Daniel Byrne was on his own.

'It was Daniel Byrne. He said that he was taking over from his father and that the club would be branching out. You know, selling pills and shit. He said it was supply and demand. I've been saying for ages that the demand for this shit was huge, but I wouldn't just take it upon myself to bring it into the club. Daniel Byrne set it all up, and he told me to keep it on the down low. Not say shit to anyone about it. I thought that Gem must have known.'

Feeling Alfie pushing him further over the balcony's edge, his back curving awkwardly as he dug his nails into the wall hoping to grip onto something as the birds continued to fly obliviously above him, chirping loudly.

It was dawn now, and light outside.

People would be waking up soon.

Jenson really didn't want to die.

'He wanted to trial it out, see how much money we made from it all. Ecstasy, Special K and GBH. That sort of shit. It's what everyone's doing these days on the clubbing scene, so I didn't even question it. I just assumed that Gem was in on it too.' Jenson was mumbling now. Frightened for his life as he glanced over to where Reece was sprawled out on the bed. The bloke would no doubt never walk again. 'I swear down, Mr Harris, I had no idea that Reece was going to stick a pill in some young girl's drink. By the time I found out, he'd already done it… it had fuck all to do with me.'

Alfie had heard enough.

'You "swear down"?' he roared. 'And what happened then, huh? When you found out she was off her fucking head? Then what did you do? 'Cause I heard you took my daughter to some grotty fucking toilet cubicle. Is that how you get off, is it? Trying to sleep with girls young enough to be your daughter? 'Cause let me tell you now, if your cock went anywhere near my daughter I'll slice it off and take great pleasure in forcing you to eat it!' Alfie could barely breathe now. His face puce with rage, his heart thudding loudly in his chest.

Never in all his days had he felt so fit to murder someone as he did with these two tonight. These two fuckers had ruined his daughter's life. They'd snatched it away from her without so much as a second thought. Thoughtless, selfish scumbags. There wasn't anything that the bloke could say to redeem himself now. The damage had been done and it was irreversible.

Jenson could see it in the man's eyes. The finality that flashed there. The lengths this man would go to avenge his daughter's hurt tonight.

'See him? He's going to live out the rest of his days in a fucking wheelchair for what he's done. He don't know it yet, but every now and then I'm going to turn up and surprise him. Remind him of what he did. Make him spend his life fearing the fuck out of getting one of his regular visits from me,' Alfie said now. Decided. 'You, on the other hand, ain't worth shit to me. Daniel Byrne might have come to you and told you to sell the gear, but you don't work for that fucking bloke. You work for Gem. And Gem works for me. You take orders only from us.'

Jenson nodded. Realising his fatal error too late.

'I get that now, boss. Honest I do. Daniel made out as if he'd squared it with Gem. I thought it was legit. A direct order—'

'But it wasn't. You fucked up, and now my little girl will be lucky if she ever sees the light of day again,' Alfie said sadly. The need to get back to the hospital as soon as he could washing over him in waves now, so angered by these two bastards. So useless at the hospital, just sitting there watching his daughter only breathing with the help of machinery, he'd had to come here tonight and sort this out once and for all. He couldn't just leave Jennifer up there on her tod. As much as he needed to sort these two scrotes out, he needed to get back to his Megan more.

His anger subsiding then, Alfie gained a bit of clarity. Back by his daughter's side where he belonged. Not here wasting his breath with this piece of scum, he finally realised.

With that Alfie Harris gave Jenson Reed one last almighty shove, enjoying seeing the flicker of realisation at what he had just done. The imminent fear plastered on Jenson's face as he fell backwards. The panic as he tried to latch on to the very man who had pushed him, as his fingertips brushed against the concrete balcony wall.

Screaming loudly as he fell to his death, he landed with a dull thud on the pavement below.

Leaning over the balcony, Alfie shook his head sadly.

'Fuck me, would you look at that, Gem,' he said pointing down to what was left of Jenson's mangled body, 'I weren't lying when I said he would make a right fucking mess, was I?'

CHAPTER THIRTY-THREE

Sam Miles was starting to feel scared now.

Daniel's behaviour had taken a rapid decline since he'd got out of the shower. He'd continued drinking, of course, and Sam suspected that was the main cause of the weird way he was conducting himself tonight. Acting all paranoid and saying that someone might come to the flat looking for him. That if they did, Sam would have to lie and say that he hadn't seen Daniel all evening.

Daniel had made Sam swear.

Then he'd begun to pace the room, stopping every few minutes so that he could peer out of the blinds, convinced as he stared out into the darkness that every shadow was really the silhouette of someone hiding out there, watching him. Waiting for him.

He was already drunk when he'd turned up here tonight, but since then, he'd managed to down over half a litre of vodka neat and Sam had lost track of the amount of coke Daniel had snorted. Enough to induce some kind of a psychotic episode by the looks of it. The man was out of control.

Sam might not be able to do anything about the drugs, but he could at least try and ensure that Daniel didn't drink anymore alcohol. Unbeknown to Daniel, he had managed to get to the kitchen and empty out the contents of any other bottles of drink that he had lying around the house without him seeing, tipping the lot down the sink as he prayed that Daniel would pass out shortly. Surely he wouldn't be able to stomach much more? He'd been drinking on and off all day. But now he was starting to talk shit too. Slurring his words, speaking in rhymes and riddles.

Sam had trouble understanding what Daniel was actually talking about. None of his conversations were making any sense. It was just mindless ramblings. Ranting and raving about anything and everything that came into his head. Though this latest outburst was suddenly silenced. Interrupted by a noise at the front door.

'Did you hear that?' Daniel said. Placing his finger over his lips, indicating to Sam to be quiet.

Though to be fair, Sam hadn't heard a thing.

'There's no one there, Daniel. You're hearing things!' Imagining things more like, he thought. The man was coked up to his eyeballs. He watched as Daniel peered through the crack in the blinds once more.

'Fuck. He's here.' His eyes wide, alert as he searched for something to use as protection. A bat. A pole. Anything.

Sam didn't have fuck all like that in his flat. The bloke was under the illusion that a poxy intercom on the door was enough to deter burglars or unwanted house guests, that's how naive and deluded Sam could be. The bloke lived on another planet.

Grabbing a small wooden stool and holding it above his head, Daniel peered out of the front door's spy hole.

Waiting, holding his breath.

'There's no one there, Daniel,' Sam said, walking up behind him, before taking a look for himself. His eye peering out into the empty corridor. Then, as if to prove his point, Sam opened the front door. 'Look, see. There's no one out here.'

'What the fuck are you playing at?' Grabbing Sam roughly by his arm, Daniel dragged him back inside. 'Are you fucking stupid or something?' he bellowed, slamming the door behind them both before throwing Sam up against the wall. 'Are you trying to get me fucking killed? I said don't open the door. Don't go anywhere near it. Do you understand? Not for fucking anyone.' Holding Sam tightly now by his throat, unaware of the strength behind his attack, Daniel was too far gone to care. 'I said "do you understand"?'

Sam nodded. Relieved when Daniel loosened his grip and let him go.

'This is bullshit. I can't stay here,' Daniel said, knowing full well that it would only be a matter of time before Alfie Harris caught up with him. As much as he'd told Jack Taylor to smooth things over for him, to make things right, Daniel didn't have much faith in the man actually doing so. Jack was supposed to be keeping him in the loop, letting him know what had gone on. But he'd heard nothing from the fucker, and he wasn't answering his phone either, which spoke volumes to Daniel.

The fucker was a snake.

The fact he'd kept quiet about Daniel killing his own father, one of Jack's oldest friends, was testament to that. Picking up his phone, he dialled Jack Taylor for the umpteenth time. Only surprise, surprise. He still didn't pick up.

'He's avoiding me!' Daniel said, moving across the flat again, walking erratically, as if, if he didn't move he'd combust from the rage inside him. 'It wouldn't surprise me if the fucker tried to stitch me up now, too. I bet that's what's fucking happened. Alfie Harris is on the warpath and Jack Taylor's probably up the man's arse, hoping that he catches up with me.' He cursed himself for pushing Jack Taylor too far.

'Who are you talking about? Why is Alfie Harris on the warpath? What the fuck's going on?' Sam said, hoping that Daniel would burn himself out soon. Until then, he needed to try and talk him down from this mood he was in. Try and restore some normality to his flat tonight. Try and get Daniel to at least start talking some sense.

'Jack Taylor. The bastard thinks I won't talk, but I fucking will. If he thinks that I'm going down for this on my own, he's got a shock coming his way. He'll do time for my father's death too. He was there.'

'Your father's death?' Sam said, horrified now at what he thought Daniel was saying. 'What do you mean he was there too? Did Jack kill him?'

Sam didn't like the sound of any of this. He knew how Daniel's father's murder had fucked up his boyfriend's head. As much as Daniel did his hardest to try and hide the fact that he was suffering, Sam knew. He'd heard him having nightmares. Screaming out his father's name in his sleep. Waking up in pools of sweat, claiming that he couldn't remember anything, and Sam had never had the guts to broach the subject with him afterwards, worried that he might upset him, or worse still, make him angry.

Sam figured that Daniel would talk about his grief when he was ready. Only, Sam didn't know how much longer that was going to be. Instead of dealing with his feelings, Daniel just seemed to bottle them all up. Blocking them out with any means he could, which, lately, had been mostly alcohol and cocaine. He'd been drinking heavily and snorting coke every day, without fail. It wasn't until Daniel mentioned that his mother had been an alcoholic that Sam had started to wonder if this was more than just his way of mourning. Perhaps alcoholism and drug addiction was some kind of genetic illness that had been passed from parent to child.

And Daniel was quickly spiralling out of control.

It didn't help that Daniel was a nasty drunk either. The man seemed to be constantly goading for a row. That was the part that Sam found the hardest to take: how Daniel would always hit out at him. Making his comments and jibes so personal.

'Fuck me, Sam, for some rich little Chelsea boy you really are thick as fuck, ain't you? All that money your parents dished out on those university fees are going to be wasted on you!' Daniel was sneering now. Turning on Sam, which was exactly what he had been trying his hardest to avoid.

Daniel had been doing this more and more lately. Starting rows. Taking out his angst on him and he wasn't sure that he was able for much more.

'Look, Daniel. I don't want to fight with you—'

''Course you don't. You know why? 'Cause I'm capable of some sick and twisted shit, Sam. Stuff that you know fuck all about.'

'What the fuck are you talking about?' Sam said now in despair.

'I'm talking about me, Sam. The fact that you haven't got the first fucking clue about me! You think you're so smart, so fucking superior, but you're nothing.'

Sam closed his eyes, knowing that there was no point in trying to reason with Daniel when he was in this kind of mood. Enough was enough. He couldn't do this again tonight. Or any other night.

'Don't you think you've had enough to drink now? I don't think you should stay here tonight if you're just going to keep drinking that shit. It ain't good for you, Daniel. It fucks with your head. Maybe you should go home tonight?'

Daniel started laughing. Really laughing. So hard that tears rolled down his cheeks. Sam stood there not knowing what the joke was that he'd clearly missed.

'You're asking me to leave?' Daniel chuckled. 'Oh behave, Sam. You don't get to tell me to do shit. If you don't like me drinking then I'll tell you what, why don't you fucking leave?'

Rolling his eyes up, Sam knew he was going to have an almighty argument on his hands soon if he didn't put a stop to this now.

'Daniel. It's my flat. You can't chuck me out of my own flat.'

'Who said I was going to chuck you out?' Daniel said, getting up and lunging at his new so-called boyfriend, sending him crashing to the floor, as he lay on top of him. His hands wrapped around Sam's throat.

'I could just kill you,' Daniel said then. Tightening his grip as he watched for the fear in Sam's eyes. 'I could strangle the last breath out of your whingey fucking throat and then dump your dead body in the bathtub. And leave you there to rot.'

'Daniel you're hurting me. Stop messing about,' Sam said. Fighting for breath. Trying to make light of Daniel's threat. Though Daniel was starting to shit him up a bit now. He was acting crazy, and he was beginning to wonder just what Daniel really was capable of doing, especially when he was in one of his moods.

'That's just it though, Sam. See what you just did there? You underestimated me? That's what I've had to put up with my whole life. People thinking they know me when they don't know anything at all!'

'I just know you and you're not a fucking monster.'

'Oh but I am. That's just it. I'm capable of things you know nothing about. Things you couldn't even fucking imagine.' Daniel was really pissed now, and he was enjoying the horrified look on Sam's face. The way that the man was trying to talk him down and pacify him. It was wholly entertaining, though a little insulting if Daniel was honest.

As if Sam Miles could control him?

No one told Daniel what to do. No one.

'I wasn't mugged tonight. That blood that I was covered in wasn't mine. It belonged to some poncy-looking barman in some bender's pub in Soho. The type of bloke who fucking loved himself, you know. Thought he was a real fucking player.' Daniel grinned now at the memory. 'He didn't even ask me my name, and yet he was quick enough to get on his knees and suck my cock. He actually disgusted me. Especially afterwards when he started acting as if I owed him something in return. So I killed him. I beat the living shit out of him. Stamped on his fucking head until there was nothing left.'

Sam stared at Daniel, willing him to make some kind of a joke. To say that it wasn't true, but Daniel wasn't laughing. He wasn't even smiling now. Instead he was staring Sam dead in the eye, telling him the truth. Getting off on the fear that was etched on Sam's face as he listened to Daniel's admission.

'Daniel. Stop talking shit. You're drunk.' But he knew it was true, deep down, that Daniel wasn't fucking about with him. 'You don't know what you're saying!' Sam said, knowing that Daniel shouldn't be telling him all this. He couldn't tell him all of this. Otherwise Sam would be in danger himself; knowing Daniel's deepest, darkest secrets he'd become a liability.

'That's just it. I do know what I'm saying, and I know what I'm doing, too. I'm proving every fucker out there wrong. They all said that I wasn't good enough. Do you know that. My father pretty much said so to my face. How I'd never be as clever or fucking successful as Nancy. How he was ashamed of me for being gay. He used to look at me with such disappointment and disgust.'

Daniel picked up the bottle of vodka from the side and took another large swig. Staring in through the glass with disappointment as he realised it was coming to an end.

'Only I showed him, didn't I?'

He was laughing now. Sliding down the wall. Slumped over with the bottle of vodka between his legs. He looked pitiful, almost. And for a second Sam felt the same pull he'd felt for Daniel when he first met him. He saw just a flicker of vulnerability that made Sam want to try and fix him.

It was only fleeting though. Quickly replaced by anger once more. Looking up with that twisted hateful smirk that Sam had started to loathe about him.

'Who do you think it was that helped to blackmail my cunt of a father? Me and that guy he was seeing. Gavin Hurst. Gavin was the same age as me, can you fucking believe that? My dad was knobbing someone the same age as me!' Daniel shook his head with disgust. 'My two-faced, hypocrite of a father underestimated me too. He had no fucking clue that all along me and Gavin were setting him up. The job was supposed to be so simple. Gavin filmed them both having sex so we could blackmail him, only, my father found out and he killed Gavin. He beat the living shit out of him. Stamped on him until he was nothing more than a bloody pulp. Just like I did to that bloke tonight. See. We were two of the same me and my dad. Only my dad couldn't fucking stand me. For him it must have been like looking in a mirror. I don't know what happened, but when I went to collect the money from my father that night, something just clicked inside me. I dunno what it was. Because he rejected me, he hated me? Fuck knows! The gun was in my hand. My finger pressing against the trigger and then, next thing I knew, I just did it. I shot him. It was as easy as that. I don't even think I meant to kill him, you know. I just wanted to hurt him, like he'd hurt me. Just wanted to see some fear on his face for once. Some real emotion instead of the fake bullshit he insisted on showing the world each day. I just wanted to see his mask slip.'

On hearing Daniel's confession. Sam felt physically sick. Daniel was going around killing people because he was fucked up in the head about the way his dad had treated him? Fuck! He'd just confessed to killing Jimmy Byrne too. His own father. And here he was, stuck alone, in his flat with the man.

A murderer. Confessing all his sins.

Sins which Sam didn't want to hear about.

He wouldn't be safe now.

If Daniel trusted him, it wouldn't be an issue, but Daniel Byrne didn't trust anyone.

'You don't know what you're saying, Daniel. You don't mean any of this. I'm sure it didn't happen like that. I mean, come on. You're not like that,' he said, giving Daniel the easy option out of this, the chance to backtrack on what he'd just told him. Now that Daniel had confessed, what would he do to Sam to ensure that he didn't start talking now too?

'Why aren't you fucking listening to me, Sam? I just told you. I am exactly like him. But now I can't seem to stop. Look at that guy from the bar tonight. That's exactly what my dad did, isn't it? He beat the shit out of Gavin Hurst. Murdered him. How ironic life is, eh? My father acted like he hated me, when all along it was because we were the fucking same. Both gay. Both liars. Both sadistic fucks!'

Sam could feel the bile rising at the back of his throat. Suddenly scared to even be in Daniel's company.

He was right about his last statement. He was a sadistic fuck. A psychopath.

This was bad. Really bad.

If Daniel was capable of murdering his own father in cold blood, he wouldn't think twice about hurting Sam. Really hurting him. Killing him even.

Feeling the panic building inside of him, he glanced towards the front door, trying to calculate how quickly he could get to it. Daniel was drunk; he'd have a few seconds delay as he tried to get to his feet.

The lock! Shit! He remembered now that Daniel had double locked it. Paranoid about keeping Alfie Harris out. It would delay him, slightly, but there was still a chance that he could make it.

But looking back at Daniel, and seeing he was already reading his mind, that Sam wouldn't have time, he made a run for the bathroom instead. Grabbing Daniel's phone from the chair as he fled, before he barricaded himself in. Bolting the door just in time to hear Daniel beating his fists against the door.

'That's right, you hide away in there, you soft little prick,' Daniel shouted. Saddened that Sam couldn't hack hearing the truth about him. That said about as much as Daniel needed to know about Sam Miles. The useless waste of space was just as bad as the rest of them.

There was no real love lost between them, he was certain of that. For him, Sam had been an easy ride. Somewhere to stay for a few days now and again, while he needed to get away from his overbearing family. Someone he could boss around, who wouldn't stand up to him.

The truth was, Daniel didn't even really like him anymore. Sam had been grating on his nerves for weeks. Acting all paranoid and possessive. Constantly asking where Daniel was going and what time he'd be back as if he was his keeper.

Hence why Daniel had sought out other men in the first place. Sam was a bore. The other men at least gave him pleasure before Daniel returned the favour by inflicting immense pain on them.

He could do that with Sam tonight too, now, he thought.

Put the fucker out of his misery one final time.

He smiled then, deciding to let the bastard sweat it out in the bathroom for a little while longer. Let him fear for his life for a while more. That was all part of the fun.

Daniel had more pressing matters to attend to, for now, like finishing off that bottle of vodka that he'd made a start on and keep an eye out for that sadist bastard, Alfie Harris.

The fucker hadn't turned up here yet, but it was only a matter of time.

And Daniel would be ready for the fucker when he came.

He'd be ready for them all.

CHAPTER THIRTY-FOUR

Going through Daniel's phone contacts with trembling hands, Sam Miles found the number he'd been looking for.

'Come on, come on,' he said, almost silently as he pressed call, praying that Daniel wouldn't overhear him, that he hadn't noticed Sam had taken his phone. He didn't know what else to do. He couldn't just stay here, cowering in his own bathroom, and the mood that Daniel was in, he knew that it would only be a matter of time before Daniel summoned him out, or worse still, until he came in here looking for him.

The phone was ringing now. But the sound of Daniel banging about in the kitchen was drowning it out. Daniel had lost his head. Getting more and more riled up as he continued to smash the place up.

Shit!

He shouldn't have tipped the rest of the alcohol down the sink. He should have just let the man drink himself into oblivion. Into a coma. At least then Sam would be safe, instead of hiding out in his bathroom. Afraid for his life.

And he really was afraid.

There was no doubt in his head now that Daniel Byrne was a murderer.

'Daniel?' Jack Taylor's voice came through, causing Sam to close his eyes with relief.

'No, it's Sam. Sam Miles. Daniel's boyfriend,' Sam spluttered now. Aware that he didn't have much time. That the second

Daniel heard him making this call he'd come crashing through the bathroom door to stop him. 'I'm sorry for calling you, Jack, but I didn't know who else to phone. I'm with Daniel, but he's not right. He's not right at all. He's pissed paralytic and he's smashing my flat up—'

'For fuck's sake!' Jack Taylor said with irritation.

'He's just fucking lost it, Jack. He's saying some real fucked-up stuff too,' Sam said, unsure if he should repeat word for word what Daniel had told him. But something told him that he should be straight with Jack. The man might have the Byrne family's interests at heart, but he was still first and foremost a police officer. A detective inspector at that.

Jack Taylor would know what to do, Sam was certain of it.

'Tonight, he came home covered in blood. He told me that he killed someone. Some barman in a bar in Soho.' Sam was crying now. Filled with panic at being alone in the flat with this madman, he was petrified. 'He said he could do it to me too, that he could snuff my life out. That he was more than capable of doing it.'

'Okay, Sam. Calm down,' Jack Taylor said, recognising the panic in the younger man's voice. He knew himself what Daniel Byrne was capable of, and he didn't want to scare the kid anymore than he already was. 'Where are you now? Are you safe?'

'I'm in the bathroom. I've locked the door, but if he wants to get in, he will. You haven't seen the state of him. It's like he's just lost it.'

'Okay, Sam. Give me your address. I'm coming over. Okay!'

Sam recited the address, then holding the phone nearer to his mouth, he said, remembering the other things that Daniel had confessed to him: 'Shit, Jack. He said other stuff too. I don't know if it's true or not, but he said that he killed his dad. I mean, he wouldn't just make that up, would he? Do you think that's why he's so fucked up? Do you think it's true?' The man was a monster. A lunatic. There was no doubt in Sam's mind that Daniel Byrne had lost his.

'Listen. Stay in the bathroom, okay. Do not come out until I get there. I'm on my way. Just stay put where you are.'

Hanging up the phone, Jack Taylor smashed his fist against the bar. Fucking Daniel! The bloke was a complete liability. With all the shit they had going on right now, this was the last thing that they needed to be dealing with. Though Jack knew that, once and for all, it did need dealing with. And properly.

The only problem was, he was currently tied up on a call over in Soho himself. Having gone straight to The Karma Club after leaving Nancy, he'd then been called out to investigate a murder in a gay bar over on Dean Street. Another gay man murdered in cold blood. It had all the markings of a serial killer on the loose. *Shit!* Jack closed his eyes as he recalled Sam Miles's last words about Daniel confessing to killing someone in a bar in Soho.

Staring across the crowded room now, as the forensic pathologist and the team of Crime Scene Investigators continued to process the crime scene for any clues on the perpetrator, Jack felt a sinking feeling in the pit of his stomach. Looking down at the twisted, disfigured body on the floor.

Jack knew exactly who the murderer was.

Daniel Byrne.

The man had been on a killing spree right under Jack's nose. Killing gay men, purely for the sake of it. Another fucking mess that Jack would have to sort out for the fucker. There was no way that Jack could just leave the scene of the crime, but at the same time he needed to get his arse over to the flat and fast. Before Daniel did something really stupid like try and kill Sam Miles too. Before the rest of the police force were called out to deal with all the drama and commotion.

If that happened, it was guaranteed that Daniel would then take the opportunity to well and truly stitch Jack up then too.

He would have no qualms in dragging Jack down in the shit with him.

His only other option right now was that maybe he could send someone else over there to try and help Sam get out of the flat. The only person that he could think of was Nancy, and even that was a gamble. Jack wasn't sure that he could trust the girl not to take things into her own hands, and Jack couldn't risk letting Nancy just wade on in there unprepared for what she was really dealing with. Jack was going to have to let the girl know the truth now.

That Daniel Byrne was a murderer. That he'd killed her father. And that Sam Miles was now in grave danger.

CHAPTER THIRTY-FIVE

Staring in through the window of Megan Harris's private room in the Intensive Care Ward of St George's Hospital, Nancy Byrne stood in silence, watching as Alfie Harris sat at his daughter's bedside, an attractive blonde lady sitting beside him. *His girlfriend?* Wrapping her arm around Alfie as he held onto his daughter's arm. A solemn look etched on the man's face. Staring at his child with such determination, he looked as if he was physically willing her to get better.

Nancy watched as the woman leaned in. Kissing Alfie on the forehead, before he hung his head and began to openly sob.

Reaching her hand out for the handle, she froze. *What was she even doing here?* she thought suddenly. Coming here and interrupting this family at such a harrowing time. *What would she even say?* That she'd heard what had happened. What her brother had done. That she was here to offer her condolences, her support. That was bullshit, and even Nancy knew that. She was here to make sure that Alfie Harris knew that what happened to his daughter tonight had nothing to do with her. It had been solely Daniel's doing.

That was the truth.

That her brother was a liability. But here and now wasn't the place to air her grievances about Daniel. Of course it wasn't. *What had she been thinking?* Fuck. This had been a stupid idea, she thought as she eyed the machinery and equipment in the room.

The tubes, and monitors that Megan Harris was attached to. Her gaze going to the nurse in the room with them. Standing at the foot of the bed, writing something down on the clipboard. Her expression looking just as solemn.

Nancy couldn't do it. She couldn't go in there. She was too scared to face the man whose daughter seemed to be clinging on literally to dear life and, in fairness, she was probably the last person that Alfie Harris wanted to see right now, and she could understand that. Of course she could. This wasn't the time and place to bring up her grievances about her brother.

Turning on her heel to leave, she heard the sound of her phone ringing out loudly, echoing throughout the cold, sterile corridor. Shit! Scrambling about in her bag, cursing herself for not remembering to turn the thing off before she'd come into the ICU, she mouthed the word sorry to a passing nurse, who, in turn, shot her a disapproving glance. Turning to face the wall, Nancy answered the call.

'Hello?'

'Nancy? It's me. Jack.'

'Jack! What's happened? Did you go to the club? Did you find anything out?'

Pushing away the thoughts of what they'd both done together just hours before, Nancy tried to stay focused.

'The dealer and the bloke that gave Megan Harris the gear have been dealt with. Alfie Harris saw to it personally. I guess Daniel will be next.'

'I guess so,' Nancy said, not bothering to add that Daniel seemed to be off the hook for now. That Alfie Harris was back at the hospital, at his daughter's bedside. That once again her brother was getting away with fucking murder.

'Though your brother is still intent on causing ructions of his own, Nancy. I just had Sam Miles on the phone. Seems like

Daniel has really fucking lost the plot tonight. The poor kid's locked away in the bathroom. He said Daniel is saying some fucked-up shit.'

'Like what?' Nancy said, closing her eyes, knowing full well what was coming next.

'Look, I hate being the one to say this, and fuck knows if it's even true, Nancy,' Jack said cautiously, knowing that once he spoke it would be out there forever and there'd be no coming back from it. He just hoped that Daniel Byrne didn't drag his name down too. 'Daniel's told Sam that he killed your father. He said that it was him and Gavin Hurst that had both blackmailed him. He said he's killed others too?'

Nancy was silent. Finally her brother was admitting it out loud. It must have been getting to him. Eating away at the mad bastard just as she had hoped that it would.

'Where is he?'

'You can't face Daniel on your own, Nancy. Sam said that he's off his fucking head. He said that he thinks he murdered someone tonight. That Daniel said as much, that he'd come home covered in blood. I've just been called out on a job. A murder investigation. Some poor bastard in a bar in Soho was beaten to death late last night, and I think Sam's right. I think Daniel was behind it, Nancy. It's not safe. I'm over here now, but I can be with you in forty-five minutes. We can deal with Daniel when I get there. Properly. For now, I just need you to get round to Sam's place and see if you can get him out of that flat. The kid's terrified.'

'Give me the address,' Nancy said, without missing a heartbeat.

'Promise me, Nancy. You won't confront Daniel. I mean it—'

'I promise I'll wait for you to get there before I go in. I'll just help Sam,' Nancy said. 'What's the address?'

Jack recited the address that Sam Miles had given him.

'I mean it, Nancy. Do not go in there. I'll get there as quick as I can,' Jack said, worried now that Daniel would tell Nancy the truth.

That's the sort of thing the bloke would do.

If Daniel Byrne was going to go down in flames, you could guarantee that the fucker would take every other bastard down with him.

He'd love that.

Telling Nancy how Jack had known about Jimmy's murderer all along. How Jack had been there. How he had seen it all and, worse still, how Daniel had paid him off for his silence.

And then there was the attack on Nancy too.

Fuck!

He was taking a massive risk letting Nancy go there on her own, but what choice did he have? For now, he had to stay here at the scene of the crime they were investigating. He'd have to slip away as soon as he got a chance. Then he could deal with Daniel properly. Silence the fucker for good.

'Don't go in until I get there, Nancy, promise me.'

'I promise,' Nancy said, hanging up the phone.

Placing the phone back inside her handbag, she felt for her father's gun.

She'd lied to Jack.

She had no intention of waiting for him to arrive. Nancy decided that it was high time that she put an end to this shit with her brother once and for all. He needed to pay for what he'd done, and she was going to be the one to do it.

A voice behind her, startling her, made her jump out of her skin.

'Well isn't this a nice surprise, Nancy Byrne?!'

It was Alfie Harris, standing in the doorway behind her, a look on his face telling her that he'd been listening to every word.

CHAPTER THIRTY-SIX

'Where is he?' Nancy said, keeping her voice down as she entered the flat.

She hadn't been expecting Sam Miles to be standing at the front door waiting for her when she arrived. She thought that she'd be turning up to chaos. To Daniel on the warpath, and Sam still locked in the bathroom.

'He finally passed out. I was going to leave, but Jack said he was on his way.'

Nancy nodded. 'Yeah he is. Are you okay?'

Sam Miles nodded, but Nancy could see the younger man was anything but.

'He's in there,' he said, nodding towards the sitting room where Daniel had finally passed out on the sofa. 'I can't do this, Nancy. He's fucked up in the head. All the things he was saying. About the other men, about your dad. Were they true?'

''Course they weren't, Sam,' Nancy said through a tight-lipped smile, not wanting to freak Sam Miles out anymore than he clearly already was. 'Look, you're right about Daniel. He's a mess. He hasn't been right for weeks. I think my dad's murder has tipped him over the edge. He's having some sort of a breakdown.'

Sam nodded. This was exactly what he wanted to hear. He knew it wasn't the truth though, but he wasn't going to argue about that. He'd seen the blood all over Daniel. He'd heard the malice in the man's voice when he'd admitted to murdering his own father. The same malice he'd used when he'd threatened to snuff out Sam's own life, too, tonight. Still, Sam was doing the smart thing and playing along. Eager to get Daniel the fuck out of his flat and out of his life for good. Now Nancy was here, she could happily deal with him in any way she saw fit.

'Tell you what, Sam. Why don't you make yourself scarce, yeah? Let me deal with Daniel. I'll have him out of here for when you return later this morning, yeah? Have you got somewhere you can go?'

Nancy Byrne was being polite, but her tone told him that she wasn't asking him. She was telling him.

'I guess,' Sam said, realising that it was almost 6 a.m. now. He was hoping that Nancy would just wake Daniel up, and take him with her. Though he figured it wasn't going to be as simple as that. Nancy Byrne looked fit to kill, and if what Daniel said was really true then he wouldn't put anything past the woman.

'I'll go to my parents' place.'

Nancy nodded, glad that Sam Miles was complying. Then she stepped aside, giving him the hint to leave.

'Now? Oh, right. Yes, I'll get out of your way,' he said, still shocked and dazed from the night's events. He quickly grabbed his coat and shoes, picking up his car keys from the kitchen side, glancing back to where Nancy stood in the doorway, watching over her brother with those cold steely eyes. The only resemblance she had at all to Daniel, Sam thought.

'I'll get out of your way then,' he said as he slipped past her, acting as if he was the one that had suggested it.

The relief hitting him, just like the cool air did the second he was outside the flat. He had no idea what fate awaited Daniel now, but he did know that he was glad to be rid of the mad bastard.

Daniel, and his family with all their fucked-up secrets.

Sam Miles never wanted to see another Byrne as long as he lived.

*

Staring down at her brother as he lay comatose on the sofa, passed out, in his drunken slumber, so blissfully unaware of the nightmare that awaited him when he finally opened his eyes, Nancy thought about the last time she had done this. How she'd stood over her brother as he'd slept, holding a gun in her hand. But then she hadn't been ballsy enough to fire the damn thing. She deeply regretted that now. For not being strong enough, and ferocious enough to avenge her father's death like she'd promised herself that she would. For not making Daniel pay for what he'd done.

Now she was going to put all of that right.

She had to.

Picking up a glass of water from the coffee table, she poured it over Daniel's head. Watching the man leap from the chair, shouting out in shock as the cold water cascaded all down him.

'What the fuck are you doing?' he bellowed, thinking it was Sam being a cunt to him. Teaching him a lesson for falling asleep drunk on the sofa again.

But it wasn't Sam. Seeing his sister's flaming red hair and that stern look on her face, her piercing green eyes boring into his, he did a double take.

'What the fuck are you doing here? Where's Sam?'

Nancy stood there for a few minutes, taking in the puzzled expression on her brother's face. Watching him as he tried to piece together what the hell was going on here tonight. It was amusing to watch. How thick her brother could really be. How hard he was trying to figure everything out. It was almost as if she could see the rusty cogs and coils twisting and turning inside his head.

'Sam's gone,' she said simply. 'The poor fucker got out while he could, and I don't blame him really. Not after everything you told him.'

Daniel didn't even flinch at that. Instead he shook his head.

'Oh, I get it. Sam's just the type to go around telling fucking tales. Is that why you're here? Sam rang you and told you everything and, typical fucking Nancy, you never could resist the opportunity to poke your fucking nose in where it wasn't wanted, could you?'

'He said you murdered someone tonight. That you came home covered in blood,' Nancy said then. The rage she'd felt inside her for all these past weeks suddenly subsided. The shake in her voice replaced with only calm as she locked eyes with her brother now. Finally laying everything out on the table between them.

'You also told Sam that you murdered our father. I want to hear you say it to me!'

Daniel laughed then. Though the noise sounded false, lingering in the back of his throat.

'Oh fuck off, Nancy, will you? Don't tell me you're wearing a wire or something,' he said, wondering what this was all about: why Nancy was insisting on having a bullshit conversation with him, why she was staring at him so intently. Still drunk, and half asleep she was unnerving the fuck out of him. Though even his sister wouldn't stoop as low as involving the police. This was just his sister being her usual control-freak self. Wanting to know everything as per; well Daniel would give the stupid bitch exactly what she wanted, in great detail.

'What do you want to hear, Nancy? Huh? You want me to tell you that it was me, do you? That I shot Dad.' Daniel laughed. He could see the physical pain flashing in his sister's eyes at his words. The hurt he was inflicting on her, and he was glad.

She fucking deserved to hurt.

'Oh come on, Nancy! Fucking hell. You're acting like Saint fucking Jimmy was the fucking pinnacle father or something. The man was a liar, a cheat. He spent his whole life, our whole lives, lying to us all. He fucked young boys, Nancy. Men younger than me.' Daniel was enjoying every bit of this. Finally, he was letting Nancy know the truth and it felt fucking good. All that rage that he had inside. All those years he had sat back and watched his father place Nancy on a pedestal. The golden child. His favourite. While their father had never so much as given him the time of day.

'He was just like me!' he snarled. 'Do you know that. We were two of the very same. Not only was he bent, but he was a fucking murderer too, Nancy. Gavin Hurst was only one of his victims. There were others too, though. Mum told me. When she was drunk at Nan Edel's funeral. How our father had murdered someone on the night of their wedding. How even Nan Joanie knew about it too. But they all covered it up. That's why Mum was so fucked up for all those years, do you know that? The man had so many fucking secrets.' Daniel smiled then. 'That night, when I went to meet him to take the money that I blackmailed him with, something in me just snapped. I was looking at him, and I was thinking that he's no better than me. Not really. He knew it too. That's why he spent all the years we were growing up belittling me. Making me feel shit about myself. Even when I went to him and told him I was gay, he knew all along. And yet he made out I was disgusting. He made me feel so ashamed. I just snapped. I pulled the trigger and, do you know, it was the best thing I ever did. I've never felt so fucking free since that cunt died.'

Unable to stop herself, Nancy hit out. The palm of her hand slapping violently across Daniel's face, leaving welts in the shape of her fingers across his cheek.

That only made Daniel smirk harder.

'A reaction from the fucking Ice Queen. Well I am flattered,' he sneered, his face throbbing under his own hand.

'I should have shot you when I had the chance,' Nancy said. 'Nothing would give me greater pleasure than to snatch your life away from you the way you did our father's. My biggest regret was that I didn't get to watch you as you took your last breath.' Nancy could feel her tears then.

Her face burning as her rage returned. Daniel was just standing there with that stupid twisted smirk on his face. Looking at her like he couldn't give two shits what he'd done. Like none of it mattered.

But it did matter to her. It mattered more than anything.

'You haven't got the guts, have you, Nancy? That's why you're nothing like me. Or him, as it happens. You're the gutless one. It's you that's weak.'

Nancy shook her head.

'No, Daniel. That's where you're wrong. I'm exactly like Dad. You see, unlike you, we were clever. That's what set us worlds apart from you. That's why Dad didn't want you involved in the business. You're lazy, and self-absorbed. Your work is sloppy. You leave a trail for people to find you. You leave a mess.' She stared at Daniel with utter hate in her eyes, glad that she was finally getting to tell her brother exactly what she thought of him.

'Me? I'm smarter than that. I knew all along that you killed our father and vowed to get my vengeance on you, and now I finally have. Here's a lesson on being clever, Daniel. There's no mess, and no comeback.'

Daniel narrowed his eyes, confused.

'You took it upon yourself to change the supplier at the club, didn't you? Thought you'd do a deal behind my back, and cut me out? Well, you've really fucked things up this time, Daniel. Megan Harris is in a fucking coma because of you.'

'Because of me? Bullshit!' Daniel spat. 'She's a kid. She shouldn't have even been in that club. Maybe Alfie Harris needs to take a closer look at his parenting skills.'

Nancy shook her head then.

Her eyes flashing with disgust, and something else.

Triumph.

Her brother had just unwittingly sealed his fate with his last words.

'Like I said earlier, I'll regret not seeing you take your last breath, Daniel, but I'll live out my days happily knowing that you have finally taken it.'

Opening the front door to the apartment, Nancy Byrne stepped outside, just as Alfie Harris stepped in.

'Do what you want with him! He's all yours now.'

CHAPTER THIRTY-SEVEN

As a stream of sweat trickled down his back, underneath his now blood-soaked shirt, Alfie Harris wiped his forehead. It had been a long night and he was lagging now. His energy depleting after two hours of vigorous revenge – inflicting extreme torture onto the piece of shit in front of him.

Staring at Daniel Byrne, the man strapped to the chair in the middle of an abandoned warehouse tucked away up an old dirt track behind The Karma Club, Alfie knew he had picked the perfect location. This place was set so far back in King's Cross's badlands that no one would be able to hear this fucker screaming here. And boy could Daniel Byrne scream!

It had taken the bloke a while though.

Begrudgingly, Alfie Harris had to give the fucker his dues. Daniel Byrne had fought it hard at first. Refusing to react or show his suffering. He had been determined not to give Alfie the satisfaction of hearing him beg and plead for his life. Alfie had known that it would come eventually. He'd been intent on making sure of that personally. Though he'd been surprised at just how much Daniel Byrne was prepared to endure before he caved in.

Intent on being an obnoxious bastard right up until the end.

And the end would be here very soon.

Alfie Harris had to hand it to Nancy Byrne. The girl had turned out to be every bit as ruthless as her old man. When the girl had told him that she didn't know about Daniel's plans to change their supplier at the club, that Daniel had gone about it without letting her know, Alfie Harris had believed her. Nancy Byrne didn't give a shit about the drugs side of the business, in fact, she'd said that she wanted to step away from The Karma Club completely. That she wanted out. Exactly as Alfie Harris did too. Then she'd told him about the phone call she'd just taken at the hospital. That Jack Taylor had called her and told her that they'd found out who murdered her father. That it had been Daniel of all people.

This piece of shit had killed his own father in cold blood. No wonder Nancy Byrne had been only too happy to hand Daniel over to him.

There was an awful lot of blood now, Alfie thought, taking in the amount of claret that dripped down Daniel's tortured body, forming a deep red pool at the feet of his chair. The cowardly piece of shit had passed out a few times, but that was okay. Alfie had waited patiently for the man to come back around before he went in for the next round of brutality.

Though he knew that Daniel wasn't going to stay conscious for much longer.

Alfie was going to have to end this shortly. He stared down at his phone that he'd placed on the floor in front of him: he'd spent the past few hours willing it to ring, praying to God that Jennifer would call him and tell him that Megan was gaining consciousness, that he needed to get his arse back up to the hospital, to be back at his daughter's bedside.

Only his phone hadn't rang once.

His little girl wasn't going to be all right ever again. And it was all this piece of shit's doing. This man was going to pay, and he was going to pay soon.

Daniel was near death now. After the torture Alfie had inflicted upon him, his body was slowly shutting down. The man could barely keep his eyes open; his head was sagging down to one side. Drifting in and out of consciousness.

'You know, the worst thing of all is that you haven't even asked me how she fucking is,' Alfie Harris snarled through gritted teeth, his temper taking over; he could feel himself about to lose control. 'You haven't even hinted that you're fucking sorry for what you did. What you've done.'

He realised that was the biggest insult in all of this. That this prick in front of him had begged and pleaded for his own miserable pathetic life but not once had the fucker said he was sorry, not once had he shown any form of remorse towards his daughter.

Daniel Byrne really didn't give a shit. Megan's life meant nothing to him. Nothing at all.

'You should see the state of her. She's plugged into a machine, do you know that? A poxy machine! That's what's keeping my little girl alive. She might not survive. My beautiful little girl might die.' Alfie was crying now. Snot and tears pouring down his face as he finally said the words out loud that he feared the most.

'If she lives – and I say IF, because the doctors have said that her chances are fucking slim to none, she'll be a vegetable – can you even fucking imagine that? A life stuck sitting in a poxy wheelchair. Sixteen years old and unable to walk or speak. Having to be fed through a fucking tube. What sort of quality of life is that huh?'

Staring down at the row of neatly lined up surgical tools on the table next to him, Alfie toyed with which one to use for his grand finale. He picked up a blowtorch. Pointing it towards Daniel's right eye. His finger over the trigger.

'Say her name,' Alfie said clearly. He could see the fear on Daniel's face then. The man barely coherent as he tried to speak. To plead with Alfie. Only, his throat was filling up with blood and, instead, he choked. Spraying Alfie's face with blood and phlegm.

Alfie wiped his face with his hand, disgusted.

'I want to hear you say it. I want my little girl's name to be the last thing that ever comes out of your mouth. So you know the reason why you are going to die.'

Daniel groaned. Incoherent now, unable to find the words. He stared at Alfie through vacant eyes.

'I can't fucking hear you!' he shouted, grabbing Daniel by a fistful of his hair and dragging the man's head backwards. He held his finger down on the blowtorch, the blast of heat exploding out the top as he moved it closer to Daniel Byrne's face.

'Megan. Megan Harris.' Daniel's words were shaky. Muffled. His throat dry, coarse. He sounded every bit as defeated as he looked.

Finally, a broken man.

Alfie was glad. That was something, at least. It was over now. Time to end this once and for all.

Picking up the petrol can down on the floor by the barn's doorway, Alfie made his way back over to Daniel now. Glad that his temper hadn't got the better of him, and he hadn't taken this fucker's life the second that he'd set eyes on him. Though it had taken every bit of Alfie Harris's restraint. He wanted Daniel to be awake for this. To see and feel everything. To suffer every second of pain possible, just as he had inflicted pain upon Megan.

'You stole my little Megan's life. So now you're going to pay with yours. I'm going to burn you alive. I want you to suffer as much as you've made me suffer. As much as you've made my Megan suffer.'

Dousing Daniel in the fuel, Alfie struck a match and tossed it towards the man, watching for a second as the flames grew higher and higher. The stench of burning flesh filling the room, just as Daniel Byrne's agonising screams were too.

Walking away from the man that had ruined his daughter's life, Alfie Harris didn't look back.

He needed to be with his daughter.

That's where he should be right now.
Daniel Byrne could burn in hell.

CHAPTER THIRTY-EIGHT

Sitting behind Alfie Harris's desk at The Karma Club with his feet up and a Scotch in his hand, Gem Kemal felt like the cat that had got the proverbial cream. This was it. He was really on his way now. He'd worked hard at gaining Alfie Harris's trust and finally it had paid off. He was his right-hand man. The man holding it all together this past few weeks, in Alfie Harris's time of need.

It had been a close one, though, double-crossing his boss, even Gem could admit that. Having to stand there and face Jenson Reed as the cheeky fucker tried to drop him in it, and claim that Daniel had said Gem had cleared the new supplier. Fuck knows how Gem had kept his head, but somehow he had. Denying all knowledge of knowing anything about the deal that he and Daniel had made, making out that he knew nothing about Ecstasy being sold in the club. That Daniel had done this all on his own and, thankfully, Alfie Harris had believed him.

Of course he had; Gem had done nothing but prove his loyalty and commitment to the man in helping Alfie sort out the entire mess. He'd worked tirelessly here at the club, stepping up just when Alfie Harris needed him the most.

Staring down at the photograph that Alfie had in pride of place on his desk, Gem looked at the young girl in the photograph. He had to hand it to the girl, it turned out that Megan Harris was a real little fighter. The Harris bloodline clearly ran strong, it seemed, as against all the odds that had been stacked up against her, Megan Harris was well on the road to making a full recovery.

Gem was glad about that. He'd never intended for anyone to get hurt when he'd executed his plan to drop Daniel Byrne well and truly in the shit.

Alfie needed Gem now more than ever. He was so busy tending to his daughter, refusing to leave his child's side, which couldn't have worked out any better for Gem. He was free to get himself properly established at the club. He was getting the kudos and the respect that he finally deserved as Alfie Harris's right-hand man and, on top of that, Alfie Harris was paying him good money. More money than Gem could have wished for.

He could provide for Miyra and the kids again. They could move out of their dodgy bedsit and have a decent life here now.

He'd been a desperate man, but his gamble had paid off.

Lighting up a cigarette then, Gem breathed out a grey plume of smoke rings above him, watching as they quickly disappeared into the air. Grinning to himself with satisfaction of the genius of his little plan.

Though it wasn't all his own doing, he knew that.

He had help, of course.

But it had all worked out perfectly in the end.

Alfie Harris had got rid of all the dealers and distributors from the club. He'd forbidden anyone here from selling gear at all. The Byrnes were completely out of the picture, and the icing on the cake was Gem still had the added bonus of having full access to all of Jimmy Byrne's drop-off points and contacts now, thanks to Daniel Byrne. And Gem knew that he wouldn't be seeing that fucker again, not after Alfie Harris had caught up with him.

It had been almost two weeks since Daniel Byrne had gone on the missing list. Fuck knows what had happened to him, but

Gem would lay a guess on the fact that Alfie Harris had wiped the man from the face of the planet.

That made him smile too. He hadn't liked Daniel from the second the bloke had walked in here for their very first meeting. He was far too cocky for Gem's liking. Too full of himself.

Still, it was true what they said: the bigger they are, the harder they fall. And Daniel, the big-fucking-I-am had fallen from astronomical heights.

The bloke had no idea that he was being set up all along.

As if Gem would want to work alongside that twat.

Gem had never really cared for Daniel's father, Jimmy Byrne, nor his gobby business partner, Alex Costa. He had never dealt with either man personally. Those two arseholes had made a point of steering clear of the likes of Gem and the rest of the Turks working in London. Jimmy Byrne hadn't ever given Gem so much as the time of day, and Gem had taken it exactly as it had been intended. Personally.

After spending the past few years working the doors of several top London clubs and being shunned by two of the biggest players, fuming at their exclusion, Gem Kemal had had no choice but to sit patiently and wait his turn. He'd thought working here and being promoted to head of security would have changed all of that, but still Jimmy and Alex had chosen to exclude him.

To treat him as irrelevant, when he was clearly anything but.

Eyeing the security cameras then, Gem cast his gaze across the packed-out dance floor. Taking in the breathtaking sight of the hundreds of men and women that filled the place tonight. The place was buzzing. He could hear the music thudding through the floor. DJ Georgie Kissking was in the house and didn't every fucker in here know about it.

Gem eyed his team that were dotted around the club, watching as they discreetly went about their business of selling Gem's gear.

Not the shit that Gem shafted Daniel Byrne with. The shit that Daniel had brought in here was laced with PMA, a chemical notable for its high toxicity. It was supposed to fuck punters' heads up. Make them sick and paranoid for up to 36 hours after they'd taken it.

Now Gem was in charge of the merchandise being sold in the club, he was only dealing in the best quality drugs available.

Grade A.

That way, he'd have free rein of the place. There would be no comeback or problems, and Alfie Harris need never get wind that the drugs were still being sold here.

Though there was one last bit of business that he needed to sort out before he could relax.

One last deal that still needed to be settled.

Eyeing the security camera, he homed in on Nancy Byrne as she crossed the club and made her way down the steps towards the office. He looked up at the clock. Dead on midnight and not a second later. Punctual as ever. He smiled.

A few minutes later, Nancy walked into the office.

Standing up, to show his manners to the lady, Gem offered her a seat.

'Nancy! Glad you could make it!' he said, sitting back in the office chair, enjoying the sense of superiority that it gave him.

Taking the seat, Nancy placed the bag on the table.

'I take it that it's all there?' Gem said smugly. Knowing that he'd stuck to his side of the deal and done exactly as Nancy Byrne had asked him to. It was payday. Time to reap the rewards of a job well done.

Sliding the bag across the desk, Nancy didn't speak. Instead, she waited as Gem Kemal took his time looking inside. Watching his eyes scan the contents, before they narrowed.

Gem shook his head.

'What the fuck is this?' he said, annoyed. 'This is not what we agreed. We said a hundred thousand. There's not even a quarter of that here?'

'It's £20k,' Nancy said bluntly. Not bothering to try and dress it up. Personally she didn't like Gem Kemal one bit.

'But this is not what we agreed, Nancy? You don't get to make the rules up as you go along. We had a deal, remember?'

'Oh, I remember,' Nancy said, her eyes flashing with fury. 'But you fucked that deal when Alfie Harris's daughter got caught up in the firing line. You were supposed to set Daniel up. That was the deal. You said you would make sure that Alfie Harris dealt with him. What you didn't say was that an innocent kid would get hurt in the process! Megan Harris nearly died!'

'I thought you were supposed to be the smart one?' Gem said, leaning back in the chair and eyeing the woman with disdain. Losing his patience now.

When Nancy Byrne had approached him, and asked him for a way to get rid of her brother, Gem had seen a golden opportunity to get the job done without having to get his own hands dirty in the process. All he'd had to do was lay out the bait. Daniel had snatched up the opportunity with both hands, getting Jenson Reed to distribute the gear without so much as a second thought. 'What did you think would happen? That Alfie Harris was just going to go after your brother for simply changing suppliers? Of course not. We had to put someone in the club at risk. How else were we supposed to alert Alfie Harris to the fact that the distributor had been changed? Of bringing shit to his doorstep. He doesn't get involved in the drugs side of the business. Your father and Alex had always taken care of that. He needed to know what was happening.'

'Oh, well he soon found out what was happening, didn't he? Jesus, Gem! You almost killed a child!'

'Well that was unfortunate. That wasn't the plan. The dodgy batch was supposed to make a couple of people sick. Dehydrated. Maybe given one or two people a minor seizure.'

'A "minor seizure"? Megan Harris was in a coma for over a week and just because she's come around now doesn't mean she's out of the woods yet. The doctors still haven't determined if there are any long-term effects. She's a fucking kid, for God's sake. She nearly died. You deliberately set out to poison someone?'

'Oh come on, Nancy. This is fucking Ecstasy you're talking about. Everything's poisonous if you take enough of it,' Gem spat, drumming his fingers on the desk then. Beyond agitated now. 'And who the fuck's fault is it that Megan Harris came to the club in the first place? She shouldn't have been there. How could I have foreseen that? It was unfortunate that it was the girl that took the tablet, Nancy. But Megan Harris more than served her purpose and, what's more, she's okay. Where's your brother now, huh? Answer me that.'

Nancy shook her head. She had no idea. She'd handed him over to Alfie Harris, and knew better than to start asking any questions about her brother's fate.

It had been two whole weeks now. There had been no sight or sound from Daniel.

Her brother was gone for good. That was all that mattered.

Gem was right. It was what Nancy had planned all along. From the second that she'd set this deal up with him, she had known that her brother was going to be written out of the equation once and for all. She hadn't been able to kill him when she'd had the opportunity, but she'd made damn sure that someone else would.

'You see?' Gem nodded, glad that he'd made his point now. 'You got what you wanted, and so have I. Megan Harris lived. And I want my money.'

'Well, this is all I'm prepared to give you. I'm not paying you a hundred grand when you almost killed an innocent child. That was never part of my plan. That was your error. Your fuck up. You're lucky that you are even getting this,' Nancy said, staring at the man with her steely green eyes, her expression deadly serious – not prepared to move so much as an inch on her final offer. 'This is the only deal that I'm giving you. Take this money and you can keep all the contacts and use the drop-off points that Daniel gave you. I never wanted to be part of the drugs side of my father's business. You can have it all. Or, you can decline my offer and choose to go to war with me instead.' Nancy sat back in her chair then, resolute in what she was saying, showing the man that she didn't fear him one bit. 'But I warn you, Gem, I fight dirty. The second that Alfie Harris finds out that you were in on this too, that you were the one that set Daniel up, that you were the real man responsible for almost killing his daughter, you'd not only lose all of this, but you'd lose your life too.'

Gem shook his head. The gall of Nancy Byrne, the cheek of the woman. It was almost fucking hilarious. She had him though, and she knew it too.

Not accepting Nancy's deal was too big a risk to take. Twenty grand was better than nothing, he supposed. Besides, he had full rein in the club now to do as he pleased. He had the Byrnes' old contacts regarding the import and export for the gear he was intending on bringing in, and he had their drop-off points too.

He was all set to go.

'You know what you are, Nancy, you're just like your father. Fucking ruthless,' Gem said as he slid his hand over the bag of money and pulled it towards him.

Nancy smiled then, getting up from her seat.

'Well, I can't disagree with that, in fact, I'll take that as a compliment!' she said, before getting up and waltzing out of The Karma Club.

Her business here finally dealt with.

Glad that she'd never have to do business with a low-life like Gem Kemal ever again.

CHAPTER THIRTY-NINE

'Thank fuck you're here. I'm sorry to call you back home, Nancy, when you're busy working but she just keeps asking for you. She's acting bat-shit crazy,' Michael said as he led Nancy and Jack Taylor through to the lounge where he'd managed to persuade Joanie to sit down quietly, pacifying her with the fact that her granddaughter was on the way over. 'Do you know what I caught her doing last night? Climbing out her bedroom window. Stark bollock naked she was too. She was away with the fairies, Nancy, I tell you. She kept saying that someone was coming to get her, and she had to get away. Then this morning, poor Colleen went to take her in a nice pot of tea, only to find Joanie had barricaded herself in her bedroom. She'd pushed some of the furniture up against the door. Christ knows where she got her strength from, she'd been that determined. It took me over half an hour to persuade her to let me in, and when I did…' Michael closed his eyes then. Genuinely worried about the state of his wife's mental health. 'She just wasn't right at all. Crying and shaking. Repeating herself over and over again, that convinced someone's after her. I think she's lost her mind,' he said with all sincerity, before opening the lounge door.

Nancy nodded, glad for the heads-up from her grandad. She'd been so consumed with sorting out the flat over at Bridge Street that she hadn't been home much at all this week. She made a mental note to keep more of an eye on her nan.

Though as she stepped into the front room, nothing could have prepared her for the state her dear old nan was in.

'Nan! What happened to you?' Nancy gasped. Taking in the vision of the woman sat huddled under a blanket in the armchair in the corner of the room. Her mottled skin now black and blue.

As if she'd been beaten?

Nancy looked at her grandfather and her mother questioningly.

'She had a bit of "an episode" and then fell down the stairs,' Colleen said, shaking her head sadly.

'I didn't fall, I was tripped. Someone tripped me up on purpose,' Joanie screeched, forcefully.

'Who, Nan?' Nancy said protectively.

Joanie shrugged. 'I don't know. I can't remember. I think I saw a foot. But I can't remember now,' she said, shaking her head. Her expression looking vacant. The woman was clearly confused.

'Me and your grandad don't know what to do with her, Nancy. It's like she's just gone into self-destruct mode now. She's constantly falling down or tripping up. It's only a matter of time before she really hurts herself.'

Nancy nodded at Colleen in agreement. Her nan was getting on now. In her early seventies, she wasn't able for all these accidents to be happening.

'What are we going to do with you, Joanie?' Michael Byrne said, sitting down next to his wife and, for the first time in his entire life, he started to openly cry.

Such a rare, genuine show of emotion that Nancy felt like crying too.

'She's just not herself anymore; these past weeks she's rapidly gone downhill,' Michael sobbed. Scared now. Having watched the gradual decline of his bolshy, vibrant wife to virtually nothing. In her place sat this mere shell of a person. Confused and vulnerable. A complete stranger.

'I don't know what to do with her, Nancy. It's like she's not here anymore. She can't remember much, and she keeps having accidents. Falling over and getting dizzy spells. It's like she's lost her mind. As much as me and Jimmy didn't get on, I wish to God he was still here. Your nan can't cope without him.'

Michael Byrne was blubbering like a baby. No longer caring what his family and Jack Taylor all thought of him as he broke down in tears. So consumed with guilt that, at first, he'd found Joanie's immense suffering somewhat amusing.

Though now it was starting to scare the life out of him.

She wasn't right at all. This couldn't just be grief surely? Both in their seventies, maybe this was it for the woman. Maybe this was the start of what was to come. Old age finally setting in? Dementia? Fuck knows what it was, but Michael Byrne just wanted his Joanie back to the way she used to be. He never in his lifetime ever imagined saying that, but there it was. The truth.

He'd give anything in the world right now to hear the woman scold him for something that he supposedly had or hadn't done. For her to shoot him one of her scathing looks.

But he doubted he'd ever see that old Joanie again.

'She pushed me down the stairs,' Joanie said, suddenly awakening from her trance and pointing her trembling frail finger at Colleen.

'Oh Joanie. Please,' Colleen said sadly, shaking her head. 'Don't you remember what happened? You thought you heard Daniel come home? You were running down the stairs, weren't you? That's when you fell.'

The sound of her grandson's name set Joanie off then.

'Daniel. Where's my Daniel gone? Haven't you found him yet?' she said, looking up expectantly at the faces in front of her.

Nancy shook her head sadly, before looking over at Jack.

'I'm sorry, Joanie. We're still doing all we can to find him. No one's seen him. We've got no leads,' Jack said, not sure that the woman even understood what he was telling her.

'I told you, Nan, he's probably gone off somewhere for a while. You know what he's like. He's probably met up with some friends and got caught up having fun somewhere. You know how spontaneous he can be,' Nancy said, though she knew no one in this room was buying her story. Not really.

Daniel had been missing now for weeks. No one had seen or heard a thing from him. Jack Taylor had been keeping an eye on the missing person's report that Joanie, Michael and Colleen had all insisted be filed. Only, they had no leads. No clues as to where he might be, or what might have happened to him.

Nancy knew that she couldn't leave her family in limbo, forever wondering what had happened to Daniel. Soon she'd have to get Jack to concoct a story about him being seen abroad somewhere. Jack could pretend that they found intelligence suggesting he was living somewhere exotic.

Her family might believe that.

That Daniel had just gone off somewhere. That was the kind of selfish crazy shit her brother would do. Though Nancy knew the only place her brother would be visiting right now was Hell, and she was glad about that.

'What about my Jimmy? Where's my Jimmy?'

Nancy shook her head then, thinking she'd misheard her nan, but she knew she hadn't.

She looked at Colleen.

'Did she bang her head?' Thinking that maybe the woman had a concussion.

'She took quite a fall, Nancy, but she's been saying things like this a lot the past few days. It's as if she forgets, you know, that he's gone…' Colleen said quietly. 'I stopped telling her any different as she always finds it too upsetting.'

Nancy's eyes filled with tears as she sat down next to her nan and took her hand.

'Nan? Dad passed away. He died, Nan… you remember that don't you?' Nancy was worried as she saw the realisation sweep across her nan's face. Her lip began to tremble. An almighty wail escaping her mouth.

'What's happening to me?' Joanie cried then. The fear written all over her face. 'My Jimmy's dead. My boy. How could I forget that? I'm losing my mind. I'm going mad.'

'I think you need to go and call the doctor, Colleen,' Nancy said, realising the severity of the situation. That her nan might be right.

Guessing that Joanie was having some sort of a mental breakdown, Nancy wasn't sure what they were dealing with yet, but she knew that they couldn't deal with this on their own. Her nan needed help. Professional help.

'We don't need a doctor. I'm perfectly capable of looking after her. She's just having a bad morning, that's all. She'll be all right after she gets some proper sleep,' Colleen said, looking visibly hurt that they had to call for help. As if Nancy was insinuating that Colleen wasn't doing a good enough job of looking after the woman.

'And you're doing a great job, Colleen,' Jack Taylor said, butting in and trying to play Devil's advocate. 'Anyone can see that. But Joanie isn't well, Colleen. She needs a doctor.'

'She's going to end up killing herself if we don't do something soon,' Michael added in full agreement, for once thinking only about Joanie and what would be best for her.

'We can get someone in to help me. A carer. Someone to keep an eye on her when I'm doing the household chores; maybe she won't have any more accidents then…' Colleen said. Worried now that if Nancy called a doctor they'd all find out what Colleen had been doing. That she'd been drugging the woman. She'd been filling her head full of stories too. Telling her that the people who killed Jimmy would be coming for her too. She might have been responsible for a couple of Joanie's falls as well. But it was nothing that the older woman didn't deserve. Joanie might look weak and frail now, but Colleen knew full well what the woman was really capable of.

'If you call a doctor out, they'll take her away. They'll put her in some institution somewhere. You can't just give up on her like that,' Colleen said, doing her best to sound indignant about Nancy's decision; but, seeing the determined look on her daughter's face, Colleen knew that Nancy wouldn't be swayed now that she had made her mind up.

'It won't be forever, Colleen, but she needs help. Now.'

Colleen nodded, defeated. 'I'll go and make the call.'

'I'll come with you and make some tea or something. Anything to make me feel useful,' Michael said, glad to tear himself away from the sight of his wife for a few moments. He needed to pull himself together.

'I'll give you a hand, Michael,' Jack Taylor said, guessing that Nancy wanted to be on her own with her nan. 'We'll leave you two for a bit. See if you can calm your nan down before the doctor gets here.'

Nancy smiled then. Appreciating the gesture.

Joanie did too. Waiting for everyone to leave the room before she spoke.

'What's the matter with me, Nancy? It's like I'm going mad. I keep forgetting everything. But how could I forget that, eh? How could I forget my own son?'

Nancy didn't speak. She couldn't, not without the answers her nan needed to hear.

'I can't remember trying to climb out of the window, or falling down the stairs. I mean, I get confused. I thought that Colleen might have tripped me up, but that woman's done nothing but be kind and good to me.' Looking down at her bruises on her arms and legs, feeling the pain from the swollen limbs. 'I'm going mad, aren't I?' Colleen and Michael were telling the truth. They must be.

Nancy shook her head.

'Don't be silly, Nan. You're not going mad. You've just been through a lot lately.'

'Are you going to send me away?' Joanie sobbed, accepting her fate.

'Of course not! We're going to get you better, that's all. You need some rest. Some proper rest, and you need to be looked after. I know Colleen and Grandad have been doing their bit, but I think we need to let the doctors look after you for a while. It won't be for long, I promise. Just a little while. Just until you're feeling better. We just want to get you well again. You want to get better, don't you?'

Joanie nodded then and Nancy could see it. The real determination in the woman's eyes. A glimmer of the old Joanie. Determined and strong. She was still in there. Nancy knew it.

'And you will, Nan. I promise you. You'll get some help, and before you know it you'll be back to your old self again.'

Joanie patted her daughter's hand.

Right now she really hoped so, more than anything else in the whole wide world.

'Thank you so much, Doctor Dolan,' Nancy said as the doctor walked back up the driveway towards the house now that he had settled Joanie in the back of the car. Michael Byrne was sitting on the back seat next to her.

Jack Taylor had his arm around Colleen who, surprisingly, had been inconsolable. Not in the least bit happy about the doctor wanting to admit Joanie to one of the top psychiatric hospitals in London. Colleen had been admitted to the very same place over the years. Nancy wondered if that's where her mother's real angst was coming from. That her mother knew what those places could be like. Though Colleen had protested so much about Joanie being admitted that even Nancy had begun to question whether or not she was making the right decision.

'You are doing the right thing, Nancy,' Dr Dolan said, sensing the anguish on the younger girl's face as he held out the paperwork for Nancy Byrne to sign. 'I would hazard a guess that your nan has had a breakdown, but we won't know the extent of her mental well-being until we've carried out some tests on her.'

Nancy nodded.

'She'll be in the very best of hands, Nancy. The Nightingale Unit has a very dedicated team of consultant psychiatrists and therapists. We'll put your nan on a specialist inpatient programme and we'll have a diagnosis done within the next few days. After that, it will be just a case of deciding what treatment will work best for her and getting your nan well again.'

Signing the paperwork, Nancy made a silent promise to herself to visit her nan every single day. They had to get her nan better. No matter what.

'Thank you, Doctor. Here let me walk you out,' Nancy said, handing over the paperwork and leading the doctor back out on to the driveway.

Losing her footing, Nancy would have toppled over if it hadn't been for the quick thinking doctor grabbing at her arm and holding her upright.

'Are you okay, Nancy? Do you want to sit down?' Doctor Dolan asked, concerned for Nancy now too. He knew the family history of the Byrne family. The fact that Nancy had recently buried her grandmother Edel, and also her father who had been murdered. Now her nan was sick too. The extreme stress that they had all been under lately was clearly taking its toll on all of them.

Nancy Byrne included.

'I'm okay.' Nancy smiled. Grateful of the help. Feeling silly now as she saw Colleen and Jack both turning and looking at her. Both of them looking equally concerned for her as she steadied herself on her feet. Stepping back and holding on to the doorframe for support.

'Are you sure you're okay?' Doctor Dolan said.

'Honestly. I just felt a bit dizzy, that's all. It's nothing. It's been happening a lot lately. I haven't been sleeping that much…'

The doctor nodded.

'Well, I'm happy to give you an examination. I could come back tomorrow? Just to make sure you're okay?'

'No, honestly, I'm fine it's nothing.'

Dr Dolan laughed. 'You say that, but sometimes it's worth checking. Only yesterday I got an emergency call out from one of my patients. The same as you, she'd been complaining of exhaustion. Zapped of all energy. She couldn't keep a thing down. The poor woman told me that she'd been meaning to call me to book in a check-up, only she'd convinced herself for months that she was dying of some terrible illness… it only turns out that she was pregnant. The poor woman didn't actually find that out until 3 a.m. in the morning when she'd started going into labour while sitting on the toilet. At least her story had a happy ending though, eh? Are you sure you don't want me to at least examine you? And check your blood pressure?' Dr Dolan said, glad that his story had made Nancy smile at least. 'You do look awfully pale.'

'Honestly, I'm fine. If it happens again, I'll call you,' Nancy said. Not wanting to cause the doctor any further fuss, nor wanting the added attention. 'Thank you so much for coming out and seeing to my nan. I'll let my grandad settle her in, and I'll come by first thing tomorrow morning and see her.'

Doctor Dolan nodded and made his way back to the car. Getting in and starting the engine.

Nancy watched as they drove away, praying that her nan would be okay, as her mother and Jack walked back towards the house now.

'I'll go and make us another cup of tea, shall I?' Colleen offered as she stepped inside the house.

Nancy offered her mum a small smile in return. She knew that Colleen and Joanie had grown close this past few weeks. That Colleen genuinely cared about her nan. What's more, the woman had finally stepped up, it seemed. Maybe it was time to put her grievance with her mother to bed, once and for all. Nancy was done with all the drama.

Closing the front door behind them all, Jack looked at Nancy.

'Are you sure you're okay?' he asked, having seen Nancy take a tumble outside.

Nancy nodded.

'I'm fine. Even Doctor Dolan said it was probably just the stress of everything that's happened. Honestly, it's nothing a lie-down won't fix.'

'Okay. I'll leave you to it then,' Jack Taylor said, taking the hint that Nancy probably needed some space right now. 'I'll go back to Bridge Street and make sure that everything's ready for tonight. I'm sure Bridget will have it all in hand. She's loving this promotion you've given her. Though, it might be going to her head a bit. She's asked the other girls to call her ma'am. She can fuck right off if she thinks I'm going to follow suit.'

Nancy laughed at that.

'I'll come back over in a few hours. After I've got my head down for a bit.' She smiled, glad that the awkwardness that had lingered between them these past few weeks seemed to have dissolved now.

Nancy saw Jack out, closing the door behind him before she leant up against the door and closed her eyes, the doctor's words still swimming about in the forefront of her mind. Dizzy and nauseous, that's what the doctor had said. The story he'd told her about his other patient. The woman had been exhausted, so drained.

It all made complete sense now.

Nancy had been thinking that she was under too much stress, that she was grieving and tired.

Physically and mentally exhausted.

But now Nancy Byrne knew. Without a single doubt.

She was carrying Jack Taylor's child.

CHAPTER FORTY

'He's stabilised for now.' Staff Nurse Louise Langton spoke softly as she led the new junior nurse down along the ward, towards the private room where their patient was currently being treated.

She could see that the younger girl was nervous. It was only natural, of course. It was the girl's very first day on shift. Talk about throwing the poor thing in at the deep end. Young Marie Huston looked as if she was just about to be fed to the lions and, in some ways, she was. Having worked on the Burns Unit at Chelsea and Westminster Hospital for just over five years, Nurse Langton was all too aware of how traumatic it was going to be for her having to see and deal with such a badly burnt patient for the first time. She still remembered her own first day working here as if it was yesterday and she knew from her own experience that there wasn't a textbook, or university in the world that could have prepared her for the shock of it.

'Are you ready?' she asked, standing outside the door so that she could give the younger nurse a few more moments to gather herself before they went into the room.

'The doctor and the trauma surgeon have just finished assessing the patient's wounds. He's been heavily sedated so he won't be very responsive, but that doesn't mean that he won't know that we are there. So be careful what you say – it's always a shock when you first see a patient so badly burnt,' Nurse Langton warned. 'Chances are, the patient will more likely remain in an induced coma, but you never know. We need to stay professional at all times.' The nurse spoke softly now. 'Walking in to this room today will be the hardest part of your career.'

'How bad is he?' Nurse Huston asked, her voice tiny. Her face drained of all colour now, the poor woman looked petrified.

'He's suffered significant burns to his entire body. The doctors have noticed other injuries too.' The nurse held back then. Not wanting to mention that the patient also had possibly been tortured. That he had other wounds on his body that they'd have to tend to – missing toenails or fingers on the man's feet and hands.

'A dog walker found him. Out by an old abandoned warehouse behind the old railway lines in King's Cross. The police think that it was possibly a premeditated attack. That he was doused in petrol and that somehow he'd managed to roll around on the floor and put himself out; though how he survived is beyond us all. He didn't have any ID on him when they brought him in and, so far, we have no idea who he is.'

Nurse Langton and two of the other senior nurses had already tended to this patient for the past couple of days. Excising his burns, cutting away any dead tissue from his skin to prevent any further infection. They needed to keep the wounds clean now. Changing his dressings regularly and keeping the wounds clean was a harrowing job. Especially to a nurse who was new to all of this.

'If you feel a bit queasy, and you need to leave the room at all, then please do so,' the nurse said sympathetically pointing towards the toilets opposite, before placing her hand over the door handle. 'Okay. You ready?'

Nurse Huston nodded. Following the older nurse into the room.

'Jesus,' she muttered despite herself and Nurse Langton's words of advice just seconds earlier. The scene before her looked like something out of a horror movie. The dark charred body of a person lying in the hospital bed, his skin black and blistered. The stench of burning flesh in the room all around them.

She could hear an awful noise, too. A low, deep groaning that rang out in the room around them. It sounded animalistic. Like that of nothing she'd ever heard before. Pure agony.

The two senior doctors were leaving the room, nodding at the senior nurse and her assistant to take over.

Nurse Langton got to work.

'Okay, we're going to apply the patient's new dressings now. Are you ready?'

Nurse Huston nodded, but really she felt physically sick. Swallowing back the acidic burn of bile that churned at the back of her throat. Eyeing the bottles of saline and tubes of paraffin. The endless rolls of dressings. Reaching out her trembling hands towards the trolley, she froze.

'I don't think I can do this.'

'Of course you can,' Nurse Langton insisted as she passed the younger nurse the first rolls of dressings.

Nurse Huston took them. Trying her hardest to banish her nerves, she set to work, mentally making the wound assessment in her head, reminding herself which dressing would be required for each area of the patient's body, just as the patient flung himself forward in the bed. Sitting bolt upright suddenly. Staring right at her.

His head had ballooned to double its normal size, making him look deformed. Abnormal, like some sort of an alien. The blistering skin on his face was flaking off in strips, striking such contrast between the sickly bright pink flesh and the charcoal black burnt tissue.

His eyelids, swollen, closed.

A loud alarm screaming out across the room, quickly followed by Nurse Huston's own scream.

'Hold on!' Nurse Langton ordered, immediately running to the other side of the bed and adjusting the patient's ventilator. 'He's bucking the ventilator. Quick, help me ease him back down onto the bed,' she called out, knowing that time was of the utmost essence.

But Nurse Huston shook her head.

That was the only movement she was capable of making. Her feet were glued to the spot. Her skin prickled with terror. She'd never seen anything like this before, and hoped that she never would again.

'Nurse Huston. Now!'

The older nurse's stern voice quickly brought Nurse Huston out of her panic-induced trance. Doing as she was told, the two nurses lowered the patient back down onto the bed, relieved that the initial panic was over.

'"Bucking the ventilator"?' Nurse Huston said, confused as the two women stared down at the man lying on the bed. His breathing had fallen back into rhythm with the ventilator. The wheezing and the whirring both merging together as one. The initial panic over.

'The ventilator disconnected,' Nurse Langton reminded the young nurse. 'It happens sometimes.'

Nurse Langton busied herself preparing the dressings. Passing a roll to the younger nurse she said: 'He can't feel anything. Not with the amount of morphine and Valium we've administered. Though once he's conscious again it will be a very different story. Especially when his dressings are being changed. That's the worst bit. Re-exposing the burn to the air can feel excruciatingly painful but we'll do our best to control it for him.'

'Is he going to survive?'

Nurse Langton wasn't able to answer that question. Instead she skirted around it. 'The important thing for now is that we make sure he doesn't go into shock. We need to keep his fluids up and his temperature down. He's been placed on a drip and he's receiving around-the-clock care. The next twenty-four hours are critical. We need to keep a close eye on him.' She prepared to apply some saline wash to the patient's skin. 'The good news is that there seems to be no sign of any internal damage to his throat from smoke inhalation, so that's a good sign. The burns always look worse at first, but the skin is an amazing organ, you know. Capable of healing really well; trust me, I've seen many a miracle working here in my time.'

Nurse Langton knew that she was being optimistic. This patient was by far one of the most badly burnt that she'd seen in the unit for years: sixty-five per cent burns meant that, technically, the patient shouldn't even be here. This would affect him for the rest of his life. He'd be badly scarred, disabled possibly. And even after all of that there would be countless operations and skin grafts needed. Physiotherapy on his affected muscles, but not only that, there were the other scars to deal with too. The scars on the inside. The panic attacks. The never-ending anxiety as the patient relived the torturous memories. And worse than all of that, there was always a chance that the patient might not recover at all. That the injury and damage to his internal organs was just too severe for him to survive.

Until he started the healing process, they wouldn't know the extent of what they were dealing with. But until then, they just had to try their hardest to keep the patient as comfortable as possible.

As the two nurses set to work side by side in silence, both of them concentrating solely on their patient, they both knew that all they could now was their very best to try to keep him alive.

Though for this patient, Nurse Langton couldn't help but think, the kindest thing might be to just let him die.

*

Daniel Byrne was trapped in a lucid dream, or a nightmare? As yet he was unable to distinguish between the two.

He couldn't move.

He couldn't even open his eyes.

Unsure if he was awake, or if this was even real.

He felt as if he was floating in and out of his body. Experiencing short bursts of an epic euphoria before constantly being plunged back down into a deep all-consuming pit of crippling pain.

It was constant. Rhythmic.

Euphoria, then agony once more. Over and over.

He tried to concentrate on the voices that he could hear around him. Close? Far away?

There was a shrill sharp beeping of alarms echoing around him too.

Where the fuck was he?

He tried so hard to try to remember. To piece together the jigsaw puzzle.

A huge crippling wave of pain washed over him, his skin feeling as if it was being instantaneously stabbed with a thousand needles.

As if he was on fire.

Fire.

He remembered then. Being strapped to the chair in an old warehouse at the mercy of Alfie Harris. The torture that he'd endured. The petrol that had been poured over him, before Alfie had left him to die alone out there.

Daniel couldn't remember anything after that.

Homing in on the noises around him. The sounds of monitors and alarms. A thick plastic tube inside his mouth.

He must be in hospital, he thought.

He was in a bad way. He knew he must be, because he couldn't wake himself up. And the pain was unbearable. So intense that Daniel just wanted to succumb to the sweet allure of nothingness. Anything, so this agony would go away.

Desperate to escape it, he tried to sink inside himself. Tried to breathe, to focus. How easy for him to just give in to death, he thought.

But then he thought about his sister Nancy.

How that bitch had set him up. She'd done all of this and when she was finished, she'd handed him over to Alfie Harris so willingly. This was her payback for their father's death. Nancy would be willing him to die now. Willing death to take him and that alone was a reason to live, Daniel Byrne thought with a newfound determination.

He was going to fight this, and he was going to survive.

He had to.

Because then he was going to repay his cunt of a sister for all that she'd done to him, if it was the very last thing that Daniel Byrne ever did.

A LETTER FROM CASEY

Thank you for taking the time to read *The Broken*. I really hope you enjoyed it! If you fancy leaving me a review, I'd really appreciate it. Not only is it great to have your feedback (I love reading each and every one of them), but adding a review can really help to gain the attention of new readers too.

So, if you would kind enough to leave a short, honest review, it would be very much appreciated!

If you enjoyed reading about Nancy and the rest of the Byrne family – a twisted family if ever there was one! – and you want to read more about Jimmy and Colleen, and go back to where it all began, please check out *The Betrayed*.

I'm currently working on the third book in the Byrne series so if you'd like to stay in touch and find out about when it's due to be released, or you just want to drop by and say 'Hello' I'd love to hear from you!

Casey x

OfficialCaseyKelleher

CaseyKelleher

www.caseykelleher.co.uk

ACKNOWLEDGEMENTS

Many thanks to my fantastic editor Keshini Naidoo for her amazing editorial skills. Your brilliant ideas and suggestions have really helped to make *The Broken* into what it is today. Thank you so much for everything, it's a pleasure to work alongside you!

I'd also like to thank Oliver Rhodes, Kim Nash and Noelle Holten for all their continued help and support, along with all the lovely Bookouture authors I've been so lucky to meet along the way. For all the giggles, and for keeping me sane!

Huge thanks also to all of those at the scene of the crime. You know who you are!

To all my fantastic readers, thank you so much for all your kind words about my books. You are the very reason I write, without you, none of this would have been possible. I love receiving your feedback and messages, so please do keep them coming!

To all the fantastic book-bloggers, and online book clubs. You all offer such fantastic support for us authors – thank you!

As always I'd like to thank my extremely supportive friends and family for all the encouragement that they give me along the way.

The Coopers, The Kellehers, The Ellis's.

Special thanks to my Bestie, Lucy and also to Laura. I always appreciate your honest feedback and thoughts as the first readers of the books. (Even if you do torture me with silence until you've finished them.)

Finally a big thank you to my husband Danny

Our three children Ben, Danny and Kyle.

Not forgetting our two little fur-babies (Princess) Sassy and Miska (Boo).

Printed in Great Britain
by Amazon